Praise for *Between Wild and Ruin*:

"What could be a corny premise turns into an exhilarating, fun ride in Edelson's adept hands. Her characters are smartly drawn, and readers will easily identify with Ruby, a strong yet insecure young artist on the verge of adulthood, who is still recovering from her tragic past . . . Fans of *Twilight* and modern fairy tales will fall in love with Ruby and root for her eventual romance."
—*Blue Ink Review (Starred Review)*

"*Between Wild and Ruin* is a stunning story of legends, romance, and destiny with themes of starting over, small towns, beauty, and community . . . Edelson perfectly breathes new life in mythology by honoring the oral tradition of a small community and the ruins that bring to life Ruby's destiny." —*Manhattan Book Review*

"Highly recommended to mature teens through new adult and adult audiences, this is a story that lingers in the mind long after its final revelation." —*Midwest Book Review*

"Author Jennifer Edelson's on-point dialogue, multicultural characters, and atmospheric setting, keenly conveys New Mexico's rich cultural roots and narratives, weaving a story that incorporates both folklore and romance into an engrossing, unforgettable YA story." —*Ryan Sprague, Author and Host of 'Somewhere In the Skies' book and podcast, co-host of the The CW's 'Mysteries Decoded*

D1399894

"*Between Wild and Ruin* is, beat for beat, very close to Stephanie Meyer's Twilight saga . . . which, thirteen years ago, captured the hearts of high school and college-aged girls everywhere, except instead of vampires vs. werewolves, it's cops vs. demons vs. mountain lions with a bit of a twist at the end." —*San Francisco Book Review*

"Descriptions of the New Mexico landscape are rich and atmospheric, arousing the senses with references to the scent of smoke and juniper, the predatory roar of mountain lions, and the brilliant dazzle of stars in the desert sky . . . The writing conveys a sense of timelessness, making it easy to believe Ruby's sense that the land is spirit-haunted and that Leo, the handsome young man she encounters near the ruins, is somehow connected to it all." —*Clarion Forward*

"An intriguing historical tale and an over-the-top love-quadrangle romance." —*Kirkus Reviews*

"The paranormal aspects of the tale are credible and richly steeped in traditional lore, and the plot is finely crafted . . . *Between Wild and Ruin* is most highly recommended." —*Reader's Favorite (5-Star Review)*

BETWEEN
WILD & RUIN

JENNIFER G. EDELSON

Published and distributed by Bad Apple Books
Santa Fe, NM 87506

This is a work of fiction. All of the characters and events portrayed in this novel are either products of author's imagination or used fictionally. Any resemblance to actual events, organizations, or persons, either living or dead, is entirely coincidental.

For information regarding bulk buys, or educational, promotional, or business inquiries, please contact BadAppleBooksinfo@gmail.com

Publisher's Cataloging-in-Publication data

Names: Edelson, Jennifer G., author.
Title: Between wild and ruin / by Jennifer G. Edelson.
Description: First trade paperback original edition. | Santa Fe [New Mexico] : Bad Apple Books, 2020. | Also published as an ebook.
Identifiers: ISBN 978-1-7335140-0-2
Subjects: CYAC: Romance fiction. | Paranormal Fiction. | New Mexico—Fiction. | LCSH: Paranormal romance.
BISAC: YOUNG ADULT FICTION / Romance / Paranormal.
Classification: LCC PN3448.L67 | DDC 813.6–dc22

Cover design by Heather Vine-Giffin

Interior design by Victoria Wolf

For every untamed dreamer and romantic.

For every person who ever thought to look below

the surface and ask 'why.' For Elijah and Gabriel,

the wildest dreamers in my life.

CHAPTER ONE

IN LA LUNA, WE REST

TOWARD THE BACK OF THE SMALL STORE, a tall endcap filled with assorted cookies catches my eye. Crouching over the scuffed tile floor, I grab a pack of Double Stuf Oreos from the bottom shelf, teetering on the balls of my feet while I squeeze a red plastic grocery basket against my side. When Mom was alive, she made us live like health freaks. Over the last ten months, I've made it my duty to support the junk food industry.

Down the aisle, something flashes. For a split second, I see my mother standing motionless between two shelves of cereal. Then just like that, she's gone, phantom to ether. Startled, I shoot up and look around, but the aisle is so empty I can hear my own breathing.

Pinching the bridge of my nose between my fingers, I briefly close my eyes. *It's bad enough you're stuck riding out senior year in the middle of Nowhere, New Mexico. Now you're seeing your dead mother, too? Nice, Ruby.*

Dim lighting casts creepy shadows over the aisle. Still

shaken, I whip around, knocking into something fleshy and solid.

"Oh, I'm so sorry!" I squawk.

A boy with a face like a car crash stares bullets at me. Our eyes meet, and I freeze, startled by the damage.

"Excuse you." He crosses his arms over his chest impatiently, glaring as if I knocked him over.

I want to apologize again. I really do. But instead, my mouth drops open.

"Let me guess, you flunked out of charm school," he says curtly.

The boy's large frame blocks the aisle. He's proportioned, and muscular, but his face is unreal. Knotty skin twists across angular planes, forming jagged boundaries around smooth glossy patches of skin near his mouth and cheeks. Near his hairline, a scar stretches down between his eyebrows, cutting along the center of his nose to his chin, dissecting his features.

"Didn't your mother teach you it's rude to stare?"

"I ... yes," I say, trying to stop gawking.

The boy's intense eyes pin me to the spot. "Yeah, I can tell."

I feel like a jerk for being so rude and more than a little mortified.

"Next time try paying attention," he scowls.

I start to say sorry, but the boy turns and stomps off down the aisle toward a cash register. After a moment, I manage to unstick my feet and follow him, almost tiptoeing toward my aunt, Liddy. I poke her in the side as we wait in line, surreptitiously pointing him out. "I almost knocked him over," I whisper. "It really pissed him off."

"Smooth move," she whispers back, giggling at the blush spreading across my cheekbones. "You okay? It's been a long drive."

I poke her harder, talking between my teeth. "Did you see his face?"

"Sad." She nods.

"I wonder what happened."

"Something terrible, I'd gather."

My stomach churns while I watch the boy pay for his groceries. His anger is palpable; I feel it physically, like a leash that tethers him to me, bridging the distance between us. And his face makes me sad. Thanks to Mom, a.k.a. former model extraordinaire, I've always hated that people care so much about what other people look like. I hate knowing that appearances matter. Even more, I hate other people thinking *I* care about the surface of anything.

"Don't feel bad," Liddy whispers. She flares her nostrils, flattening the sharp tip of her nose exactly the way Mom used to whenever she was caught between amusement and irritation.

Liddy rubs the small of my back, then pulls several bills out of her purse when the checker begins swiping our items. Two lanes over, the boy finishes paying and glances up at me. He grabs his bag off the checkout belt, glares for what feels like an hour, and marches out of the store. Through the front window, I watch him load groceries into a worn black pickup truck. Slamming the tailgate, he turns and squints at me, then jumps into the cab, revving up the engine before squealing out of the parking lot like a banshee.

Liddy raises a manicured eyebrow at the checkout clerk.

"Ezra." The clerk nods toward the window. "That guy's got

a heck of a chip on his shoulder." Under his breath, he adds, "Asshole."

Trailing behind Liddy, I silently pray that the next time I meet someone new, I'll be smoother—or at least that the rest of La Luna's residents aren't as touchy. Leaving my friends back in Los Angeles sucked. Starting over in a remote town full of people who hate me when I still suffer from bouts of self-doubt myself would be horrible.

Liddy drives toward a pine dotted butte, heading through the pass above La Luna. Lush and wooded with piñon, La Luna is a haven nestled against the Sangre de Cristo Mountains. It's a small town but compared to the village we drove by on our way into the pass — blink-and-you'll-miss-it Glorieta — it could be Los Angeles.

"We're almost there," Liddy says, pointing at the looming mountain ahead of us. "Didn't I say it was breathtaking?"

I nod my response, mesmerized by the craggy peaks framed by the windshield. It just isn't the home I'm used to.

"You okay?" she asks. "You've been pretty quiet all day."

Alongside us, tall junipers, and ponderosa pines line the road, swaying in the wind as we drive. "I thought you liked quiet," I whisper, awed by nature's abundant use of green to mask the desert. "Isn't that why we left Los Angeles?"

"We left so we could start fresh." Liddy's already pouty lips purse into a frown. "And last I checked, you were all for it."

"I'm fine, Lid. It just all looks so different." I inhale, breathing in sage and piñon. "And it smells ... odd."

In the foothills above La Luna proper, Liddy pulls into a long gravel driveway and stops in front of a secluded wooden house, letting the car idle for a moment. Majestic pines frame the rectangular wood-sided structure. From this angle, it looks like it grew out of the bottom of the mountain.

"Liddy," I exhale. "You never told me."

"I tried, babe. But your mother always sabotaged the conversation."

"I can't believe she didn't want to move here. It's so beautiful."

"It's not urban enough." Liddy tips her head slightly, as if in deference to Mom's memory. "At least, that was her excuse. You know how she was."

We unload the Volkswagen. There isn't much to bring inside. Liddy already packed and sent forward almost everything we own a few weeks ago. She flew out to New Mexico, settled things with the university, where she'll join the Chemistry Department in the fall, and enrolled me in my new high school. *Always go into battle armed with a breadth of information and an organized mind*—that's her motto.

After we unpack our groceries, we gorge ourselves on frozen pizza and junk food around our old table in our new kitchen. Neither of us say much; it's been an achingly long few days between here and Los Angeles.

"I guess I'll go to bed, Lid," I finally say. "If you don't mind."

"All right." She drums a burgundy nail on the table. "But let's go into Santa Fe this weekend. We'll do a little shopping and get some dinner."

"Deal." I smile.

I toss our plates into the trash, stopping near the table before heading upstairs. Stretching over the back of Liddy's chair to reach her face, I kiss her pale cheek and brush a long piece of copper hair out of her eyes. Liddy has a beautiful head of wild hair that she almost always wears loosely down her shoulders.

"I love you," I whisper in her ear.

She leans back against the chair and smiles up at me, raising an arm to brush my cheek with her fingers. "I love you too, babe. Good night."

For the first time in my life, I have my own bathroom. Upstairs in my underwear, I stand in the small yellow space and quickly brush my teeth, turning away from the mirror. I know my face as well as I know Liddy's. But I can't look at my chipmunk cheeks, or at my nose, which has a small rise at the bridge, or at my chin, which I've always thought seems a little sharp, without seeing my mother. Except for my green eyes, everyone used to say we looked identical.

I find a pair of sweats in an unpacked box near my bed and throw them on. Uncertain, I stand in the middle of my new room, staring at the pale beams of near-flawless wood lining the floor and ceiling, offsetting brilliant red walls. My easel and a large box of paints lie against the wall under the rectangular window overlooking the backyard creek, and my fingers itch just staring at them. Washed in moonlight, the backyard looks ethereal.

Uncomfortable in an unfamiliar house, I kill the lights and linger near the picture window, gazing down at the pines and creek below. Vast as the forest seems from the safety of my new bedroom, it's a little intimidating. Beams of moonlight pierce the windowpane, staking my bed to the floor. They cast shadows over everything.

I rub my eyes, something Mom used to nag I shouldn't do if I want to avoid crow's feet. For the briefest moment, colorful sunbursts pop in the windowpane. Then my eyes adjust, and

I notice a figure stirring near the creek. A dark blotch casts a shadow on a boulder near the banks of the stream. Uneasy, I step back out of the window frame as the shadow stands and stretches. When silvery light illuminates its face, I realize I'm staring at a mountain lion.

The longer I watch the lion, the worse the night plays tricks on me. The forest comes alive, and the lion tilts its head, angled up toward my window like it's looking for something. Ghostly shapes fade against the sky, then spring to life when I blink. Eventually, my eyes grow so tired of trying to focus, night becomes an inky smudge. The lion disappears. I have no clue if it's still out there. But I'm not so keen on the idea that *it* might be watching *me*.

Clouds obscure the moon, shadowing the backyard. City girl that I am, I freak and dive for my bed, pulling the comforter over my head. Burying my face into my pillow, I mumble, "Stupid, Ruby." After everything, I don't need a shrink to tell me that I'm overtired and excitable, and probably making mountains out of molehills.

I close my eyes and try thinking about the long drive from California to New Mexico. Then I think about my mother. We weren't close. But I loved her. And I'm not always sure who I am anymore without her around to tell me. If she were alive, I'd find her and tell her the lion scared the bejesus out of me. I'd tell her how nervous I am about starting over in a small town like La Luna. Ten months have passed since Mom died, but in my new room, hiding under the pile of blankets shielding me from both my new life and the secretive night outside my window, it feels like forever.

CHAPTER TWO

THE MOUNTAIN SPEAKS

LIDDY HANDS ME A BAGEL, then slides a tub of cream cheese across the table after it. "Want to drive up to Las Vegas?" she asks, staring absentmindedly out at the creek through the kitchen's bay window.

"When are you going?" I follow her eyes to the creek that cuts our yard in two, itching to explore the woods behind our house. The kitchen is warm and cozy, but the gnarled junipers and ponderosa pines lining the backyard's border are more enticing. It's almost as if I can feel the forest's pull.

"It depends on whether you want to come."

Whenever Liddy travels, she makes it a priority to seek out the area's historic Jewish neighborhoods. Once upon a time, Las Vegas was both New Mexico's biggest city and the seat of the state's Jewish population. I understand why she wants to visit. But getting to know yet another new town doesn't sound like the best way to spend my last two days of freedom.

"You know, I think maybe I'll just grab lunch in La Luna or take a hike or something."

She squints at me. "How are you going to get to La Luna?"

"Walk?" I shrug.

"It's at least three miles." She frowns.

"I hiked all the time back home." I shoot her a super-exaggerated you've-got-to-be-kidding-me eye roll for good measure. Before Mom died, the Santa Monica Mountains were my home away from home. Three miles will be like walking up the driveway.

Liddy shakes her head at me as though the fact that I'd rather hike than connect with my heritage amuses her. But her compassionate smile makes me feel bad. *She's* stuck with me, not the other way around, and *Duh, Ruby, you don't need to constantly remind her.*

"Fine," she says cheerfully. "Just be back by dinner please."

Eager to get outside after being stuck in a car for three days, I quickly finish my breakfast and pack up the compass Mom bought me for my eleventh birthday, along with my pocketknife for good measure. Outside, I stop for a moment at the base of the mountain near our property's border, at the beginning of what looks like a path leading straight up into the forest. From the backyard, our wood-sided house seems to merge with the bottom of the Sangre de Cristo Mountain Range. Tall pines blend with its frame, and I inhale in awe, breathing in the late summer scent of lavender.

After walking through dense stands of pine trees, I follow the remnants of what may have been a trail toward the top of the mountain. Higher up, the pines and junipers dappling the mountainside grow taller, but there aren't as many. As they thin, small gusts of wind whistle through the forest, echoing through the trees. Otherwise, the forest is completely silent.

Closer to the top of the mountain, the rocky ground levels off and the land spreads across a plateau below the mountain's peak. Unlike the forest, the plateau is more like a jungle, marked by thick hanging moss and clusters of tall, unidentifiable conifers. Trees stand like sentries several rows deep. Beyond them, fallen logs lie scattered among overgrown shrubs and boulders in circular bands like rings on a tree. I walk through it all, making my way past thick brush into a clearing.

Fresh sap and damp earth assault my nose. Under bright sunlight, large, rough-cut slabs of glittery rock blanket the otherwise bare field. Some lie stacked on top of each other like the crumbling remains of a building. Awestruck, I circle the structure, running my fingers over what looks like a ruin.

"Incredible, isn't it?"

A voice behind me sends my heart racing toward my throat. I jump, whipping around to find a young man leaning casually against a pine near the clearing's perimeter, looking off to his left as though listening for something.

Even in the shade, his face glows. He smiles, showing off teeth that gleam like snowflakes between perfect lips. Hair as dark as Liddy's French roast coffee falls around his face in unruly waves. His features are angular but refined, and his high, rounded cheeks soften the striking juxtaposition.

I blink, then blink again. *Ruby*. I rub my eyes. *You're hallucinating*. But he's still there, staring at me.

While I gawk, he pushes himself off the tree. "Not many people make it up here." He smiles broadly.

A soft, purple-hued halo circles his golden irises, catching fire in the sunlight. They settle on me, and my heart stops, completely paralyzed by his faultless storybook features.

I exhale, trying to swallow inconspicuously. "It's definitely a hike."

"Who are you?"

"Who am I?" I sputter. "Who are *you*?"

"Leo." He grins.

"I'm Ruby."

"Ruby." My name rolls off his tongue with a smooth "R" and a musical lilt. Somehow, he even manages to make it sound appealing. "First time up?"

"Yes. We just moved to La Luna."

"La Luna," he repeats. "Welcome."

"Thanks," I mumble.

Earth to Ruby, I mentally smack myself. *Since when has any boy made you senseless?*

"You okay?" He smiles like he knows I'm not. Like he knows *why* I'm not. "Do you want to sit down? The altitude can be a bitch if you're not used to it."

"No. I mean, yes, I'm fine. No, I don't want to sit down. You just really startled me. You should announce yourself next time."

"Next time?"

"Next time you sneak up on somebody."

Leo raises a perfect dark eyebrow. "But then it wouldn't be sneaking, would it?"

My cheeks flush, and I suddenly want to drop through a hole in the ground. I choke out, "Ummm," and something incoherent and then stare at my toes like they hold the keys to my future.

Leo extends a hand. "Come here," he motions. "I want to show you something."

Mesmerized by both Leo and the ruin, I follow him through the decaying structure, not caring that he could be a serial killer or lunatic. He leads me through a small section of the wall to a boulder with a flat notch near the center of the roofless building.

"What is it?" The boulder is almost magnetic, and I feel myself taking a step closer.

"A ruin."

"*Really?*" I answer, raising an eyebrow.

"You mean what *was* it?"

I nod. Some people are so hung up on semantics. "What *was* it then?" I correct myself, rolling my eyes without thinking.

His top lip pulls slightly to the left. "Some say it was a pueblo storehouse. Others say, well, other things."

"Other things?" I wrap my arms around my bare shoulders, smoothing the baby hairs on my upper arms standing at attention.

"Some folks think it's a gate." He pauses, apparently waiting for me to suck in my breath or something. "Not many people know it's up here, but some of the old-timers, they say it leads to the Land of the Ancients."

"What's the Land of the Ancients?" I ask skeptically.

"Depends on who you ask."

"I'm asking you." I smile sweetly, pretending I'm not a little unsettled.

"A spirit realm," he says.

"Like Heaven?"

"Nope. More like a motel. Someplace you stop on your way to someplace else."

I smirk, not at all convinced he's serious. "So, The Land of the Ancients, it's what, the River Styx or something?"

"I wouldn't knock the veil between the living and dead, Ruby."

"Well," I say, trying to hatchet my unease, "You'd think the Ancients would put their gateway someplace more ... convenient."

Leo smiles something wicked. "It's just a story."

Leo's tall tale reminds me of Liddy's love affair with facts and science. She'd have laughed him off the mountain. "What do *you* think the ruin is?"

He shrugs. "Probably a holy site for the Pecos. See the stones in the ground?"

I hadn't before, but once he points them out, I do.

"They radiate out from the center of the ruin. A few lead to the edge of the mountain. Some of the bigger pueblos in New Mexico, like Chaco Canyon, have thousands of them. They act as a bridge for a tribal shaman's spirit travels."

"Seriously?"

He cocks an eyebrow. "Every culture has its witches."

I stand completely still, taking everything in. The site *feels* sacred. Even the air, which hums like a transformer, feels hallowed against my skin. Dropping my backpack, I walk closer to the notched boulder at the center of the ruin. As I move to sit down on it, Leo dashes over and grabs my arm, stopping me.

"Don't."

"Oh, right. Because it's sacred?"

"Because it's sacrificial."

"What do you mean, 'sacrificial'?"

He raises his eyebrows, then pulls his fingers across his throat, pretending to slit it.

I shudder. "I thought that only happened in Mexico and Central America? You know, like with the Aztecs and Mayans."

"Before the Ancients restricted the gate to spiritual travels, the Aztecs made pilgrimages here to exchange their souls for things like a better life on Earth or for passage to a different dimension." His violet eyes glimmer, underscoring his sly smile. "Apparently, the gods and demigods of Ottomundo weren't above trading for Earthly curios."

"Ottomundo?"

"The Otherworld." Leo's face relaxes. "It's what my grandpa called it."

"So I can't just sit down and barter my soul away?" I ask, maybe more amused by his fanciful story than he is.

"You could try. But when Awonawilona the Creator discovered that the gods were interfering in mortal affairs, she assigned a Watcher to guard it. I doubt you'd last a minute. Anyway, sacrifice isn't always about death." He shrugs. "Natives worship the Earth. It's a symbiotic relationship. We make our own kinds of sacrifices."

I stare at the rock suspiciously.

"If you don't believe me," he adds, "you could always test your luck. Otherwise, I'd stay off it."

Except for a few incised glyphs around the boulder's base, it looks so unobtrusive. I try to imagine someone's head resting on the surface before being hacked off. The image makes me shudder. Sacrifice is one tradition I have a hard time swallowing. Killing for some supposedly bigger purpose reduces life to a catalyst rather than revering it for what it is in the here and now—a gift.

Apprehensive, I turn back to Leo. Between his unreal face

and the ruins, I still feel a little speechless. "I'm not much of a gambler."

"Smart choice." Leo winks.

The sun shifts, casting shadows over half the structure. As Leo stares at the timeworn ruin, I clear my throat. "So, do many people come up here?"

"It's not a very promising tourist spot. There are plenty of ruins in New Mexico you don't have to work up a sweat to get to."

"Do you come here a lot?" I ask.

"Is that a pickup line?"

"Umm ... it would be if I was trying to pick you up," I say, a little more adamantly than I mean to.

"I do." He laughs. "It's a good place to reflect." Leo's eyes sweep my face and body appreciatively. He isn't subtle. After a long minute, he points to a large log lying in the shade. "Come sit with me?"

I hesitate, fully aware we're in the middle of nowhere and that he's a stranger. But mental debate is pointless. Stranger or not, I already know I'm going to sit down with him.

"Fine," I sigh. "For a little while."

I follow Leo to the gnarly log and sit down, shuffling to my left when he sits down close beside me.

"You all right?" he asks when I scratch at my ears.

"Yeah. That buzzing's just driving me crazy."

"Buzzing?"

"You don't hear it?"

He shakes his head slowly, looking at me with his curious eyes. "No."

"It's like the ground is humming. Or, like cicadas or something."

"It's the altitude," he reassures me. "Your body equilibrating."

"You think so?" I first noticed the drone when I stepped into the clearing, but now my ears are throbbing.

"I know so." He meets my eyes. "Now tell me why you moved here, Ruby."

Leo is a stranger, and we're alone in a completely foreign place, but the urge to talk to him is so strong it's almost like he willed it out of me. Without even really thinking about it, I tell him about moving to New Mexico, skirting around Mom's death. He asks how I like La Luna, and I tell him how weird it is being so far from the coast. He asks about school, and I admit that the idea, starting Pecos High in a few days, ranks right up there with eating moldy cheese. I talk for an eternity, not at all sure he wants to hear even half of my stories.

"Do you live around here?" I finally ask, hoping to change the subject.

Leo points north. "Yes."

"Did you go to Pecos High School?"

He smiles. "Did I? Or do I?"

"Do you?"

"No. But I did."

"You graduated?"

"Yes," he answers evenly. "I graduated."

"Did you like it?"

"Not really."

Leo doesn't seem all that interested in answering my questions. And he isn't quick to volunteer anything either. But I keep prying. "Have you lived in the pass for a long time?"

"All my life."

"Do you go to the university? Or work? I mean, what do you do?"

"Lot of things, Ruby. What do you do?"

I sigh, frustrated with his evasive responses. "How old are you?"

"Old enough to know what I want." He dips his head and meets my eyes, staring at me thoughtfully. "Like you."

"Funny you think that. A year ago, I had my life all planned out. Now, not so much. Actually, I don't know that I want anything anymore."

Leo scans my face, sweeping over it like a searchlight. "Who broke your heart?"

I pull back. "What makes you say that?"

"Not wanting anything makes life easier. But spirited people don't think that way. With spirited people, something has to break them before they trade wanting for complacency. And you, Ruby, you seem like a girl with fight."

"I assure you." I place my hand on my chest, holding it there tightly. "My heart is intact."

"Oh?" He raises a dark eyebrow and tips his head. "Well, I'm glad to hear it."

Leo's arrogance annoys me. I hate when people assume things about my life, even when they're right. *Especially* when they're right.

"I've been up here awhile," I mumble. "I should probably start back."

He stands up. "I'll walk you part of the way."

"I'll be fine," I answer tersely.

Leo chuckles. "I'm sure you will be. *I'd* like the company."

Arrogant or not, Leo makes my heart twitter. I nod and pull my compass out of my backpack to mask my nervousness. As I hold it steady, the compass spindle moves east, then west, then halfway between both before wobbling slightly toward Leo. I shake it, but the spindle bobs erratically.

Leo holds out his hand. "Here. Give it to me."

He takes the compass and taps the glass with a long finger, then hands it back. In my own hand, the spindle settles just shy of north, pointing me left down the mountain.

"Thanks," I frown. "That was weird."

"Must be those spirit lines."

"Must be." I laugh.

"You don't need the compass anyway. I know the forest as well as I know my own face."

I shake my head and smirk. Leo's face is unforgettable. He must really know his way around the mountain. "Lead then."

Leo walks beside me. More than halfway home, after assuring him I have my bearings, he stops, and points left. "I have to go that way, Ruby. You sure you know the way back?"

"I know where I am. It was the plateau that confused me."

Smiling slyly, he rolls out, "It was a pleasure meeting you. Maybe I'll see you around."

I nod my agreement, but my brain isn't feeling quite so courteous. *That's it? Maybe I'll see you around.*

Standing close, Leo brushes a strand of hair off my cheek. "Until then."

My mouth opens but nothing comes out, so I smile and shake my head, hoping to at least *look* unaffected.

Leo winks and walks off through the forest. When he's gone, I exhale, surprised to find I've been holding my breath. No one, and I mean no one, has ever made me feel so unraveled. Most of my friends went stark raving boy-crazy by tenth grade, but that madness somehow skipped me. Boys always seemed like too much heartache.

A thousand could-have, might-have, should-have-said-to-hims follow me home. Walking past boulders, and blankets of pinecones, and lightning-charred tree stumps, I focus on the forest and will myself to stop thinking about Leo's stupid face. But it's a useless endeavor. Like a broken record, my mind won't stop replaying the glorious moment I first saw him.

Over dinner, I tell Liddy about Leo and the ruin, recounting every detail I remember while she doles out food from a bunch of takeout cartons.

"Okay, you found a ruin," she says cheerily, as if stumbling into a ruin in the middle of nowhere is the most normal thing.

"It's almost two miles up. Don't you think that's weird?"

"Not really." She shrugs. "New Mexico's full of them."

I pick at my paper plate, pushing my dinner around. "I think the heat killed my appetite."

Liddy pops a jalapeño into her mouth and makes an "O" at me with her lips. "So, this Leo boy, was he nice?"

"Not exactly. But I liked him."

"And?" She narrows her grey eyes at me.

"I don't know. I mean, I wanted to tell him things. I felt like I knew him. I was almost too comfortable all things considered."

"Hmmm," she says.

"Hmmm, what?"

"You're right."

"I am?" I choke.

"You were up there all alone, babe."

"So?"

"So ..." She hesitates. "You said it, he's a stranger. You were definitely too comfortable."

I look past her out the window toward the mountains. "I'm not Mom."

Liddy's voice softens. "Sweetheart. It's not *you* I don't trust."

"Seriously, Liddy, how often do I meet someone I *like* like?"

Liddy stifles her smile. "Let me see." She puts a finger over her lips as if contemplating. "Ruby, dear," she laughs, "you're the only almost eighteen-year-old I know who will go out of her way to avoid the opposite sex if you think anything will come of it."

I cross my arms over my chest. "You're jumping the gun anyway. He didn't even ask for my number."

Liddy looks sympathetic. But also amused. "Why didn't you ask for his?"

"Seriously, you didn't see him. I couldn't. I would've died."

"It's not like you're chopped liver."

"No. Really. *I mean it.*"

"So do I."

"Why do you do that? I can't just bat my eyelashes and get whatever I want."

"Oh, Ruby." Liddy holds her hands up in surrender. "You're so clueless."

She stands up and clears the table. I join her at the sink, washing dishes while she dries. *Bad Ruby.* I know I'm being defensive. But I can't help myself.

We work together quietly until Liddy turns and smears a handful of bubbles on my nose. "Want to go to breakfast tomorrow morning? You can ask about Leo in town."

I shrug.

Liddy swats my butt with a dishtowel, jumping back in time to miss the dishwater I propel out of the sink at her. "You'll have to be faster than that."

"Oh?" I giggle as water splatters her nose.

"So, breakfast?"

I nod yes.

"And you'll ask about Leo?"

I shake my head no.

Her eyes twinkle. "Your loss, love."

CHAPTER THREE

GHOSTS OF GLORIETA

THE DRIVE INTO TOWN FEELS shorter than last time. Pines whizz past beneath a dense layer of black clouds leading the way through the pass. When we reach La Luna, Liddy stops the car in front of Margarita's, a diner across the street from the sheriff's station on bustling Luna Street.

"Save me a seat. I'll be back in an hour," she tells me.

Being a newbie makes me feel like an interloper, but I kiss Liddy on the cheek and get out of the car anyway, hopping on to the sidewalk with as much verve as I can muster.

"Try not to break any hearts, sweetie!" she calls after me.

Dumb as it is, that always makes me smile. She's been telling me not to break any hearts since I was five years old. To date, as far as I know, I haven't. I've never had the opportunity.

As Liddy pulls away, I head toward a small, grassy park at the end of Luna Street. A smattering of shops and businesses line the south side of the road, and I walk slowly, window-shopping along the way. Most of the small storefronts are clean and orderly, but a few, with their dusty displays and dim interiors, remind me of the long-forgotten towns boarded up off the side of the highway between California and New Mexico.

At the park, I find a bench and sit down, inhaling the scents of juniper and lavender. The sun is a half-moon over the lush hillside and viewing downtown from the commons, the main drag looks like a colorful ribbon cutting through the mountains. Pickups rumble toward the highway, and people walk between the small office buildings sandwiched along the block. Compared to Los Angeles, La Luna is minuscule. But in a few serene moments, I try the town on for size and find it fits my somber state of mind perfectly.

Content to people watch, I pull a sketchpad out of my backpack and balance it on my thighs. My hand instantly takes on its own life, filling page after page with sketches of the hillside above Luna Street. I draw until my stomach starts growling, then finally give in and walk back to Margarita's.

Inside the small diner, charred wood and fried food smells fill the air. The room is abuzz with people, most of whom, with their cowboy hats and turquoise jewelry, look like regulars. Clutching my sketchbook, I walk down the main aisle to a booth next to a window at the back of the diner. Sliding in as inconspicuously as possible, I grab a menu off the table, pretending I'm completely engrossed by dishes like green chili omelets and huevos rancheros while I try to blend in with the walls. Over the menu, I peek at the patrons, killing time until Liddy shows up.

"What'd you get?" Liddy asks when she arrives, sliding into the booth beside me.

"I didn't. I waited for you to order."

As if on cue, a stout young woman walks over to our table.

She smiles, and her black eyes light up. Together with the two long black braids hanging over her yellow shirt, she seems childlike and entirely approachable.

"You the newbies?" she asks. "Moved into Chriso's old place out near Apache Canyon?"

I stare at Liddy before answering. "Yeah."

"Thought so."

I bite my lip. "Are we that obvious?"

"It's a small place." She taps her pen against her chin absently. "Folks saw you 'round town the other night. They're already talking about *las recién llegadas*."

"The newcomers?" Liddy asks.

"Yes." She grins.

"How do they know we're not tourists?"

She nods sideways at Liddy. "You went around and introduced yourself last month. People remember those things. And my sister, Racine, saw you guys in the market the other night. Her bigmouth girlfriend came in here yesterday talking about the new girl with eyes like Spanish olives. Anyways, you're big news. And news around here travels fast. There's not much else for people to get excited about. You'll see. Welcome though." She tucks her pad and pen into her apron and crosses her arms over her chest. "I'm Daisy."

I smile at her and nudge Liddy under the table, unsure how I feel about being so conspicuous. Too bad for La Luna, if people knew us, they'd realize we're probably the least exciting big news this week. "Thanks." It comes out awkwardly. "I'm Ruby, and this is Liddy."

"You in high school, Ruby?" Daisy asks.

"A senior."

"My sister, Racine, is a senior. I'll introduce you."

"I'd like that." I grin, hoping she means it.

Daisy coughs abruptly, as though suddenly aware she has a job to do. "Anyways, can I get you ladies something?"

"Want to share a red chili omelet?" Liddy asks me.

When I nod, Daisy writes it down. "Great. I better get to it then."

She hurries off behind the counter and shoves a piece of paper at the cook, then leans over and whispers to him, nodding back at us. Around the diner, people steal little glances at our table. It's sort of like being a sideshow amusement, though no one seems to mind us being here. We're more curiosity than freak.

After Daisy brings us coffee, Liddy pulls out the Sunday crossword and positions it between us. "You going to ask about Leo?"

"Hell no."

She raises an eyebrow and starts scribbling in words, but when Daisy comes back with our food, she whispers under her breath, "Go on. Ask her."

"Ask me what?" Daisy smiles.

"Nothing," I say briskly.

Liddy shoves her elbow into my waist. I shoot her my fiercest scowl, then look up at Daisy. "Do you know a boy named Leo? He said he used to go to Pecos High School."

Daisy looks toward the ceiling, then shakes her head. "Name doesn't ring a bell."

"He's *really* good-looking," I add.

"*Really* good-looking? Nope. But I'm not near as nosy as some folk think I am, *Jim*," she stresses under her breath, scowling at a man sitting a couple of seats down the counter. "Ask Racine when you meet her. She knows everyone."

Daisy walks off to take another order. When she's out of earshot, Liddy whispers, "You can breathe now."

I poke her. It's true I want to meet Leo again, but as a rule, no boy is worth hyperventilating over, drop-dead gorgeous or not. "You're a riot."

"You going to eat that?" She reaches out and steals the only piece of toast on the plate before I can answer.

"Do I have a choice?"

"Not really," she mumbles cheerily with her mouth full.

"You sure you're not pregnant?" I mutter.

Liddy coughs through her bite, then grins at me. "You're more than enough, sweetheart. Anyway, when would I have had the opportunity?"

Talk about an understatement. My whole life, I've watched Liddy watch the dating boat sail by. Forty-three years is a long time to give up romance to care for someone else's daughter.

"Don't make that face," she says. "You worry too much."

"I swear, Lid, if the teaching gig doesn't go well, you have a future in mind reading."

"It's no big secret." She laughs. "Your face is like a neon sign."

"Then you have eyes on the side of your head. You weren't even looking at me."

"Ruby, love." She places a hand on my knee and squeezes. "You're like my own daughter. I don't need to look at you to know what you're thinking."

She's right. Constitutionally, we're nearly identical. She just has about twenty-five years on me.

Liddy gives my forearm a squeeze, finishes off breakfast, and goes back to the crossword. While Liddy fills in words, I sit and read the *Santa Fe New Mexican* while I listen over its pages to the diner's ambient chatter. All around, things clank, and scrape, and sizzle.

A small string of bells hitched to the front door adds to the din, and when they jangle violently enough to mimic church bells, I look up from my paper. A gust moves through Margarita's, and the boy I ran into at the market marches in, moving like he carries the weight of the world on his shoulders. He meets my eyes briefly, keeping his face lowered as he makes his way toward the only space left in the diner—the booth right across from ours. Curiously, everyone seems to purposely disregard him as though his presence is, but shouldn't be, bothersome. They ignore him, but the tension coming off at least a few of Margarita's patrons is palpable.

Mom always said, *You can catch more flies with honey.* I never listened much when she was alive, but I still feel terrible about gawking at him in the market, so it seems like a good time to start. Mustering my nerve, I lean over the table toward him and say, "Hi."

The boy barely glances up from his paper, squinting as he stares past me. "What do you want?" he finally grumbles.

"Ezra Lucero. *Guácala!* Be nice!" Daisy demands from behind the counter. "Pay no mind to Ezra, Ruby." She shakes her head at him. "His bark is worse than his bite, though I wouldn't heed either." She comes around and refills our coffee cups, giving him a death stare before walking back to the counter.

Liddy looks up from her crossword, cocking her head at me inquisitively.

"I just wanted to say sorry about the other day in the market," I continue quietly. "I mean, bumping into you and then ... well, the way I acted."

"Fine," he answers curtly.

"Maybe we could buy you a cup of coffee?"

Ezra drops his paper on the table. He tilts his strong but scarred chin and looks me dead in the eyes. "Why?"

"I just thought ..."

"Well don't think." He drops his voice a notch. "It isn't very becoming."

From all over the diner heads turn toward our table. Their eyes pierce holes through my body. Self-conscious, I pull my sweater away from my neck as a flush of heat spreads from my throat to my cheeks.

"Oh," I whisper at the tabletop. "I'm sorry."

Ezra looks around the room. He shakes his head, then goes back to reading. After a moment, he drops his paper, grabs his keys off the table, and slides out of the booth. "Cancel my order, Daisy," he grumbles on his way out of the diner.

When Ezra walks out of the restaurant, everyone stares. Mortified, I try to slink under the table, riding out the hush that settles over the room.

"Don't worry about Ezra. He's a jerk."

Liddy and I turn around at the same time. Two sheriffs fill the booth behind us, sprawled in their seats like they've settled down to watch the Sunday game. The youngest of the two smiles, crinkling his lucent green eyes at me.

"Angel's right." The sheriff across the table from him nods. "That boy hasn't been right in the head for years."

The sheriff closest to us holds out his hand. "I'm Angel. This old coot over here," he points to his partner, "is Torrance."

Angel has a friendly face. His smooth, tanned skin and broad cheekbones dress up his wide, welcoming smile. He also looks a lot like Torrance, except Torrance is wider, and graying slightly at the temples, and maybe fifteen years older.

"I'm Ruby." I lean over my seatback and shake his hand.

Liddy smiles and nods her head. "Liddy."

Angel pats the empty seat beside him. "Why don't you come on over here and sit with us."

Before I can answer, Liddy's out of the booth and on her way over to their table. She slides in next to Angel. Hesitantly, I leave the booth and slide in beside Torrance.

"You just moved into Chriso's old place, right?" Torrance's smile radiates warmth.

"Right," Liddy answers.

"Have you settled in?"

"We have for the most part. Thank you for asking."

Torrance's hazel eyes twinkle. "My sister considered buying it for all of ten minutes when it first went on the market. Been empty now for a while though."

"Mom didn't want to live so far outside Santa Fe," Angel adds.

That's why they look so much alike. The minute I glance between them again, I see it. Angel is Torrance's nephew.

As if on cue, Daisy comes over, refills our coffee cups, and places a hand on a rounded hip, holding the coffee pot in the air with her other hand. "Most folks don't want to live up in Paso de Demonio."

"Demon's Pass?" I ask.

Torrance winks as if to excuse Daisy's snooping. "That's

what the old-timers call the forest up near where you live."

"They claim it's haunted," Daisy adds. "The forest don't take well to intruders. They say that unless you got ties to the land, maybe some Pecos or Apache blood, it'll snuff your soul. Tall tales you know, like white folks' fairies and leprechauns."

"People have been yapping about everything from ghosts to aliens living on that mountain for decades now." Torrance raises an eyebrow. His face lights up, punctuated by a huge grin. "These days, though, most of the stories come from kids out sneaking around with Jack and Jimmy Beam. Nothing like a pint of Jack Daniel's to stir up urban legends."

Remembering what Leo said on the mountain, I shiver despite my sweater. *Great*. I've exchanged smog and rush hour traffic for a possessed forest. "Fantastic," I mumble, turning to Liddy. "You never told me."

Angel puts his coffee cup down and leans in closer. "It's all just superstition, Ruby. You know how people are. Something scares them, and they find a way to turn it into more to justify crapping their pants. Besides, people around here just love their stories."

"Ruby isn't worried," Liddy assures him. She turns to me, raising an eyebrow playfully. "Despite her mother's flights of fancy and penchant for moonstones, I raised a skeptic."

Daisy pulls her dark eyebrows into a knob above her nose. "You should be. That forest has secrets. May not be little green men, but it's a strange place." She taps the table with her pen to drive home her point and walks off to take another order.

"Daisy is a little sensitive." Angel nods Daisy's way affectionately.

Torrance lets out a hearty laugh. "And a little bit messing with you."

"Oh. Duh," I fumble. But thinking about the ruin and what Leo told me, it's no wonder people tell stories about the forest. How could it not be haunted—even if only by history?

Angel adjusts himself on the seat, leaning in over the table. "So, what's your plan, Ruby?"

"Well, school starts tomorrow."

"You going to the university?"

"No," I blush. "Senior year."

Angel looks surprised. "How old are you?"

"I'll be eighteen in two months, in October."

"Man, I sure as heck don't envy you." He laughs. "It's been four years and I still hate high school. I couldn't get out fast enough."

"You're both pups." Torrance stretches backward and pats his stomach. "What I wouldn't give to be a youngster again."

Angel snorts. "You'd think we already buried him. Torrey acts like he's a hundred, not the ancient age of forty-two."

Liddy grins, and I know what she's thinking. Time hasn't treated Torrance poorly at all. He's handsome enough as it is. I can only imagine what he looked like at Angel's age. Although looking at Angel, I have a good idea.

"Mind if I ask you why you moved to La Luna?" Angel asks me.

I glance at Liddy, who half smiles. "We don't mind you asking," she tells Angel. "But it's a long story."

"Got it." Angel winks at me and swipes the last of his eggs off his plate with a tortilla before wiping his mouth with a napkin. Sensitive to Liddy's answer, he leans back against the seat, crackling like static across the table as he tells us about all the teachers he had at Pecos High, as well as which classes to avoid. Listening to him, it takes me maybe two minutes to figure out I enjoy hearing him talk; his mellow personality complements his mesmerizing voice, laced with Southwestern charm.

"So, what did you say to Ezra anyway?" Angel finally asks me. "I haven't seen him that riled up in a while."

"I don't know? 'Sorry'?" I shrug. "I bumped into him at the market and sort of stared. I felt bad about it, so I tried to say 'sorry.'"

Torrance gives me a sympathetic nod. "Don't feel bad. Ezra was about as nice as a horse's ass before his accident." He looks to Angel. "Now he's a nightmare."

"Ezra's always been a jerk," Angel agrees. "None of his family have ever been particularly friendly. Ezra's grandparents were *so* antisocial, some of the old-timers still claim the whole bunch of them are witches."

Torrance shoots Angel a look. "*Angel.*"

"What happened to him?" Liddy asks.

"No one knows," Torrance says. "But he used to be a handsome kid. The girls loved him. Though no one loved Ezra more than himself. I think that boy would've stapled a mirror over his forehead if he could've."

Daisy leans over the Formica counter and rests her chin in her palms, joining the conversation from across the aisle. "I don't think Ezra ever loved himself, Torrey. I don't think he has it in him to love anything." She comes around the counter and fills our cups again. "Angel and I, we went to high school with him. He followed some rich-ass society chick out east on scholarship after graduation. *Cague cabeza* never stopped talking about his Little Miss Perfect. But he came back two years later with his tail between his legs and a face that looks like someone stomped on it."

"He was in some sort of accident," Angel says. "But he won't talk about it."

"That's terrible," Liddy murmurs.

"You ask me," Angel nods, "he got what he had coming."

Torrance clicks his tongue disapprovingly at Angel, then grabs the bill off the table. He pulls his wallet out of his back pocket and holds out a wide palm. "Gimme yours."

"That's very nice of you, but we're fine," Liddy says politely.

Torrance is exactly how I imagined small-town friendly, but I'm also not surprised Liddy declined. Liddy would die before she let anyone, much less La Luna's hot sheriff, pay for our meal.

"We've been filling you up with wild stories. Not a very good welcome wagon, you ask me. Hand it over," he insists.

"It's okay, Torrance," I interject. "I would've sat around complaining to Liddy about Ezra if you hadn't invited us over. You have no idea how much we appreciate the company." I'm not just saying it to be polite either. Ezra's abrupt exit felt a little like being pummeled by a boxer.

Torrance wrinkles his nose. "Maybe just humor me." He sets his fine lips in an obstinate scowl, and I suspect arguing won't make one iota of difference.

Liddy sighs, hesitating before saying, "Only if you let us make it up to you."

Liddy and I stand up to let them out of the booth. Torrance gets up and throws a few bills on the table. He positions his hat on his head, then tips it as he half bows at Liddy, looking dashing in his tan uniform. "It'd be my pleasure."

Angel grabs his own hat off the seat and holds it under his arm, waiting for me to step aside. After promising to give me a tour of La Luna in the near future, he semi bows and trails Torrance to the door.

When they leave, I nudge Liddy. "You like Torrance."

Liddy squints at me, pursing her lips together.

"He's very handsome," I tell her.

"And Angel?"

"I guess he's handsome too. Anyway, I think Torrance was into you."

"Yeah?"

Liddy reminds me of a seventh grader, giddy about the prospect but too full of pride to admit it. It makes me laugh. Sometimes she's so oblivious. "Do I have to remind you that you could have any man on this planet if you wanted?"

"Oh, would that were true." She laughs. "And why do you say that like it's a bad thing?"

"I don't ..." I trail off. "You just ... you reminded me of Mom for a second."

"Because I like that he may like me? Ruby, it's not like I said I want to jump him."

"Thanks for the visual," I grimace.

Liddy and I barely ever talk about sex. The longest conversation we've ever had about boys was when I had sex for the first and last time. Liddy gave me an excruciating *use protection, be choosy, don't let a boy push you into something you don't want* speech, and then neither she nor my mom ever mentioned sex and me together in a sentence again.

"Can we go now?" I groan.

Liddy gives me a look. Ignoring my frown, she shrugs

toward the door. On our way out, we say goodbye to Daisy, who hands me a napkin filled with scribbly numbers.

"My sister, Racine's, cell. I'll tell her you'll call tonight. You let her show you around."

Smiling, I tuck the number in my pocket. "Thanks, I will."

Outside Margarita's, the dark clouds that hung overhead earlier have dissipated. Bright beams of sunlight hit the sidewalk, igniting glittery flecks of mica embedded in the cement. The air is still crisp, but if the last two days in the Southwest are any sign, it will be sweltering by three.

"So, we live in a haunted forest," I say as Liddy drags me to the car.

"Isn't every battlefield haunted?"

"Battlefield?" I choke.

She pulls her burnished eyebrows together, cocking her head as if to say, *Duh, Ruby.* "You didn't know the pass through the Sangre de Cristos here was a Civil War battlefield?"

"No. I didn't realize the Civil War made it this far west."

"Really? I thought for sure you'd read up on it before we moved." She shrugs and points east, sweeping her arm in an arc. "The Union fought off the Confederacy in Apache Canyon. The skirmish stopped the Confederates and the Civil War from moving beyond the New Mexico Territory."

I swallow. "You could've told me that before we moved."

"Like I said, Ruby, I thought you knew."

Liddy is right. Before Mom died, I would have researched the area to within an inch of its subterranean geography. "Guess I just never got around to it."

"Well, you've had other things on your mind, sweetie." She grabs my hand, twining her fingers with mine. "Anyway, how many people live in a supposedly haunted forest? It's pretty cool."

'Supposedly haunted' is as far as Liddy will go. She doesn't believe in much beyond biology, beakers, and test tubes. "Ghosts *and* witches," I snort. "The name, 'Paso de Demonio,' it's creepy, right?"

"Let's rename it," she says.

"Okay." I bite my lip and glance sideways at her. "Any suggestions?"

"How about El Vidente?"

"'The Seer'?"

"Yeah." She smiles. "Just imagine what it's witnessed."

"Great. Shall we take a vote?"

"All right," she agrees. "I make a motion that we rename the pass El Vidente. Anyone willing to second the majority?"

"I'll second," I pipe in.

"All in favor of El Vidente, raise their hands."

Liddy and I both raise our hands simultaneously.

"Good. Motion granted." Liddy claps for effect. "El Vidente, it is."

When Mom was alive, that's how the three of us made decisions, especially when we couldn't all agree. We've been doing it for so long, I guess it hasn't sunk in yet that two out of two is always a majority.

"What do you think it's seen?" I ask.

"El Vidente?"

"Yes."

"Everything."

I sigh. "Lucky."

"Life wouldn't be much of a surprise if you were El Vidente, love. What fun would that be? Anyhow, seeing is only one part of the equation. What really matters is that after you see, you let your eyes give way to your heart."

"Feelings shmeelings."

Liddy stops me on the corner. She puts her hand on my shoulder and squeezes. "You're not a machine. Don't even think about pulling that I'm-tough-as-nails routine with me anymore, got it? We're here now, clean slate and everything."

I salute her. "Yes, sir."

Liddy swats me over the head gently.

"The thing is, Lid, I could do without surprises for a while, you know?"

She nods. "I do, love. Indubitably."

I snort and sigh hard for effect, shaking my head as I step out into the crosswalk. Why are the simplest things so hard to talk about?

"Ruby!" Liddy grabs my arm, pulling me back just as a dirty, black pickup speeds past. "Pay attention!"

The driver hits his brakes, squealing to a stop in the middle of the street. I meet his eyes, sucking in my breath as I shake free from Liddy's grip.

Of course. Ezra.

CHAPTER FOUR

OVER AGAIN

WAITING ON PECOS HIGH'S front quad for Racine, my outsider flag is about as obvious as the United States flag whipping in the wind beside me. Kids merge in clumps in front of the main building, forming excited groups of hoodies, backpacks, and skateboards, talking about who did what scandalous thing to whom over the summer. Some of the kids closest to me stare, but they're polite enough to pretend they aren't when I catch them looking.

As the quad starts thinning out, someone calls my name, and a small, bubbly girl rushes up to me with a bouncy jog that makes me long for another pot of coffee. A jumble of petite features, shiny black hair, and dark sapphire eyes fringed with even darker lashes, she proclaims, "You must be Ruby! Look at you." Smiling, she grabs a lock of hair off my shoulder and waves it in the air like a tassel, then pulls me into a hug. "I'm Racine."

"Hi," I answer, grateful she found me.

"I love your dress," she gushes.

I stare down at the grass green wrap dress I've awkwardly tied around my body. Liddy bought it for me without asking and then made me promise to wear it. She claims it complements my eyes, that it makes my flax-colored hair look like buckwheat honey, that it makes my waist look tiny and my hips look so curvy they put Botticelli's Venus to shame. She was full of compliments, most of them baloney.

"Thanks," I sigh, secretly eyeing Racine's more flattering black sundress. "I feel like an overripe pear."

"Oh no," she assures me. "You look fantastic."

Racine grabs my hand and pulls me along into the building, talking at high speed about her classes, where to sit during lunch, and whom to avoid like the plague. She keeps on talking, though I barely say a thing. But she's comfortable to be around, and I know right away I want to be her friend.

"So, meet me for lunch?" she asks when we stop in front of my classroom.

"Sure. In the cafeteria?"

"Near the lunch line."

After I nod yes, she hugs me again. "Mr. Peterson's pretty cool." She waggles a finger toward my classroom, then grabs a brush from her purse and quickly pulls it through her long, straight hair, which she wears tucked beneath a wide red headband. "You'll love him. Anyway, see you at twelve." She squeezes my arm and runs off down the hall, waving over the sea of students that swallows her.

Except for a short break, the next four periods pass like a Tilt-A-Whirl. By the time lunch rolls around, I have a headache of Ulysses-sized proportions. I need aspirin in the worst way and turn my purse inside out, looking for relief. But all I find are a few scattered jellybeans and a half-eaten Twix.

"Ruby," Racine says after I follow her to the lunch line. "What's up?"

I rub my fists against my temples and squint. "My head's killing me."

Racine digs around in her purse and pulls out a small plastic bottle, handing me two white capsules. "Here. They may make you loopy, but they'll do the trick."

I take them from her and shrug quizzically.

"I get migraines."

I look at the capsules with longing. "I don't want to make a fool of myself."

She shrugs. "Keep them then—just in case."

"I really appreciate it," I add. "Just believe me, I'm loopy enough as it is."

Racine utters a soft, "Oh," then tells me to hold on. She hops out of line and rushes toward a tall girl near the cafeteria's entrance. They whisper to each other before Racine walks back, rolling two aspirin in her hand. "Take these," she orders. "If they don't help, take the Midral."

"Racine," I gush goofily, "I *so* owe you."

"You gave me an excuse to ignore Marta this morning. We're totally even."

"Marta?"

"You'll see."

I pay for my lunch, take my pink tray, and follow Racine outside to a scrubby area of quad alongside a football field that borders the mountains. Racine leads us to a picnic table and sits down beside two other girls already spread out on its benches.

"Ruby," she says, swooping her arm across the table. "This is Ashley and Marta."

They all start talking at once. Obviously, Racine warned them I was coming. They ask about Los Angeles and how I like La Luna and Pecos High. Ashley, who looks a little like a greyhound with a sleek black bob, asks if I've ever met Brad Pitt. She shivers as she says his name, breaking out in giggles. "He's a babe."

Marta frowns. "He's old."

"Whatever, he's still a massive hottie."

Marta raises a dark eyebrow and looks at me. "What Ashley means is, she totally wants to do him."

"Like you don't?" Ashley pouts, then turns and gives me a syrupy smile, showing every one of her large, square teeth. "Marta will *do* anything."

"Amen," Racine agrees. "Speaking of." She turns to me. "Daisy claims Angel's got it for you."

I swallow and bob my head from girl to girl. They all look back expectantly.

"Um, I don't think so." I mean it to sound convincing, but I blush.

Marta's brown eyes sparkle. "Oh, he likes you, Ruby."

"How do you know?"

"Beside the fact that you're new meat?" Marta pulls her long chocolate hair into a ponytail and twirls it into a bun, playing with the ends as she speaks. "He's my second cousin. I hear everything."

"He's sweet," I admit.

Racine gives me the once-over. "Sweet?"

"And handsome."

"Handsome as sin. And I hear he's good in bed." Ashley grins.

"Ashley!" Marta balls up her napkin and chucks it at her. "Barf."

"I'm just saying." She shrugs.

The three of them banter relentlessly, lobbing insults at each other like pros, obviously tight-knit friends. When the insults peter out, Racine throws an arm around my shoulders.

"Well?" she prods, turning back to me.

"Well what?"

"You gonna go out with him?"

It's fair to say I don't feel like explaining my lack of experience with boys to strangers. On the other hand, at least one of those strangers is trying to get to know me. I'm lucky to have even one new acquaintance to show me around.

I shrug, unsure how to answer. Angel is sweet, handsome, and definitely easy to be around. I just didn't feel that same oh-my-god factor around him like I did around Leo.

"I just moved here," I mumble.

Racine polishes an apple on her sundress and takes a bite, talking while she chews. "So what, you just moved here? How long does it take to decide whether you like a guy? It's not like it's rocket science or something."

"I like him. I just don't know if I like him *that* way. You know?"

Marta stares at me like I've sprouted wings and levitated over the table. Ashley looks thoughtful, and Racine just smiles. "Well," she says. "No one says you have to marry him."

"Really?" I ask sarcastically.

"Really," she deadpans.

"You looking for your soul mate, Ruby?" Marta scoffs.

I choke on my soda. "Good god, no. I just don't want to waste my time."

"How is going on a date wasting your time?" Ashley asks. "I mean, if you like him. Just think of him like, well, like man candy."

"Man candy?" I giggle. "What do I do with that?"

"If I have to tell you," Ashley smirks, "then maybe you better let me take a stab at him."

"Be my guest." I laugh.

"She's chicken." Marta speaks to the group, but her tone is unmistakably challenging.

I look her dead in the eyes, trying not to blink despite my pounding head. "No. I just have other things on my mind."

"Like what?" Racine asks.

"Like unpacking my room. And settling in."

"You *are* chicken." Ashley giggles.

"Oh, snap." Racine laughs.

"Maybe." I frown and rub my forehead. "Maybe not. Maybe he's just not the right guy."

"Angel's everybody's right guy." Ashley sighs.

"I don't know. I mean, I met someone I sort of liked this weekend while I was hiking."

Like. Funny. I haven't stopped thinking about Leo since Saturday.

"Spill," Racine demands.

"His name is Leo. Said he went to Pecos High. You guys know him?"

"Leo ..." Racine looks up at the sky for a moment. "That's right, Daisy asked me about him last night. Nope, name doesn't ring a bell."

43

I try to describe Leo as best I can, but he isn't easy to put into words. Incredibly, spectacularly, beautiful seems like an understatement.

"You're a dork," Marta snickers when I'm done.

"He sounds scrumptious," Ashley says.

"You met him hiking?" Racine asks.

"Yeah. A couple miles from my house. Up the mountain."

She bunches her mouth into a knot. "In Paso de Demonio?"

"Racine's superstitious." Ashley takes a bite of her sandwich, talking through a mouth full of peanut butter. "She believes every little thing people say about ghosts, and aliens, and, like, Bigfoot."

"Remember last time we were out near Pigeon Ranch?" Racine asks her. "You said yourself, it freaked you out."

Ashley throws a nut at her, pulling her small, heart-shaped face into a sour scowl. "That's because you kept talking about all the dead Confederate soldiers' ghosts walking around."

"There is kind of a weird vibe up the mountain," I admit. "But I also kind of like it."

"You believe in ghosts?" Ashley asks.

"Not really." If Liddy had her way, the only thing I'd believe in is compounds and beakers. The closest she even comes to considering the mystical is when she makes fun of Schrödinger. "Though I guess I'm open to it."

Racine looks at me sternly. "Yeah, well, just because you don't believe doesn't mean they don't exist." She crosses herself. "Just be careful up there, Ruby."

Marta snorts just as the warning bell rings. Ashley squeezes the life out of me and runs off to the bathroom, but Marta walks away with barely a wave over her shoulder. When they're gone, Racine tugs on my sleeve. "Way to go, Ruby, you survived."

"Survived?" I ask, though I have an idea.

"Las Gallinas."

"The Hens?"

"Yep."

"They weren't so bad."

"Not at all," Racine agrees wholeheartedly. "But I've known them forever, especially Ashley. She's been my neighbor since, like, kindergarten. It's not so hard for me to deal with their nosing around."

"I didn't mind."

"You're a good sport."

"You're great to show me around."

"Any time, *mi nueva amiga*," she smiles.

Next period, Racine and I manage to snag seats beside each other in the Media Tech room. Media Tech is one of three classes we share, and I'm grateful; she definitely makes being the new girl easier. Toward the end of class, when she sees me pushing my knuckles into my forehead across the aisle, she taps on my desk with a pencil.

"Hey," she whispers, "take the Midral."

Nodding, I dig around in my pocket for the pills, shove them to the back of my throat, and dry swallow. But on the way to sixth period, I warn her to keep an eye on me. "Just in case I fall asleep on the desk or, like, drool." I shudder.

My head feels a little like someone filled it with helium, but I manage to make it through AP Ancient Civilizations with barely a dribble. I even sort of enjoy it, despite the pounding.

Except for sewing back in tenth grade, which I took on a lark, I've liked almost every subject I've ever had in high school.

When the bell rings, Racine walks me out to the front quad, where we meet up with Ashley and Marta.

"You taking the bus home, Ruby?" Marta asks.

"Most of the time. Yeah. But I think I'll walk today."

Ashley's eyes pop. "Didn't you say you live *above* La Luna?"

"I do. But I like walking." Racine's medicine has definitely started to affect me; the wind feels like icy pinpricks against my skin, but my muscles are warm and happy.

"Racine drives." Marta scowls. "But the bitch lives like fifteen miles that way," she points north, "and won't take us home."

"That's not true," Racine snaps. "I just won't drive *you* home. Besides, I work today."

"If I had a car, I'd drive you home, Marta," I lie.

"That's mighty nice of you, Ruby." Racine speaks in an affected voice, doing a spot-on John Wayne impersonation.

I laugh a little overenthusiastically. Clearly, I'm not all in my right mind.

"What?" she chirps. "My dad loves westerns."

"No problem, lil' lady," I answer, attempting my own less-than-stellar impression.

"Great. Now we have to put up with two idiots," Marta mutters.

Racine hugs me after Marta gets on the bus, waving as she walks off to her car. When the bus pulls away, I stand with Ashley near the empty quad, inhaling piñon-scented air, holding it in until my lungs feel like bursting. I stand and stare up at the mountain range, focusing on the craggy green peaks and rutted mesas looming over the valley.

"It's so pretty," I murmur absently.

"It really is," Ashley nods. "It'll be hard to leave next summer. New York and me, I kind of can't imagine it. I've never been out of New Mexico."

"Really? You're moving to New York?"

"Acting," she shrugs. "Theater. It seems like the best place for it. But it also kinda scares me."

"I know what you mean."

Secretly, I already sort of hate the thought of moving to Northern California to attend Stanford—Liddy's pick for me. Then again, I never really imagined that I'd like living in a place like La Luna either and it's definitely charming.

After Ashley leaves, I stand in the same spot on the quad. Behind me, engines rumble in the school parking lot, filling my head with noise. The sound tickles my ears, whispering nonsense that makes odd sense in my addled mind. For a moment I drift away, daydreaming about Leo and the ruin. Then I realize I'm standing stiffly, staring up at nothing with my mouth slightly open, and pray people aren't thinking the worst about me as they walk by.

Looped up on headache meds, I start my trek back to La Luna. Overhead, black cumulus clouds follow me as I walk under the highway overpass toward Frontage Road. I try to keep my eyes on the street. But my mind wanders.

Except for my headache, the day has gone about as well as a person could ask for. Racine is like the Tiffany Diamond, and Ashley is a gem, though the verdict is still out on Marta. Still, I'm lucky they've taken me in. Marta could be Medusa for all I care, as long as I don't have to wade through a sea of new faces on my own.

Closer to the interstate a strong wind tears through the pass, intensifying the sharp, earthy scent of mountain rain. It whips my hair into a nest and feels cool, and crisp, and electric against my skin. Somewhere close by it thunders. I pull hair out of my eyes and glance north, turning in circles on the side of the road.

Over the mountains, it looks like night punched a hole through the sky. Long black clouds swallow white threads, coming together in a grey blur over the horizon. I watch, mesmerized, while leaves and dirt and an errant flyer blow past my bare legs.

In a blink, the storm moves overhead. The sky opens and a blanket of rain rockets toward the street, falling in sheets that pelt my head and arms. It stings, but I feel alive. With my face to the sky, surrounded by a drum line of falling rain and thunder, I barely notice the black pickup that pulls over beside me, idling on the shoulder.

"What the hell are you doing?" the driver yells out his partially open window.

"Standing!" I yell back, still looking up at the clouds.

"Jesus, Ruby, get in the truck."

My name snaps me back to reality. I jerk my head toward the road, peer through the truck's rain-obscured window, and vehemently shake my head no, when I realize it's Ezra.

Ezra leans across the cab and opens the passenger door from the inside, motioning for me to climb in. "I don't live that far from you. Come on."

His damaged face grimaces at me, but he looks earnest, if not a little bit anxious that I'll decline. "Fine," I harrumph. I climb into the cab and drop my soaking wet backpack on the floor, dripping all over his seat. "Umm, I'm wet."

"I see that." He frowns.

"Sorry."

"What were you doing?" he asks irritably.

"Walking home."

Ezra shakes his head. "Figures."

"How do you know my name?"

He raises his brow, pulling the waxy area over his eyes up toward his hairline. "Daisy called you Ruby when she bitched me out."

Ezra shifts his truck out of neutral and pulls away from the side of the road. He looks forward and keeps his mouth shut, peering through the triangular patch of transparent space trailing the windshield wipers.

I survey his uneven face while he drives, following the knotty skin over his features. Near his left eye an unblemished patch of skin crosses the bridge of his nose. He still has a pronounced nose, but the cheek facing me twists in scarred scallops; it's rough and dark in places and looks almost beautiful in the muted light.

Ezra still has prominent lips, but the right side of his Cupid's bow merges with the space beneath his nose, losing its border to scarring. His eyebrows are dark and full like his hair, but the skin above them is smooth and thin, almost like tanned wax paper. And though his right eye has the slightest droop at the outer corner, his violet-brown irises are still striking. Whatever happened, his thick, shoulder-length hair looks like something out of a shampoo commercial; he wears it pulled back, though a few loose locks fall over his face like a curtain.

"Stop staring," Ezra says matter-of-factly to the road.

My fingers twitch, inadvertently moving for the sketchpad in my backpack. I want to draw him. "Why?"

He shakes his head tersely and frowns. "Because it makes me uncomfortable."

"My mother's whole world was her face. She was beautiful. Then she died. Lot of good it did her."

Ezra pauses before speaking. "I'm sorry to hear it."

"She was a model," I tell the windshield feebly. "Anyway, I don't care what people look like. It doesn't matter."

He glances sideways, then snorts. "You don't think so?"

"I know so," I insist.

Ezra nods curtly, obviously finishing the conversation inside his head. After a moment, he asks, "Why were you walking in the rain?"

"Why are you driving in the rain?"

"Because I want to go home."

"Well?"

"You're very difficult." He sighs.

"I'm not really."

Ezra briefly meets my eyes. He looks both amused, and annoyed, and entirely unconvinced by my proclamation. "Why didn't you take the school bus?"

"I didn't feel like taking the bus. Besides, how do you know I'm coming from school?"

He chuckles but keeps his mouth shut.

"Because everyone here knows everything, right?"

"Something like that."

"I have to repeat senior year!" I blurt out.

He grins and covers his mouth with a hand, speaking through his fingers. "You're that stupid?"

"Like minds," I mumble. When he ignores me, I add, "You're a jerk."

"I never claimed I wasn't."

"So, what happened to your face?"

"How do you know I wasn't born like this?"

"And you call *me* difficult." I sigh.

I keep my eyes on the street and my mouth shut the rest of the way home. Raindrops bounce off the road, leaving behind seismic rings that spread out centrifugally across the tarmac. Each ripple is its own distraction. Given Ezra's complete stonewall, I'm grateful for it.

When we pull into my driveway, I realize I haven't told Ezra where to go. "How'd you know where I live?" I ask him.

"I'm right up over the hill there." He points through the forest. "I know who all my neighbors are."

"Oh. Right. Angel said you live close by."

"*Angel*." He swallows like the name tastes bad. "I'm sure that's not all he told you."

"He also said I'd get used to your attitude."

"Of course he did."

I sit in Ezra's truck, dripping on his seat, doing my best to give him the evil eye and feeling a little sorry for him even as I do.

"You can get out of my truck now," he announces.

"Well thanks for the ride, I guess."

Ezra's eyes fall on my face, narrowing while they focus. When I make no move to get out, he reaches across my waist and unlatches the door, swinging it open. "Goodbye."

His harsh send-off makes my cheeks sting. He may as well have slapped me, then pushed me out. I jump down and slam the truck door as hard as I can, eager to suck some of the wind out of his overinflated sails.

Angel is right. Ezra wears the term "jerk" like some people wear their letterman jackets. It fits him well. But then, I also kind of respect his bluntness—despite how badly I want to clock him.

CHAPTER FIVE

GUARDIAN ANGEL

MY HEAD HUMS AS I STAND UP, brushing pine needles and dirt from my jeans. Scratching at my ears, I toss my stumpy charcoals into my backpack, wishing Mother Nature had it in her to grant me just one more hour to sketch the ruin. Pre-twilight transforms the plateau into a fairyland. I want to draw the ruin in shadows, but I'm afraid of looking more like mountain lion meat than Ruby Brooks once twilight sets in.

Sunset turns the mountainside golden, igniting the dried flora covering the forest floor. As I lean over to collect an escapee drawing, a patch of crimson pine needles catches my attention. The needles spread out in a piecemeal path that leads me toward a maroon mess near the center of the ruin, to the rock Leo claimed was once an altar. Against the drab ground, the patch looks like dried blood. I pick up a pine needle, scratching at it, watching curiously as a crusty substance flakes off its root, like rust crumbling between my fingers.

A faint metallic scent fills the air, popping my imagination into overdrive. Turning in circles on the empty plateau, I suddenly feel exposed, and maybe a little afraid of being something's dinner.

As I stare at the rock, the humming grows louder, vibrating between the ruin's crumbling walls. I paw at my ears, then rub my eyes, waiting for my head to explode as my vision turns the forest into blurry chunks of light and outlines. Off to the side, between the trees, something moves. Startled, I whip around, squinting to see better.

In the shadows between two tall pines, I see my mother.

Already unnerved, I close my eyes, trying to forget Daisy's haunted forest stories. My mother died ten months ago. It's got to be the altitude. There's no way she's standing there like an ephemeral stump near the ruins. Still, my mind takes off running, moving from ghosts, to demons, to being sure I'm about to face down another mountain lion.

Shaky and suddenly mindful of Leo's story about Ottomundo, not to mention just about every news report about mysterious animal attacks I've ever seen, I rush to my backpack. Quickly gathering all my art materials, I turn toward the sloping hillside, refusing to look back before running at breakneck speed down the mountain to the creek.

Inside my kitchen, at the table, I collapse over my backpack. Did I really just sprint down the mountain? *Seriously, Ruby. Jeez.*

Ghosts. What a joke. *Embrace the unknown. Have some fun. Don't be such a freaking baby.* If Mom was alive, that's exactly what she'd tell me.

Rationalizing the plateau's oddities over a bag of Cheetos and a hot shower, I try sketching the ruin from memory afterward to unwind. A couple of sketches and a couple of Oreos dipped in milk for good measure, do the trick. My fears are easy enough to explain. Whether blood or sap, altitude does funny things to a person; ears ring and heads spin. Animals hunt and the things they hunt bleed.

By nightfall, as I park on Luna Street, I manage to move on to stressing about more important things, like my outfit and being the new girl in town. Racine and Ashley planned a girls' night out, and walking toward La Cuesta to meet them, my nerves go a little wonky. The ruin and its strange hum fall off my map. Starting over is just as frightening.

I notice Racine immediately. Under La Cuesta's neon sign, she lounges against the wall in a thin red sweater dress and high-heeled tan sandals that match her handbag. Ashley stands next to her in a gauzy blue mini. Compared to Racine, she looks almost mousy.

"Hey!" I wave at them.

"Ruby!" Racine rushes over and grabs my bare shoulders. "Look at you!"

Guessing in advance that they'd wear dresses, I dug up a billowy yellow skirt and violet halter top earlier. Liddy says they don't match. But I've never taken her or Mom's fashion advice very seriously.

Twirling in a little circle, I hold my arms out at my sides. "Okay?"

Racine purrs, "Divine."

"Hose me down." Ashley waves an open palm at her face. "I can't even."

Racine swats Ashley's butt and hooks an arm through my arm, sandwiching herself between us. From the sidewalk, I hear the cover band playing inside La Cuesta clearly. Inside, the noise is deafening. People crowd every square inch between La Cuesta's four walls; they dance on the dance floor, hover over pool tables, and pile into booths, yelling over each other enthusiastically.

"Ruby!" Racine shouts in my ear once we make it past the entrance. "Come up to the bar with me and order for us. Ash will look for a table."

"Why me?" I yell back.

"Word is Jack doesn't card. But just in case, you're new in town, and you look older, and you're gorgeous."

I look Racine over. "You're not exactly chopped liver."

"Please, Ruby. You're such a cool cucumber. I giggle when I'm nervous."

That's a new one to me. I don't feel anywhere near as composed as Racine looks. "I might pee my pants," I complain with a straight face.

She raises her eyebrows. "I have Handi Wipes in my purse."

"All right, come on." I grab Racine's hand and drag her to the bar, nudging us between two men standing at the railing. "Excuse me." I smile coyly.

One of them smiles back. "No excuse needed." He clears a space and lets his eyes wander over my face and body.

"See," Racine whispers in my ear.

Ignoring my neighbor's prying eyes, I lean over the bar. "Hey!" I call out to the bartender.

"Hey yourself." The bartender nods appraisingly. "What'll it be?"

Racine elbows me in the ribs. She wants a Bloody Mary. But me? I have no idea. I've never been much of a drinker. "Make me something special?" I ask, smiling just enough to seem flirty.

"Sure." He winks.

We leave the bar with Racine's Bloody Mary, Ashley's Cape Cod, and my Chattanooga-something. As we maneuver through a slew of already drunk people, Racine leans in and yells, "You're amazing!"

"Thanks." I grimace. Being my mother's daughter means I know how to work a room. By the time I was six, I'd learned "charming." By twelve, well, Mom had already taught me to use everything in my arsenal. Though I never felt good about it—manipulating people always makes me feel dirty.

We comb the tavern until we find Ashley at a booth near the back of the tiny dance floor, already surrounded by boys. They make room for us around the table.

"Hey, Ruby," one of them says when we sit down. *Henry*, I think. "How do you like Pecos?"

"Everyone's really great."

"It's a total shithole," one of the other boys says.

"It's not," I insist.

Racine shakes her head. "You just wait."

"Pecos and La Luna suck ass. I'm out of here as soon as I graduate," Henry sniffs.

"Me too," Racine nods. "Hello, Arizona State."

Ashley rolls her eyes. "Ray, you change your freaking mind every week. I thought you were set on UNLV."

"Las Vegas is old news." She waves her hand in the air, blowing Ashley off. "Where are you going, Ruby?"

"Stanford, probably," I answer quickly, trying to downplay it. "I got in last year, then deferred. They're holding my place; it's mine as long as I finish up with decent grades at Pecos."

Racine and Ashley both looked surprised. Ashley holds

a small hand up beside her head, tilting it inquisitively.

I take a deep breath. "I'm repeating senior year."

"Seriously?" Racine gawks. She takes a sip of her drink and glances up at the ceiling as if unsure whether to pry. "Why?"

I shrug. "It's a long, boring story."

She shoots me a look. "So, are you going?"

I shrug again. "We'll see."

Mom and I used to argue about how much Stanford costs. She wanted to know why I couldn't apply somewhere local. Then, after she died, Liddy insisted on tapping into a part of her inheritance, by default my inheritance, to pay for it. Once upon a time, I had something to prove. I wanted Mom to understand I had more to offer than fading looks and charm. But after she died, I realized I'd picked a stupid fight.

Henry holds his hand out across the table. "Forget college. Right now, I want to dance. Do you dance, Ruby?"

"I don't," I answer nicely, doing my best to avoid public humiliation.

Racine pokes my waist under the table. "Go," she insists.

Henry jumps up and snatches my hand, pulling me into a standing position. I grab my drink, downing it in one gulp while I glare at Racine.

The limited space on the small, packed dance floor makes it hard to move, and that's a blessing. I stand very close to Henry, swaying instead, which given the setup is about the best anyone can do. Henry talks over the music, but I barely hear him. So I just nod here and there and look around the room.

After what seems like a decade, Henry smiles and steps away, bowing majestically. I'm about to curtsy back when someone taps my shoulder.

"Ruby, you look incredible!" that someone shouts.

Out of uniform, I barely recognize Angel. His dark, worn jeans and untucked black button up dress him down. But he wears casual the way Mom walked the runway—with aplomb.

"Thanks." I swallow.

"Dance with me?"

"Do I have to?"

"Yes." He laughs, grabbing me by the waist.

Angel looks down into my eyes, moving his hips to the music. He puts his wide hands on my shoulders and runs them down my arms, raising goose bumps despite the hot dance floor. When he reaches my hands, he grabs them and hooks my arms around his waist, holding them at the small of his back. His body feels strong, and for a moment, my own body defects; it really, really wants him. But I'm not sure if I do.

"Angel." I break away from him. "I think I need to sit down."

Angel smiles ruefully and takes my hand, leading me to our table. Over the din, we talk about the upcoming Maize Festival, and someone's pot garden that Torrance and Angel recently busted, and Pecos High's football team. We talk about Ashley's brother, serving his third tour in the Middle East, and about Racine's crush on Giovanni, who so far hasn't come by the tavern. Outwardly at least, everything falls into place. But I feel like I've projected myself to the other side of the bar and am watching our table from a distance.

As the night wears on, the booth clears out, but Angel stays put. By midnight, I know the way I know one plus one is two that Racine and Marta are right. Angel likes me.

"So," Ashley says when there's no one left in the booth

but the four of us, "ever find that guy you were asking about? Leo?"

"No. I went back up to the ruin a few times, but no dice."

"Ruin?" Angel asks. "You mean the Pecos Monument?"

"Nope. The one near my house."

Everyone looks confused, so I point south up the mountain. "That way. Above La Luna. You guys don't know it?"

They all shake their heads no in unison.

"Really? There's this tiny ruin a couple miles up the mountain behind my house. It's beautiful. I've been up there sketching all week."

Angel twists sideways in the booth. "I take it you're not too worried about Paso de Demonio then?" He grins.

"Not so much," I lie. The forest does make me nervous, just not enough to stop visiting the ruin.

Racine's eyes bloom. "I said it before, that doesn't mean you should be caviler about it. I've seen ghosts in the pass, Ruby."

Angel gives her the once-over, then laughs. "The forest isn't haunted, Ray."

"I saw one, too, once," Ashley volunteers. "I think. It was kind of foggy out."

Angel snorts, leans across the table, and scrubs the top of Ashley's head with a fist before twisting sideways in the booth, shooting me a cocky grin. "Next you'll be telling her to watch out for El Maldito."

"El Maldito?" I echo.

"*That's* an urban legend," Racine says authoritatively.

"Like hell," Ashley squawks. "I've seen it! Freaking lion is as big as a freaking car."

"You did not." Racine shakes her head, shooting Ashley a cut-it-out look.

"You mean a mountain lion?" I ask.

"Yeah. A giant, man-eating mountain lion," Racine smirks. "Roams the pass looking for prey. But seriously, it's New Mexico, Ruby. Who hasn't seen a mountain lion?"

"Yeah, but not one that big," Ashley adds.

I stare between them, thinking about the lion I saw in my backyard.

"Locals love to exaggerate." Angel squeezes my forearm, letting his hand linger. "Bears, deer, bobcats. Wildlife is par for the course out here. Just keep an eye out after dark."

"Like you're the expert?" Ashley gently socks Angel's arm. "Whatever, I'm tired of your abuse, Angel. I'm calling it a night." She nods toward the pool tables at one of the boys I met earlier. "Jorge said he'd give me a ride home."

"What about you, Ruby?" Racine asks. "You need a ride?"

"I had one drink, like, three hours ago. I'm fine. Thanks though."

"You sure? You can leave your car overnight. I'll give you a ride back into La Luna on my way to work in the morning. I have to be in Santa Fe by nine."

"I'll take you home," Angel offers.

"Thanks, guys. For real, it's fine. I can drive."

Angel cuts Racine off before she can answer. "You shouldn't be here to begin with. You're underage. You all are." He frowns. "Let me take you home, Ruby. Racine can drive you to your car in the morning."

I look at Racine, who shrugs. I look at Angel, whose handsome face makes it hard to resist his offer. "If you don't mind bringing me back here in the morning, Racine."

Racine answers, "Not at all." But she silently mouths, "Are you sure?" afterward.

I quickly jerk my head yes. If Angel guesses I'm nervous about being alone with him, I'll die.

Racine walks us outside to Angel's white Ford Bronco. When Angel opens the passenger door, and I notice the Sheriff's emblem on the side, I cross my wrists and hold my arms out. "Think he'll cuff me?" I whisper in Racine's ear when she moves to hug me goodbye.

"Good Lord, I hope so." She giggles.

Angel looks at us sweetly and smiles, waiting for me to climb into his vehicle. After Racine walks off, he takes my hand and helps me up into the front seat, grinning like a jack-o'-lantern.

"Handcuffs?" He looks at me askew, raising an eyebrow as we drive out of La Luna.

"I mean, I've never been arrested." I smile coyly at him, hating how flirty I'm being.

"So, did you have fun tonight?" he asks.

I hiccup, then giggle. "Sorry," I blush. "I'm a terrible drunk."

"I thought you said you could drive."

"Okay, I'm a terrible wanna-be drunk. It's more of a contact high."

Without asking, Angel grabs my hand and tucks my fingers into a ball in his palm, squeezing them tightly. "You know, I really could arrest you just for being in La Cuesta."

"But you won't ... will you?" My eyelashes bat at him without my permission, and I seriously want to smack myself for being my mother reincarnate.

"Not this time." He grins. "Just do me a favor, don't go back again. As happy as I was to see you tonight, it put me in an awkward position. Ray and Ash should know better."

I bite my lip, embarrassed. "I'm sorry, Angel. I won't go back." Waving two fingers in the air, I aim them at my brow. "Scout's honor."

He laughs. "Were you a scout?"

"Not for long. My mom made such a fuss about our Brownie outfits, they kicked me out."

Angel laughs and then looks at me, still smiling. "So, now that we're alone, tell me, how are you *really* getting along so far?"

"Good. Fine. Everyone is so friendly." *Except Ezra*, I think fleetingly. "I'm really lucky Daisy hooked me up with Racine."

"Ray's a great girl. I'm glad to hear it."

He keeps his eyes on me, only peripherally watching the road.

I poke his arm. "What?"

"I'm worried about you, Ruby."

"Me? Why?"

Angel squeezes my fingers again, which are still encased by his large hand. After a very long minute, he says, "You didn't tell me about your mom. But Liddy told Torrance, and he told me." He looks sheepish for a moment. "I know why you moved here."

"Great," I snap, my standard knee-jerk reaction when it comes to talking about anything that has to do with Mom's death. And what is Liddy doing talking to Torrance anyway? "So now the whole town knows?"

"No. Torrance isn't like that. He doesn't gossip."

"Then why'd he tell you?"

"He knows I like you."

"And why'd Liddy tell him? Wait, you do?"

"You know I do."

I swallow, totally blanking.

"It's okay." Angel turns back to the windshield, speaking softly. "There's no rush. Anyway, I won't tell anyone. I just thought moving here, repeating senior year after everything, it must be hard for you."

"I'm fine. I like it here. Let's just leave it at that for now, all right?"

"Sure, Ruby. But if you do want to talk, I'm here."

I nod, smiling tightly. *Self,* I tell myself, *don't take it personally. He's not prying.*

"I'm sorry, Angel. It's not you. I don't mean to be so uptight. I just don't like talking about what happened. I'm still really sensitive about it."

Angel drives up my driveway and shuts his truck off. In the dim light, the half-moon turns his eyes to serpentine, a hard green dappled at the center with brown flecking.

"There's no reason to apologize," he says quietly.

Between Angel's handsome face, his sweet disposition, and the late hour, I really want to kiss him. But I'm not at all sure it's a good idea.

"Hey." He hooks a finger under my chin, lifting my face.

"Hey." I smile back shyly.

Angel slowly leans forward, staring at me the entire time. My logical self screams, *Pull back!* but when his lips meet my lips, my uncooperative self takes over. I lean into his soft, warm mouth and close my eyes, ignoring the alarm going off in my head. I kiss him back, indulging the me who doesn't want to rationalize until something rustles outside the Bronco.

"Angel!" I jerk back and point to a silhouette between two tall pines maybe a hundred feet off the driveway. Angel follows my finger, leaning forward.

"Jesus. That's one hell of a big cat."

"I think it's the same one I saw in our backyard last week."

"El Maldito?" Angel wiggles his eyebrows playfully and reaches back to grab a rifle from its mount. "Wait." I touch his wrist. "What are you doing?"

"Scaring it off."

I point to the gun. "Then why do you need that?"

"In case it doesn't scare off easily."

"Just give it a minute." Running my hand up his forearm, I gently rub my thumb against the crease near his elbow. Guns scare me as much as mountain lions. "Please."

Angel sighs plainly exasperated. I scoot toward him until our thighs touch. A metal passenger door may stand between the cat and me, but I've seen plenty of horror movies. I'm the new girl sitting in a truck kissing a townie.

"That's an awfully ballsy lion," I whisper.

Angel snakes an arm around my shoulder. "You're not much of a threat, Ruby."

"I wish it would go away," I gulp. "It's giving me the creeps."

"It's just a mountain lion."

"It is huge." I shudder. "They only come out at night, right?"

He chuckles. "Usually."

"Right." I let my breath out in a long, noisy sigh.

"It probably doesn't even notice us," he assures me.

"You're so calm."

"I've lived here all my life. Like I said before, you sort of get used to them." He runs a hand over his cropped head, grinning. "The Devil has really good timing."

"About that." I glance nervously out the window. "I really like you, Angel. But ..."

"But?"

"I just moved here. And I'm still a mess after last year, you know? For now, at least, I think I should focus on school."

He sits back, looking thoughtful. "I like you, Ruby. I'd sure hate to waste this kind of chemistry."

"I just ... I'm not sure I'm ready."

"I get it. But maybe tell me when you are?" he asks sweetly.

I nod and squeeze his knee before self-consciously pulling my hand back. As I sigh, the lion walks off, disappearing into the dark forest. "This sucks. I've never been so aware of being in the middle of nowhere."

"It takes some getting used to," he says quietly.

"What if I see it again?"

Briefly, Angel strokes my cheek with the back of his hand. "Then you call me. No matter the time. I'll come over."

I turn to him, feeling bad for leading him on, for being so wishy-washy. "You're a nice guy, you know that?"

Angel smiles. "I do."

"Friends?"

He nods. "Friends. For now. Absolutely."

CHAPTER SIX

HISTORY LESSONS I HAVEN'T LEARNED

THE NEXT MORNING IS A full-pot-of-coffee affair. My head throbs, and my skin feels so tight it threatens to peel off in sheets. The dry, hot weather is taking its toll. Factor in my morning-after pallor and I may as well be a walking billboard for drought management.

A brief glance in the bathroom mirror confirms that dark circles have roosted under my eyes overnight. My face looks drawn and a little grey, but a dab of concealer and lipstick isn't the answer. I need water. And coffee. Lots and lots of black, steaming coffee.

"You came in late," Liddy tells her newspaper when I walk into the kitchen, dragging myself like a slug to the full—*Thank you, Liddy*—coffee pot.

"Not really." I shrug.

"And you're up early. Considering Angel brought you home after one last night."

I plop down into the cushioned alcove looking out at the

creek. The bay window is the best thing about the kitchen. Sitting inside the cozy space feels like being on a small, safe ship floating on a sea tethered to my own private island.

"How'd you know Angel brought me home?" I mumble.

"His truck woke me up. I looked out the window."

"Racine will be here soon," I blurt out. "I left the car in La Luna. I hope you don't mind."

"Ruby! What if I needed it this morning?"

I bite my lip, feeling bad about leaving it in town without asking. "Angel insisted on giving me a ride home."

She gives me a look. "Because you drank too much?"

"No. Because he's Angel."

"You shouldn't have left the car."

"I don't want to fight, Lid. If you're going to ground me, just do it."

"I'm not going to ground you, Ruby. I'm just surprised."

"Up until Mom died, my grades were great. I brush my teeth. I'm not pregnant. Can't I please just be a normal teenager once in a while?" I jump up and plunk my yellow coffee mug down on the table, effectively ending the conversation.

She looks bemused. "When will you be back?"

"Never, if I can help it."

Liddy squints one eye and raises the other along with her top lip, waiting.

"When do you need the car?" I finally ask.

"Lucky you, I'm not going anywhere. But I thought we'd catch a movie and dinner later. Like we talked about."

"You still want to go with me?"

Liddy takes a bite of toast, answering with her mouth full. "Why not?"

"Fine. I'll probably go see the Pecos Monument or something. I'll be back early."

"Want company?" she asks casually.

"Not really."

"All right. Try to be back around four."

On my way out of the kitchen, I wave halfheartedly, feeling guilty. Liddy means well, and I love her. She isn't Mom and hallelujah for that. But sometimes her ability to equalize on cue drives me crazy.

Quickly, I throw on a pair of jeans and a tank top, pretty much dismissing the fact that I resemble a half-mashed raisin. Outside, warm air assaults my skin. Arid heat has already burned through the pass and the minute I step onto the sunny porch, my neck starts sweating. I pull my hair back, winding it into a ponytail, and am about to go inside to get a bottle of water when Racine pulls up the driveway.

"Morning," she chirps when I hop into her beat-up Civic. "You look like crap, sweetie."

"I feel like it too. It's so flipping hot this morning."

Racine nods sympathetically. "September's the worst, but it'll rain by two, and it'll cool off in the next few weeks. So," she hesitates. "What happened?"

"Liddy and I got in a tiff," I tell the window.

"I mean last night. After you left the bar."

"Oh." *Last night.* Of course. But Racine means *what happened* the way Liddy means *do it and I'll kill you* when she says, "Don't you think we should talk about it first?" The statement is both a question and an answer.

"Well," I hesitate. "He kissed me."

"And?"

"I kissed him back."

"You *do* like him then?"

I scrub my face, rubbing roughly at my lips. "I'm not sure. But we talked about it afterward."

"*Afterward?*" she squeaks.

"That's all that happened, I swear! But believe me," I moan. "It wasn't easy."

Racine gives me a knowing nod, then smiles. "You probably broke his heart."

"I doubt it. I'm sure there's a long line of nicer, prettier girls behind me."

"He's not a player, Ruby. And he really is a sweet guy."

A *really* sweet guy. She's right. "I'm a moron, I know."

"What are you scared of?" she asks, looking at me curiously.

I shrug, staring out the window at the street. "Caring maybe."

For the first time since leaving my house, Racine focuses on the road completely. She speaks to the windshield, but her voice is soft and genuine. "I don't know what happened to you in LA, you know? But if you want to talk about it, I'm a good listener."

"Thanks, Racine."

"You've got friends here. You can trust me."

It hasn't escaped me that I've struck like the friendship pot o' gold. I want Racine to know that. It just isn't so easy to tell her. After Mom died, I pretty much turned my emotions off. "I'm not trying to be evasive." I sigh. "You have no idea how grateful I am to have met you. I'm just tired of dissecting everything. You know? Of wondering why things happen when there aren't any answers that make sense."

"Was it bad?" she asks softly. "I mean, the reason you moved here?"

"Kind of."

Racine reaches out and squeezes my arm. "All right, my mysterious friend. Just don't forget, when you're ready to talk, I'll be here."

Racine flips the radio on. Otherwise, we drive to La Luna in silence, but it isn't uncomfortable. Being with Racine is so easy.

As we pull up in front of my car, she grabs my shoulder. "Wait, you didn't tell me. Is he a good kisser?"

"Seriously good," I groan. "Thank God for El Maldito. It saved me."

"What?" she cocks an eyebrow.

"We sort of ran into a mountain lion. It was just standing between the trees near my driveway."

Racine's eyes pop. "Seriously? How weird. You must have freaked out."

"Strange timing, right? I almost gave Angel a reason to blow *me* off. Pee-pants aren't so sexy." My exaggerated pout and big doe eyes make her laugh, and that makes me giggle.

Before I open the car door, she reaches across her seat and hugs me. "See you on Monday?"

"Absolutely. Have fun at work." She lets me go, and I give her hand an extra squeeze before hopping out. "You're the best, Racine."

Racine waves as she drives away, leaving me standing in front of Liddy's Volkswagen. After a quick visual inspection—Liddy would never forgive me if something happened to her car—I head into Margarita's.

From the looks of it, La Luna is a town full of early risers. The only booth left in the diner is a four-top near the back, and lucky me, right behind Ezra's. Ezra sits slumped against his seatback with a newspaper and a cup of coffee. When he notices me walking toward the booth behind him, he pulls his straw cowboy hat down over his face and slinks into the seat even further, hiding behind his paper.

I scan the diner, hoping to will someone out of a different booth. When that doesn't work, I finish my trek, walking as stealthily as I can, pretending I don't notice him.

Daisy brings me a coffee cup immediately. She nods sympathetically, filling the cup to the brim. "You look like you need this."

"I could kiss you." I smile up at her.

"Yeah? Do me a favor and don't. Next thing you know, we'll be the talk of the town. Trust me." She winks and waves her free hand around the room, clicking her tongue disdainfully.

"I don't mind." I grin. "Besides, who on Earth would blame me?"

"No one." She smiles crookedly and tugs on a braid. "But you try explaining it to the old-timers."

Daisy takes my order, lingering at the table while I briefly recap my first week at Pecos High. When she comes back to drop off my breakfast, she asks, "You went out with Racine last night, didn't you?"

"Yeah. We had a great time."

"From the looks of it, I believe you." She raises an eyebrow, reminding me of Racine. "You see Angel?"

I squint at her before answering. "Yes."

Leaning over, Daisy whispers conspiratorially, "You know,

regulars been taking bets on whether you'd be back after your run-in with Ezra." She pulls her pad out of her maroon apron and turns it over, scanning the backside. "Looks like Angel won the kitty."

"The kitty?" I whisper back.

"Angel wouldn't comment on Ezra, but he bet five bucks you'd be back this weekend, which means he was hoping to see you again. I'll wager you all my tips he'll be in soon just to check."

Daisy laughs and straightens up. She refills my coffee cup, then leaves me perplexed and alone with an enormous bowl of oatmeal. While I eat, I stare out the window, trying to ignore that Ezra's behind me. Instead, I think about the people walking by. I give each of them a secret identity. *Computer hacker. Cheeto addict. Internet porn star.* It's what Mom and I did when I was a kid and we had to wait in line. Back then I thought that if those everyday humdrum people could be spies, and diplomats, and members of secret witches' covens that met on the sly at the Magic Castle, then I could be anything I wanted. When I see Angel's Bronco pull into his assigned space in front of the Sheriff's Department across the street, I give him his own secret identity: professional sweet-talker. Last night he proved he could charm the pants off just about anyone.

Out on the sidewalk, Angel is harmless. But as soon as he turns and heads for Margarita's front door, my throat constricts. After our driveway kiss and Daisy's counsel, I'm not ready to face him. Panicking, I grab my cereal and coffee, hop up, and slip into Ezra's booth uninvited. "Mind if I join you?" I ask nervously.

Ezra drops his paper only slightly. "Will you go away if I say I do?" he asks from under his hat.

"No," I answer politely.

"Then whatever." Ezra pulls the paper up tautly, so it covers his face again. I reach over the top and peel it down. "Is this why everyone hates you?"

"*Hates me?* Are you serious?"

I bite my lip. "Kind of?"

Ezra starts laughing. Not condescendingly like I expect but for real. "What do you think, Ruby?"

"I think you're kind of a jerk. But I already told you that." I nod earnestly, as though the answer to my inquiry is in doubt and I'm somehow enlightening him.

"Then I guess you answered your own question."

"You do know that people don't like you? That people talk, that is."

He snorts. "I've lived here all my life. I may be ugly, but I'm not deaf. People talk. I don't pay attention."

I eye him, curious to know if he means it. "You can't be as bad as people say."

When his pupils narrow and he meets my stare, I cover my mouth. *Dumb, Ruby.*

"I may not listen, but that doesn't mean the talk isn't true."

"You say it like you're proud."

"No," he snaps. "I just don't care."

"You know, your face isn't a very good excuse to be a jerk to everyone."

Ezra looks both angry and surprised. For a moment, I think he might throw his coffee cup at me. But then he of good timing steps up to the booth and interrupts whatever it is Ezra is contemplating.

"Ruby." Standing over the table in his crisp beige uniform,

Angel winks at me. "How are you this morning?"

"Good." I swallow, still dodging Ezra's glare. "Great. You?"

"Fantastic. I had a fine time last night."

"Oh ... yeah ... me too," I stutter, feeling like a taxidermied deer. Angel nods at a now-empty table near the entrance. "Do you want to join me?"

Maybe Angel likes my company. But I also get the distinct impression he thinks he's rescuing a damsel in distress. "No. I'm good here. Thanks."

"Really?" He pulls his head back into his neck, knotting his eyebrows together. "You sure?"

"Positive. Right, Ezra?" I give Ezra a little kick under the table.

"Right," Ezra says casually, with just the slightest hint of amusement. "Ruby and I were having a delightful conversation."

"Oh, well." Angel sounds surprised. "I'm glad you're okay. I know we had a great time last night at La Cuesta. But after the whole driveway incident, I thought you might want a little company this morning."

As Angel speaks, I realize he's choosing his words carefully for Ezra's ears, not mine. "Well, I do have company. But maybe we can talk later?" I ask nicely, emphasizing the word "later" so he'll go away and let me die of embarrassment.

"Have dinner with me this week?"

"Um, can I check my calendar first?"

"Sure. Call me." Angel tips his hat at us and walks off toward Daisy.

Across from me, Ezra is doing a lousy job of hiding his delight. "Your calendar? Didn't you just move here?"

"Whatever."

"La Cuesta. I guess that explains it."

"What's that?"

"Why you look like shit."

I squint at him, admonishing his bad attitude with a curt nod of my own. "Thanks. You don't look so hot yourself."

Ezra chuckles. "You're a gem. You know that? I bet that's why you're named Ruby."

"Actually." I sigh. "It's not. My mother named me after Jack Ruby."

Ezra raises his eyebrows quizzically.

"Because he was a Jew with balls." I smile broadly, then cover my mouth. "At least that's what she told me."

Ezra reminds me of a caged beast, gloriously feral behind a controlled exterior. It isn't exactly that I want him to like me, and I don't exactly like him, but trying to get inside that cage without being torn apart is a compelling challenge.

Ezra smirks, opening the paper's sports section. He holds it up in front of his face. "You can go now."

I pull it down again. "Why?"

"You came over here to avoid Angel."

"Yes."

"Yes?"

"I said yes," I snap.

"He's gone now."

"Well, now I don't want to leave."

"You really do look like crap." He frowns at me.

"Fine. I look like crap. Surprise." I throw my hands up. "The bar was dusty. And I didn't drink enough water. It all kind of had its way with me."

"You were there with Angel?"

"Yes. I think I gave him the wrong impression."

"You think?" He cocks an eyebrow at me.

"Can you please stop repeating me?" I look down at the table at the uneaten bowl of oatmeal I brought over. The more I think about going to the Pecos Monument alone, about being alone all afternoon, the more I don't want to be.

"I have a weird question for you," I tell him.

"Lovely."

"Will you come to the Pecos Monument with me when you're done eating?"

Ezra drops his paper on the table and looks at me curiously. "Why would I go to Pecos with you?"

"Because I asked."

He shakes his head, grabs his coffee cup, and stares at its bottom for a second. When he looks up again, I can tell he's waiting for something.

"I really don't want to be alone," I admit.

"What's wrong with being alone?"

"It's lonely."

"Imagine that," he sighs.

My jaw flexes. It's probably better he declined anyway; calling him a grump is an understatement of epic proportions. "Just forget it."

Ezra fixes a hard stare somewhere past my face. His eyes never roam, and he never blinks, but eventually, he nods. "All right," he answers quietly. Ezra dumps the paper on his seat, throws a few bills on the table, and stands up. He towers over the table, tapping his boot on the flecked linoleum floor while he waits. "Are you coming?"

When I stand up and follow Ezra, quickly waving goodbye as I rush past Angel out of Margarita's, everyone, and I mean *everyone*, stops what they're doing. I can almost hear the chattering inside their heads.

Outside, Ezra stops on the sidewalk, looming over me. "You know you just gave everyone a mouthful to talk about, right?"

Nodding, I hook my arm in his and semi drag him toward my car. The gesture probably gives at least a few of Margarita's patrons angina. Although, if they're that set on making a meal of it, they probably have it coming.

Ezra stops my march forward and points down the street. "I'll drive."

I shrug indifferently and follow him to his truck.

Compared to the outside of the dusty black pickup, the cab is surprisingly clean. As I buckle up, Ezra takes his cowboy hat off, throws it on the seat between us, and drives away from La Luna with both windows down. He takes main roads to the Pecos monument instead of the highway, driving slowly, but the warm wind whips his shoulder-length hair around his face as if he was speeding.

Ezra's hair, which lacks a part but still seems to fall equally on either side of his face, masks a lot of his scarring. He has beautiful hair, dark and glossy like wet ink. It definitely adds to his magnetism—a trait that surprises me, considering his messed-up attitude.

As he parks near Pecos's Welcome Center, I pull my own hair out of its ponytail and run my fingers through it, combing out the knots that formed while the tail snapped out the window. While I smooth it, Ezra stares at me. For someone who claims *I* should learn some manners, he sure stares a lot at people.

"What?" I ask, squinting at him.

"You should wear it down more."

Ezra hops out of his truck and walks toward the ranger station. Without checking to see if I've joined him, he stops and stands near the entrance with his hands stuck in his pockets, staring up at the mountains. From a distance, it's hard to miss he has a nice build. His worn jeans and checkered shirt fit his tall frame and broad shoulders perfectly. With his hat pulled down so far over his face, it's easy to imagine Ezra before his accident. From afar, I completely see the guy he was. And for maybe the first time since we met, I feel more than a little sorry for him.

"You waiting for an invitation?" he shouts across the parking lot.

I scramble out of the cab. At the entrance, Ezra turns and walks into the building without me, making a beeline for a rack of postcards, where he tries to blend with the fixtures. A ranger hands me a map of the Pecos Monument, staring past me at Ezra while he briefly explains the things we'll see.

In the middle of the ranger's speech, Ezra slips outside, waiting near the beginning of the trail. When I catch up with him, I hold out a pamphlet. "Here. You read."

"I don't need a guide." He hands it back to me.

"*I* haven't been here before. I want to know what happened, about its history."

"I'll tell you." Ezra motions for me to follow, and I walk alongside him to the first crumbled structure rapt as he begins explaining the monument and its people. "Once upon a time, Pecos was the largest pueblo in New Mexico. Before Pecos, Natives built rock and mud villages in the valley here. They lived in pit houses along drainages off the Pecos River." He sweeps an arm across the plain in front of us. "By the 1400s, they'd gathered into a singular group. When Coronado passed through in 1540, the Pecos Pueblo was near 2,000 Pecos strong."

I close my eyes, trying to picture a great big dwelling rather than the grassy piles of rubble surrounding me. "It's hard to imagine."

"The Pecos built their pueblo at a midpoint in the pass through the Southern Sangre de Cristo Mountain Range. Strategically speaking, they ran the trade path between the pueblos of the Rio Grande and the plains tribes. Plains Indians—mostly Comanche and Apache—they traded their goods here. Look." He points toward a hard patch of barren land outside the rubble. "You can still see tipi ruts in the earth. The Pecos refused Plains Indians entry inside the pueblo, so the Plains tribes set up camp outside the perimeter during long spells of bartering."

Walking the trail with Ezra is like walking back in time. At the next clearing, he stops and stands behind me, pointing over my shoulder at the remnants of a crumbling rock wall. "Look over there. Pecos had sketchy relationships with other tribes, especially the Comanche. The wall signaled they weren't allowed beyond that point."

He walks on ahead, stopping again in front of a crumbling adobe mission. Catching up, I pull him down beside me on a wooden bench and grab a small pad and a piece of charcoal out of my backpack. "Do you mind?" I ask. "I want to sketch it. The sun's casting crazy shadows over the adobe."

He looks at me kind of funny. "You want to sketch it?"

"Just for a minute. But don't stop talking."

Ezra's momentary silence adds to the pueblo's quiet mystery. The air is dead still for a couple of minutes before he starts again. "Governor Oñate came through here in 1598. He called the pueblo 'Santiago' and assigned Pecos its first permanent missionaries. They built the mission there around 1617."

I look up from my smudged paper and scratch my nose. "What happened to everyone? It says in the ranger station that the pueblo was completely abandoned by the 1800s."

Ezra gazes at the mission, but really past it, as if the answer lies among its ruins. "You want history or lore?"

"History first," I tell him.

"Pecos played a big part in the Pueblo Revolt against the Spaniards. A lot of Pecos died fighting for their freedom. The rest were under constant attack by the Querecho Apache. By the mid-1700s, between the two, only about 600 Pecos remained. After that, from what I understand, contaminated well water finished them off. The few Pecos left moved up to the Jemez Pueblo. Only a handful of people still have Pecos blood today."

Sitting in the completely silent, oddly stirring monument that even abandoned still manages to hold so much magic, I'm struck by the fact that a whole distinct group of people just disappeared. Absently, I wipe my black fingertips on my jeans, feeling morose. "How does an entire culture just vanish like that?"

"That's history." He shrugs.

"Yeah, well, chalking something up to history doesn't make it any easier to swallow. What if historians said that about the Holocaust?" I roll my eyes. "That's history; let's just write it off."

Ezra leans over and smudges my nose with a thumb. "I wasn't writing it off," he answers calmly, wiping charcoal on my jeans. "It is sad. But there's no point crying over spilt milk. We learn our lessons and move on. It's all part of a process I have no control over. Anyway, it's a leap to compare what happened here to the Holocaust."

His levelheaded response is completely logical. Listening to it, I know he's right. But it still feels wrong. It's like saying my own life doesn't matter because it's fleeting, that no one will remember me unless I somehow manage to make an indelible imprint. Even after Mom, it's still hard to grasp that once you die, life moves on.

"Were you a history major?" I ask, purposely changing the subject.

"What makes you think I went to college?"

"Word is you went away after high school and came back like ..."

"This?" He tilts his head up and meets my eyes, daring me to look away.

"Yes," I whisper. "Sorry."

"You've been asking around about me?"

"No. I mean, well a little ... I guess I'm curious."

"I went to college for a while." He nods. "I studied astronomy."

"Not history?"

"I just said astronomy."

"Did you pick it all up living here then?"

"You're worse than the Inquisition," he sniffs.

"I'm just really impressed you know so much. Most people don't. Or they don't care. I'm ..."

"Curious?" he cuts me off.

"Yes."

"Ever hear the saying 'curiosity killed the cat,' Ruby?"

"I'm not a cat."

He looks at me and chuckles. "No," he says. "You're not."

His stare makes me uncomfortable. I have a habit of being too blunt, and until Ezra, I've never met anyone else as straightforward.

"So ..." Using my backpack as a diversion, I pull out an orange, a bag of Cheetos, and a Snickers bar. I split the Snickers in two and hand him half. "Hungry?"

"Not the Snickers." He nods. "The orange."

I stare longingly at the orange and hand it over. Considering the tour he just gave me, it's only right. Ezra peels the orange slowly, dropping small pieces of peel on his blue jeans. He seems pensive and a little lost in our surroundings.

"So, what's the lore?" I ask.

"Lore?"

"You said there was lore. About the pueblo."

Ezra turns his stony face toward the mission. He chews on the edge of an orange segment, taking his time before answering me. "Some of the elders from other pueblos today will tell you that Pecos was full of witchery, or that the Pecos people were enchanted. They're flush with stories."

"Like?"

"Like that before Montezuma went back to Mexico, he lit a sacred fire at Pecos and entrusted the Pecos people to keep it lit until he returned. Depending on which Pueblo elder you ask, the Pecos either neglected to keep the fire burning, and then fled for their lives or taxed their people to the point of death and exhaustion tending to it. In one version, the Pecos kept a giant snake god who helped them kindle the flames. The Pecos sacrificed newborns to the snake in exchange for prosperity and protection. But when they got lazy and stopped feeding it, it cursed the pueblo. Some of the Spaniards back in the day believed the Pecos were agents of the Devil. And there are still Pueblo elders today that think Pecos fell to ruin because shamans from rival pueblos cursed it."

Ezra stops talking. I can't tell if he just paused or finished telling me the story. I want him to go on, but he looks the slightest bit uncomfortable. "How do you know so much about Pecos?"

"I read a lot."

"Really?"

"Yes, really."

"Books about New Mexico and pueblos?"

"You're a pain, you know that?"

"I've been told," I mumble self-consciously.

He pops the last piece of orange in his mouth, chewing slowly. "How about I tell you more on the way back?"

Ezra stands up, waiting for me to follow him through the rest of the monument back to the truck. On the way, he occasionally stops to point something out or to tell me about the people who came to the pueblo to escape the Inquisition, or about the Civil War and the now infamous—in my mind at least—Glorieta Battlefield, just miles to the west. He talks all the way to the parking lot and half of the way back to La Luna. When he's through, he drops his head against his headrest and sighs heavily, as though totally spent.

"Ezra, do you know anything about the ruin near my house?" I ask.

"Near your house? You mean up the mountain?"

"Yeah."

He sighs. "It's old."

"I guessed that." I give him a look. He doesn't seem surprised I know about it, but he isn't excited either. "Do you know who built it?"

Ezra shakes his head. "But it's tucked away for a reason," he says gruffly.

"Really? What's that?"

"If whoever it belonged to wanted people around, they wouldn't have built it so high on the mountain." He sets his mouth in a scowl. "Be careful up there."

"Why? Because El Maldito might get me? Or the ghosts of Glorieta?" I joke.

"Just because, Ruby."

"You think the forest is haunted?" I ask, a little amused by his somberness.

"I'm big on leaving things that aren't meant to be meddled with alone."

Ezra stares straight ahead as he drives, but he keeps his mouth shut. I think about asking him more about the ruin or maybe about Leo, just in case, but his expression makes it clear he isn't interested in talking.

After a while, when the silence starts to feel a little heavy, I start babbling. "Even if you didn't study history, you must have a soft spot for it."

"Not really," he says. "Just sometimes, despite what I said about moving on, the past makes more sense to me than the present."

"Nothing makes sense to me lately." I roll down my window and hold my hand out. "I think that's why I love history. It just is, independent of what I think. Independent of my longing to make it mean something. Like God. Or space." I turn away from him, toward the scrubby mesas out my window. "History reminds me that humanity is so much larger than just me and the little world I've wrapped myself in. That my life is inconsequential in the grand scheme of things. It sounds weird, but I find the idea seriously comforting."

Ezra makes a sound like snickering. "Pretty girls shouldn't think so much."

"That's a shitty thing to say!" I stare at him, amazed and a little dumbfounded.

"You think it's shitty I think you're beautiful?"

"Are you serious, Ezra?"

"It's true," he answers. "But I'd lay odds you already know that."

"That's right." I exhale harshly. "I forgot. Daisy did call you a chauvinist."

"Daisy doesn't know me very well."

"Seems like she was on point."

"What do you know about me, Ruby? Really?" he asks defensively.

"Daisy said that you were an ass before your accident. That you treated girls like garbage. She said you never gave a crap about who you hurt and that everyone knew it. And you know what, Ezra, it's not that hard to swallow."

Ezra's jaw clenches, his knuckles tight and ashy where he grips the steering wheel. He inhales slowly through his nose and opens his mouth like he may say something, then closes it and purses his lips together, letting his breath escape in a stream. He seems angry, and I sense what I said hurt him. And that surprises me.

"I'm sorry," I whisper. "That was crappy."

The rest of the drive into La Luna, Ezra watches the road like it might disappear. He doesn't speak or even blink, as far as I can tell. And he certainly doesn't acknowledge me. When we pull into town, he quickly finds my car and parks behind it. But he doesn't open the door like he did when he gave me a ride home from school last week or tell me to leave. Instead, he loops an arm over his steering wheel and turns sideways on his seat.

"Daisy is right," he says evenly. "I wasn't very nice. But I'm not a chauvinist. And what I did before you moved here isn't your business."

My throat tightens, but I make myself look into his eyes. Even if he is as horrible as everyone says, it doesn't give me an excuse to behave so poorly. "It's not my business. You're right. I'm sorry." I grab my backpack and move to open the door, but Ezra puts his hand on my knee.

"Wait." He looks down at the stitching in his upholstery. I can almost hear him counting the threads, following a path with his eyes to the end of each seam. "If you want to know something, ask me. Daisy may be right about a lot of it. But there's plenty people say that isn't true. You want to come to a conclusion, come to it honestly. Then you can feel free to judge me."

His eyes are alarmingly clear, and in them I see the makings of a real, honest friendship. "If you promise to stop being so evasive all the time, you've got yourself a deal."

"I wasn't exactly bartering."

"And I can't *exactly* come to my own conclusions if you won't *exactly* talk to me."

He sighs, signaling defeat. And in that moment, I genuinely like him. "All right. I'll do my best. Just ease up on the interrogation a little, Ruby."

"Interrogation?"

He crosses his arms over his chest and sits stiffly, pursing his lips.

"Okay. No interrogation. Maybe just, like a little interview here and there?"

"I'll think about it."

I hold my hand out to him. "Truce?"

Ezra takes it, grips it firmly, then places it on my knee. "Something like that."

"You're the best tour guide a girl could ask for. Thanks for coming with me."

His smile is small but genuine. "I didn't really have a choice. You kidnapped me."

I flush a little, then look at the seat. "Maybe we can do it again sometime."

"Maybe," he nods. "We'll see."

CHAPTER SEVEN

CHERRY PIE FOREVER

FROM OUT OF NOWHERE, a green blur grabs me before first period, dragging me into the girl's bathroom. "Did you really leave Margarita's with Ezra on Saturday?" Racine squawks, circling me in a billowy jade dress. "Everyone's talking about it."

"If everyone's talking about it, why ask?"

"Come on," she insists. "Tell me."

"He showed me around the Pecos Monument."

Racine looks at me askew, tilting her face to the left as though pinning her thoughts down. "I can't believe you went out with him."

"We definitely did not *go out*. I saw Angel outside Margarita's Saturday morning after you dropped me off, and I panicked. I totally ambushed Ezra's booth. Believe me, he wasn't all that thrilled about it. Then I bullied him into going to Pecos."

"Why?" Her eyes narrow to slits.

I shrug. "I didn't feel like going alone?"

"I can't believe he went with you."

Racine pulls a brush out of her purse and runs it through

her long black hair a couple of times. Patting the sides down with her palms, she pushes it behind her ears, letting a swath of bangs fall into her eyes.

"He's not as bad as everyone says," I assure her.

"Oh?"

"And why is everyone so surprised?"

"Well," she smiles sheepishly, "when I say everyone, I mean Daisy. Daisy tells me everything. She's the gossip mill's main motor."

"So, I'm not, like, the morning news?"

"Not yet." She grabs my sleeve, pulling my purple T-shirt toward her. "Your hair's a mess, Ruby. Do you fix it in the dark or what?"

Racine tugs my hair out of its rubber band and brushes it until it's smooth. Pulling it off my face, she wraps the elastic neatly around my new ponytail. Beaming, she turns me toward the mirror.

"Thanks," I mumble, quickly turning away again.

Racine rolls her eyes but keeps her mouth shut. She locks an arm in mine and drags me out of the bathroom. "Let's find Ashley. She's dying to know why you were out with Ezra."

"You just said no one knows."

"I'm the one who told her. Ezra dated her sister back in the day. I think it's fair to say that Ash isn't fond of him. He totally played Cassie."

I sigh. The more I learn about Ezra, the less I understand him.

Ashley makes herself scarce until lunchtime, and thankfully, Racine knows enough to keep my visit with Ezra to herself around Marta. While Las Gallinas compare their weekends, I watch the sky over the mountains. In a breathless rush, they tick off who went where, on what date, and with whom. They gossip about how their dates looked. And what they wore. And what they ate. And said. And how often they breathed and used the bathroom. They pore over carefully compiled checklists, meticulously marking off each detail like every little facet is the most important thing since the invention of lip gloss or Cheetos. Eventually, the queue gets around to me. They all want to know what I did with my weekend—or more specifically, what I did with Angel when we left the bar on Friday.

Marta grins, stretching casually. "Davis told me you left with him."

"Who's Davis?" I ask.

"Davis is the dude with the spiky blue hair and labret piercing. You know, the one who sat with us for a couple minutes before Daniel came over," Ashley answers. "He's Marta's brother's best friend."

"Oh. Well." I pause. "Angel gave me a ride home. That's it."

Racine smiles at the table. Marta looks disappointed. "What a waste." She frowns.

When the fifth-period bell rings, Marta follows Racine and me into the main building. "Hey, Ruby," she says, sort of thoughtfully. "I'm throwing a party in a couple weeks. You and Angel should come."

I nod yes, hopeful the invite is a sign Marta is thawing. "Thanks."

"I mean, I'm inviting him anyway," she adds. "Come or don't. I'm just saying."

Racine clutches my elbow and steers me down the hall toward Media Tech. "We'll call you!" she shouts over her back.

Before class starts, she sits on my desktop leaning toward me. "Ignore her. She'll get over it. She just feels a little threatened."

"Why?" I squint up at her.

"What do you mean, why? Seriously, Ruby? You're the pretty new girl." She shakes her head and looks toward the blackboard like someone wrote the answer across its chalky surface. When I snort, she bonks me on the head.

"I'm sorry, I don't get it," I tell her. "It's not like Marta's Quasimodo or something."

"You don't, do you." She sighs. "Just give her a break for now. That's all I'm asking."

"Of course. I mean I *am* the new girl. Duh. And pissing off Marta isn't on my agenda, I swear."

Racine smiles and hops off my desk. After class, she sings Angel's praises on the way to sixth period, and after that, while we wait on the front quad for the rest of Las Gallinas.

"I get it." I finally stop her. "You want me to come to Marta's party with him."

"You may as well. It's totally going around that you're an item."

"But we're not. We haven't even gone on a date." I'm not sure what to say about the rumor, but I feel like I need to say something, or maybe just change the subject. "We never got a chance to talk to Ashley about Ezra."

"I'll talk to her. Just, Ruby, if Daisy knows, everyone knows. Or at least they will soon."

"Then they will." I shrug.

News, even fake news, travels fast in the pass. Since Angel and I are apparently already on the brink of betrothal, I spend the next couple of days waiting for one of Las Gallinas to grill me about Ezra, especially Marta. If anyone is going to say something obnoxious, Marta is it. But she doesn't ask. No one says anything, not in town or at school. Not until Thursday afternoon, when I run into Angel at the library in downtown La Luna.

"Hey." He smiles when he notices me. "What're you doing?"

"Hey yourself." I smile back. "I'm trying to find some info on the ruin near my house. Though I'm supposed to be studying for a calculus exam."

"Any luck?" he asks, sitting down beside me.

I stare down at the book in front of me. The library's overfilled stacks cram the compact building, but except for a few texts about the Santa Fe Trail and the Battle of Glorieta, most of the library's regional collection focuses on the area's Native American culture or the nearby Pecos Pueblo.

"Not really. Though I'm learning more about New Mexico's ruins in general."

"I called you last night. Did you get my message?"

"Uh," I pause, debating whether to lie or not, "I did."

Angel throws an arm around the back of my seat. "So how do you feel about going into Santa Fe with me tomorrow night for dinner?"

How I feel is nervous and unsure, which is why I never called Angel back, but I'm not about to tell him that. Instead, I look into his green eyes and nod yes.

He smiles. "Did you just accept my invitation?"

"I guess I did."

Angel raps his knuckles on the table lightly. "Great. I made reservations at this restaurant Torrance told me about. And I was thinking we could stop by my mom's place first. She owns a little cafe out on the south side of Santa Fe."

"Great," I mumble. If he *already* made reservations, he either hedged his bets or was pretty damned sure I'd agree. Either way, the boy has initiative.

"So, I've been meaning to ask ..." he hesitates.

I nod, flipping through my notebook while I wait.

"What happened after you left Margarita's with Ezra Saturday."

"We went to the Pecos Pueblo."

Angel tips back in his seat. "I'm not sure why he went with you, Ruby. But I'd be careful."

"Thanks," I grumble. "I guess I am lousy company."

He flicks my ear playfully. "That's not what I meant. I'm saying he's not very social. It's not like him to spend time with anyone. Even someone as charming as you, princess."

"I'm persuasive," I insist. "And don't call me princess."

Angel's laugh comes from his stomach. It's hearty and genuine and echoes through the near-empty library. "I'll buy that."

I meet Angel's eyes. "I get that Ezra's not very popular. But we don't have any history. I'm giving him the benefit."

"I like that about you. Maybe he does too. Just be careful, okay? Ezra is what he is, whether you have history or not."

I nod. *Ezra is what he is.* But then I'm not sure who that is yet.

"So, what are you doing here?" I ask.

"I told Torrance I'd pick him up a Tony Hillerman novel. One of the perks of being La Luna's finest—you get dibs on library books." He cracks a broad smile and tips his hat. "I've got to go, Ruby. But I'll call you tonight."

Watching Angel walk out of the library, I think about how my yes sort of tumbled out without my permission. Hanging out with a group of friends is one thing, spending the whole evening alone with Angel is another. I like him a lot. And I'm not sure yet if that's a good thing.

Later, over leftover tamales and coleslaw, I tell Liddy how I feel about going out with Angel, and how I kind of wish I'd said no instead. Amused, she makes her patented get-a-clue face at me. "It's easier to say no," she chirps. "Much safer."

"What do you mean by 'safer'?"

She chews on her lip. After a few seconds, she sighs like I asked her to explain the meaning of life in Pig Latin. "I mean, I imagine you're not gunning to put yourself out there right now. And I can't say I blame you. It's been a hard year."

Liddy always makes sense, even when I don't want her to. "But you think I should go?"

"I think you should, yes. If you're not ready to date you're not ready, but that doesn't mean you can't have fun. You're allowed to move on. Go out and live your life, Ruby."

My gut says she's right. There isn't any good reason not to go into Santa Fe with Angel. I mean, I went to Pecos with Ezra and *we* had fun. And Angel is a hundred times easier to be around. Not to mention better looking.

I promise Liddy I'll go. End of story. But by the next morning, the prospect of spending an evening alone with Angel, excites me about as much as Mr. Peterson's first-period ode to Lord Byron. I'm one-quarter interested, and three-quarters mortified.

Doubt creeps back on plodding feet. My only saving grace is Racine, who insists on coming over after school to help me get ready. A lifesaver to the infinite degree, she's seriously better than any stupid boyfriend.

Rifling through my clothes after school, Racine squeals,

"Ruby, some of these dresses are amazing!" She pokes an arm out of my closet and holds up a long, sequined gown.

"Thanks," I sigh. "They were my mother's. But it's not like I have a lot of places to wear them." My closet is stuffed with dresses, skirts, and tops I coveted while Mom was alive, the kind of clothes people wear in movies or high-fashion magazines.

"Shit, Ruby, she has really good taste."

"Yeah," I say. "She did."

"Did?"

"She's dead."

"Oh." Racine looks up at me with wide eyes. "Oh, Ruby, I'm sorry."

"Me too."

"When you said you lived with your aunt, I assumed your mom traveled or something. Or, like, that you didn't get along. I wish you'd told me."

"I don't like talking about it."

"Did it happen recently?"

"Last November. Right after Thanksgiving."

"God. What about your dad?"

I shake my head. "No one knows who he is."

"Really?" Racine scrunches her face into a ball.

"Mom wouldn't tell us. Truthfully, I'm not even sure she knew. She was kind of liberated. At least that's what she'd say."

Racine looks at the dress and absently shuffles through the rest hanging in my closet. I can tell she isn't sure what to say, and that she wonders whether or not it's all right to ask me questions. But I wait out her silence. I don't want to encourage the conversation.

After a few moments, she pulls out one of the last things my mom bought before she died and holds it up for me. "How about this? It'll look awesome on you."

Racine waves a silky emerald dress that cinches at the waist in my face. It's a little clingier than I like and definitely low-cut. Mom wasn't flat, but she wasn't curvy like I am. And she had, like seven inches on me.

"I don't know ..." I start before Racine cuts me off.

"Try it," she insists.

Grimacing, I pull off my jeans and T-shirt and yank the dress over my head, then let Racine zip it up in the back. It's a little too long, falling past my knees rather than above, and the bust is too tight.

"Wow." I look down at my cleavage. "It looks like someone squashed a melon into an eggcup."

"Wait." Racine walks behind me and unhooks my bra. "Now take it off."

"It's not going to look any better with a strapless."

"Ruby, just take the stupid thing off, okay?"

I pull my bra straps down, sneaking out of it without taking off the dress. When I drop it on the ground, Racine comes around and starts pulling at my bustline. She adjusts the dress's straps in back and tells me to bend over. "Just maneuver up a little. The dress will take care of the rest."

When I'm through "maneuvering" and upright, Racine whistles through her teeth.

"Bad?" I grimace.

"You won't be able to keep him off you."

"*Racine.*" I blush.

"You do know how pretty you are?"

"That's gracious coming from *you*," I joke, meaning it with all my fiber.

"And you're not at all stuck up about it." She smiles.

Racine brushes my hair and straightens it with the flat iron she brought over. The way she acts, futzing over me like a mother hen, you'd think she was sending me out on my first date. Though truth be told, there haven't been many others.

When Racine finishes, I grab my purse and a cardigan and head down the hall to dig for a pair of Liddy's heels. Foot size is about the only physical attribute we have in common.

"Wait!" Racine calls, racing down the hall after me. "You didn't even look in the mirror."

"You're a genius, Ray. I trust you."

"Okay," she answers hesitantly, giving me one of those who-are-you-really looks.

She helps me choose a pair of scarlet high heels. Given Liddy's arsenal of shoes, it figures Racine would go straight for red. They're kind of flashy. But I also like how confident they make me feel.

"Perfect!" Racine exclaims on her way downstairs. "You look like a million dollars." She grabs her bag off the couch and heads for the front door. "Just don't do anything to mess up your makeup in the next ten minutes, hear me?"

"I'll stand here in the hall. I won't even breathe. I promise."

Racine laughs. She crosses her eyes and blows me a kiss. "Remember to use protection!" she calls on her way out.

"As if!" I yell back. I agreed to a date but given my body's sociable response to Angel, and its tendency to go all anarchistic around him, I plan on keeping a polite distance.

Angel pulls up the driveway at six, sharp. Since Liddy is still at the university, I quickly jot down a note and leave it on the table. Then I run outside. When Angel sees me, he stops dead in the driveway and fixes his eyes on my dress, embarrassing the heck out of my already awkward self.

"Ruby," he draws out, "you look beautiful."

"You don't look too shabby yourself." I blush.

He doesn't. Against his loose white button up and dark blue jeans, his chocolate hair and caramel skin glow. He looks flawless, and edible, and not at all like someone I should be alone with.

Angel walks around to the passenger door and holds it open. He takes my hand as I step up into the Bronco and buckles the seatbelt across my lap. The gesture is a little old-fashioned, but then Mom taught me to always appreciate a true gentleman.

We talk nonstop during the drive into Santa Fe. As the land changes from densely foliaged mountains to scrubbier hills and rocky mesas, Angel describes his deputy's duties. He delights in the details, like how his colleague Chuck never shows up on time and how he's always pulling cats out of overgrown cholla gardens and dogs out of the Pecos River. In a way, Angel is a maverick. He subscribes to these textbook ideals and believes in justice to a hilt, but also likes doing things his way, even if it means breaking the rules. Listening to him talk, I realize I like knowing there's some rebel beneath his glossy exterior.

In Santa Fe, we drive to his mother's restaurant off Cerrillos Road and park outside a small adobe café named, Rojo. Inside the café, Angel pulls me into the kitchen, calling out in Spanish. Near the stove, a tall, commanding woman turns toward us, holding a dishtowel and knife. She waves the knife in the air and yells, "Angel, *mi corazon, viene beso su mami!*"

"*Sí, sí,* Mama," Angel mutters fondly. "Patience." He pulls the knife from her hand and hugs her tightly, picking her up off the ground. "Mama, this is Ruby." He smiles, waving his hand toward me. "Ruby, this is my mom, Viviane."

"Hello," she says warmly. "Please, make yourself at home. I'm so happy to meet you."

"Thank you, Ms. Ruiz." I almost curtsy. She has so much presence, she's almost majestic.

"Ruby. Please. Call me Viviane," she insists.

Viviane walks us around the kitchen. She's chatty, and sort of quirky, and not at all like Angel, who seems more levelheaded. Over the next half hour, she also repeatedly tries to feed me. The café smells wonderful, but Angel keeps refusing her, giving me the eye whenever I try shaking my head yes.

"Don't encourage her," he whispers in my ear. "We'll never get out of here."

Rojo is packed so staying for dinner seems like a really good idea. But since Angel is adamant about eating downtown, I smile and decline every time Viviane asks, covertly shooting him the evil eye when he isn't looking. When Angel announces it's time to go, Viviane walks us to the front of the crowded dining room and gives me a hug. "*Hasta próximo tiempo,*" she whispers in my ear. "Please, come back, anytime."

"I will. I swear," I promise. "I'll bring my aunt."

We say our goodbyes and head for downtown Santa Fe, stopping for dinner at a fancier restaurant Angel picked near the Plaza.

"So, what's wrong with your mom's place?" I rib him when our food comes, staring over the balcony at the people walking below us on the street. "Don't you feel like a traitor?"

He laughs. "She would have hovered all night, trust me."

"What's wrong with that? I like her."

"You don't know my mom. One dish would have turned into fifty. We'd be there 'til closing time."

"You guys seem close."

"We are. Very. But she's nosy."

"She's also really sweet. You're lucky."

"I am," he nods.

"My mom traveled a lot." I try to sound indifferent. "She'd take off for days. We weren't even sure where she was half the time. I never saw her."

"That must have sucked."

"Even when she was home, she was kind of a stranger. Anyway," I shake my head, mad at myself for bringing her up, "what was Viviane like when you were a kid?"

Angel nods sympathetically, reaching across the table to squeeze my fingers. The gesture makes my stomach roil, and I gently pull my hand away. I hate it when people feel sorry for me.

"My mom was always there," he says. "I barely knew my dad. He took off a lot. And he left for good when I was about four, so mostly, Mom and Torrance raised me."

"Torrance is pretty cool," I tell him.

"What about Liddy? I take it she was more like your mom then?"

"Can we change the subject?" I ask.

"Why?"

"I don't want to talk about me, Angel."

"Then tell me about Los Angeles."

"I don't want to talk about Los Angeles either," I insist. "Tell me more about your family."

Angel drops his eyes for a moment, then sits back in his chair. "I will if you tell me why you moved to New Mexico."

Except for the fact that Liddy bought the house in La Luna without telling us a couple of months before Mom died, I'm not sure myself. Until Liddy decided we should move, I wouldn't have guessed she even knew where La Luna was on a map.

"Liddy found an ad for the house sitting on the table one day. Mom had been going on about getting out of LA for so long, Liddy figured it was her way of finally manning up. She assumed Mom left the listing for a reason, so she went out and bought it. She was going to surprise her."

Mom often protested living in the land of silicon and smog and traffic so dense you could practically lean out your car window and kiss another car's bumper. She loved to wax on about packing it up and riding out of town with the sunset. But honestly, Mom was always more talk than action.

"Just like that?" he asks.

"She really wanted Mom to be happy. But when Liddy finally told us she bought the house, Mom was pissed. She was capricious about everything though, so it wasn't surprising. Still, Liddy was angry. She almost sold it. She was looking for an agent here in New Mexico when Mom died. Afterward, I guess Liddy just thought it was a good place to start over."

Angel's small smile crinkles the corners of his eyes. "I really wasn't trying to get you to talk about her. I swear."

"I sound angry, don't I?"

"A little bit."

Angel's eyes are so friendly. They stay locked on mine, encouraging me to go on. I'm comfortable around him, it's just that Mom isn't a comfortable subject.

"I really don't like talking about her." I sniff, then smile, trying to soften my tone. "So, I've been wondering," I say, purposely redirecting the conversation, "What do *you* think happened to Ezra?"

He frowns, dismissing the question with a wave.

"You never wonder?"

"Not anymore."

"If you had to guess?" I prod.

"What's up with you?" he asks.

"Now *you* sound mad."

"I'm not. I just don't understand why you're interested in Ezra."

"I guess I feel bad for him."

"You shouldn't. He doesn't deserve it."

"How well do you know him?" I ask, feeling defensive for no good reason.

Angel cocks his head curiously and crosses his arms against his chest, sitting back in the tan patio chair. "Better than you do."

"He's really not *that* bad, Angel."

He sits very still, as if waiting out a small, impudent child. "People don't like him. I don't like him. And for good reason. It's fair to say I don't understand why you want to hang out with him."

Instinctively, I pull back against my seat, putting a few more inches between us. "It really sucks to be alone. I know that."

"Has it occurred to you," he answers, "that maybe he's alone for a reason?"

"People change."

"Do they?" He shakes his head. "Maybe they do. But far as I can tell, Ezra hasn't."

I stare at him, almost angry.

Angel looks off at the twinkling lights hanging from the trees over the sidewalk on the Plaza, avoiding my eyes. "He's a user. It's his MO, Ruby. He'll gain your trust, get what he wants, then kick you to the curb when he's done. That's what he does, did with every girl unfortunate to fall for him."

"I guess I'm safe then. Because I'm not planning on falling for him."

He exhales, clearly exasperated. Sighing, he leans forward over the table. "I'm not kidding when I say old-timers still talk about his family."

"Maybe, but Ezra's not his family."

"If he takes advantage of you, I swear I'll arrest him."

"You'll arrest him?" I cover my mouth, stifling a laugh.

"If he hurts you, yes."

"Angel." I lean closer. "You're very sweet. But you barely know me. Don't you think you're being a little overprotective?"

"You act like it's a bad thing. You're my friend. I take care of my friends."

"I'm just ... I just don't understand why you think I can't take care of myself."

"I'm sure you can take care of yourself. But you don't know Ezra."

"I'm not two!" I snap. "I resent people treating me like I am."

"Look, I'm just saying, you're not taking me seriously enough when I tell you the boy's got issues. Ezra's not someone you want to be blind around."

"I'm not blind," I insist. "Maybe everyone else is."

"What's that supposed to mean?"

"It means that most people don't bother to look beneath the surface." I meet his eyes defiantly, silently accusing him of being most people. "I shouldn't have to explain myself for wanting to give Ezra a chance. And I really don't want to sit here and listen to a speech about my judgment. I mean, you don't really know me either."

Angel stares at me like I grew three more heads. He glances around, as if embarrassed by my outburst. "I didn't know it meant that much to you," he says softly. "I'm sorry."

I inhale deeply and close my eyes. Right or wrong, Angel doesn't deserve a lashing in the middle of some fancy restaurant during a date he planned to impress the lame girl he likes. Reeling myself in a little, I bat my eyes, showing all my teeth for effect. "I just hate knowing that something like looks matters so much to people. You can blame my mom for that."

Angel stares down at the table. "How was your food?"

"It was good, why?"

He shrugs. "Maybe we should call it a night."

Slick as ever, I've managed to alienate Angel in just a couple of hours. I want to stay longer and try to salvage things, but I nod instead, assuming he wouldn't have mentioned leaving if *he* wanted to be with *me* any longer.

Angel pays the bill and takes the stairs down to the Plaza before me, walking a few steps ahead until we reach the street. Neither of us speak on the way back to the parking lot, and the wind whistling down the narrow porticos connecting the Plaza accentuates the silence.

"You okay?" Angel finally asks when we stop at his truck.

I shiver and shrug. "I'm fine."

He opens the passenger door, waiting for me to climb in, then takes off his coat and hands it to me. "Ruby, I know you've been through a lot. I have no business pushing you. But I really like you. And no matter how it plays out between us, and no matter how strong you are, I'll still worry. It's the way I'm built."

He shuts the door and walks around to the driver's side before I can answer.

On the way back to La Luna, I lay my cheek against the leather headrest and focus on his profile, hoping he'll glance at me and give me the opening I need. But he doesn't. So, I speak to the side of him instead. "I'm really sorry, Angel."

Angel does this seriously cute thing with his mouth before sighing. "Don't apologize. I like that you say what's on your mind. Whatever it is."

"I'm still sorry." I pout sweetly for good measure. "Even if I am right."

Angel finally glances over at me. "Maybe, Ruby." He shrugs. "But if it turns out you're not, I get bragging rights."

"If you promise not to arrest Ezra, you've got yourself a deal."

"Torture maybe?"

"I'm a pacifist." I grin.

"If you're so sure, why not just agree to my conditions and be done with it?"

"Principle."

Angel slips his hand into mine, intertwining our fingers. "You drive a hard bargain."

Our hands lie together in a ball on my lap. I look down at

them suspiciously. When he squeezes my fingers and smiles at me like a lost puppy, I can't help but go with it. It's not like he suffers in either the looks or the intelligence department.

"Do you want to go home, or do you want to grab a piece of pie?" he asks.

I nod. "At Margarita's?"

"Where else?"

We pull onto Luna Street and park in Angel's spot across from the diner. Humming, he comes around and opens the door for me, slipping an arm around my shoulder while we walk. Near Margarita's, we run into Ezra on the sidewalk. He stops and tips his cowboy hat when he sees us.

"Evening, Ruby," he says quietly.

"Figures," Angel mutters.

I open my mouth to ask how Ezra's evening is, but all I manage is a clumsy squeak. For some reason, seeing him makes me nervous.

Ezra and I stare at each other, both fixed to our spots on the sidewalk. He examines me like he's never seen a real live girl before, until Angel tightens his arm around my shoulder and mumbles, "Cat got your tongue?"

Ezra glances from me to Angel, then down at Angel's arm around my shoulder. Streetlight glints off his eyes and for the briefest moment his irises look golden, shifting along with pupils that contract so fast it has to be a trick of light.

"Well, I better be off," he finally says, walking toward his truck before I can answer.

After he's out of earshot, Angel mutters, "Jerk."

I turn toward him. "Not really."

He looks down at my face, cocking an eyebrow.

"At least, not to me. How's that?"

"You want to be friends with the guy, that's your deal."

I wonder how long they've disliked each other. I'm not certain that Angel's animosity is mutual, but judging by Ezra's response whenever I mention Angel, it seems likely.

"Were you ever friends?" I ask.

"Not really."

"Were you jealous?"

"You mean of the way he looked?"

I nod.

"Everyone was."

"So, you hate him because he used to be hot?" I joke.

"No." He shakes my shoulders playfully. "I hate him because he's awful. He's always been obnoxious. We played football together. Dude was a constant headache."

"You played football?"

"Quarterback."

"And Ezra?" I just can't imagine it.

"Running back."

"I wish I could have seen you in those pants." I giggle.

"Remind me, I'll show you my yearbook sometime."

Imagining them high fiving and slapping each other on the ass makes me laugh, which quickly spirals into hysterics. Liddy likes to joke that my runaway fits have something to do with repressed feelings. I think I'm just better at appreciating the absurd.

Angel maneuvers my shaking body through Margarita's front door. He slips me into a booth and sits down beside me with a startling *thwump*. "Cherry pie!" he yells to the waitress across the counter. "My date's having a fit, so please, Mary, step on it."

"A fit?" I giggle.

"A moment?" He slinks an arm around my shoulders.

"A moment," I choke. "I like that. Too bad it's fleeting."

He grins. "It doesn't have to be."

"No, it doesn't, does it." I hiccup. "But it always is."

"It's all about your outlook, Ruby."

Angel is right. I was born a silver-lining type of girl. But my mother's death left its own pall, and in the last year, that lining took on a little tarnish.

"Well, right now," I swallow, working through the tail end of my laughing fit, "I'm all about looking out for my cherry pie."

"Cherry pie forever." He smiles. "That works."

"Cherry pie forever," I agree, knowing even as I say it, that cherries have pits and that in the grand scheme of things, like everything else in life, pits are mostly unavoidable.

CHAPTER EIGHT

IF I ONLY COULD

SUNRISE SETS THE HILLSIDE ON FIRE making embers of the yellowing leaves and rusty piñon needles blanketing the mountain. The sky glows, brilliant with first dawn, and alone in Apache Canyon with nothing but the scenery for company, my paintbrush comes alive. Each brushstroke highlights the pecked wood on an otherwise perfect juniper, smooth rocks jutting from a jagged outcropping, and a swath of red leaves in a sea of yellow birch droppings.

When the sun climbs above the mountains, I drop my palette and brush on the grass and lie down near a set of ruts etched into the hard ground—remnants of the original Santa Fe Trail. For hundreds of years settlers, Native Americans and explorers traveled over this very spot. Knowing it gives me goose bumps; Apache Canyon met them all.

Like a bird in flight, I stretch my arms and legs as far I can over the ground. Turning my face up toward the sky, I close my eyes. The morning air cools my bare legs, and occasionally a breeze flutters across my cheeks, tickling my lashes. Faint sounds surround me, the natural world in perfect disharmony. Lulled by sap and lavender smells I drift, daydreaming about history. Until a voice startles me back to reality.

"Odd place for a nap," it says from above me.

Surprised, I open my eyes, shielding them from sunlight that suddenly isn't there.

Leo stands over me, looking down into my face with the most amused expression. "Mind if I join you?" he asks.

I move my head against the scrubby grass and feel my hair catch in its blades. *You're awake, Ruby. He's not a hallucination.*

Leo drops to the ground, lying down beside me. He stretches out his long frame and turns his head sideways. Like the first time we met, his beautiful face leaves me utterly speechless.

"How are you?" he asks casually. "Other than happy to see me."

I didn't think we'd meet again. So I'm surprised. And happy. I'm just not thrilled he knows it. "Okay," I answer.

Leo looks straight into the sun without shielding his eyes. "I missed you up at the ruin this week," he tells the sky.

"I was up there."

"Looking for me?" he asks bluntly.

I start to say no, but for some reason answer yes. "For the ruin too," I add.

Leo turns on his side, planting his elbow in the dirt. "Well, here I am."

"Yes, here you are." I sit up and pull my legs to my chest, using my knees as a chin rest. "I wondered if I'd see you again."

"Because you wanted to," he says, not even pretending it's a question.

"For real?" I sniff. "Yes, I wanted to."

Leo smiles. "I'm not surprised."

"To think I was worried you were insecure."

He chuckles but doesn't say anything, and his focused gaze makes me uncomfortable. "It's quiet up on the plateau," I say, eager to change the subject. "Don't you think? I mean, I've never even seen a squirrel or a bird up there. It's a little unsettling."

Leo narrows his beautiful eyes, peeking at me through thick black lashes. "Don't get too comfortable thinking you're alone up there, Ruby. There's life on the mountain. It sees *you* regardless."

"Right, like El Maldito," I joke.

His eyes fall on my face, lingering on my mouth. "Mountain lions are good luck," he says absently.

"Really?" I bite the inside of my cheek. "They also kill for the sake of killing. I looked it up."

"I wouldn't worry about it," he sniffs. "You're not much of a meal."

"I also read they usually only come out at night." I sweep my arms out in front of me. "Though obviously, I'm not that worried."

"How often do you hike up to the ruin?" he asks.

"I went a couple of times after school last week. It clears my head. Don't laugh," I titter nervously and look right at him, "but sometimes it's like I hear the ruin in my sleep. That noise I told you about last time? It's like it's calling me."

Leo stares, focusing on me like a laser beam, but otherwise he's inscrutable.

"You think that's strange?" I ask, feeling insecure.

"A little."

"I'm really into sketching it. But maybe I just like the solitude." I shrug. "I don't know."

Leo's eyes blaze in the sunlight as he slowly picks single blades of grass from the ground, rubbing each between his fingers before discarding one blade for another. For a few moments, he seems perfectly content to sit with me in silence.

"So, how do you like it here so far?" he finally asks.

"Here in Apache Canyon?"

"No. Just here. La Luna, Glorieta, Pecos."

"I think it's magical."

"Magical," he repeats, with a lilt that elevates the word. "That's perfect."

"Thanks." I blush.

"Do *you* believe in magic?"

"I used to believe. But I gave it up. Quit cold turkey."

Leo's laugh comes out heavy and a little stiff. He leans back again, settling on both his elbows.

"Do you believe in magic?" I ask him.

"Definitely. Look around."

On the drive out to New Mexico, I was sure living in La Luna would be like eating dirt—dry, bland, and hard to swallow. But that isn't true; I feel a sense of permanence in the pass, as if I finally fit my surroundings.

"It feels right." I nod. "The way home should."

"That *is* magic." He grins.

"I belong. You know? I've never really felt that before."

Leo raises a polished eyebrow. "Fate?"

I try not to giggle. "I'm not a big believer in providence."

"Will is a powerful thing, but it's good to know your place, Ruby. Sometimes," Leo plucks a blade of grass from the ground, "there *is* a grand design."

Leo keeps talking, telling me about growing up in a culture

that barely makes sense to the outside world but that his elders still take seriously. "Sometimes it feels like I'm two people stuck in one body," he says. Leo smiles, like the thought amuses him. "Who I'm supposed to be and who I am. They don't always coexist well."

"I know the feeling." I sigh.

"Do you?"

"My mom was really superficial. She was all about appearances and popularity. When I was with her, I usually felt like an imposter in my own skin. I had a hard time making friends because of it. Guess you could say I'm combative sometimes, even though I'm a lot like her—probably because I'm a lot like her."

"How did you deal with it?"

"There's a Yiddish proverb: 'God created a world full of little worlds.' So, I tell myself there's room enough for all of us to do our own thing. Most of the time thinking that keeps me going. I'm trying to be okay with being me on my own terms *and* her daughter. Besides," I shrug, "in the long run, we're all just human, aren't we?"

Leo laughs. "I hope so, Ruby."

He stands up and holds out his hand, and I let him pull me upright.

"Will you walk me back?" I ask.

Leo lingers in front of me, erect and proud, like he's never had a weak moment in his life. But he doesn't answer.

"What?" I ask, brushing dust off my face while he stares. "Stop gawking at me."

He takes a step closer, looking down at my face, tracing it with his eyes. The canyon is so quiet I can hear my heart pounding.

"Leo," I exhale, too aware of how close he is.

With a single finger, Leo lifts my chin. "You are beautiful, Ruby."

Before I can protest, he kisses me.

Leo's lips are dizzying. I forget that I'm standing in the middle of a remote, supposedly haunted canyon. I forget that I'm Ruby Brooks, niece of Lydia Brooks, daughter of the formerly gorgeous, now very dead, Serephine Brooks. And I want to forget. And I want to kiss Leo so badly, I feel it in every inch of my body. The feeling grows through me, and out of me, and into the ground, taking root beneath the soil. Yet, I barely know him. And that's a terrible thing.

"Leo," I breathe, pushing against his chest, "Stop."

"Why?" he whispers, tugging me back.

"I hardly know you."

"You know enough."

His body feels hard and strong, but his eyes are soft. When he looks down at my face, I feel like a wet noodle, ready to collapse into his arms. He kisses me again, and the contact is electrifying. I could lose myself. It would be so easy. But a quiet voice buried beneath all my want warns me to proceed cautiously.

"Leo!" I step back abruptly, losing my balance.

Leo catches me and quickly lets go, as calm and collected as ever. "We obviously crossed signals."

"I think they crashed into each other."

"Maybe."

"Don't be mad," I tell him.

His lovely face breaks into perfect fractions. "Why would I be? It's not personal."

Leo is beautiful—like a Caravaggio painting. But he's also the cockiest boy I've ever met. "It's completely personal! You almost devoured me."

"Devoured you?" He laughs. "I don't think so."

"You kissed me."

"And you kissed me back."

The sun is so intense it's nearly unbearable. It beats down on my nose and shoulders, smashing my skin flat against my bones. For a brief moment I feel mean and skeletal. I'm sure that like my mother, Leo isn't used to people telling him no, and knowing it makes me angry.

Crossing my arms over my chest, I glare at him. "You shouldn't have."

"Kissed you? Don't sweat it. Come on. I'll walk you part of the way back."

I speed walk over to my easel and start packing up. *Don't sweat it? Seriously?*

From behind, Leo places a hand on my shoulder. "I'm impressed."

"I am impressive," I tell him, shrugging his hand off.

"How long have you been painting?"

"Since I was little. My mom bought me a set of paints in grade school. Whenever I had a tantrum, she made me go outside on the patio and 'paint my feelings out.'"

"Ever think about selling your work?"

"Not a chance." I have a closet full of paintings. Liddy wants to hang them on the walls in the new house, but I refuse. They're more like therapy. For my eyes only.

"You could, you know."

I turn and face him. "Right. Because you're the expert."

"You're intuitive." He grins.

I shake my head, exasperated. "And you're frustrating."

"Because I kissed you?"

"Because you're cocky and blasé, like you couldn't care less."

"You're wrong there," he says.

I balance my canvas against my leg and put my hands on my hips, annoyed enough to say what's on my mind. "Then why don't you meet me in town and take me out?"

"I would if I could, Ruby. But I'm very short on time lately."

My mouth drops open a little. Not because he said no exactly. But because he just kissed me. Kissing is fine but going out on a date isn't?

"Wow," I exhale.

"Maybe in a couple weeks. I'm not saying I don't want to. I do. I'm saying I can't."

I turn away from him, speaking over my shoulder as I start toward home. "I understand."

Leo catches up and grabs my hand, stopping my steady clip back to La Luna. "You don't." His eyes sparkle. "Take my word for it."

I close my eyes and start counting backward from ten. At six, I open them again. "Okay," I say, knowing I'll regret it. "I'll take your word for it."

"Why don't you meet me up at the ruin after school on Thursday?"

"You sure you can find the time?" I sniff.

"An hour or so. For you, Ruby, I can do that." Ignoring my sarcasm, Leo focuses his golden eyes on my face so intently, I swear he can see my insides. His gaze makes me shiver. I both hate and love the attention.

"You're staring again," I tell him.

"Can't help it."

I raise my eyebrows. "Try a little harder, maybe?"

"Okay, Ruby." He cocks his head. "When's your birthday?"

"My birthday?"

"Yes. The day you were born."

"Halloween."

His plush lips pull across his face, breaking into a wide smile. I sigh, waiting for him to ask the inevitable, like whether I'm really a goblin or a demon. I've heard it all; people are so predictable.

"Samhain," he says.

"S ... what?"

"Samhain. The Celtic New Year. When the veil between this world and the next is at its thinnest, and the dead return to mingle with the living."

"Nice," I grimace. "Your grandfather tell you that?"

"As a matter of fact, he did."

"Why'd you ask?"

Leo's sudden frown is more like a tick. "Just had a feeling."

"Now you're psychic too?" I snicker under my breath.

Leo doesn't answer. Silently, he follows me back through the canyon to the frontage trail. But about a mile outside of La Luna, he stops. While he checks his watch, I admire his strong tanned arms, trying to make out what looks like a tattoo peeking out from beneath his black shirtsleeve. Without thinking, I reach out and lightly trace a longish rectangle.

"What is it?" I ask.

Leo lifts his sleeve, showing me the colorful imprint on his tanned shoulder. "A totem." When I lean in close, he touches one of the interlocking faces that make up the tattoo. "My spirit guide."

The abstract tattoo vaguely reminds me of animal faces, but they could be anything from toucans to sloths. I'm still curious, but when I start to ask *what* his totem is, he taps his shoulder and lets his shirtsleeve drop.

"I have to go, Ruby. Next week?"

I nod, and he gives me a quick hug before sprinting off.

I watch him go, thinking about all the questions I forgot to ask. It annoys me how being near Leo rewires my brain; how I forget about simple things most people think about, like where he lives, and his last name, and whether or not he goes to college.

"My head is like that strainer when I'm around him," I complain to Liddy during breakfast the next morning, pointing to the colander near the sink.

"I don't like you hanging out with a stranger in the woods." Liddy frowns.

"Ooh, Liddy, 'Stranger in the Woods.' Isn't that a book?"

Liddy gets up and refills her coffee cup. "Why are you always so sassy?"

"Why are you always so paranoid?"

"I worry about you." She runs her fingers through her hair and takes a sip of coffee. "Speaking of boys, what about Angel? You never told me about your date Friday night."

"I really haven't seen you. But it was fine, I guess."

"Fine?"

I sigh. "Tell me about Torrance instead."

"Torrance?" She frowns.

"You went out with him this week, didn't you? I mean, you saw him Wednesday and again last night."

Liddy looks embarrassed. "We had dinner. He's really easy to talk to, Ruby. And we have a good time."

I move to the kitchen alcove and spread out over a pile of pillows. Outside, fat black rain clouds mask the sun. "You like him?"

"We get along."

I raise my eyebrows, sure "we get along" means something else. "Glad to hear it," I mutter. "What did you guys do last night?"

"We had dinner in Las Vegas. Then we went back to Torrance's house—to watch a movie," she adds.

"I went to bed at two. You weren't back yet."

"It was a long movie," she smiles. "And we had a lot to talk about."

Liddy gets up, stretches, and then comes over to the alcove to sit down beside me. She puts her hand on my knee and looks out the window. "Torrance is a gentleman. For your sake, I found myself hoping Angel is as wonderful."

I put my head on her shoulder. "He is."

"But?"

"I don't know?" I shrug. Truth be told, I can't stop thinking about Leo.

"Well, between Angel and your mystery man, it's not like you're bereft of choices. Just remember Stanford next year. A boyfriend may not be the best idea, for obvious reasons."

I pretend to choke, then plunge my ears with my fingers, letting my mouth fall open. Liddy and Mom started pestering me to get out and date the summer before tenth grade. They were always like, *Why don't you have a boyfriend, Ruby? Why don't you go out more, Ruby? Stop studying so much and have some fun, Ruby.*

Liddy laughs. "I'm just looking out for your best interests." She gets up and heads for the stairs. "I'm going to take a shower. I still have a mountain of work to do this morning, so if you want the car, it's yours. Just be back by six."

"Thanks." I get up and kiss her, then walk back to the kitchen, pausing for a minute before plunking down in the alcove again. "Liddy," I stop her, "I meant to ask ... we never really talk about why you bought Mom a house in New Mexico of all places. I was wondering about it the other night."

Liddy freezes. When she turns around, she looks a little crestfallen. "When we were younger, Sera used to take off a lot. She had friends in Albuquerque; they hitchhiked all over New Mexico. She fell in love with it."

"Did you know where she was?"

"Then? No. She'd disappear and call me somewhere from the road."

"Some things never change," I mutter.

"She came out this way now and then after you were born, but she never wanted to talk about it. Honestly, love, your mom was always a bit of a mystery. There was a lot more than I knew going on inside her head."

Liddy looks so sad. I stand up and go to her, hugging her so hard she gasps. "You're suffocating me," she laughs.

"I didn't know." I step back. "You must have worried a lot."

"It's a full-time job." She shrugs, pretending like I often do, that she's invincible. "I'm going upstairs, love. Are you all right?"

"Yeah, I am." I blow her a kiss and head back to the alcove. "Go."

"Ruby." She clears her throat, pausing on the bottom stair.

"This is probably a bad time to say this, so don't kill me."

"What?"

She draws her lips back over her teeth and rushes out, "Iin-vitedTorranceandAngelover."

"What?" I shriek. "Liddy! When?"

"For dinner. Tonight. Sorry."

"Yeah, I'll bet." I want to be mad, but she so reminds me of myself, I can't even pretend I don't understand. "Fine. But I'm not cooking. And I'm not, like, putting on a dress."

"I'll cook. And you can come in your PJs. How's that?"

I shake my head. "If you're lucky, I'll be home by five-thirty."

Liddy bites back a smile, trying to look serious. "You do that."

She walks upstairs, shaking her head for effect. When I hear her bedroom door close, I run upstairs after her and quickly dress. My heart already feels like it's tied in knots. Thinking about Angel confuses me; thinking about having dinner with *both* Angel and Torrance makes me feel like I may throw up.

CHAPTER NINE

THE PEOPLE WE BECOME

I DECIDE TO DRIVE INTO LA LUNA. Near Margarita's, I pass Ezra on the street and wave, pointing to the parking spot I plan to grab a few rows up. He stops, waiting on the sidewalk with an impatient scowl.

"You looked lovely Friday night," he grumps when I catch up.

"Thank you," I answer graciously, knowing he's full of it. "Where are you off to?"

"My truck."

"Come to Margarita's with me?"

Ezra's face is perfectly immobile. He stares at me passionlessly as if observing a beetle on the sidewalk.

"Please?"

"Why? You feeling lonely again?"

I raise an eyebrow, Liddy-style. "Did I do something?"

"No," he scowls.

"Then stop being a jerk and come in with me," I scowl back.

"I have things to do."

"What things?"

"Stuff."

"That's brilliant. 'Stuff.'" I put my hands on my hips. "What if I promise to only drive you crazy for a couple of minutes? I'll buy you a piece of pie to top it off."

Ezra makes a heavy noise that hangs in the air between us. He drops his shoulders. "Fine. For a couple minutes."

Inside Margarita's, fewer people stare at us, but it's obvious everyone thinks I'm nuts for hanging out with him. Ezra heads for the back of the diner and plops down in the booth farthest from the door. He slides toward the wall, then squashes up against it when I slide in beside him.

"There's a seat over there." He points across the table.

"Yeah, but I thought we could do the crossword together."

From the side, Ezra looks like he isn't sure whether he wants to smile at me or push me out of the booth. When I pull the crossword out of my backpack, he mumbles, "The crossword takes more than a few minutes," and grabs it out of my hands. After we order pie and coffee, he takes my pen and swiftly begins filling in the boxes.

"Are you just guessing?" I ask.

"Nope."

"Give it to me." I pull the paper over and glance sideways, a little amazed he's gotten so many so fast. "Wow, you're good."

Ezra grins. "I already did it this morning."

"All right, let me rephrase that. Wow, you're an ass."

He chuckles. "I thought we already established that."

"Why do I feel like you really enjoy annoying me?" I ask, sort of joking.

Though Ezra is being his normal prickly self, something between us feels different. He sits closer as we work on the puzzle and leans toward me when he speaks. Beneath his grumpy façade, he seems comfortable.

"Because I do."

"Well, you know what they say about boys who like to annoy girls."

"I don't," he says. "Tell me."

"Forget it."

Ezra turns sideways in his seat and rests an elbow on the table. "You're blushing."

"I'm not."

Suddenly, he reaches over and brushes hair out of my eye, surprising us both. Just as abruptly, he sits back and clears his throat. "So, what's going on with you and Angel?"

I swallow, startled by his brief display of affection. "Why?"

For a moment, he stares, looking thoughtful. "You're too smart for him."

"Wait. Was that a compliment?"

"I'm just being honest."

"And are you actually trying to give me advice?"

"I'm trying to be a friend." He shrugs.

"Thanks, but I wouldn't worry too much."

"No?"

"We're just friends."

"I think he has more than friendship on his mind."

"Maybe." I sigh, still fazed Ezra's touch affected me. "But that's all it is right now."

Ezra stares at me like he doesn't get it. "You don't think he's attractive?"

"He is. But that doesn't mean I want to date him. Don't be so superficial."

"Don't be naïve. Appearances matter."

"To some people, maybe."

"Really?" He squints. "Then you must be an exception."

"Coming from you, I'll take that as a compliment."

Ezra's mouth tugs just a twitch to the right. "Ruby, if you're determined to drive me crazy for longer than a few minutes, maybe we can take it somewhere else."

"Like where?"

"Have you been to Villanueva State Park? It's just past Pecos."

"No."

"Do you know how to fish?"

"Not really."

"Do you want to learn?"

"Sure." I shrug. "I guess. As long as I'm back by around five-thirty."

"Come on." He throws a ten on the table over my protests, gets up, and walks out of Margarita's, assuming I'll follow. "I'll drive," he says over his back.

I follow Ezra down the street toward his truck. He climbs into the cab and opens the passenger door from the inside. Not very smooth. And very un-Angel-like. Comparatively, Ezra's lack of decorum is almost funny.

Scattered fishing poles and tackle clutter the back of his pickup, and I realize that he'd probably been on his way to Villanueva when I attacked. "Thanks for inviting me," I chirp. "I've always wanted to learn."

Ezra turns to me with a genuine smile. "No, you haven't."

I wrinkle my nose and smile apologetically. "I have for at least the last five minutes."

Ezra explains the how-tos of fishing while he drives, speaking in a smooth, mesmerizing voice about balance tackle, and bail pickup, and downriggers—words I've definitely never heard used in everyday life. When we get to the park, he piles my arms full of fishing gear. I trail behind him, helping carry his poles and cooler, and a chair, and his tackle box down to the river.

Near the bank of the river, he puts a fishing pole in my hand and stands right behind me, wrapping his arms around my shoulders so he can maneuver his wide calloused palms over my grip. But he seems stiff and a little uncomfortable.

"Do you mind?" he asks.

"Um, no." I hesitate. "Whatever."

He pulls my hands back along with the reel and says something about "hauling," then whips the rod toward the river. The line flies across the water, glinting under the sun like drops of silver floating over the river's surface.

When it stops, Ezra exhales. I feel his warm body move against my back, and I am completely comfortable *and* painfully aware of his immediacy. He keeps his hands on mine until a few moments after the lure sinks, like we're one body, until I nervously clear my throat. Then he abruptly lets go and steps to my side.

"Spot-on." He smiles down at me.

"There's no way I can do that on my own," I gulp.

"You will. Eventually, you'll go from hooking the grass to making it across the river. It just takes time."

Ezra casts his own line and plunks down on the bank next to the spot I staked out. He grabs a soda from the cooler, holding a bottle of Dr Pepper up in the sunlight. "My only vice."

We sit for a while, passing the bottle back and forth when things get too quiet—until Ezra's line rattles.

Ezra jumps up and wrestles with his pole, pulling up a strange-looking fish the size of Texas. "Channel catfish." He looks back at me. "They usually don't come out until dusk."

The catfish bounces furiously on Ezra's line. When I move to touch its barbs, he stops me. "Don't. They're sharp. And venomous."

Pulling my hand back, I shudder. "Yikes."

He puts the fish in a smaller cooler then recasts his line, propping the reel in a hole he dug in the ground next to the one he dug for mine. Ezra grabs a sandwich and splits it in two, offering me half. While we eat, I think about his incredible mind, marveling at how he knows so much about so many interesting subjects.

"Hey." I bump his shoulder with my own. "You never did tell me how you got to be such a history buff."

Ezra stretches his arms out over his knees in front of him, dangling his sandwich above the grass. "My mother knows everything. And she's fond of sharing it."

As he speaks, my line moves downstream. Faster than lightning, Ezra jumps up again, taking my hand with him. He throws me at my pole, positioning himself behind me much the same way he did when we cast it. Moving gently, he tugs and releases in increments until the line pulls up a sleek fish with smooth, mottled skin.

"Cutthroat trout," he says behind me.

"Can we throw it back?"

"Are you kidding?" He looks down over my shoulder, tilting his face sideways to see mine.

"Well ... no? I'm not sure how I feel about killing it."

"It's a fish, Ruby. You take it home and eat it. I'll show you how to clean it before we leave." He lets go of me and unhooks the fish, adding it to the one in the cooler.

After Ezra helps me set up the line again, he sits down on the bank. Grabbing my sandwich off the ground where I left it, I sit down beside him and lean sideways into his shoulder. "So, your mother passed along what?" I prompt, hoping he'll continue where he left off.

"Our history."

"*Our* history?"

"Pecos. Remember when I said there are only a few people left with Pecos blood? My mother's ancestors came from the Pecos Pueblo."

"Seriously? That's awesome." Knowing Ezra can trace his family history back to an extinct culture adds mystery to his already complex personality. Liddy says we can trace a handful of our ancestors as far back as my great-great grandfathers from Ukraine and Russia, but after that, it's speculative at best.

"My great-grandfather about nine times removed came over from Spain during the Inquisition. He married a Pecos woman and stayed down at the pueblo until he died. My great-great-great grandfather's family secured a land grant, land we still own, when the pueblo collapsed. The rest went up to Jemez."

"So, most of your family live in Jemez now?"

"Just my mother. She's Shiankya Pecos. That was her clan. Far as I know, other than us, there aren't any others left. My dad was half Navajo. He died a couple years back. He has family all over the Southwest. I've got cousins all over New Mexico, but we're not close."

"You live alone? On your land?"

"Ever since my mother moved up to Jemez."

"She left you the house?"

He nods. "I took it over after I came back."

"From school?" I ask hesitantly.

"Yes."

"What happened? I mean, why'd you leave Boston?"

Ezra stares at me curiously. "How'd you know I went to college in Boston?"

"I heard." I shrug.

"You ask a lot of questions."

"I'm sorry. I ... I just want to know you better."

He slumps a little and sighs. "I'm sure you've heard stories."

"People say you were in some kind of accident. And that you came home around the end of your sophomore year. But that's it."

He drops his head sideways on his knees, which he's pulled close to his chest. His ear meets his blue jeans, and he leaves it there for a long time, staring off into the distance.

"I'm being nosy. I'm sorry, Ezra."

Ezra lifts his head and meets my eyes, looking past my speed bumps and guardrails and all the infinite stop signs, seeing me more clearly, I'm sure, than most of the people who've known me all my life. "Tell me about your mother, first."

Surprisingly, I find myself wanting to tell him. Even the things I've never said out loud before because they make me feel like a mean or hateful daughter. "She was gone a lot. I used to think it was my fault, like she didn't want to be with me or something. Liddy assured me it was just Mom's way, but I never believed her. I'm pretty sure I reminded Mom of what she gave up. Before me, she was on this fast track to supermodel stardom. Then, like that," I snap for emphasis, "she wasn't."

He frowns. "You know that's not your fault."

"Mom was a drama queen, Ezra. Swan diving off a pier in front of hundreds of people proved it. In her world, everything was bigger than life."

"She drowned?"

"That's what they say."

He looks at me inquisitively.

"She fell off the Santa Monica Pier. But she knew how to swim," I say softly. Other than Liddy, I've never talked about my mom's "accident," with anyone. "She was an all-state swimmer in high school."

"That is dramatic."

"Mom always had to have the last word, even when she knew she was wrong. She said she made sacrifices to stay in Los Angeles with us, but she was full of it."

Ezra stares at me. He looks genuinely interested, and it makes my heart swell. "You all lived together?"

"Yeah. My grandparents died when Mom was fifteen. Liddy was nineteen. She raised her after that."

Ezra runs a hand through his hair, closes his eyes, and tilts his face toward the sun. "You think she jumped?"

I drop my head, staring at the scrubby hillside. "Sometimes I think she just got tired of herself."

"I can relate to that."

"Whatever it was, she left us."

Ezra scratches his cheek and adjusts his legs, fidgeting with a few dry blades of grass beneath him. "Is that why you flunked senior year?" He looks at me with what seems like sympathy.

"Before she died, I was a straight-A student. Afterward ..." I sniff and face him. "Yeah."

"That's tough."

"You must think I'm an ass," I say, wiping a tear away.

"I don't." Ezra scoots closer and wraps an arm around my shoulder. Stiffly, he pulls me tightly against his side, dipping his head down to meet my eyes. Hair falls in his face, and he tucks it behind his ear, cocking his head sideways with a pensive smile. "There's no one way to feel when someone dies. Be angry for as long as you need to, but then find a way to purge it from your system. It's never good to hold grudges against the dead, Ruby. Trust me."

I rub my nose against his shoulder, then push my face against his arm, into his checkered blue shirt. His reaction is surprisingly tender; he puts his hand on my head and gently combs his fingers through my hair.

"I'm such an idiot," I mumble. "See why I hate talking about her?"

"It's no crime to cry." After a minute he lets go of me, putting about ten inches of space between us. "You okay now?"

"Yes, thank you. Still friends?"

Ezra smiles. "You're awfully insecure for someone so pretty. Yes, Ruby. We're still friends. Not for much longer, though, if you keep asking me stupid questions."

"You think I'm pretty?"

"Not really." He laughs. "But that's what you tell a girl when you want her to feel better, right?"

Small rocks dot the scrubby soil. I grab one and playfully chuck it at him, then jump up and run along the river. Faster than a jet he catches up and grabs me, dragging me toward the bank, where he dangles me over the water. When I finally break free, shrieking like a warbler, I pull him down the slope. We land near a pile of boulders about an inch from the river.

"That was close." I giggle.

"Not close enough." He sits up forcefully, projecting me into a couple of inches of water. Deep laughter breaks from his chest, pitching him forward. He shakes his head and covers his mouth. "You're wet," he says, stifling his delight.

Half soaked, I jump up and kick water at him, spattering his long-sleeved shirt with droplets. I do my best to look perturbed, but the truth is, I feel ... untethered.

"You suck!" I yell, laughing at the same time.

He stands up, wearing an amused smile that softens his scarred face and motions at me to come over. "I do, don't I?"

Ezra raises the hem of his shirt, lifting it to wipe my face. As he mops water off my forehead, I catch a glimpse of his stomach. Smooth brown patches of distorted skin run in lengths up his sides, but the muscular contours between his pelvis and chest are still visible. When he's through, he wipes water from my left eye with a thumb before stepping back, leaving his wet shirt half tucked above a large silver belt buckle.

"Good as new."

"Th ... thanks," I stutter.

I suddenly feel nervous in this way that sends my stomach on a roller-coaster ride. But it's Ezra standing in front of me, not Leo or Angel, so I don't exactly understand why.

"You ready to go?" he asks.

"No. But I guess I should if I'm going to get back in time."

Ezra holds out a hand and leads me up the bank to the cooler, where he teaches me how to clean my fish before we leave. As I pack up two newly gutted fish monsters to take home—a process I'll never in a million years be able to get through on my own without puking—I remind him that he hasn't told me why he dropped out of college.

"Can we save that for another day?" he asks quietly, looking off toward the mountains. "Like maybe next week?"

"Next week?"

"I'm going into Grants to pick up an order for a client out near El Morro. It's incredible country. If you've never been, you should go."

"Are you inviting me to come with you?" I ask awkwardly.

"Do you want to?"

"Um ... all right?"

"I'm thinking of pitching a tent near the El Morro Monument Saturday night."

"So ... you want me to ... camp with you?"

Ezra laughs. "If I only had a recorder."

"I just ... I'm not sure."

"Look at me." He points at his face. "You don't have much to worry about. I think we both know that."

"Ezra, that's not it."

"Do you want to go or not?" he snaps.

"Yes," I snap back.

Ezra throws his fishing gear in the truck bed, shooting me a look before hopping into the cab. This time he doesn't even open the door for me from the inside. When I climb up, he switches the radio to some dreadful country station. Except for his humming along, that's pretty much that; not a word leaves his mouth until La Luna.

On Luna Street, Ezra pulls his truck up right behind my

car. "I want to leave early," he says. "It's about a three-hour drive from here to Grants."

"What should I bring?"

He pinches his lip, pulling at it so a little pocket of space forms near the upper corner. A square patch of white tooth gleams through the small cavern. Somehow, it makes him look both dreadfully vulnerable *and* unquestionably confident.

"I'll bring everything we need. Wear something light, but bring something warm to sleep in."

"Do you camp a lot?" Seasoned hiker aside, my skills don't extend to surviving in the desert overnight.

He chuckles and nods. "My mother says I'm better suited to wilderness than society."

"I feel that way sometimes when I'm up the mountain."

Ezra's intense eyes fall on my face. "You still hiking up to the ruin?"

"Yeah. I go up to sketch it." That at least, is half true.

Ezra looks out the window, speaking to the street. "Be careful up there, Ruby."

His concern surprises me. "I am. I will be." Gathering my stuff, I open the car door. "I guess pick me up at my house Saturday morning."

As I jump out, he coughs. "I'm glad you're coming."

"I'm glad you're glad. I'm really looking forward to it."

I take my fish and get out of Ezra's truck, waving as he drives off. I smell like fish and river, and don't have a whole lot of time to shower before dinner, which is maybe a good thing considering the company. But I do want a moment to straighten up. My catfish and I share a similar look, mottled and shiny.

CHAPTER TEN

IN-BETWEEN

ANGEL'S BRONCO IS ALREADY in the driveway. As soon as I walk inside the house, I hear him laughing with Liddy and Torrance in the kitchen.

"Ruby, is that you?" Liddy calls out. "You're late."

"Yep. Sorry." I run into the kitchen and drop my package of fish on the counter, nodding hello at Angel and Torrance.

Liddy stares at me curiously, wrinkling her nose. "Where were you? I tried to call."

"Fishing."

"Fishing?" She chokes. "What the ... no wonder you smell so funky."

"Sorry, Lid. My cell phone barely gets reception outside of La Luna."

Liddy rolls her eyes. "Ruby." She takes a deep breath. "Just wash up and sit down." She points to the sharply set table, accented by a huge salad and crusty loaf of bread, along with what looks like brisket. *Brisket*. She obviously really likes Torrance.

Torrance and Angel sit across from each other at the table. While I wash my hands, Torrance points to the lump of newspaper-wrapped fish on the kitchen counter. "Looks like you caught a few. What'd you get?"

I bite my thumbnail, trying to remember. "I think Ezra said I caught a catfish and a trout." I toss the fish into the refrigerator. When I turn around, they're all staring at me.

Torrance sits back in his chair. "Well, that's quite a haul. Too bad you didn't get here earlier. We could've fried 'em up."

Angel chokes on his sentence before he gets it all out. "You went fishing with Ezra?"

Narrowing an eye, I focus it on him. "Don't start."

"I thought you were thinking about going into Las Vegas," Liddy says.

"I was, but I ran into Ezra. He invited me to go fishing." I nod at the brisket and pull the platter toward me as I sit, attempting to maneuver a big slice between the platter and my plate. "What'd you guys do?" I ask through a bite.

Angel and Torrance tag-team talk through dinner, sharing their day with a kind of verve that's contagious. After we stuff ourselves, and I help Liddy clear the table, Liddy and Torrance retire to the living room to build a fire. Angel stays in the kitchen, insisting on helping me wash dishes.

"Don't be annoyed." I flick bubbles at him. "You promised you'd trust my judgment."

"I'm not annoyed. Just surprised." Angel snaps my back with the dishtowel. He holds up his fists in victory. "And he scores. Twenty points."

"You sounded like it at dinner."

"I guess I don't understand the attraction—on either side."

"You don't understand why he'd want to hang out with me?"

"We've already gone through this. No, Ruby. I don't. He doesn't like anything. Especially not people."

"You forget." I wiggle my eyebrows at him. "I'm special."

"Special needs, maybe." He dumps the dishtowel by the sink and wraps his arms around my back. "Let's go in the living room."

Angel maneuvers my body down the short hall, plunking me down on the couch next to Torrance and Liddy. But trying to converse with either of them is pointless. They're so absorbed in their own conversation they barely notice us.

After a while, Angel winks at me. "Want to go for a walk?"

"Yes, please. Just give me a sec to change."

I run upstairs and quickly exchange my fish-infused clothes for something a little less rank, and we head through the back of the house, walking down to the stream. Overhead, the sky is filled with stars and because of the almost-full moon, saturated with light. It sweeps over boulders and water, illuminating them under a blanket of night.

I listen to Angel talk for a while, sitting on an outcrop of rocks by the bank while he tells me more about his father, Mick, and how Mick left for good when Angel was almost too young to remember. Angel makes it clear: Torrance has always been more like a father to him than anyone.

"Torrance seems like a really good guy," I tell him.

"Yeah. He is. And he really likes her." Angel nods back toward the house.

"Liddy? Did he tell you that?"

Angel doesn't answer, but he smiles, his teeth glowing in the moonlight.

"I'm glad. Liddy deserves someone really special."

"What about you?" he asks.

"What do you mean?"

"Don't you deserve someone special?"

"I haven't taken care of my messed-up sister and her screwy daughter all my life. Liddy gave up a lot for us, including having her own family."

"You're avoiding the question."

"I'm not sure I've earned the right to make that claim. I don't 'deserve' anything yet."

"You're hard on yourself, you know that?"

"Yeah. Liddy tells me all the time."

Angel stares quietly at the brook while I watch the sky, searching for shooting stars. When two fall at nearly the same time, I wish with all my might I can forgive my mother.

"You want to see a movie Tuesday?" Angel asks. "I have the day off. We could ride into Santa Fe after school. Or maybe Saturday, if that doesn't work."

"Tuesday sounds good. I'm going camping Saturday."

Dammit. Of all the things to just blurt out.

"Camping? With Racine?"

My heart speeds up, anticipating Angel's reaction. That it shouldn't matter is another story. My brain and heart aren't quite working together yet.

"With Ezra."

Angel makes one of those almost funny confused faces. First, he jerks his head, then scrunches his nose, then sort of opens his mouth. He stands up and moves closer to me, then bends forward a little, grabbing a stone off the ground that he throws into the brook. "So what? Do you like him?"

"Yeah, he's funny."

"That's not what I mean."

"Oh. No. Of course not."

But after the day we just shared, I sort of do. I just don't understand it. Ezra is mean sometimes, especially when he feels cornered and goes on the attack. And he isn't exactly handsome. But there's something about him that overshadows all that.

"Angel ..." I start, but the trees behind us rustle.

We both turn toward the sound. Angel holds his finger to his lips and shushes me.

Suddenly, a smudge behind a tree about sixty feet from the bank leaps into the open, morphing into a mountain lion. It stops and sits perfectly still, looking up at something unseen by our human eyes. Beneath the moon, its fur gleams as if polished by starlight.

"Don't move," Angel whispers.

The lion lingers near the tree long enough for me to appreciate its size. It's broad and long-limbed, and its muscled haunches ripple as it sways in place, mesmerized by whatever it sees in the treetops. It's so close. Close enough that under moonlight, I can see its dappled peach nose and haunting mustard eyes. Close enough to see its long white whiskers saluting the night.

Angel and I sit motionless, Angel's hand on my wrist to steady me. But I'm not scared as much as spellbound. Not until the lion's eyes turn down from the sky and settle on us. Then my breath hitches, sending my heart into an unsteady, dizzying rhythm.

"Don't look away," Angel says between his teeth. "Don't turn your head. They won't attack from the front."

I stare at the lion, caught in a standoff. For a moment, it doesn't blink or even move. Then it takes several steps forward, maintaining eye contact. By the time it's close enough for me to really start worrying, I'm convinced I'm going to have a heart attack.

"I think it wants to eat me," I whisper.

"If it gets any closer ..."

"We run."

"No, Ruby. We stand up and throw rocks and yell. Spread yourself out wide so you look big. We'll lock arms, so we seem like one person. All right?"

Angel slowly grabs my hand and pulls our arms out like we're flying. He steps away from me a bit, creating a void between our bodies. Then he uses his toe to shuffle rocks my way, close to my feet.

"If it gets any closer, *you* run."

"What about you?"

"Just do it."

The lion stands its ground, staring me down like a couple days' worth of dinner. Finally, it breaks eye contact. It opens its huge mouth, baring teeth the size of Liddy's stilettos, and yawns. The lion seems so bored by our display, it makes me laugh. I cover my mouth and try to stifle hysterical giggles.

As I stand with my hand welded to my mouth, the lion gives me the once-over. Then, as suddenly as it appeared, it turns toward the trees and lopes off.

"Come on." Angel pulls my hand and dashes for the house.

I react like an automaton, running like the wind until we're inside. Past the door, I start hyperventilating. Crouching down on the kitchen floor, I try putting my head between my knees but lose my balance.

Angel drops down on the floor beside me and starts laughing. "You okay there?"

"Am I conscious?"

"That was a big sucker."

"I think it's the same one we saw before."

"I think you're right."

"That's the third time I've seen it, Angel."

He nods. "We should call the BLM and have them send out a conservation officer."

"To trap it?"

Angel scoots behind me and rubs my shoulders. "If they can find it, yes. They'll tranquilize it and move it to an unpopulated area. But until we get someone out here, do me a favor and stay in the house after dark."

"You don't need to convince me, officer. I really thought I was going to be its evening meal. I almost had a heart attack."

Angel drops his chin on my shoulder. "I'm pretty sure you'll live."

"I totally owe you."

"You do, don't you." His smile is clear in his voice. "It's settled then; we'll go to the movies after school on Tuesday. You can buy me a bucket of popcorn for starters."

CHAPTER ELEVEN

REALLY, REAL, REALITY

"YOU'RE SERIOUSLY GOING CAMPING with Ezra?" Ashley asks, waving her corn dog around in the air.

"She also has a date with Angel after school today and a date with Leo on Thursday," Marta adds, tapping her long fingernails on the wooden lunch table.

"You know that how?" I look at Racine, who shrugs sheepishly.

"Who are you bringing to Marta's party?" Racine asks.

Ashley snorts. "As long as it's not Ezra. I can't stand him."

"Ezra's her *project*," Marta quips. "And Leo hasn't really asked her *out* out. I'm betting on Angel."

"Jeez, Racine. Is there anything I told you yesterday that you kept to yourself?" I get up, gather my trash, and head for the wastebasket.

"Ruby, wait." Racine stands up and runs after me. "I'm really sorry. I told Ashley about Leo and the camping-with-Ezra thing. I should have known she'd have a big mouth about it. But everyone knows you hung out with Ezra again on Sunday, just like they know Angel and Torrance were at your house. I promise to keep it zipped from now on, but you sort of have to deal with it. Otherwise, just don't do whatever it is you don't want people to talk about. At least not in public."

Racine follows me through the main building to the bathroom. "Seriously, tell me you haven't heard all about how I made out with Giovanni Friday night. I know you have. By tomorrow, it'll be all about how I ripped his clothes off and threw him down in the middle of the party we were at."

"You did?" I croak.

"No! That's my point. That's just how it is around here."

"I hate the way Marta acts around me, Ray," I tell her through the stall door.

As soon as I come out, she pulls a hairbrush from her purse and starts tugging at my hair. "She *can* be a total bitch. But she can also be really kind. She's not that bad when you get to know her. Cut her a little slack. I mean, Ruby, you know she's just jealous."

"She's not."

"Like hell, she's not. You've been here a month, and you've already got your own fan club. And the fact that you barely seem to care aggravates it."

"What's that supposed to mean?"

"Just that sometimes, you act like being gorgeous is a curse. Or you're just plain oblivious. To someone like Marta, it comes off as stuck-up. Most people do care about what they look like, and they make an effort. Marta thinks you're trying to show us all up."

I suck in my breath and pull away from her brush. "I didn't know you felt that way."

"Don't get in a tizzy about it. *I* know you're not. And I don't think you're stuck up. Look, I'll talk to Marta, but maybe keep in mind how she feels as well. Okay?"

Racine's sapphire eyes are as open as her face. She has my back *and* told me the truth without padding it, and I admire her for trying to sit on the fence between us. Not to mention I know she's at least partially right. "Fine, I'll do my best."

We kill the last few minutes before fifth period in the bathroom avoiding Las Gallinas. After school, Racine and Giovanni wait with me for Angel on the quad near the parking lot. Ashley and Marta join us while they wait for the bus, but they keep their distance.

"I'm sorry I was so crabby at lunch," I tell them, hoping to smooth things over. "I'm nervous about seeing Angel. I have, like zero experience when it comes to boys. I'm lame like that."

"Amen," Marta snickers.

"Shut it, Marta." Racine elbows her in the side.

"If you don't want to go out with him," Marta says, shooting Racine a look, "then don't. But don't act like you don't when you really do. That's what's lame about it."

"Marta," Racine starts.

"No," I interrupt. "She's right. It's like I want to see him, even though I don't. Like there are two Rubys inside me, and they both want different things. It makes it harder to decide."

Marta tilts her head sideways and glowers. "You make everything so complicated."

As if it's not bad enough Marta already thinks I'm an attention hog, Angel pulls into the roundabout, flips on his lights and siren, and waves at us.

"I'm so going to murder him," I mumble under my breath.

He calls me over and Racine giggles. "Show off."

Angel gets out and opens my door, grinning like the Cheshire Cat. Mortified, I walk over and climb into the passenger's seat, trying to ignore Marta and her evil eye while I wave goodbye.

"Sorry I'm late," he says as I blow Racine an exaggerated kiss. "I had to wade out into the middle of the river to rescue another stranded dog."

"Seriously?"

"Sadly, yes. Tough work, right?"

We drive to his mother's restaurant in Santa Fe first. In Rojo's kitchen, roasted meat and chile smells tickle my nose. Viviane and two other cooks hurry around pots of sauce, and colorful slabs of vegetables, and meats that litter every inch of counter space. When she sees us, she waves us over to a huge oven.

"Help me chop?" she asks, holding out an apron.

Viviane stands me in front of a heavy chopping board and wraps my hand around the sturdy handle of a blocky knife. While I attempt to chop unfamiliar root vegetables, she talks up a storm about the best kinds of oils to sauté food in. After I finish and arrange each root by color in a circle on the board, she finds us a table near the back of the restaurant.

Always a gentleman, Angel pulls out a chair for me. "You were right at home in there."

"What about you? Ever help your mom out?"

"Sometimes. When she needs me. But I'd rather eat than cook." He takes the menu out of my hand and places it on the table. "Let me order?"

The restaurant smells so good I'm not sure what to choose, so I nod my head.

Viviane comes back and sets a basket of frybread on the table. As she walks away grinning, Angel shoves a piece in his mouth. "How's school?" he asks, chewing slowly.

"Good, though I hate Mr. Haggis." Listening to my calculus teacher drone on ranks about as high as having botulism.

"Who doesn't?" He toys with a piece of ice, clinking it around his water glass. "Are you going to Marta's party?"

I pick at a piece of frybread, twisting a frayed sliver of dough into a scaly thread. "I know she's your cousin, Angel, so no offense, but I don't like her. And I'm pretty sure it's mutual."

Angel laughs. "Second cousin. And you're not in the minority. No offense taken."

"I don't know if I'm going. Though if Racine has her way, I suppose I'll be there."

"If you want company ..."

"I'll let you know," I finish.

We eat and talk politics, which leads to an argument about war. Where I'm a humanity-knows-no-boundaries pacifist, Angel has more of what Liddy would call a shock-and-awe mentality: hit the enemy hard when they least expect it, and then beat them into submission.

After dinner, we see a movie that's almost as awesome as Viviane's food, and by the end of the night I'm glad I agreed to go out again with Angel. But I'm even less certain about our status.

"Want to sit on the front porch?" he asks after he parks in my driveway.

"You're not worried about the lion?"

He leans back and pats the rifle mounted in the back of his Bronco. "I'll bring Tess."

"Tess?" I laugh. "You named it?"

Angel shrugs. "Doesn't everyone?"

The moon is high over the horizon, and when I step outside, I look up toward the mountains behind our house. Hazy light washes the forest, casting shadows in the spaces between the trees climbing the foothills. For a moment, it's silent in a way life never is.

"You okay?" Angel asks.

I shake my head. "I'm okay. Let's just sit down."

I plunk onto a porch step beside him, staring at the pines across the driveway. Tall trees rise like sentries from the scrubby ground, leaving pockets of dark space between each trunk. After Daisy and Leo's stories, it's easy to imagine things that go bump in the night. Way too easy.

Angel wraps an arm around my shoulder and pulls me close. But when he tries to kiss me, I maneuver his kiss toward my forehead.

"Sorry." I smile.

"It was worth a try." He shrugs.

"I had fun tonight, Angel."

"But?"

"I like you, obviously. But I'm still confused about what I want."

My arms prickle, and I suddenly *feel* something watching me. The bushes off the driveway rustle and I jump up, standing paralyzed on the porch step. Being a skeptic by day is a cinch. But in the dark, ghosts and El Maldito don't seem quite as fantastical.

Angel grabs Tess and pulls me closer, shushing me with a finger. As my ears adjust, homing in on the forest's night music, I hear the ruin's hum—almost like a whisper.

"Do you hear that?" I swallow.

He looks down at me. "What?"

"That noise?"

Angel squints at me, then looks out at the driveway. After a minute he shrugs. "Nothing."

I'm about to tell him maybe we should go inside, but something moves off to my side. "Angel!" I gasp, pivoting on the step. Out of the corner of my eye, I glimpse what looks like a smudge of a horse riding across my driveway. "Did you see it?"

He shakes his head. "You're seeing shadows, Ruby."

"It looked like a man on a horse. Like a see-through man on a horse made of smoke." Whatever crossed the driveway, I'm 100 percent certain it wasn't just a shadow.

"I think Daisy's stories are getting to you."

"Maybe." I make a face at him.

"You should probably go inside," he says, concern tainting his voice.

"I saw *something*, Angel. I'm not crazy."

"I don't think you're crazy," he laughs. "I think you're tired. Plus, I already blew it once tonight. I'm thinking if I get you inside now, I might still be able to recoup my losses."

I rub my eyes again, straining to see down the driveway in the dark. "It's not that I'm not interested."

"It's just that you're not interested," he half smiles.

Why does Angel have to make it so hard? Why can't he be just the tiniest bit jerky, or stuck-up, or have bad hygiene or something—some trait that makes it easier to pull away when he turns on the charm. Because I do like him. For some reason, I just can't bring myself to commit to more. "You know what, you're right. I'm just tired."

"Don't stress, Ruby." Angel holds a hand in the air as if swearing on the Bible. "I want it to work. But I don't want to push either."

"I *must* be crazy." I sigh.

"You must be." He gives me a tight hug and turns me around, giving me a gentle push toward the door. Like a true gentleman, he waits on the steps until I get inside.

For the most part, Angel is perfect. And I like being with him. So, what is it, I wonder, when it comes to love, that makes two people get on like a house on fire?

When I ask Racine the next day, she claims to have less than a clue. She's never seriously even been in lust with anyone before Giovanni. Ashley doesn't have much to offer either. Marta, on the other hand, is full of wisdom.

"It's not Angel," she says. "It's you. You wouldn't click with an amoeba. You're too busy rationalizing your feelings." She holds her hands up, adding air quotes to the word "feelings."

"Marta!" Racine makes a show of kicking her under the lunch table.

"It's fine," I say. "Whatever."

Marta will probably rot in Hell anyway; there isn't any point in fueling her fire. But her lame remark does make me wonder. Rationalize, rationalize, rationalize—that's how I survive. What if she's right? What if I just listened to my heart once in a while?

After the last bell of the day, I escape to Margarita's with my homework. But instead of working on calculus, I sit in my booth and stare out the window, wondering what makes some people love you and others not. Wondering, I suppose, whether Marta knows more than I give her credit for. I've never been in love. Maybe my heart made the preemptive choice to break on its own. Maybe after my mother, it's incapable of falling for anyone.

As people shuffle around Margarita's, my mind wanders, but when Ezra walks in and passes my booth on his way to an empty table without saying hello, I cut myself off. Dwelling is getting me nowhere. Besides, it probably isn't wise to dig very deeply. Mom always warned that if I dig too far, I'll just hit bottom and fall out.

Across the diner, Ezra flips through a menu while he pretends to ignore me, which makes me wonder if I'm not somehow projecting. Daisy takes his order. When she's done, I walk over to his booth.

"Now I have leprosy?" I ask.

"You're better off over there." He nods at my table.

I sit down across from him anyway.

Ezra scowls. "Go away, Ruby."

"Pick up your crap and come sit with me."

He finally looks up, growling something unintelligible under his breath. But he grabs his hat and keys and follows me back to my table.

When Daisy comes over to refill my coffee, she looks only slightly puzzled. "Should I bring your food over here?" she asks Ezra.

"Does it look like you should?"

Daisy shoots me a look. "Why do you put up with him?"

"You said it before. His bark is way worse than his bite." I lower my voice and whisper, cupping my hand around my mouth conspiratorially. "Ezra doesn't like this getting out, but he's secretly nice."

Daisy's eyebrows jump to her hairline. For a moment, she looks worse than perplexed. "I went to school with him, Ruby. I don't recall no nice guy living in that bigheaded, stuck-up, sorry excuse of a person."

Ezra clears his throat. "I am sitting here, Day."

"Yeah, I know, Ez. I just keep trying to forget it."

"You guys are like fourth graders," I reprimand them. When Daisy is out of earshot, I lean across the table and whisper, "What'd you do to her, Ezra?"

"Probably something terrible."

"Maybe you could try being nicer?"

Ezra leans toward me unremorsefully. "Why? Not a single person within a twenty-mile radius has been even remotely decent since I moved back."

"You don't have to stoop to the same level."

"I'm not stooping. I'm just not going to jump through hoops like a miserable dog for a bunch of no-good assholes."

"Is that how you see me?" For some reason, my eyes well with tears, but instead of wiping them away, I leave them clinging to my lashes, afraid to draw attention to the fact that I'm being emotional.

Ezra relaxes his full mouth, letting his angular jaw go slack. "No. You're *not* most people."

"But you can't make an effort for anyone else?"

"I am who I am, Ruby. If you don't like it, you're free to stop stalking me."

Giving him my harshest look, I sigh to mask a sniffle. "Why'd you ignore me when you walked in?"

He crosses his arms over his chest. "I'm not in the mood to be stared at."

"Maybe if you were nicer, people wouldn't stare. You're not a bad person, Ezra. You want everyone to *think* you are, but you're not. I bet that's because it's safer. Because then you don't have to explain yourself."

Ezra sits up straighter, glowering at me. "Or maybe if you left me alone, that would solve my problem. No Ruby, no nosy people wondering about her pet."

"God you're a pain in the ass to argue with!"

Ezra flares his nostrils. "Don't tell me who I am or ask me to be someone I'm not, and you won't have to."

Quarreling with him takes effort. I deflate like a punctured balloon, slumping slowly into the seat. "Can you just try? Because I'd *really* appreciate it."

Defeat settles in his posture when I ask, surprising me. He relaxes his back and drops his elbows on the table. "Around you. How's that?"

"*Ezra*," I grimace.

"I'm not going to meet you all the way."

There isn't a doubt in my mind he means it. And as much as it feels like I lost a battle, I know I've won ground that's never belonged to anyone else. I nod okay, but a deep sigh feels like the most appropriate answer.

A ghost of a smile touches Ezra's mouth. "You're something."

"Is that like a left-handed compliment?"

"There's nothing left-handed about it."

As he stares, his words carry this unfamiliar message to my heart. Ezra confuses me. The way I feel when I'm with him confuses me. Unlike Angel, Ezra comes off rough and uninviting. But with Angel, I feel lost. When I'm with Ezra, I feel right.

"You barely know me," I swallow.

"I know that it's hard for you to take a compliment. And that, though you're thoughtful most of the time, you're still hard on yourself. And I definitely know you shouldn't argue with me. Because no matter what you think you know, I'm always right."

"Umm ..." I choke.

He looks almost satisfied.

"Are ... are we still on for Saturday?" I stutter, flushing a little.

Ezra's spotlight eyes settle on my face, searching for something more than my outward response. "Why wouldn't we be?"

"I don't know. Because you changed your mind?"

"No. I still think I can handle your company."

His tone is almost smug. But after his off-the-cuff compliment, I'm not in the mood to fight. "So, what are you up to for the rest of the week?" I mumble.

"I have to restore a chair. Otherwise," he shrugs, "I'll probably run down to Albuquerque to pick up an armoire from a client."

"A client? Is that what you do? I mean, your job?"

"That's it. I restore furniture. Sometimes I build from scratch. But I limit custom orders. They're a real pain in my ass when I'm not in the mood to take on a project."

"Really? Furniture?"

"Carpentry. Family business. I picked it up when I moved back. It's not exactly lucrative, but I don't have much overhead. And I work for myself. I enjoy it. Some of the pieces are really beautiful."

That Ezra has a creative streak surprises me. "I paint," I volunteer.

"Paint what?"

"Everything. What I see or feel. It depends on my mood."

Ezra seems pleased, but not surprised. "Do you paint as well as you draw?"

"I guess." I shrug.

"I'd like to see your work."

"You mean like when hell freezes over?"

He looks at his watch. "I'm not particularly patient to begin with, Ruby. Don't you think that's asking a lot?"

Ezra's mind is whip sharp, but his intelligence is understated. While he stares at me with an almost-smile on his face, I realize I'd be happy to sit with him forever. And I might have, but when I grab his arm and playfully peek down at his watch, I see it's nearing seven o'clock.

"Crap. I told Liddy I'd be back by now." I gather up my notebook and throw my books into my backpack haphazardly. "She hates it when I walk in the dark. Come to think of it, lately I hate walking in the dark."

Ezra grabs my backpack and stands up. "Come on. I'll give you a ride."

"Thanks," I tell him on the way to his truck. "In Los Angeles, there's enough light pollution to power a small planet. I'm not used to how dark it gets in the pass."

"You afraid of the dark?" he asks.

"Uh-uh. El Maldito. And haunted forests." I laugh.

"Right. The Damned," he says.

"What?"

"Maldito. It means 'damned'."

"You believe the stories?"

"Definitely." He nods.

"Really?" I giggle. It's not the answer I expected. "The way you talked about Montezuma's snake god, I thought you thought it was crap."

"New Mexico's founded on folklore. Why not?"

"Because things like ghosts and snake gods don't exist."

"Maybe not in your world."

"Ezra, you're totally messing with me, right?"

Ezra hops in his truck, glancing at me peripherally as I buckle up. He grins as he pulls away from the curb. "Maybe. Maybe not."

"I keep seeing the same mountain lion. And I swear I saw a horse in my driveway last night, so I'm not being totally paranoid. Angel saw the lion Sunday night too. He agreed—it's a big sucker."

Except for the slightest twitch, Ezra's usually dynamic face is immobile. "You went out with Angel Sunday night?"

"No. Liddy invited Angel and Torrance over for dinner. I saw them after we went fishing."

"Oh."

Oh. That's all he says. But it hits me as though he shouted.

Ezra pulls up my driveway and stops the truck, idling near my front porch. He smiles again, quietly speaking to the windshield. "I'll see you on Saturday, Ruby."

My stomach turns unexpectedly. Only this time, I kind of know why. "I didn't tell you Angel was coming over later Sunday because I didn't think it mattered."

"It doesn't."

"Ezra ..."

"I have to go." Like the first time he drove me home, he leans across the cab and opens my door. "I'll be here early Saturday. Around seven."

Ezra waits for me to hop out. When I'm down, he drives backward down the driveway, taking off before I make it into the house. In the foyer, I slip off my flats and drop my backpack on the tiled floor before running to the window, trying to ignore the knots in my stomach as I watch his headlights disappear into the dark.

"I'm in here!" Liddy shouts when she hears me.

In the den, Liddy sits hunched over a stack of bills. She sees me standing in the doorframe and holds up an envelope, waving it in the air. "Your first payment to Stanford."

"That's almost a year away."

Liddy pushes her reading glasses up the bridge of her nose. "I'm trying to be a little more forward-thinking. Got a problem with it?"

"No. I just ... I'm not even sure I want to go anymore."

"Since when?"

"Since lately. I'm thinking about applying to UCLA or the UNM in Albuquerque."

"You're going. You got in, and we can pay for it. Ruby, you almost fainted when you got your acceptance letter. Whatever's going through your head now, it'll pass."

Liddy's face says it all. She's already plotted out the rest of my life, starting with my graduation from Stanford. I'll go there, and then on to graduate school at some Ivy fortress, and then secure some great science professorship, like she did. It's pointless to argue. *She's* made up her mind already.

"Sorry I'm late." I sigh. "What's for dinner?"

"Let's fry up that fish," she chirps, also signaling that the topic—Stanford—is officially off limits. "Give me a minute, and I'll meet you in the kitchen."

Family photos plaster the den's burnt umber walls, of my grandparents, and my mother and Liddy, and Mom and I together at various stages in our lives. The den is cozy, and I want to stay and talk with Liddy about Ezra, but instead, I go and wash up.

CHAPTER TWELVE

FALLING TO RUIN

SITTING OUTSIDE WITH LAS GALLINAS, watching the Pecos football players collide like steam engines on the football field, I still can't stop thinking about Ezra. About what he said to me at Margarita's, and how I felt it physically when he gave me the cold shoulder in his truck.

"Earth to Ruby." Racine snaps her fingers in front of my face. "You meeting Leo this afternoon?"

I drop my sandwich—leftover fried trout between two slabs of wheat bread—and answer yes. But that's all I have to say about it. Ezra confuses me. And because of it, I'm not as excited as I was to meet Leo up at the ruin.

"Pop quiz. You're alone together in the woods." Ashley smirks. "What do you do?"

"What do I do, or what do *you* do?" I answer politely.

"Oh, we all know the answer to that one," Marta squeals.

"Marta!" Ashley snaps. "Bitch!"

"And you wouldn't, Marta?" Racine says. "*Toma uno saber uno.*"

Marta pulls back her long hair and giggles. "A lady never tells."

Ashley gives me the once-over. She grabs a five-dollar bill out of her purse and smacks it on the table. "I'll bet you five Ruby's not like that."

"Like what?" I ask.

"Easy," they say in unison, breaking into giggles.

"It's not like I haven't thought about it."

There's no way I'd tell them about kissing Leo in Apache Canyon. Racine knows, and with Racine alone, it will stay. I trust the rest of them about as much as I like doing laundry.

"Would you?" Ashley's eyes pop. "I mean, up the mountain, all alone?"

"Probably not."

Marta looks at me as if staring down a dim child. "Of course she wouldn't."

"That's a good thing," Racine cuts in. She purses her lips, maintaining an expression so serious she reminds me of someone's mother. "You're crazy enough hiking alone in that forest to begin with."

Marta clicks her tongue. "Ray, enough of the spooky forest thing."

That they think I'd consider sleeping with Leo in the middle of the woods almost makes me laugh. I mean, I *have* considered it, in some detail. But chances aren't good that I'd lie down in a pile of leaves with anyone.

"It's kind of exciting," Ashley says. "I mean, what if he's the ghost of a Confederate soldier?"

"Union," Marta corrects her. "If Ruby's gonna mack on a ghost, he better be Union."

"He's not a ghost."

"How do you know?" Ashley's playful eyes grow. "I mean, what if he cast a spell on you?"

"He's not a ghost." I laugh. "I can't see through him."

"Then bring him to my party," Marta challenges.

"A ghost would be better than bringing Ezra," Ashley mumbles under her breath. "That jerk broke Cassie's heart."

I clear my throat. "Ezra isn't a jerk."

"Except for his face, the dude was a total waste of space before his accident," Marta sniffs. "Without it, he's nothing."

"I'm not dense. I know none of you like him," I tell my sandwich. I drop my head into my hands and rub my eyes. Defending Ezra all the time tires me out. "But people change."

"At least with Ezra, you know what you're signing up for." Racine waggles a finger at me. "I mean, this Leo guy, for all you know, he's a serial killer."

Racine is right. Leo is completely inscrutable. Worse, no one knows him.

Just what are you signing up for, Ruby? Why did you agree to meet Leo alone in the middle of a haunted forest? Staring past Racine, I shake my head at the sky. Prudence is my MO. Back in LA, I'd almost always been careful.

After school, the same questions dog me all the way up the mountain. Puzzling out Leo's enigmatic effect on me gives me a headache, and it doesn't help that the buzzing on the plateau is at an all-time high. I walk slowly, and by the time I enter the clearing, my head is spinning.

Near the ruin, I spread out a wool blanket, hoping to equilibrate before facing him. Laying down, I close my eyes and think about mountain lions and ghosts, and the story Leo told me about the Otherworld, until the hum turns to more of a crackle. A whispering sound emanates from the ruin walls. Faint singsong syllables form drawn-out nonsense words that taper off without ending, raising the tiny hairs on my neck and arms.

Unnerved, I poke a finger in my ears, rubbing while I swallow.

Cicadas? The wind? What the hell?

"Ruby, what is this fascination you have with the ground?" Leo asks from above me.

Startled, I snap up, focusing on Leo's brilliant face. My mind is full of steel wool, and in the few moments it takes to slip into gear, Leo could probably get me to do anything. He's like a Siren; I feel like a ship following him straight to the edge of the planet.

"Everything okay?" he grins.

I smooth my hair, which has spread out around the blanket and collected its own little pile of sticks and leaves. "Yes," I whisper. "I was just listening to the wind."

Leo sits down on the blanket next to me and crosses his legs. He lies back, partially resting on his elbows. "What did it tell you?"

"Nothing that made sense."

His brown arms are strong and defined beneath a tight black T-shirt that flexes in all the right places. My earlier conversation with Las Gallinas comes to mind, about being reckless, and I quickly look away, red like a tomato.

"You're a funny girl," he says. "Why do you do that?"

"What?"

"Act like you don't notice me?"

The contents of my stomach turn, making a hard right in search of my esophagus. I swallow and answer him the best I can without stuttering. "I notice you. Obviously. We're sitting here having a conversation, aren't we?"

Leo smiles wickedly, raising both his eyebrows.

"What?"

"That's not what I meant. You're beautiful. I enjoy looking at you. I'm not embarrassed to admit it."

"Oh, I see. You're asking me if I think you're good-looking. Or wait. No. You're *telling* me that you're good-looking and wondering why I don't slobber all over you."

"Something like that."

I shake my head forcefully, but truthfully, I'm trembling inside. Even at his cockiest, I can't pretend I don't find Leo unbelievably, almost unbearably, attractive. "A girl could do worse, I guess."

"You're so transparent. But if you want to pretend," he throws his hands up in the air and falls back on the blanket, "then be my guest."

"You're full of yourself, you know that?"

"Yes." Leo grabs my wrist, pulling me off-balance. He tugs me down flat on my back.

"Leo ..."

"Tell me what the wind said."

"I just did. Don't be mental." Leo's grin is infuriatingly smug. I take a deep breath and let it out slowly. "Fine. It said, 'Ruby, what the hell are you doing in the middle of nowhere with such a conceited boy?' Then it called you something I can't repeat."

Leo's brusque laugh surprises me. "Okay, Ruby. Now tell me about the boys you knew back in Los Angeles."

"There's nothing to tell."

"Make it up then."

"Seriously? I dated a boy named Tyler for, like two minutes."

"What happened?"

I grimace. "I drank too much at a party and jumped his best friend."

Grinning, Leo turns on his side, leaning slightly over me. "And since then?"

"There isn't more to tell. For the most part, I avoid the lesser species."

"Lesser species?"

"It's a challenge just to speak your language."

"We'll see about that." He snickers.

Leo lowers his face above mine, and his hair brushes my cheeks as his strange golden eyes memorize my features. His smell, like cut wood and wet earth, drives me crazy.

When Leo's lips touch mine, and he runs a calloused hand along the side of my face, down my neck, and over my shirt, the contact sends electric shivers through my entire body. But when he bunches my shirt, tracing a finger up my bare stomach to my rib cage, I stop him.

"Hey." My heart is beating so fast it's difficult to speak. "I can't."

"Why?"

"I don't ... you know why," I swallow.

"But you want me."

I stutter, shocked by his confidence. "I do ... but ... there has to be more."

"There's more." He smirks. "Trust me."

"I mean more, like, more between us."

Leo's lips twitch. "What's wrong with having fun?" He leans into me again, pressing me backward as I try to sit up.

"Leo, stop!"

Leo snaps away from me. He looks at me like a fly in his soup, wrinkling his nose. "If that's what you really want."

"It is what I want," I say out loud, reminding myself as much as anyone. I adjust my shirt and straighten my hair. "You really are full of yourself."

"And?"

"*And?* God. Remind me what it is I like about you?"

"My wit and charm?" He grins.

Leo stands up and holds out his hand, but I refuse it, making a show of standing on my own. My mind is a ball of confusion, and Leo's behavior is only making it worse. I'm not sure if I like him, but it's hard to keep my hands off him, even though not keeping my hands off him goes against everything I know about myself.

"It's not the end of the world, Ruby." His face is completely unemotional, bringing home the casualness of his statement. "But I have to ask, what were you expecting?"

Leaning over to gather the blanket and my backpack—and to hide my face while I speak—my answer comes out wobbly, which makes me hate myself. "I didn't *expect* anything, except maybe to get to know you better."

"Then we want the same things," he answers lightly.

"No. You want to sleep with me. Big difference."

"It's just sex. Don't make a capital crime out of it. If you don't want to do it, you don't. Either way, it has nothing to do with whether I want to know you better."

"You really believe that? That it's just sex?"

He looks at me blankly, then shakes his head. "Yes."

When sunlight hits his face, highlighting features so achingly beautiful I could die, I wonder if there is some force in La Luna that sent Leo to me out of spite—for being a bad person, or niece, or daughter.

"I don't think we should meet like this again."

"But you still want to go out with me," he sort-of asks.

I swallow, staring at Leo's strong arms and sturdy hands, which he's tucked into his pockets. *God*, I think, *what's wrong with me? Please don't answer yes.*

"I don't think so."

"How about Saturday?"

"I just said no, Leo."

"You said, 'I don't think so.'"

"Fine. No. I can't."

"Like I said, you're a funny girl." Leo pulls his hands out of his pockets and puts them behind his head. "First you want me to take you out, then you turn me down."

"I already have plans, this Saturday."

"Then break them."

I stare at him incredulously. "I don't want to." And the truth is, I don't. I've really started looking forward to my camping trip with Ezra.

Leo gives me the once-over, clearly not accustomed to people turning him down. "What are you doing this weekend that's so important?"

"Camping."

He shoots me a larger-than-life grin, showing off polished enamel. "Maybe I could come along."

Looking at him, I'd swear on a Bible that the men in the pass are all crazy. "Are you insane? First, you have, like no time for me, and then you go and invite yourself on my camping trip. Forget it."

"Who are you going with?" He shoves his hands back into his pockets and steps backward. "Maybe I know her."

"*His* name is Ezra."

"Okay, Ruby. Now I get it." He grins even wider. "You want to have your cake and eat it too, don't you?"

Leo's words drip with innuendo, and I hate him for it. "Are you serious?" I gape at him.

"As a heart attack."

"You're so frustrating!" Seriously pissed, I whip away fast enough that my head spins.

Suddenly, a flash like an explosion lights the sky, followed by a radiant purple hue that expands overhead, billowing across the forest like an inkblot. Disoriented, I push my palms against my lids and close my eyes.

When I open them again, Leo is gone, but my mother is standing in front of me. A blur of ephemeral wavy features, she moves her mouth, rippling while she speaks. She yells, and I hold an arm over my face as her words cull up a gust of wind that whips my hair into a frenzy.

Watchers are forbidden to mix with True of Heart!

Her body flickers, fading against a now-black sky as cascades of tiny violet sparks light the dark spaces between each tree, vanishing, then pulsing back to life. They expand, swallowing me in blinding light. Until Leo's voice brings me back, and I look up and see his panicked face and realize I'm on the ground and that we're still in the clearing.

"Ruby!"

I sit bolt upright, gasping. "What the hell was that?"

Leo hovers over me. "Jesus, are you all right?"

"What just happened?"

"I think you fainted."

Mom's words echo in my head. *Watchers are forbidden to mix with True of Heart.*

"Ruby?" He shakes me.

"I must have." I blink.

"It's probably the altitude. You're not used to it yet."

With Leo's help, I stand and steady myself. "How long was I out?"

"Less than a minute."

"Jeez, Leo. You actually look worried."

"You dropped like a rock. Why in the hell wouldn't I be?"

"Because you're a jerk," I mutter. Thinking about how Leo's stupid face made my knees shake just ten minutes ago infuriates me.

"You're white as a sheet," he says, following me slowly away from the ruin. "Are you sure you can walk?"

I rub at a lump rising behind my ear. "I think I hit my head."

"You should have someone look at it."

I nod, eager to get away from him. Hitting my head hard enough to hallucinate probably isn't a good thing. Hallucinating my dead mother is unnerving.

Ignoring my screaming headache, I make my way down the mountain. Half of me hopes Leo will follow, half hopes he'll drop through a rift in the ground.

Silently trailing behind me for a while, Leo finally stops on a woody slope about a quarter mile above our backyard. "You sure you're going to be all right?" He asks. "I really should get going."

I stop walking, nodding unconvincingly. Dragging my shoe through bits of broken leaves, I suddenly feel displaced. My heart feels unsettled, like it's not sure where it belongs.

"Go," I tell him.

Obviously, making things right isn't one of Leo's priorities. What's worse is that it shouldn't be a surprise. Leo may as well be a ghost because he's definitely the ultimate stranger.

CHAPTER THIRTEEN

WILD OPEN SPACES

"THAT BOY COULD COME UP TO THE DOOR and knock like a decent human being!" Liddy yells from the kitchen.

Ezra's beat-up truck rumbles in the driveway, Ezra inside it, hitting his horn in annoying spurts, as if the first few beeps weren't enough to announce his arrival. I grab my duffle bag and backpack and quickly run down the stairs, rushing past the kitchen toward the door.

In the hallway, Liddy stops me. Decked out in her fuzzy green bathrobe, she puts her hands on her hips and strikes an intimidating pose. "No way. You're not going anywhere until I officially meet him."

We lock eyes, two trains headed straight for each other. Liddy wins; I jump track first, sighing heavily as I drop my bags on the porch and run to Ezra's truck to drag him back into the house. Ezra doesn't argue, but he isn't thrilled about it either. Still, he shuts the engine, climbs down, and shuffles to the porch.

At the steps, he tips his straw cowboy hat at Liddy and smiles. "Ma'am."

"Liddy," she replies, a little short because Ezra called her by a title, she, herself, reserves for octogenarians. She scans his face before she speaks again, but appropriately, not in horror and not for too long. "It's good to finally meet you. Ruby has said a lot of kind things."

Ezra coughs, covering his mouth, hiding what looks like a smile. Liddy is just being nice, but Ezra isn't dense either. "Likewise."

"Ruby tells me you live nearby."

"Yep. About a mile east off Sawtooth Road. In the densest part of the forest—about thirty acres worth of dense actually."

Liddy's face turns cloudy, morphing from her normal unruffled expression to concern. "You live up there alone?"

He nods slowly. "Yes, ma'am. Liddy."

"For how long?"

"For a couple of years. The land's been in my family since before the Civil War. I grew up there." His voice is light, but his tight-lipped smile is a tipoff; he isn't particularly happy about being interrogated by an attractive but pushy woman in a fuzzy green bathrobe who has only heard bad things about him from most everyone else.

"How old are you, Ezra?"

"Twenty."

Twenty. I wasn't sure myself.

"You're awfully young to live up there all alone."

Ezra inhales and grins awkwardly. "I get along just fine. And I'm not alone. I've got the ghosts of Glorieta to keep me company. They're almost like family. But a lot less judgmental."

Liddy squints and takes a sip of her coffee, holding the mug to her lips for a moment longer than it takes to swallow. "Do your parents live in New Mexico?"

"My mother lives in Jemez. My father's dead."

"I'm sorry."

"Don't be," he answers evenly. "No one else is."

Liddy flares her nostrils disagreeably and looks him up and down, taking in his frame while she searches for a psychological hole to peg him in. She isn't used to being spoken to so acrimoniously by anyone but me. Best guess, he's either earned her respect for holding his own while she questions him, or majorly blown it for being so condescending. With Liddy, there isn't always a whole lot in-between.

"Um," I break in, "Ezra, don't you think we should get going?"

Liddy answers before Ezra can. "Are you camping at El Morro or somewhere else around Grants?"

"There's a campsite at the monument. We'll set up camp before we head out. We'll be in, or near the park the whole time. Tomorrow we'll drive into Grants before heading back to La Luna. I'll make sure Ruby calls you."

"Fine." She kisses my cheek and relief floods through me. It wasn't my intention to turn one little overnight trip with a friend into a battle. Liddy and I have enough on our plate between us already.

Ezra and I say our goodbyes, throw my stuff in his truck bed, and then head off down I-25 toward Grants. We don't talk much at first; Ezra's face is hard to read and at times he seems downright sullen.

"I'm really sorry, Ezra," I tell him after we pass Santa Fe.

"For what?"

"Liddy."

He smiles. "She was just doing her job."

"That's a gracious way to put it."

"Still think you'll make it through the night?" he asks.

"You mean with you?"

"I mean roughing it."

"You think I can't?"

Ezra smiles wickedly. "I have every confidence in you."

"I may be from LA, but I know what I'm doing," I assure him. "I'll be fine."

He sighs. "Why'd you come with me, Ruby? To piss Liddy off?"

Rather than answer, I stare at his profile for a good long time, willing to bet he knows that isn't the reason. Willing to bet he knows that despite his face, he still has this charisma that draws me—an allure I still don't understand.

On the radio, a woman wails on about how she stood by her husband while he hit the bottle, then her, and then left her for an RV park and a redheaded waitress with high-class hands. Ezra fiddles with the dial, turning up the song while he simultaneously pulls his hat down, as though covering his face to block out the shame of it all. Maybe trying to drown out my stare as well.

"What a load of crap," Ezra mumbles.

"It's why I hate country."

He chuckles. "It's why I love it. Just when I think my life couldn't be worse, along comes the lady with the drug-addled, alcoholic, sex-addicted husband. It's like watching reality TV— only slightly less annoying."

"Misery loves company, right?"

Ezra twitches and turns to look at me. "What makes you think I'm miserable?"

"You act like it."

"No, I don't. You just assume I am."

I shoot Ezra a sidelong stare, debating whether or not to argue. Maybe he isn't. I don't believe him. But it's true I don't know him very well.

We drive through Albuquerque without speaking, merging from I-25 onto I-40. Near Acoma, as the land turns from a sinuous golden brown to more rugged ochre, Ezra turns the radio off and sighs deeply, as though marshaling up the energy to talk to me again. I hold my hand out the window, resisting the wind, waving at eroded earth and the cornflower sky.

"You know, I followed a girl a lot like you out to college."

My heart skips and my stomach tightens. I've wanted to know more about Ezra since Pecos, but I've never mustered the nerve to ask again.

"What do you mean, 'a girl like me'?"

"Attractive. Smart. Mouthy."

"Thanks, I guess." I pull my legs up on the seat and turn toward him, resting my cheek against the seat rest. "What made you think of her?"

Ezra shrugs. "Caroline was a real ... well, let's just say she was high-maintenance. But she was gorgeous, so I did my best to ignore her tantrums."

"You think I'm high-maintenance?"

"No. *You're* beautiful." Ezra turns and meets my eyes. "Honestly, Ruby, you're surprisingly unaware for someone so beguiling. It's hard to believe that you're really as unassuming as you come off."

Beguiling. That makes me blush fiercely.

"How'd you meet her?" I ask softly.

"She transferred to Pecos in eleventh grade, from Denver. Every boy on the football team had it for her. I know it's hard to believe, but once upon a time, when I wanted something, or someone, I got it."

"I've heard," I mumble.

"Caroline wasn't particularly nice, but she was sharp, and she looked good on my arm."

"What happened?"

Ezra looks away, facing the mountain range lingering, on its peaks for so long I think he's decided to stop talking. He takes his hat off and throws it on the mat at my feet, then runs a hand through his dark hair, pulling at the ends. "I'd planned to go to the UNM in Albuquerque. But she asked me to apply to Harvard with her instead."

"And you got in."

"Yes. I got in, and I followed her. Though I shouldn't have."

"Why?"

"I loved her. At least I thought I did."

"You loved her?" I bite back my smile; he seems so serious. "What's so bad about that?"

"She didn't love me back. By the time I found the nerve to tell her how I felt, she was already in love with one of her professors. I'd been too busy lauding my successful conquest to notice."

I rub Ezra's knee. His voice is heavy with resignation, and I suddenly want to hug him. "Did you come home because you broke up or because ..." In the air, I circle my face with a finger.

"Both. I couldn't get over the idea that *she* broke up with *me.*

Until then, girls came easy, they never left."

"From what I hear, Ezra, *you* did a lot of leaving."

He sets his jaw in a scowl and stares at the road. "You might call it poetic justice."

"That's not what I meant."

"It's true though, isn't it? And it's what you were thinking." He grips the steering wheel with both hands, glancing over at me. "Until I fell in love with her, I never thought much about people beyond what they could do for me. Even after we broke up, I was more or less ticked she had the gall to leave when I still loved her. It never occurred to me to think about *why* she didn't love me back—not until later."

"After she left?"

"After this happened." Ezra tips his chin at his reflection in the rearview mirror.

"What did happen?" I ask tentatively. "I mean, if you're ready to tell me."

His grip on the steering wheel is so tight his knuckles turn ashy. I look away, at mountains that give way to plains that give way to cascades of pockmarked lava, frozen in time. Off the side of the highway mounds of solidified black rock rise and fall in waves, transforming the landscape into a haunting memory of the once active El Malpais region, a chain of volcanoes stretching some twenty miles west of Grants out to El Morro.

"I'm not even sure I really loved her. Being with her made me feel valuable. I guess I made the mistake of believing that her being with me meant *I* was worthy. When we broke up, it confirmed all the things people whispered about me back in La Luna. I felt empty, and I kind of fell apart. And I blamed her for it. I wasn't willing to look very deep, you know? But somewhere inside, I also badly wanted to know why I wasn't good enough. I wanted to know what I did wrong. After she left, I literally got down on my knees and prayed for an answer."

"Oh ... oh no," I whisper expectantly.

"The next week, I was in an accident. I never saw her again after that. And that was fine because I couldn't bear her seeing me." He sniffs, jerking his head slightly. "In some ways, I suppose I got what I asked for."

Ezra is calm, but I realize *I* am crying. No matter how bad he was before, no one deserves that kind of punishment.

Ezra keeps his eyes on the road. His stonewall makes it easier to wipe away my tears and gather my faculties. After several minutes that hang between us like a wet towel, I breathe a long breath, expelling much of the tension I've been carrying around since he first invited me to go to Grants. Steadily it leaves my body, unraveling like a sweater until there's nothing left but fine, loose threads.

"I'm so sorry," I finally whisper. I don't know what else to say. Words alone won't convey how sad I am for him, just like words can't express what it must have been like to lose everything—because really, from what I've gathered, Ezra's face was his life.

Ezra coughs, clearing his throat. "I'm sure you are. You know, you're maybe the only person I know who really understands what it means to be seduced by the surface of things. How utterly useless the surface of anything is."

"Beauty's a bitch." I frown.

"Ruby, my guess is you don't give beauty the credit it's due."

"No, I just don't let myself get caught up in superficialities. Real beauty is so much more than shiny objects and first impressions."

Ezra places a hand on my chin and gently nudges my face toward the passenger window. "Then look around."

When I blink, squeezing out a new batch of tears, the land comes into focus. Everything looks bigger and crisper, brighter than it did just minutes ago. We pass a field of mustard flowers so yellow they're blinding, so defined they stand out against the blue sky like cardboard cutouts pasted against a painted backdrop. The landscape flourishes. It has no agenda and no desire to impress me, and in being so unassuming, it does.

Ezra exhales. "People are ugly. I'm a prime example. But the land—there's something so pure about it."

"That's because it's inanimate."

Ezra gives me a look I interpret as a warning.

"What I mean," I quickly add, moving my hand toward the windshield, "is that it's easy to trust what you see because trusting doesn't require you to look past the surface."

He shakes his head disbelievingly. "People see what they want to, Ruby. And most folks don't see real beauty for what it's worth when it's right in front of them. Even when they do, they hoard it. Lord knows I'd keep it all to myself if I could."

"Really? I feel compelled to share it. I mean, I'd probably stop noticing all of this after a while if I didn't occasionally get to see it through someone else's eyes."

"That's the other problem with beauty, it fades quickly."

I watch his face, but he's turned back to the road and won't look at me. "I don't think so, Ezra. It's more about what you do with it. If you're selfish with it, like everything else, you destroy its integrity. Without perspective, everything looks different after a while. Sharing is a good thing. Nothing can be *all* yours without a price."

"I suppose that's why my exterior finally matches who I am below the surface." He smiles a distant smile, but his voice is cynical. "I've always been a selfish jerk."

"I don't believe that."

"You're very trusting."

"That's bad how?"

"It's naïve."

Ezra turns left off the highway onto a smaller road that leads through a field of wildflowers. Off the side of the road, a sign indicates we've reached El Morro. Ahead of us, rising above the valley, a massive sandstone bluff surrounded by sunlit pines and flowers meets the jewel-toned sky.

"I'd rather trust you until you give me a reason not to," I say quietly, awed by my surroundings. "That's not naïve. It's what friends do."

"Ruby, you don't pay enough attention when you look at me."

"I don't care about your face, Ezra. Why don't you get that? And I *don't* think it, or you, are ugly. It's the fundamental you, the you underneath all your bullshit, that stands out. I'd like that guy regardless."

His eyes twinkle. "You like me?"

"Yeah, kinda."

Ezra parks his truck in the empty parking lot near the ranger station. He walks around to my side and opens the door, offering to help me down. "Let's go in and get a permit. We can set up camp afterward."

I take his hand, holding on to it even after I climb down from the truck, and follow him into the station. We register, and a tall ranger with cornflower hair and the sweetest smile directs us toward the campsite, supplying us with maps and information about El Morro's history. She speaks to me directly, barely meeting Ezra's eyes. Her standoffishness makes me sad, and I wonder how often Ezra has to deal with clueless people.

At the ranger's direction, Ezra parks his truck near campsite number seven. Though El Morro sits squarely in the middle of nowhere, which is primordial enough, the campsite doesn't feel particularly primitive; we're allowed to pull Ezra's truck right up to the actual clearing.

Ezra unloads the truck bed, throwing duffels of junk at me that I drop on the ground by my feet. He makes fun of me while we pitch a tent. I never claimed to be a camping expert, but the way he teases, you'd think I'd sworn on a Bible I passed Advanced High Desert Camping.

After we get the tent up and I trip over its stakes several times, pulling a side down, just when we had it standing, I shrug and mutter, "Just one?"

"Do you see another?"

"No."

"Chill out," he grumps. "If you're worried about it, I'll sleep outside."

"Worried?"

"I have little intention of taking advantage of you."

"For real? I just worried I'd have to go through that again." I shake my head, pointing at the tent, then pick up a rolled sleeping bag and chuck it at him.

"Oh. Right." He looks embarrassed.

"You're such an idiot."

Ezra smiles crookedly. "Why don't we both forget the tent and sleep outside? The night sky is incredible out here."

Grinning, I throw my own bag next to the one I chucked at him. "Sounds nice."

As we finish setting up, Ezra tells me everything he knows about El Morro. The monument's place in history as an ancient pueblo, and a wagon trail watering hole, and a Conquistador's landmark sound romantic and wild, exactly the way I imagined it would be when I first saw the massive sandstone bluff rising above the valley.

When our campsite is finally up and running, we follow a path from the campground to the trailhead leading to El Morro's mesa. The elevation changes swiftly, sucking up my breath as we climb, but rewards us with sweeping views of the Zuni Mountains, the volcanic craters across the El Malpais plain, and the El Morro Valley. We don't talk much, and the silence emphasizes the awe I feel watching the scenery unfurl beneath the mesa.

At the very top of the sandstone bluff, I stop to inhale. My breath comes hard but looking around I know it isn't just the climb that's left me short. The 360-degree view is equally breathtaking.

"You look lost," Ezra says softly.

"I am." I turn toward him. "I could stand here forever. Please, please don't ever find me."

A small smile touches Ezra's eyes. He takes my hand while I drink from my water bottle, maneuvering us along the crest of the mesa to an ancient ruined pueblo at the top of the bluff. The incredible height makes the mostly unexcavated structure feel enormous. At 450 feet above the ground, I can hardly imagine living somewhere so spectacular.

"What if you could wake up to this every day?" I ask him.

"It's too high. It must have been nearly impossible to get up here before the park service carved the staircase into the mesa. Strategic but not very practical." He cups his brow and stares out at the valley.

"You're so utilitarian. I said 'imagine' it."

"I have. I think the isolation would eventually tamp all that wonder."

"You're a killjoy, you know that?" I walk away from him toward the rangers working to restore part of the pueblo. Ezra follows, standing silently beside me while I look down into the pueblo's partially excavated rooms, talking excitedly to the rangers about the crumbling adobe.

When we've seen all of it, we quietly walk the path over the mesa down to Inscription Trail. At the bottom of the bluff, next to a large protected spring recessed into the wall, a paved foot trail leads along the monolith's base, introducing us to some two thousand messages and signatures carved into its soft sandstone walls.

As we walk, I marvel at each inscription. The sandstone tablet, covered with everything from native petroglyphs to fluid Spanish script dating back four hundred years, chronicles the Southwest's long chain of frontier history, capturing the heart of New Mexico.

"You look ... wistful." Ezra smiles.

"It's so amazing, I almost can't breathe."

Nodding, Ezra opens the guidebook we bought and reads from its pages. "The one you're looking at, that was inscribed by New Mexico's first Governor, Don Juan de Oñate in 1605. Sixteen hundred and five," he whistles. "Think about it, that's fifteen years before the Pilgrims landed at Plymouth Rock."

We walk slowly, stopping at each numbered trail post to read the guide. A few of the Spanish inscriptions have been translated. Others fade into the sandstone, their meanings lost to time. We walk past prayers and blessings left by families heading west on the Santa Fe Trail in wagon caravans, and poems written by frontier explorers, and notes written by Spanish Conquistadors who later became the founders of many of New Mexico's towns and missions, and signatures from every man who built the first railroad through western New Mexico. Looking at them all, I feel like an astronaut viewing Earth from space for the very first time. It fills me with a kind of wanderlust that roots in my chest and grows into my lungs, squeezing them with longing.

By the time we finally return to camp, twilight has settled over the monument, pulling a swath of crimson clouds across the purple horizon. I feel hungry, and alive, and most surprisingly, like I belong right where I am, alongside Ezra.

Still awed by my surroundings, I plunk down onto a rock and rummage through a cooler full of food while Ezra gathers sticks for a fire. "Marshmallows?" I ask, holding up a bag.

He nods. "Can't have a campfire without them."

Together, we prop chunks of wood into a small teepee in the firepit and set it ablaze. When it's stoked enough, Ezra sits down next to the fire. I hand him a Dr Pepper and watch while he demolishes a sandwich.

"What?" He frowns, catching me staring.

"You'd think you never had a sandwich before." I giggle, waving my own sandwich in the air.

"I'm hungry."

"Obviously."

Ezra sets his can on the ground near his shoes. "Are you glad you came?"

"Immensely. Are you?"

"Yes. Watching you, the way your nose crinkles up like a wounded hedgehog when you're excited about something, it's priceless." Ezra does something with his face that may have been a pretty darned good imitation of me crinkling my nose like a wounded hedgehog, if there was enough loose skin on his face to crinkle.

"You'd think," I start, turning my nose up at him, "that you'd be a little more compassionate about my silly face. Not everyone wants to be reminded of how stupid they look, especially when it involves hedgehogs."

"Why? Because my own face is so awful?"

"Precisely," I answer.

"Your face is beautiful. You know I'm joking." Ezra grabs his can and stands up, walking over to his sleeping bag. He sits down, patting my own bag beside him. "Come here."

"What about our marshmallows?" I really want to impale a perfect white puff and watch it sizzle, but I don't want him to know how easily amused I am by stuff like campfires and junk food.

"Later. I want to show you something."

Curious, I get up and sit down beside him. Without warning, he pushes me back flat against my bag on the ground.

"What ..." I squawk.

Ezra quickly falls back beside me and points up at the sky. "I want to show you before it dips below the horizon." He points at a cluster of stars to the west, making a circle in the sky with his fingers. "My grandfather called it the Pecos Circle. All twenty-three clans united."

I count, squinting to see some of the fainter lights. Once my eyes adjust, those twenty-three stars step forward, forming a perfect circle in the night sky. I look at him and smile, marveling at how the campfire lights his face, highlighting his high cheeks and momentarily clear eyes.

"Twenty-three clans?" I ask.

"Yes." He holds his hand above his head, moving his finger in a circle. "Story goes, every star up there is its own universe, each overseen by a separate Pecos clan."

"What was your clan?"

"Shiankya."

"What does that mean?"

He turns toward me and grins. "Mountain lion."

I sock his arm. "You're a laugh riot."

Ezra stares up at the sky, mesmerized by the formation. "My grandfather was a little crazy. He really believed he'd make it to the circle someday. He even had a speech he'd written to persuade the gods to send him back home after he died."

"Like, he *really* believed?"

"Yes."

"In reincarnation?"

"Absolutely."

"That's wild." I pause for a moment, thinking about the ruin. "If I tell you something, promise you won't laugh?"

"I promise to make an effort," he says, half smiling.

"I saw my mom on Thursday. I was up the mountain, hiking, and I ... I don't know. First, I thought I fainted and maybe imagined it. She was like a ghost, but it felt so real. It was like she was trying to warn me about something."

"In the forest?" Ezra's voice is low and steady, but his eyes are laser focused on me.

"Up near the ruin I told you about."

"*Did* you faint?"

"I must have. I hit my head. Here." I grab his hand and push his fingers to the bump behind my ear. "But it's not the first time I've seen her since we moved. And I was wide awake the other times."

Ezra rubs a thumb over my lump gently, holding my focus. "Grief is a funny thing. I believe you saw her, but that doesn't mean she was real." He pulls his hand away. "You shouldn't be going up there alone. It's not safe."

"I fell a few feet. It's not like I climbed a tree and plummeted to the ground."

"But what if you had?" he asks. "My grandfather was fond of saying the forest isn't shy about warning people off to protect its secrets. Maybe it's best to leave good enough alone."

"Seriously?"

He shrugs. "I don't question things I don't understand."

"You *really* believe the forest is full of secrets?"

"I didn't say that. My grandfather did. But I do believe the universe helps guide us."

The forest behind my house feels hallowed, not threatening, but his answer unnerves me. I *did* faint. And I *did* see my mother, whatever that means. And Ezra knows a lot more about the pass and its ghosts than I do. I stare at him, peeling back layers that surprise me. Whether he believes what he's saying or just messing with me, he obviously holds his grandfather in high esteem. "Tell me more about him?"

Ezra starts out reluctantly, talking slowly until his guard melts away. He tells me about his grandfather and then his father—about the difficult relationships they had, tainted by tradition, history, and pride.

"How old were you when your dad died?" I ask.

"Fourteen."

"Oh. God. For some reason, I thought you were younger. What happened?"

"Car accident." Ezra stiffens a little. He tips his chin back toward the sky, then turns his face sideways. "He drove himself off a cliff."

"Wait, he drove himself off? On purpose?"

"Yes."

"I ... How do you know?"

"He left a note."

I swallow, staring wide-eyed. "So, he ..."

"Killed himself. Yes."

For a moment, I feel numb. "Why didn't you tell me?"

"I didn't want to diminish your mother's death with my own story. Plus, my dad died nearly six years ago. And I understood why he did it. It's not the same."

"Why?"

"Why what?"

"Why'd he do it?" I whisper.

"He didn't have much reason to stay in La Luna, but he couldn't really leave. It was his only way out. By the time he died, my mom and dad hated each other. And the two of us, at that point, we weren't all that close."

"You say it like it doesn't bother you."

"It doesn't. Not anymore."

His words are absolute, but his voice wavers slightly. Maybe he means it, maybe not. Whatever the case, his relationship with his father has clearly left its mark, and for the time being, I decide to leave it at that. It's enough knowing we have something so terrible in common.

"What about your mom? Are you close?"

He smiles. "How come you're so nosy?"

"I'm not nosy. I just want to know you better. Got a problem with it?"

Ezra shrugs before starting in without a hitch, as if happy to change the subject. When I finish asking the last of what probably seems like a million questions, his speech both speeds up and trickles off until there's nothing passing between his lips but his breath and a sigh. Afterward, he exhales heavily. "You make me feel so goddamn chatty."

I turn over on my side and smile a toothy grin, intentionally wrinkling my nose like a hedgehog. "Really?"

Ezra playfully nudges me back against my sleeping bag with an arm. He shakes his head, rubbing it against the fabric so it crackles. "I wish I'd met you a long time ago."

"Why?"

"Just because."

"Because I'm so 'beguiling'?" I tease, almost blushing again when I remember what he called me earlier.

"Something like that."

I squint at him, trying to see past his guarded eyes.

"Want to toast a few marshmallows?" he asks.

"Not yet. Tell me why you wish you'd met me a long time ago."

"Tell me more about your family and maybe I will."

"Uh-uh. Last time I made a deal like that, you skipped out on your end."

"I didn't. You know what happened to my face, don't you? You practically know everything about me."

"Yeah, but ..."

"But nothing. I just didn't tell you right away. I really didn't have the opportunity. You talk a lot. It's hard to get a word in edgewise."

"Bull." I roll on my side again and jokingly punch his arm. "The fact that I'm interesting is just a convenient excuse to back out on your end."

Ezra snorts. "If you don't want to know why I wish I'd met you sooner, Ruby, then don't tell me."

I try to stare him down. Honing my fine-tuned wiles, I stare seductively, then threateningly, then exasperatedly. Nothing works. Finally, I just give up and begin—from birth, hoping to bore him to death long before I reach high school.

I start talking, telling myself I won't get emotional, but when I get to Mom's death, predictably, I start crying. Ezra winds an arm under my back and pulls me in toward his body. With my head on his shoulder, I alternate between sniffling and storytelling until I can't talk anymore.

"You're very hard on her, you know," he says, drawing me in tighter.

"Don't you think she deserves it?" I sniffle.

"I mostly feel sorry for her. Sounds like she must have been miserable."

"She could've tried, at least. And she didn't have to be so shallow."

"She doesn't sound shallow, Ruby. She sounds lonely, and maybe scared. That's an indescribable feeling."

"No matter how you look at it, she left me."

"People leave. Like the song says, it's the oldest story in the world. No matter what you do or how good you are, you can't stop them."

I grumble into his shoulder, then pull away.

"Look, if you want someone to pat you on the back and tell you you're right, that your mother was horrible, that you have every right to hate her, then maybe you should try your hand with Angel."

"That's low," I snap.

"Then don't go all wounded-wallflower on me when you know better."

Emotionally, Ezra tugs me in so many directions it hurts, but most of all, I hate thinking he may be right. I sit up abruptly, pulling further away. At the same time, he pulls me back, tethering me to the ground with his arm and strong grip.

"No way. You're not going to ask me all these personal questions about my father, which I answered honestly, and then pull away when you can't deal with your own shit. You're entitled to mope. But anger is poison, and once you go down that path, it's nearly impossible to turn back."

Ezra rolls on his side and stares down at me, piercing my heart with his guarded eyes. He's thrown up his wall again, and as suddenly as he let me in, he's tossed me out.

"You're mad at me," I whisper.

"I just wonder what it is that scares you so much you can't even look at yourself. I've watched you, Ruby. You avoid windows. You won't look in mirrors. Half the time it looks like you dressed in the dark."

"I look like her. I see her face," I sniffle. "It makes me feel ugly."

"You didn't do anything wrong. She didn't die because of you. Jesus, you want to know what ugly feels like, try being me for a while."

"Ezra," I whisper, "it's like this constant reminder."

"Of what?"

"You want the laundry list? That I wasn't good enough to make her want to stick around. That I was a bad daughter. That I'll end up like her. Afraid to let anything matter."

Sympathy flickers across Ezra's face, rearranging his wary expression. When his pupils dilate, refocusing like they've just calibrated to the dimming light, it feels like I've known him forever.

"You aren't her," he answers softly. "You're too aware to ever give in to that kind of emptiness. It may be there," he pushes a finger against my heart, "until you let yourself live again. But you do know who you are. You know that what you see in the mirror is far less important than who you are inside."

"You should talk," I blurt out.

"You think I don't know that?"

"Do you?" I squint up at him.

"Unfortunately," his eyes crinkle, "what I see and who I am are the same."

"I don't believe it."

"Ruby ..."

"You may *think* you're ugly," I cut him off. "You may *feel* ugly. But there's nothing about you that is, not on the inside *or* out."

Ezra pulls away from me, dropping flat against his sleeping bag. "Not always," he whispers. "Not when I'm with you."

"Not always when you're with me, what?"

He looks thoughtful, and sad, and terribly conflicted. "When I'm with you, I don't always feel ugly."

"Okay, now you have to tell me."

"Tell you what?"

"Why you wish you'd met me a long time ago."

Ezra covers his face with his arm, laughing softly. "You're entirely too tenacious," he says through his jacket sleeve.

"Well?"

"I don't think I can."

"That's not fair."

"I'm not sure what I meant."

Without thinking, I sit up, pull his arm away from his face, and stare hard into his eyes. "You like me."

"I do."

"No. I mean ... you *like* me. More than friends."

He somehow manages to both laugh and frown. "You're crazy."

A strand of hair sticks to his lip, so I brush it away. When I touch him, he flinches, and I know I'm right. My chest feels tight knowing it so concretely.

"Stop staring," he whispers. "You're worse than my moth ..."

I kiss him before he can finish. Ezra's lips sting my own, and the sudden connection sends a shock down my throat that lodges in my stomach. When he realizes what I'm doing, he tries pushing me away. But I push back, refusing to budge until he admits how he feels. If I'm wrong, I'll be completely humiliated. Either way, I'm going to find out.

Ezra shoots up abruptly, knocking me to the ground. "What the hell are you doing?"

Suddenly the dirt is my ally. I stare at it as though divining my future.

"Ruby!"

Ezra sounds confused, maybe hurt. I look up at the stars, then force myself to meet his eyes, just like I'd expect him to do if the tables were turned. "I thought ... well, I guess it doesn't matter what I thought. I like you, Ezra. I mean, I really do."

"How?" he asks, dumbfounded.

"I guess because you're you," I whisper.

He presses his fingers against his forehead. "Ruby, it's not that easy."

What stands out isn't *what* he says, but that he doesn't deny he likes me or argue that I shouldn't like him. It leaves me the opening I need. "Why? We're together now, aren't we?"

"You need to look in the mirror for real because I think you've forgotten who you are."

"I know who I am. At least I do when I'm with you. And I couldn't care less what people think. They don't know you. They don't know how I feel about you."

Ezra looks so perplexed I think his head might literally whirl into a tailspin. I use the moment to pick myself up off the ground and corner him. "If you don't want me, that's a different story. Then just tell me, please. No matter what, we're friends, right? But don't tell me you don't if you do."

He opens his mouth to say something, then grabs the collar of my jacket instead, roughly pulling me forward by the lapels. When our lips meet, he kisses me back, softly at first, then with an insistence that makes me crazy. I topple him over and lie on his body, pinning him while we kiss, worried he may change his mind.

After an eternity, I roll beside him, snuggling into the side of his down-clad chest. Ezra doesn't speak. He just stares up at the sky with eyes that never waver.

"What are you thinking?" I ask.

"I don't know."

"Really?"

"Yes, really."

"Are you mad at me?"

I feel him laugh, though he does it silently. "No, I'm not. I'd say I'm more, like, happy. And maybe confused. A little frustrated with myself. Not mad at you." He rolls on his side and runs a finger across my cheek. "Take it back if you don't mean it, Ruby. Just do it now, okay? I'm not very good with heartbreak."

"I don't know how to say it any plainer, Ezra. I really, really like you."

"It's hard for me to understand."

"Maybe *you* should look in the mirror again. Because whoever you think you were, if you ever were, you're just not anymore. You don't need a perfect face. You're beautiful here." I touch his chest over his heart. "And you get me. And I trust you. You aren't decent to me because you have something to prove or because you want to get me in bed ... err, well, at least I'm pretty sure that's not it."

Ezra laughs. "I'm with you because you basically hog-tied me that first time we went to Pecos. I never had much of a chance, did I?"

"You know you did." I swat him playfully. "You didn't have to invite me out here. Look, this may sound terrible, but it's partly because of your face that I trust you. And it's because of your face that you let yourself trust me. It may not be as perfect as you'd like, but I don't see what you do. And I don't wonder who you are beneath it either."

"I wouldn't put all your eggs in one basket, Ruby."

"Ezra." I shake my head. "Don't be so cynical."

"I like you a lot, obviously. But I am still me."

Ezra can be so intense. But his reticence isn't hard to understand. Still, the attraction is perceptible, fixed to my body like my own skin. Somehow, he's already integral to who I'm becoming, even if I haven't quite figured it out yet.

"Ezra, I'm tired of talking. Just come back here and kiss me. Whatever *you* decide, I know where *I* stand with it. If you change your mind after you wake up and realize what a dopey idiot I've been, wearing my heart on my sleeve, you'll tell me."

Ezra pulls off his jacket and winds his arm under my back. He throws the jacket on top off us and arranges it to cover the top half of our bodies. Underneath, we fit together like a custom lock and key. His body feels strong and soft all at the same time as I explore it tentatively with my fingers, moving my hand lightly over his scratchy shirt and blue jeans.

For the longest time, he just lies there, rigid and wound tight, stroking my hair while he holds me. I move my hand under his shirt, over his warm chest and stomach, and he swallows or shifts but never halts my journey. We kiss, and I close my eyes. When I open them again, it's light outside, and Ezra is still sleeping beside me.

CHAPTER FOURTEEN

THE TRICK IS TO OPEN YOUR EYES

"HIYA." ANGEL SMILES, tossing a library book on the chair next to me just a little too casually. "What are you up to?"

"It's Thursday. We're in a library. What do you think I'm doing?"

"Studying?"

"Bingo," I laugh, pointing to my physics book. "What else?"

He sits down, crossing his strong arms over his starched khaki button up. "Maybe trying to avoid everyone?"

"Angel ..."

"Maybe," he places a finger on his lips, "maybe all that talk I've been hearing around town is true." He sits back in the chair, folding his arms across his chest again like a general.

"Talk?" I whisper innocently.

"Lots of talk. Everywhere I go."

"Angel, I wanted to tell you myself. I just thought ... I don't know. That you'd be hurt, or angry, or that you wouldn't understand."

He shakes his head. "I am hurt. And I don't understand."

I run a fingernail back and forth in a groove in the wood table, stalling. "I'm sorry. I really am. I knew you'd have something to say about it."

"Here's a tip, Ruby. Soon enough, all of La Luna's going to have something to say about it."

"I don't care what everyone else says. I care what *you* think, Angel."

"There's not one cell in that boy's body that deserves you," he says through his teeth. "It's beyond me what you see in him. Why would you settle?"

"I haven't settled. Ezra isn't his face. He's a good person."

Angel fiddles with my physics book, flicking a page back and forth between his fingers. "A good person? He'd have to have done one hell of a turnaround."

"You know, sometimes you act like he broke *your* heart!"

He squints at me. "How do you know he didn't?"

"*Angel*," I squawk. "Are you serious?"

"As a bullet. He had a bad habit of homing in on whoever I dated in high school. Ezra stole my ex Caroline right out from under my nose." He tips back in the chair, looking half pissed, half smug.

"Oh. I'm sorry. You never told me."

Caroline. The girl Ezra followed to Boston, who turned around and broke his heart. Ezra's words ring in my head. *Guess you might call it poetic justice.* I stare down at the table, resigning myself to the fact that I'm going to be defending Ezra for a good long while.

"I really do think he's changed," I say softly. "He knows who he was before. And he doesn't like it. He *wants* to be different."

Angel drops back on all four chair legs and leans forward,

pushing his forearms against the table. "Anything's possible, I suppose. But I doubt it."

I bite my lip. "I'm sorry if I hurt you."

"Are you?"

I bat my lashes at him a little more strenuously than usual, hating that I've reverted to Mom's tricks to soothe him. "Yes."

"I really don't get it." He scrubs the short hairs on the back of his head with both hands before dropping them heavily on the table. "All that I'm-not-ready crap, was it a lie?"

"No. I *do* like you, Angel. And I'm *not* ready. I just, I feel like myself around him. And I haven't felt like myself since my mom died."

He sighs, staring at my lip as I chew on it. "Do you even know who you are, Ruby? Maybe you feel okay with yourself around him because you don't have to work at it. I bet that boy jumps on any scrap you throw him." He sits back in the chair. "Definitely easier than letting yourself care about someone."

Angel stares at me, and I meet his eyes, trying to conceal my anger. He's my friend. But I've also never seen him act so purposefully hateful. "Ezra isn't desperate. And neither am I."

He looks at me askew. "So, what do we do now?"

"You said our friendship is important to you." I smile as sweetly as I can, pretending I'm not furious with him. "You could try supporting me."

"That's all you want?" he asks sarcastically.

"Baby steps."

Angel gets up and stands perfectly still, looking down at me. "All right," he finally says. "Baby steps. Itty-bitty baby steps."

"Still friends, then?" I ask, looking up at him.

He nods. "You're gonna need one."

I try smiling wider, but my insides hurt. I know Angel's reaction is a preview, a portent of what's to come around town once everyone knows Ezra and I are together.

"You still going to Marta's party Saturday night?" he asks.

"Maybe?" I shrug. "I'm not sure I've talked Ezra into going yet."

"Well, if I see you, I see you, I guess." He repositions his hat. "If not, good luck."

"Thanks. I hope I do see you," I say, kind of not meaning it. Angel and Ezra in a room together is a disaster in the making. On the other hand, I could definitely use the luck. As soon as Las Gallinas found out about Ezra at lunch on Monday, Marta's bad attitude kicked into overdrive. The school week so far, has been unbearable. If Marta could stop me from coming to her party without incurring Racine's wrath, I know she'd have banned me already.

Angel swaggers out of the library, and I flip my physics book shut, feeling a little morose. He welcomed me into La Luna's fold from the very beginning. I hate the thought of alienating him. But not an iota of me regrets being with Ezra.

Unable to concentrate on my physics homework, I open the book I found buried in the stacks earlier. Ezra's stories about his family have been on my mind 24-7 since El Morro. I want to understand how his background shaped him.

Flipping *Of the Pecos People* to its table of contents, I briefly skim each chapter, but the book mostly just describes in greater detail the things Ezra already told me about Pecos's history. Toward the back of the book, I find a chart mapping Pecos's twenty-three clans. Connecting clan to clan with a finger, I look for Shiankya, zigzagging across the page. A few smooth strokes between headings, and I find his clan name. Beneath it, a short caption reads: "Watchers and Guardians of the Mountain." Beneath that, a small picture stares up at me. The same picture Leo has tattooed on his arm.

A sigh escapes my lips, and my hand shakes as I close the book. Could Leo know Ezra? And didn't Mom's ghost, if it even was my mom, say something about a Watcher on the mountain last week?

"Not too many locals interested in Pecos these days. But once upon a time ..."

Startled, I look up at the librarian standing over me. She smiles and points at the book. "Back in the day, Pecos was quite the mystery."

Struggling to find my voice, I breathe out, "I was trying to learn more about Pecos folklore and why it was abandoned."

She smiles wider, showing a few crooked teeth. "When I was a babe, town folk believed the Pecos were magic. Descendants of the Ancients, they called them."

"Descendants of the Ancients?" I gulp.

"Before folks knew much about Pecos origins, common talk was that the Puebloan peoples descended from the Olmec, Aztec, Toltec, and Mayans down south—the Ancients. Until scholars started churning out their books, information people passed down stuck."

Ancients. They'd been a part of Leo's story about the ruin. Shivering, I wrap my arms around my chest, trying to remember everything he told me.

The librarian squints almost conspiratorially. "My grammy was Isleta. She said the Pecos guarded the entrance to the Otherworld, or what she called the Bone Closet. Not exactly a place you go to die, but some place you go to wait—like a recycling center. The Bone Closet keeps our secrets and souls while the Ancients decide where to send us next." The librarian blinks, stepping back. "Still gives me the creeps when I think about it."

I tap the book. "It says in the book that some Spaniards thought the Pecos were witches."

"Not much information about it, that's for sure. But there's plenty of lore in New Mexico about witchery and shamanism. Every pueblo's got theirs. Folks just don't like talking about it." She shakes her head. "There's a story Grammy used to tell us, the 'True Tale of the Demise of the Pecos Pueblo.' Story goes, all but a handful of Pecos turned to witchery and evildoing by the mid-1800s. Because of it, rivals from other pueblos prayed to the Ancients to eradicate the pueblo. Soon after, all but a handful of Pecos drowned in a great flood. The few left abandoned Pecos for Jemez, letting the pueblo fall to ruin."

Wide-eyed, I mentally add her story to my growing list of local lore.

"Working on a paper?" she asks.

"Sort of," I lie.

"There's a good book covering Pecos folklore dating back to just before the first relations between the Spaniards and the Pueblo. An anthropologist came out here in 1904 and spent a year digging up bones, and documents, and tall tales passed down from folk all over New Mexico. Not much interest in it locally, but I'm sure there's a copy housed away in Albuquerque. If you're interested, I'd be happy to check."

"Yes, please."

Still shaky, I thank her profusely, say goodbye and grab my

stuff, shoving everything into my backpack. The sun is just starting to set, and as I step outside, debating whether to call Ezra or walk home so I have time to think, he pulls up in front of the library.

"Hey," he calls out the passenger window. "Where you going?"

"Jeez, you have good timing." I open the door and hop into the cab, kissing his cheek gently. "Home, do you mind?"

Ezra nods and pulls away from the curb, heading south out of La Luna proper. "Homework?" he asks, nodding back at the library.

"Yeah." I squeeze his knee, leaving my fingers on his warm blue jeans. I'm dying to ask him about his clan, and maybe Leo. But I also want him to go to Marta's party, and I know what his answer will be if I start picking his brain first. Getting him to open up also means arming myself for battle, and a battle definitely isn't going to help my cause. "I was thinking about calling you when you pulled up. Weird, right? But I'm happy to see you. What were you doing in town?"

He nods toward the bed of his pickup. "Groceries."

Outside, surrounded by scarlet twilight and fresh air, the idea that Leo and Ezra could be from the same clan and not know it, suddenly seems ridiculous. But I'm still itching to ask.

Ezra gives me a look but doesn't say anything. After a moment, I wiggle his hand again. "Go with me to Marta's party tomorrow night?" I ask coyly.

"The only reason you want to go to that party is to show Marta up."

"That's not the only reason." I jokingly pretend I'm offended, holding a hand to my chest dramatically. "I also really want people to see us together."

"They have seen us together. All week long. Haven't you heard?" He grimaces.

"I mean my people. You know? My friends."

"Marta's party probably isn't the best way to do it, Ruby."

"It means a lot to me."

Ezra glances at me, his expression stony. "I'm not particularly good in a crowd."

"I'll hold your hand the whole time."

"It's a bad idea."

"You'll have fun. I'll never leave your side."

"I'm not worried about having fun." He sighs.

"Then what is it?"

"You really want to go?"

"I really want to go with *you*," I correct him.

Ezra stops in my driveway and lets the car idle. "Let's be clear, Ruby. Going is just asking for trouble."

I scrunch my nose at him and lean over and kiss his scarred cheek. His hair, which I pull loose from its band, falls over his eyes. When I move to push it behind his ear, he flinches. "Ezra, can you please just trust me?"

"You give people too much credit."

"You don't give them enough."

"Fine." Grimacing, he sighs hard. "I'll pick you up tomorrow evening."

I wrap both arms around him and pull him as close as I can over the break. He hugs me back anemically, and I feel his turmoil. But I know if I mention it, it'll only close him off. "Hey," I throw out casually before climbing down, "I've been meaning to ask you, do you know a guy named Leo?"

He looks at me, raising an eyebrow. "Doesn't ring a bell."

"You sure?"

"I don't. Why?"

"He's Native American."

Ezra frowns. "Half of New Mexico is Native American, Ruby. That doesn't mean we all know each other."

"That's not what I meant." I feel stupid but keep pushing. "I think he may be Pecos or from Jemez."

Ezra focuses on my face so intently my cheeks burn. "I doubt it."

"Then maybe he's a ghost."

Ezra bursts out laughing. It's so sudden, I jump. "Don't laugh at me!"

"You're adorable when you're trying to manipulate me, know that?" He bites back a smile. "Anyway, aren't you supposed to be a skeptic?"

"I prefer the term 'open-minded.'" I give him another look. "And skepticism isn't the same as dogma. Just because I don't believe doesn't mean I don't wonder."

"I don't know anyone named Leo." He smirks at me. "But if it helps, I'll ask my mom. If he's Pecos or from Jemez, she'll know."

"Thank you." I grab his hand and fiddle with his long, graceful fingers.

"So how do you know him?" Ezra asks.

"He's just some guy I've run into hiking," I say quickly.

Ezra doesn't say anything, but he doesn't look particularly thrilled either. After quickly hugging him again, I run inside, happy enough he agreed to go to Marta's party *and* that he didn't press me for a more detailed answer about Leo. My small victory is enough to quell my anxiety about making a public social appearance with Ezra, until lunch the next day, when I should know better than to bring Ezra up in front of Marta but still can't seem to stop talking.

As if Ezra's trepidation and Marta's attitude aren't already enough to make me think twice about Marta's party, Marta seals the deal. "I've been trying to wrap my mind around this all week," she complains over her greasy cafeteria pizza. "It's so jacked that you'd do that to Angel."

"I didn't do anything to Angel," I answer, reluctant to rehash the conversation for the tenth time. "I just don't want to date him."

"I don't believe it," Ashley butts in. "If Ezra wasn't in the picture, you'd be all over it."

"But Ezra is in the picture."

"You're really together?" Racine marvels. "I mean ... *together* together?"

"Seriously, yuck," Ashley adds. Her eyes bulge. "For real, do you, like, kiss him?"

I roll my eyes at her, biting my lip to stop myself from saying something rotten. "At least I'm kissing someone," I answer sweetly.

Racine kicks me under the lunch table.

"*Mee-oow*," Ashley mutters.

"I get it," Marta shrugs. "Ezra's a sure bet. He'll never leave. Unlike Angel."

I throw my hands in the air, speaking tightly through my teeth. "Listen, Marta, Angel is a good friend. Because that's what I want." Trying to explain the unexplainable to people is driving me batty. Why can't Ezra and I just be like any other new couple?

"What happened to Leo?" Ashley asks, almost snidely. "He's not in the running?"

"He turned out to be a jerk."

Marta clicks her tongue. "Who do you think you are, Ruby? Taming the one feral boy in town, just so you can say you did it. Not that anyone else would want him."

Were they not rooted to my forehead my eyebrows would take flight. I jump up, leaning across the table toward her. "You think I'm with Ezra because I have something to prove? Who do you think *you* are, Marta? What gives you the right to be so judgmental?"

"Whoa." Racine holds her hand up in the air between us, shaking her head at me. "Angel is Marta's cousin. And, Marta," she turns and glares at Marta, "Don't be such a bitch."

"If you like Ezra *so* much," Marta purrs, "then I *dare* you to bring him to my party."

Looking her straight in the eyes, I try to project confidence I don't feel. "I *am* bringing him."

That shuts Marta up, and until Ezra and I leave for the party later, I'm pretty sure I can deal. But when eight o'clock rolls around and Ezra's face drops as I drag him off my living room couch and push him out the door, my stomach rebels.

Ezra doesn't talk much on the way to Marta's, so I keep my forehead pressed against the window, mesmerized by the lucent night. When we pull up in front of Marta's house, he sucks in his breath. Too aware of all the people milling in tight groups on the lawn, he throws his truck into gear and drives up the road, parking farther down the block than necessary.

"This isn't a good idea, Ruby."

"Why?" I try to smile. "Don't I look pretty tonight?"

Ezra grabs a lock of my hair, which I've worn down like he likes, and rubs it between his fingers. "You always look pretty.

That's probably why I agreed to go in the first place. But I'm sure you already know that."

"Are you accusing me of using my feminine wiles to get you to do something?" I ask innocently.

"Yes."

"Ezra," I pout.

"Don't do that. I'll go in. I just think it's a mistake."

"Always the harbinger of doom," I tease, squeezing his hand reassuringly.

But I feel a little silly. What kind of girl drags her college-aged boyfriend to some high school party, especially when that boyfriend clearly doesn't want to be there? I touch his face, running my finger over his cheek, tracing a line to his soft lips. "Ezra, I'm being dumb. I'm sorry. If you want to leave, we can. The party doesn't mean *that* much to me."

"It doesn't?"

I sigh. "Not if you really don't want to go."

He looks conflicted, but he musters a small smile, pushing my fingers against his lips with his hand. "Why don't we go in for a half hour or so and see what happens."

"You look upset."

"I'm not. I'm just continually in awe of how ridiculously easy it is for you to get me to do things."

"Are you coming then?" I ask, a little snappier than I intend.

"Not if you're going to pout."

"I'm not pouting," I lie. "I just don't want to fight. If it's going to be an issue, you can drop me off and go home."

He shrugs, so I open the door and hop down, waiting on the curb. When it starts to feel like he might sit in his truck all night, I walk to Marta's alone, making it all the way to her kitchen with time to grab a beer before he catches up.

"You're not legal," he whispers in my ear, sneaking up behind me.

"Neither are you," I shrug, looking at him over my shoulder.

Ezra's top lip curls up over his teeth, showing off a perfect white row of enamel. "Suit yourself. Grab me a cup, will you?"

I finagle a red plastic cup off the tall tower on the table and shove it against his chest. He takes it, but then grasps my wrist and tugs me against him. "See how everyone's looking at us?" he whispers.

I survey the kitchen. Marta's guests are trying hard to pretend they don't notice him. But all around the room, people steal glances.

"Do you want to leave?" I whisper back.

He wraps an arm around my shoulders. "I can handle it if you can. Just don't be mad anymore, all right?"

"I'm not." I let my forehead drop against his chest. "I'm happy you came. I just feel bad."

Ezra fills his cup and walks us toward the patio. Kids blocking the door move aside as Ezra maneuvers us through, snaking outside to an emptier spot near a squat juniper. The crowded space feels claustrophobic, and that makes me feel like drinking. I toss back my beer, downing half in one gulp.

"Whoa, trigger." Ezra grabs my cup and holds it away from me. "Not so fast."

"I'm not two," I tell him.

He cups my chin with a wide hand. "Yeah, well, I don't want you getting sick in my truck."

Already nearing tipsy, I stand on my tiptoes and try to place an apologetic kiss on Ezra's nose, losing my balance when I hear Racine's voice.

"Ruby!" she squeals as I flip around.

Racine trots over, flanked by Marta and Ashley. She smiles affably at Ezra.

"Hey," I grin at them, linking an arm through Ezra's. "You guys know Ezra, right?"

"It's good to see you." Racine nods.

"Yeah, we all know each other," Marta glowers. "Unfortunately."

"Or at least *of* each other," Ezra counters.

Marta purses her lips but thankfully keeps her mouth shut, proving there's a first time for everything.

"How's your sister?" Ezra asks Ashley. "I heard she moved to Texas."

"She's ... good." Ashley looks at me with wide eyes, unsure where her loyalties lie.

"Like you care," Marta snips.

Ezra smiles sweetly, doing a good job of looking unruffled. "Why wouldn't I?"

"Because pigs don't fly."

Racine lays a hand on Marta's arm. "Marta, he's just being polite."

Racine smiles at me, nodding at my drink. Uncomfortable, I toss back the rest of my beer and hand Ezra the cup. "Do you mind?"

"You mean, will I go get you another drink so you can remind your friends to be nice to me while I'm gone?"

Marta snorts.

"Yes," I answer coolly. "That's exactly what I mean."

Ezra takes the cup, leaving me alone with Las Gallinas.

"So, how's it going?" Racine asks. "I mean, you know."

I look around at all the faces filling Marta's backyard, some of which stare back. "He's kind of in a mood. But he's trying."

"Well, that's something," Racine nods.

"You guys think I'm crazy bringing him here, right?"

"I think you're crazy," Marta volunteers.

"I can't believe he came," Ashley says. "He's usually, like totally antisocial."

I bite my lip. "I sort of talked him into it."

"You're a good sport." Racine smiles. "I would have totally bounced by now."

Ezra takes his sweet time coming back with my beer. While I wait, the four of us stand in the crowded space and gossip about Liddy and Torrance, who seem fast on their way to item-hood. Within minutes, a group of boys from school gathers at our sides.

"Oh hey, Ruby," Ashley cuts in when one of them mentions Halloween, "want to hike up to that ruin you talked about, on Halloween night? It'll freak the shit out of Racine." She grins at Racine.

One of the boys, Ricardo, says, "I'm totally in. What ruin?"

"Near her house." Racine nods at me. "And no, thank you. I'm not hiking Paso de Demonio on Halloween, much less ever."

"It's my birthday anyway." I look down at the flagstone patio.

"Get out!" Ashley squeaks.

Marta snorts. "Figures. You've definitely got that witchy vibe."

"Marta!" Racine gives her the evil eye. "Seriously?"

She turns back to me. "That's so cool, Ruby."

"Not really," I shrug. "People usually forget it because it's on Halloween. And you have no idea how much crap I had to put up with growing up." I give Marta my own evil look, for good measure. "And for the record," I tell her, "if I was a witch, *you'd* know already."

Marta rolls her eyes at me. Tired of her, I turn my back slightly and focus on talking to Ricardo as I scan the patio for Ezra. A couple of seconds later, I find him. Propped against the patio doorframe with two beers in hand, Ezra stares back at us suspiciously. When our eyes meet, he pushes himself off the wall and walks toward our group, exaggerating his gait and smile.

"Here." He hands me my plastic cup.

"Thanks," I say to the ground.

Ricardo keeps talking. "So, Ruby," he says. "I was wondering if you maybe wanted to go out some time."

Marta giggles. Somehow, I've attracted the only boy at Pecos High who hasn't seen me with Ezra or heard the gossip, and I've managed to do it in front of Ezra.

My eyes follow the grouting along the flagstone. I stare down at it, shifting my weight, and start to tell Ricardo 'no thank you,' but Ezra wraps an arm around my shoulder. "Well?" he says. "What do you say, Ruby? You want to go on a date with this dude or not?"

Marta and Racine clear their throats simultaneously. Ashley stares at the ground, maybe familiarizing herself with the same flagstone network.

"No. I mean, thanks, but I'm with Ezra." I lean sideways into Ezra's body.

Ricardo's mouth drops open. "Oh. I didn't know."

"Ruby keeps me locked in a closet." Ezra laughs.

"Well." Ricardo smiles tightly. "I guess I'll see you Monday."

Ricardo walks away quickly, and Ashley clears her throat, croaking out, "Um, I totally need a drink. Anyone else coming?"

"For sure." Racine nods. Marta just smiles and follows them to the kitchen, leaving me alone with Ezra.

I jab his arm. "Way to alienate my friends."

Ezra rubs his face brusquely, then drops his hand to his side. "Way to make time." He looks at his wrist pretending to check his watch. "I was gone, what, maybe five minutes?"

"You're being lame."

"It *was* kind of amusing watching my girlfriend flirt with another guy."

"Ezra!" I blurt out. "You can't be serious."

"Can't I?"

"I'm not interested in anyone else. How many times do I have to tell you?"

"A couple at least." He frowns.

Frustrated, I look him up and down. He looks really uncomfortable and I suddenly feel bad. "Listen, do you want to leave?"

Ezra shakes his head. "Actually, I think I should go."

"You mean alone?" I ask.

"Generally, that's what 'I' means."

"Ezra ..." I begin, exasperated.

"You'll have more fun. I'll see you tomorrow."

My free hand finds my hip and settles there, squeezing like it wants to rip out a chunk of flesh. "Why do I feel like you're just looking for an excuse to get out of here?"

He shrugs indifferently. "Maybe because you don't want to admit that this was a bad idea."

"Fine!" I snap at him. "Go."

Ezra's nostrils flare. He turns slightly and inadvertently steps into Angel, who appears out of nowhere.

"Of course," Ezra mumbles under his breath.

Reaching for Ezra's arm, I grab him back quickly. "If you want to leave, I'll go with you."

Ezra wrenches loose from my grip. "Fine, Ruby. I'll be in the truck."

"I can give her a ride home," Angel says.

Ezra looks like he wants to punch Angel's face in. Instead, he steps back. "If that's what she wants," he replies coolly.

"Hello?" Everyone on the patio turns to stare, and I quickly go from flushed to sunburned. "I'm not a commodity. I don't want a ride, Angel. And I no longer want to go with you either, Ezra!"

Ezra stands his ground, looking back and forth between Angel and me.

"I'm serious," I tell him.

His frown twists into a scowl. "Must suck," he sneers at Angel. "Wanting something so badly."

Angel's jaw goes so rigid you could bounce a rock off it. "You just can't help yourself, can you? Do you even like her? Or is it all just a game to you, Ezra?"

"Does it matter?" Ezra sneers. "She already picked. And you lost."

Hearing Ezra say it makes my heart skip, but I barely have a chance to react before Angel steps in his face. "If I hadn't promised Ruby, I'd give you a chance, I'd have your ass on the ground." He rolls it out smoothly. "Why don't you do everyone a favor and walk away now."

Furious, I push between them. "Are you serious?" I stare daggers at Ezra. "I'm not a toy, Ezra." Looking between them, I add, "And if I was a toy, I definitely wouldn't want to belong to either of you. You're both freaking Neanderthals!"

"If you want to go with him, Ruby, go," Ezra growls.

"I don't. But right now, I have less than zero desire to be with you either!"

Ezra shoves his beer cup at me and bows with a flourish, tipping an invisible hat in the air before stomping off.

"Great!" I snap at Angel as Ezra marches away. "Thanks for coming to my rescue."

"You're welcome," he answers sharply.

"That was sarcasm." I glare at him.

"Yeah, I know." He shakes his head. "Tell me he wasn't being an ass to you. To everyone."

"He wasn't until you showed up! And if you hadn't all stared at him like some sideshow freak, he probably would have stayed. He didn't lose his *mind* in the accident, Angel. It's not like he doesn't know how you all feel about him."

"Well, *golly*," Angel retorts. "I wonder why."

"I'm not a wilting flower. I don't need you to save me. So just back off!"

I turn to find Racine on the periphery of the patio, watching us. She rushes over and yanks at my hand before I can say something irredeemable. "Let's just go inside, fill our cups, and forget about stupid boys for the night," she coaxes. Before I can answer, she links her arm in mine, steers me inside toward the keg, and fills my red cup. "Drink," she commands.

I'm furious, and between Las Gallinas and my trusty red cup, Ezra completely ceases to exist for the next few hours. I don't even let myself think of him again until the next morning. Not until my alarm clock accidentally goes off at seven a.m. and I roll out of bed, cursing the gods for having such a rotten sense of humor.

Half asleep and bundled in a bathrobe, I shuffle downstairs in search of a strong pot of coffee. Following a serious caffeine fix, my only plan for the day involves hanging around the house in my pajamas.

At the bottom of the staircase, I literally bump into Torrance. We round the wall between the hall and the kitchen at the same time, colliding near the bottom step.

"Whoa. Morning." He smiles and holds up a mug, standing barefoot in his jeans and a rumpled shirt. "I was just bringing this to Liddy."

"I ... jeez." I close my eyes.

Torrance clears his throat. When I open my eyes, he smiles. "Ruby," he says cautiously, "I hope this doesn't make you uncomfortable."

"You mean that you never went home last night?"

He stares, waiting for me to answer the question for myself. Then he shakes his head. "Liddy's awake. Maybe you two should talk."

"No. I'm just ..." I look down at the stairs, then up at his handsome face. "I had a long night that sadly didn't include a whole lot of sleep. I didn't notice your truck last night. You just surprised me."

"You sure?"

Seeing him all sleepy-eyed and rumpled on the steps throws me for a loop. I feel weird standing in front of him in my pajamas. Suddenly, I want to get dressed and get out as much as I want to appease my inner sloth.

"Yeah," I nod. "I am. But will you do me a favor? Tell her I went for a hike?"

"Are we good?" he asks.

"Perfect." And we are, for the most part. My real problem is Ezra; seeing Torrance just reminds me that love takes two and that I'm minus my second until Ezra and I talk.

I putter around the kitchen for a few minutes until I'm sure Torrance is gone, then quickly change out of my pajamas, paying little attention to my knotty hair or pale face. I don't even brush my teeth, just grab my sweater, and backpack and run out the back door with my compass, Swiss Army knife, and a thermos of coffee. Strong coffee, I have to give Torrance that.

Crisp air zaps my skin but does nothing for my budding headache as I briskly make my way up the mountain. Closer to the plateau, I try to wipe Ezra from my thoughts. Walking out on me at Marta's gives me a perfect out. Except I don't want out. Despite everything, my heart is sure that the real Ezra *isn't* the boy who left me alone at the party last night.

In the clearing, I pull tracing paper from my backpack and absently layer it over a ruin wall. My hand moves, rubbing charcoal over the wall's grainy surface. I let my senses take over, drifting until the clearing starts to hum. Except this time the humming is crisper and more resonant, like voices, not static. I think I hear someone say, "Open it," and jump, losing my charcoals to the ground.

For just a moment, the air is so thick it's suffocating. Then something flickers near my side, like a candle petering out, and a figure darts between the trees to my right. I whip around, holding my breath. My skin tingles and I'm this close to hyperventilating.

"Seriously, Ruby," I say out loud, reaching to pick up my charcoals. "Have you lost your freaking mind?"

"Up here," a familiar voice answers, "I'd encourage you to keep an eye on it."

"Leo!" I sputter, jumping about half a mile. "I hate it when you do that!"

Leo flashes a cocky smile.

"You almost gave me a freaking heart attack."

"It's a pleasure to see you too." He chuckles.

Bits of flora stick to my everything. Fall has settled in, and the forest seems to be shedding. Shaky, I brush dried leaves from my knees, leaving my rubbings on the ground.

"How was your camping trip?" he asks casually.

Still breathless, I step back, putting a good few feet between us. "Not that it's any of your business, but good."

"Good?" He grins.

"It was great, Leo. Wonderful." I shuffle my toe through a small pile of leaves and pine needles. "What do you care anyway?"

"Why are you always so touchy, Ruby?" He raises his dark eyebrows high on his forehead.

"Why are you so cocky?"

Leo sits down on the ground and pats the dirt next to him. "Don't be like that. I just want to visit for a while."

Reluctantly, I sit down across from him, dropping my chin on my knees while I pull my legs in, curling into a ball. Above the mountaintop, the sun seems to explode against the brilliant blue sky. Everything in the clearing glows orange in hues that set the plateau on fire. Leo follows my gaze to a patch of wild lavender growing like a weed against a crumbling ruin wall, its purple deep against the brown adobe.

"Is your background Pecos?" I finally blurt out. "Or Jemez?"

"Nope."

Leo's grin irritates me. "What then?"

He smirks but doesn't answer.

"If this is how you get your girl," I sniff, "I get why you're always up here alone."

"You're obviously still attracted to me." Leo looks straight ahead, examining the ruin like I bore him. "I don't blame you."

After a beat, he leans forward, swooping in to kiss me before I can stop him.

"Leo!" I shout, slouching away. "Are you completely mental?"

Avoiding Leo's eyes, I grab my water bottle and rubbings and shove everything into my backpack. When I move to stand, he follows and grabs my arm. "You can pretend all you want, Ruby. But you can't deny there's something between us."

His bulk looms over me, but I stand my ground. "Yeah, it's called your ego."

"No." He rubs a finger against my inner elbow, sending an unwelcome spark down my spine. "It's physical."

"Are you for real?"

"Last I checked." He smiles.

I wrench my arm from Leo's hand. "You're disgusting, you know that? Newsflash—I have standards. You should look the word up sometime."

Leo closes his eyes, still broadcasting that infernal smirk. "'Standard: an accepted example of something against which others are judged or measured; a moral principle of behavior.'" He puts his hands on his hips and opens his eyes. "Who's your barometer?"

If I had something to chuck, I'd chuck it hard, aiming straight for his perfect face. Instead, I flip him the bird and run toward the middle of the ruin. A tiny part of me hopes Leo will follow so I can kick him in the balls, but when I look back, he's gone.

I turn in circles, weaving a path through the clearing.

What the hell, Ruby?

The sky shimmers like a mirage, fading to a bruised kind of black and violet. Above me, a huge sapphire orb eclipses half the eastern skyline. Disoriented, I step back and trip over the boulder, flailing as my behind hits the ground.

My mother appears over me. A blur of almost holographic features, she moves her mouth but makes no sound. Holding my hand out, I reach for her. A couple of feet divide us, and as she extends her arm to bridge the gap, a large object falls from the sky. Rough and grainy, it looks like a rock, except its bulk slowly unfolds in the space between us, unfurling spindly limbs like a giant, mutant spider.

My mother's soundless words hit me like a shockwave. Still sitting, I jump up. Her voice fills my head, and the rock-thing bursts into a million pieces of black confetti that whirl slowly like ash to the ground.

Go back! she says firmly. *And be wary of the Watcher.*

Her body flickers, rising slightly off the ground, vanishing, then pulsing to life. I desperately want to grab her and hold her down, to ask what she means, but something tugs hard on my arm. Pulling away from it, I fight while the forest fades, swallowing me up again in blinding light.

"Ruby!"

I sit bolt upright, gasping. Once again, Leo crouches over

me. He looks almost terrified. Leveraging his outstretched hand, I stand and steady myself.

"Are you all right?" Leo asks, doing a good job of faking genuine worry.

Still disoriented, I shake my head slowly. "I was here in the forest, but not. I saw planets I swear don't belong near Earth." I reach out for his arm again, using it to catch my balance.

"That's crazy," he says. Except the way he looks at me, it's like he knows exactly what I'm talking about.

Suddenly scared of Leo, I whip away from him and run down the mountain, startling at the sound my own footfalls make as I step over dried twigs and leaves. Brushwood snaps at my legs and scratches my arms, and by the time I run into our backyard, my eyes are puffy, and my legs burn like I've run a marathon.

Breathless, I wipe a shirtsleeve quickly over my face and slip off my shoes near the back door, hoping to sneak inside without alerting anyone. Even when my eyes are dry, Liddy has this uncanny ability to tell when I've been crying.

The door swings open as I reach for the doorknob. "Ruby! You have perfect timing." Liddy grabs my arm and swiftly maneuvers me past Torrance, who's sitting at the kitchen table reading the paper.

"What's up?" I ask, trying to sound indifferent.

She pulls me past the archway into the living room. Before I can protest, Ezra's straw cowboy hat catches my attention, along with his dark eyes peering out from beneath it.

"I was just about to leave," he tells the wall near the front door.

I touch my hair, which must be standing out in a million directions and pull bits of leaf off my sweater. "Then why don't you?"

"Well, I'll just leave you two. Hon," Liddy whispers as she wipes dirt off my chin, "I'll be in the kitchen."

Liddy leaves the room, and Ezra clears his throat, ruminating before speaking. "Can we talk?"

My head is still screaming, and my first instinct is to throw a shoe at him, but I grab his hand and pull him outside to the front porch. "Okay. Talk."

Ezra nods at Torrance's truck. "That Torrance's?"

I shrug, hoping he won't dwell on it. He searches my face, and I imagine how terribly messy I look through his eyes.

"Is that why you're crying?"

"I'm not."

"Ruby," he sighs.

"It has nothing to do with Torrance. I just ... I was up at the ruin. Something happened. I saw something, Ezra." I'm definitely not about to tell him about Leo, especially not after his altercation with Angel at Marta's party last night.

He pulls a hair off my lip and frowns fiercely. "Saw what?"

"My mother."

Ezra opens his mouth a little but then closes it, as if suddenly rethinking his response. "Are you okay?" he asks tentatively.

"Yeah. I'm just having a really bad morning."

Ezra sighs and fidgets with his belt buckle. I watch his long fingers flick the silver edge, scraping at its intricate design. After a moment, he reaches out and hooks my chin. "I *really* don't like you going up there."

"I'm drawn to it," I admit.

He pulls me close, breathing into my hair. "If something happened to you ..." He trails off, pulling me against him even tighter. "Ruby, I'm sorry about last night. I shouldn't have left you."

"We shouldn't have gone," I whisper into his chest.

"You mean I shouldn't have gone."

I push away, forging space between our bodies so I can see him better. "No, Ezra, I mean *we* shouldn't have gone. We're together, aren't we? We do things together. That's how it works. At least, how it's supposed to."

"Well, look how *we* turned out last night."

I wince and sit down on a porch step. The sun hangs in the eastern sky. My eyes burn, but I force myself to look at it anyway, turning back to Ezra afterward so nothing but his outline shows clearly, as though the sun erased the rest of him completely.

"Ez, you can be really charming when you want. I don't think people would be so quick to judge if they saw that side of you. Your face shouldn't define you. It does, because you let it."

Ezra sits down on a step a couple of feet away, pursing his lips together. "You think people had a better opinion of me when my face was different?"

"I don't know. Did they?"

"Except for you, no one's ever seen past my face either way." He stares at me, as though dumbfounded by my cluelessness. "People see what they want. This way at least I don't have to live by anyone's stupid rules, or conceptions, or conditions."

"Are you really feeding me that I'm-a-lone-wolf-in-a-grim-world crap?"

Ezra's grin catches me off guard. "I wouldn't say I'm a wolf, Ruby."

"Fine. A donkey then."

I expect him to argue, not beam at me affectionately. "Look, I knew how things were going to play out last night—I told you. And I went anyway. Can't you give me a little credit for that?"

"If you admit you're not as jaded as you pretend."

"You have zero idea what it's like to be stared at all the time." He exhales, resigned to a fate he obviously cares a lot more about than he lets on.

"Then tell me."

Ezra shakes his head. He takes off his hat and tosses it on the stair next to him, letting it divide us. "Ruby, it wasn't just me they were whispering about last night."

Ezra's skin near glows in the sunlight. His cheek looks soft and warm, and I reach out and touch it. "Don't worry about me so much."

He drops his face into his hands and holds it there, speaking through his fingers. "I do. Since the day you forced your way into my booth to avoid Angel."

My throat constricts a little. I croak out, "Really?" then cover my mouth, mumbling into my hand. "Why?"

"Because I'm crazy about you."

"You are?" I nearly squeak.

"Could you be more clueless?" Ezra tips his head toward the sun. "Just tell me what to do to make this right."

I push the hat away and scoot to his side, winding my arm around his broad shoulders. His checkered cotton shirt is soft and warm against my skin, inviting every atom of my affection. "You're already doing it."

"I'm really sorry," he says, searching my face.

"I'm sorry too. All I really want is for you to give us a chance."

Ezra hooks my chin with a finger again, moving in closer. "My heart is yours. I want you entirely, Ruby, even though I know I'm undeserving."

My own heart hammers out an uneven beat. Between that and my aching head, I barely hear him. "I don't always get what you see in me either," I say, pretending I'm not paralyzed, and breathless, and suddenly, unbelievably happy. "But I trust your judgment."

He takes my hand and winds his fingers through mine. "I want us to be together. Despite how wrong we are."

"It's not wrong," I whisper. "Just hard. There's a big difference."

Ezra stands up and pulls me close, wrapping his strong arms around my back near where my rear meets my spine, fitting my curves as though he's the last missing part of a near-completed puzzle.

"Like a jigsaw puzzle," he whispers into my hair.

I look up at him. "Did I say that out loud?"

He nuzzles my ear with his chin. "I don't need to see your face to know what you're thinking."

In Ezra's arms, I come alive. I stop thinking about Leo, and the ruin, and my mother. I stop worrying about whether I'm going crazy or maybe dying from some rare brain tumor. But with Ezra it isn't just physical; the attraction is intuitive and elemental. Our minds, like our bodies, are united. He holds me, and it's like I *see* the air crackle around us, sparkling in vibrant bursts of white and blue and yellow. He smells like sun and fresh air, and when he kisses me, he tastes like oranges. Right now, he could have a face like the Devil for all I care; our connection is absolute and intense, and I know he's mine completely.

CHAPTER FIFTEEN

FOUR-LETTER WORDS

A WEEK BEFORE MY BIRTHDAY, Liddy gives me a letter from Mom. Mom asked Liddy to hold it until I turned eighteen, so Liddy put it away, then in the drama that followed Mom's death, forgot about it. Until last night, when she finally unpacked the last of her boxes. From my bed, the letter glows in the morning sun. I've been staring at it, propped unopened on the ledge of my easel, for hours now, terrified of what's inside.

Wrapped in a thick blanket, I get up and shuffle to the envelope, then flop back into bed, gripping the square tightly. Across the envelope's crisp surface, the words: "To my darling Ruby" leap out at me in my mother's blocky script. My hands shake, so I bite my nails, wondering what could possibly be so important she had to write it down.

After a few anxious minutes, I rip the envelope open—fast, the way you rip off a Band-Aid, hoping to be good and finished before you realize it's off. The envelope holds a single sheet of paper, and I read it while I hold my breath.

Ruby, love, you're finally eighteen. Can you believe it? Eighteen, and really more Liddy's child than mine. Two peas in a pod you both are, and I couldn't be more grateful. My guess is, I'm not there to celebrate with you, and knowing you, you're mad. I don't blame you, sweetheart, but I want you to know nothing you or Liddy did brought any of us to this moment. I've always loved you and always will. I regret nothing, least of all you and the joy you've made of my life.

If you'll allow me, I'd like to leave you with something wise. So here it is. Don't let your head be your only guide, and don't let anyone convince you your instincts are wrong. Pay attention. Look past the obvious. Accept things beyond your control, but always fight fiercely for what's yours. Don't let anyone convince you that you don't have enough strength. It's that fight, in the end, that defines all you are and become. I want you to be happy, Ruby, and when you learn to trust yourself, you will be. You are already true. One day, you'll be True of Heart.

Happy birthday.
Love, Mom

Through tears, I read the letter over and over. Mom must have known she was going to die. Cryptic as her words are, that much is evident. I read the letter again, and then one more time, letting my heart break just a little more as I go over every line.

Distraught, I lie back on my bed, staring at the tips of the pine trees out my window where they meet the sky. Mom's words haunt me, because I don't know what they mean, even though my gut tells me they're important. No matter how I think about them, I can't purge the feeling that something is off, and that suspicion follows me around the next few days, hanging over my head like the Hindenburg.

Eventually, Racine notices. After tiptoeing around me half the week, she finally corners me on the high school's front quad.

"*Everyone's* talking about what a drag you are, Ruby," she rolls out, exaggerating the word "everyone" in this way that hints she just means herself.

As she speaks, the wind sends skeletal leaves dancing across the dying grass. A small branch clings to my foot, and I mumble as I kick it off. "I hope you told 'em all about my long, checkered past—you know, my history of homicide, and assault, and robbery."

She wrinkles her nose. "I left the assault part out, sorry."

We laugh at the same time, and for a fleeting moment everything feels normal.

Racine sighs and turns her big blue eyes on me. "What gives?"

"It's almost my birthday. First one without Mom. I'm just ... sad, I guess."

"Everyone thinks it's Ezra."

"Everyone?"

"Well, you know. The girls. And Giovanni."

"Well, it's not."

Racine shifts her backpack from one shoulder to another. "Marta saw you guys fighting in front of Margarita's Sunday."

"Oh, that."

After I read Ezra Mom's letter, pouring my heart out while he listened, I unsuccessfully tried to kiss him in front of

Margarita's. Saying he's shy about displaying his feelings for me in public is an understatement. He'd been snappy about it, and given where my heart is, my head went on an insecurity bender.

"Whatever." I shrug nonchalantly. "It was nothing."

Racine gives me a look. "Well, if you feel like talking."

"Just tell everyone it's not Ez. We're fine." As if on cue, Ezra's truck pulls up in front of the school, idling across the street.

"Speaking of," Racine mutters.

"Want a ride?"

"Nah. I'm waiting for Giovanni."

"All right. Be good." I kiss her cheek and walk backward to Ezra's truck, waving at Giovanni, headed toward us across the quad.

She grins. "I'll try."

As Ezra pulls away from the curb, I stick my tongue out at Racine through the window. Ezra turns onto the frontage road, smiling quietly to himself while he drives slowly through the pass.

"What?" I push a finger against his rib cage, twisting playfully.

He snorts. "Sometimes I forget you're in high school."

"I'm just trying to ease some tension." Leaning over, I kiss his scarred cheek. "Racine says I'm being kind of mental."

"It's nice to see you smile. It's been a few days."

"Liddy won't be home until six," I tell him, ignoring what I know is an invitation to talk about the letter again. "Come over for a while?"

"I thought you had to study."

"I'd rather study you." I grin.

Ezra pulls up my driveway but leaves the truck running when I move to get out.

"Aren't you coming in?" I ask.

"I still have a few really big units to finish up before the holidays."

"What's more important?" I smile sweetly. "Your stinking orders, or me?"

The question isn't fair. His work is important—almost therapeutic. He's so good at restoring things. I know that. I just really want to be with him right now.

Sighing, Ezra swiftly turns the engine off and jumps out of his truck, trudging behind me into the house. After I drop my backpack in the hall, he tosses his hat on a chair and grabs me around the waist, pulling me up against him. He kisses me gently and maneuvers me toward the couch, plunking me down. "Tell me about your day."

"You sure you want to know?"

He smiles sweetly, so differently from just moments ago. "I always want to know."

Ezra's lap makes a comfortable pillow. I lay my head back and kick my feet up on the arm of the couch, wiggling my purple socks at him. "I'm swamped with French homework. Ms. Lisset's class is a nightmare. You had her, didn't you?"

I look up at him. From some angles, he looks almost perfect; I can't even see his scars.

"Yeah. And I never forgot a single word of French. Between that and Spanish, my college language requirement was a breeze." He caresses my hair, brushing a strand across my forehead. "How are Las Gallinas?" he asks affectionately.

"They've been all right. But apparently, *I'm* driving everyone crazy."

"*No*," he says, his voice laced with sarcasm.

I swing a pillow toward his head, barely cuffing him. "You're lucky I'm so forgiving."

"No, I'm just lucky." He walks his fingers slowly up and down my bare arm, sending chills through my body.

"Ez, I'm sorry if it seems like I'm in a bad mood all of the time lately."

"*Seems*? I don't mean to beat a dead horse, but you're not exactly subtle, Ruby." He looks down at my face, tracing my lips with a finger. "Your birthday's in a few days, first one without your mom ... the letter ... I get it. Must feel like you're just going through the motions."

"Yeah," I whisper. "It does."

"Do you want to talk more about the letter?" He smiles meekly.

"No. Not really. Now that I know it probably wasn't an accident, I guess I'm just extra mad she left. But at least I'm not alone." I sit up and wrap my arms around his neck. "I have you."

Ezra kisses me, letting his lips linger on mine. When he pulls away, he says, "You do, Ruby. For now."

"For always."

"Everything's fleeting," he answers matter-of-factly. "Everyone leaves, eventually."

"I hate it when you do that." I hate it especially because a huge part of me fears he's right. Besides knowing I'm in love with him—even if I haven't said it yet—I'm beyond tired of holding my breath. For once, I just want to exist without needing to examine my life, to be okay without questioning if I'm doing everything right.

Ezra runs a calloused palm up my wrist to my shoulder,

moving on to trace my collarbone with a fingertip. His finger travels up my neck, under my chin, and then slowly down to my neckline beneath my shirt, raising goose bumps that make me shiver.

I sit up and lay my hands flat on his chest, pushing him back against the couch. "You think you can just charm me with that finger of yours and everything will be okay?"

"I hope so." He grins.

Climbing on top of him, I pin his body to the cushions. "Kiss me again," I demand.

Ezra wraps a hand around the back of my neck. He pulls me forward, holding my face just a fraction from his own, so close his features blur. He holds me there suspended, waiting, and then raises his head to kiss me.

The kiss is intense; he tugs at the loops on my blue jeans, pulling me to him as he runs a hand under my shirt against my bare sides. Every little baby hair on my body stands at attention. In a flash, I yank my shirt over my head, tossing it off to the side of the couch. We haven't made it much past kissing, so I'm not sure how far he wants to go, but I tug at his shirt anyway, brushing against his chest as I bunch it over his stomach.

Despite a fair amount of scarring, Ezra has an incredible body. It's lean, and long, and defined by muscle in all the right places. No amount of damage masks how genetically gifted he is. Yet when I touch him, tracing a finger to the hollow in his neck, he winces.

"Hey," I whisper. "You're beautiful." I try tugging his shirt over his shoulders, but he grabs at the fabric as it leaves his head, yanking it back.

For a brief second, before he pulls his shirt down, my eyes wander over his stomach, and broad chest, and defined arms, stalling at what looks like ink on his left shoulder.

"Is that a tattoo?" Ezra never wears short sleeve shirts. I've never seen his arms above his elbows.

Ezra nods and tries pushing me off him.

Resisting, I pull at his shirt. "What is it? Let me see."

"Nothing," he answers breathlessly.

"It can't be 'nothing.'"

"Ruby." He sits up brusquely. "Stop it."

I push him back against the cushions. "You're a tease."

"I mean it." He sits up again, locking my hands in a vice grip.

I freeze, confused by his sudden about-face. "Ezra, let go. You're hurting me."

Ezra inhales like the weight of the universe just fell on his shoulders. He briskly lets go of my wrists. "I can't do this."

"Do what?" I squeak.

He pushes me off his lap and stands up, almost knocking me out of the way. "Have sex with you."

"Who said anything about having sex?" I ask, trying to keep my voice steady.

Ezra stares down at me like I've suddenly contracted anthrax.

"If you don't think I'm attractive, then tell me," I choke out, feeling exposed. "But if it's you, Ez, I mean, if you think I'm not attracted to you, you're wrong."

He stares up at the ceiling, at the lounger in the corner near the fireplace, down the hall, but he won't meet my eyes. Looking tortured, he wraps his arms protectively around his body and walks out the front door without so much as a goodbye.

My heart thumps so hard it threatens to rip from my chest in a blaze of angry glory. Watching him walk away makes me so mad, I want to rip his heart out and chuck it at his face just to watch it splatter. "The only thing freakish about you," I shout out the door after him, "is your attitude! God, Ezra, why *would* anyone want you?"

After I slam the door shut, I start sobbing. His rejection, which has more to do with his own self-esteem than me, I'm sure, feels like bricks crushing my heart. I cry for a long time, curling into a tight ball on the corner of the couch. Until Liddy nudges my shoulder, and I open my eyes.

Outside, it's dark, and I feel number than my leg, which has stopped feeling anything twisted like it is beneath my body.

"Hey," Liddy shakes my arm. "Wake up, love. We've got company."

My heart skips before I realize she just means Torrance. "Muhumph," I grumble, throwing an arm across my eyes. "Tell him I'm dead or something."

"You've looked better." She pulls my arm off my face, tugging me into a sitting position.

"Liddy," I whine, "why are you so mean to me?"

"I'm your aunt. It's my duty."

Liddy drags me to the bathroom, sitting me down on the toilet seat. She wets a washcloth with warm water and wipes my eyes. The same thing she's always done when I'm upset since, like, birth.

"Is it the letter?" she asks softly. "I know it's been bugging you."

"Everyone leaves."

"What?"

"Everyone leaves. That's what he told me."

"Ezra?"

"Yes."

"Well, if he can't see how lucky he is, then good riddance. Anyway, he's wrong. You're stuck with *me* forever." Liddy talks tough, but she smiles sympathetically.

"Why can't it be easy?" I whisper.

Liddy crouches down and wraps her arms around me. "You're a rebel, love. You defy convention. You don't suddenly want it all handed to you on a platter now, do you?"

"I wouldn't mind a guidebook or something," I sniffle.

"Isn't that one of the reasons you like Ezra so much? Because he's a puzzle? And not particularly conventional in just about every way I can think of?"

"I like him because I like him. It feels right, Liddy. I feel right. If you think I like him because he's a pain in the ass ... jeez."

Liddy smiles, brushing hair off my shoulder. "You've always been drawn to a challenge. It wouldn't surprise me if that was just a little part of your interest in him."

"I shouldn't have to justify my reasons for loving someone," I snap.

She inhales sharply. "You love him?"

"I don't know," I choke. "I'm just saying."

Liddy stands up, looking down at me affectionately. "If only Sera were here."

"What's that supposed to mean?"

"You've never really had a boyfriend. She'd sure as hell be sorry, she missed it."

"She'd probably say I have bad judgment, or low standards, or something else totally stupid." I sigh and stand up. "I doubt she'd be sorry though. If either of us mattered at all, she'd still be here."

"Sweetheart," Liddy sighs, "we don't know that."

"Don't we?" I frown down at the floor. "Liddy, Ezra thinks it's impossible for me to love him because of his face. We were ..." I bite my lip, quickly mulling whether or not to tell her the truth. "We were fooling around, and I tried to take off his shirt, and he completely lost it. He walked out."

Liddy puts her hand on her hips, striking a formidable pose. "I hope you kicked him in the ass on the way out."

The tiled floor spreads out below me into squares that turn into four-squares that turn into rectangles. "He left before I could."

"Don't second-guess yourself. Let him know how you feel. But don't let him treat you like shit either. You hear me?"

She holds her hand out. I take it, following her from the bathroom toward the kitchen. "Mom's letter really screwed me up. I'm confused about things I thought I understood. *Especially* when it comes to my heart. It's like I want to be with him so badly I feel like I'd give up everything. And on the other hand, I'm so afraid to let him in, I think I do things to sabotage us. It makes no sense. Seriously, I feel like I barely know myself at all anymore."

"You're good at reading *other* people, love. But you've always limited your own introspection to a comfort zone. It's time you took an honest look at yourself. If being with Ezra helps you do that, then that's something." Liddy shakes my arm encouragingly. "Now come on, I stopped in Santa Fe after work and brought us all sushi and an early birthday cake."

"Torrance eats sushi?"

"Shhh!" She smacks my behind. "He's not as small-town as you think."

"I'm not what?" Torrance looks up from the countertop in the kitchen, where he's putting little pieces of colorful fish out on a plate.

"A Neanderthal," I mumble.

"Oh." He nods. "Which one of you took my side?"

"Me." Liddy raises her hand.

Torrance chuckles and places a platter of sushi on the table, motioning for me to sit down. "Just remember, my cuffs are in the truck, Ruby."

Over dinner, I fake smile and try to follow along while Torrance and Liddy talk about work and the university over dinner, but I can't think about anything but Ezra. Earlier, he switched from hot to cold so quickly. Maybe he really is *that* insecure, but my gut says there's more to the story.

Our fight keeps me up all night. The next morning it takes a full pot of coffee, a double dose of Pop-Tarts, and a bag of Cheetos to save me—just barely—from missing first period. At school, people stare as I wind my way down the main hall. They gawk like I've transformed from Ruby Brooks into a zombie. And I do look pretty horrible, but seriously.

The weirdness continues until lunch, when Marta corners me in the cafeteria line. "I'm so sorry, Ruby," she says in a breathy rush. "I had no idea."

"About?" I frown.

She grips my hand, staring at me with an expression that makes my stomach turn.

"That you've been such a pain?" I smile, only half joking.

"Yes."

"Seriously?"

"It all makes sense now."

"Did somebody slip you a roofie?" As she hovers over me, everyone in line stares. "Marta," I snap. "You're creeping me out."

"You should have told us about your mom. I feel like such a bitch now."

"My mother?" I look over at Racine, who is waiting for us at the register, watching me stiffly. Totally without my permission, my eyes start to water.

In my mind, I rip Marta's hand from my wrist, flailing my arm in the air wildly while I shout, *It's none of your business!* But as surprised and hurt as I am, all I manage is a weak, "I'm sorry."

Across the cafeteria, Racine shakes her head at me. She looks worried, but before she has any kind of chance to intervene, I rush out of the cafeteria, no doubt leaving Marta to wonder why I'm always so mental.

"Ruby!" Racine catches up with me halfway down the main hall. "Where are you going?"

"To the nearest bridge. Know of any?"

She jumps in front of me and grabs my shoulders, bowing her head to catch her breath. "Look, I just heard about it myself on the way to lunch. I know what you're thinking. But I swear I didn't tell anyone."

"You *heard* about it? That's why everyone's staring at me like I'm a freak show today?" I shake my head at a row of lockers. "If *you* didn't say anything, Ray, who did?"

"I have an idea." She walks alongside me toward the door to the front quad. "If you just hold up a minute, I'll find out."

I feel like a drama queen, but the pressure in my chest has me spinning. If I don't leave soon, I know I'll do something crazy. "People already think I'm a nutcase for dating Ezra," I rush out.

"Screw them if they don't know better. They don't know you, Ruby."

"Blah." I drop my head in my hands and leave it there for emphasis.

"I understand you want to keep your life private. But now that it's not, show them what you're made of. I mean, look how you've put your foot down with Ezra."

"How I put my foot down with Ezra?" *I should put my foot down on Ezra.*

"You knew what you wanted and went for it, even though everyone warned you."

"This is different."

"It's not. You didn't kill your mother. Things happen. Act like you know it, and everyone else will." Racine pulls me to a stop near the front entrance. "Look, just wait here a minute, okay? I'll be back."

Between the kids lingering in the hall giving me sideways glances, and my pounding head, Racine's minute seems like forever. I count to 256 before she reappears, dragging Ashley behind her.

"Tell her!" Racine barks.

Ashley stares at her toes, clicking them nervously against the linoleum floor.

"Now!" Racine shoves Ashley forward, prompting her to look up at me.

"I overheard you guys talking about your mom's letter in

the bathroom the other day," Ashley blurts out. "Everyone is saying you're so bitchy lately because of Ezra, and I thought if they knew, they'd lay off."

Hearing her, I'm not sure whether to laugh or punch her.

"She only wanted to make things better," Racine adds.

"I'm really sorry, Ruby," Ashley pleads. "For real."

Ashley looks so stricken I feel bad for her, big mouth and all. "I wish you hadn't."

"I'm totally sorry," she says again. "I'll do anything to make it up to you."

My chest feels tight for so many reasons. It isn't fair to blame it all on Ashley. And I really don't want to drag it out. "Thanks for sticking up for me, I guess."

Ashley beams. "Really?"

"Yeah, but you can carry my books for the rest of the day." Before she can answer, I dump my backpack over her shoulder, doing my best to pretend I'm done with it.

Ashley fist bumps my arm. "Props," she smiles sweetly. "I'm down with whatever."

Ashley and Racine flank me protectively as we walk to fifth period. Knowing they have my back makes the day slightly more bearable but walking down the hall is a little like parting the Red Sea. People stand to the side as we pass, clearing a ribbon of space in the otherwise crowded corridor.

By the end of fifth period, I just want to leave. Between the rumor mill and my fight with Ezra, my stomach feels queasy. I must look queasy too because when the bell rings, Racine insists that I ditch last period.

"I'll go with you," she says. "We can stuff our faces with malts and fries."

"No. It's okay, Ray. I'd rather be alone."

Racine agrees to cover for me and make up a story in case anyone asks why I missed sixth period. "Go home and eat a pint of ice cream or something," she says as she hugs me.

Walking slowly, it takes me ten minutes just to get from Pecos High to Frontage Road. I'm tired, physically, and emotionally, but alone is exactly what I don't want to be. I want to call Ezra. *He* may owe *me* an explanation, but I can probably forgive his morose mood yesterday in exchange for a few reassuring words. Resigned, I stop under a big oak tree and make myself call him.

"What?" Ezra snips when he answers the phone.

"What yourself," I snip back, surprised by his abrupt greeting. "You didn't call me."

"You didn't call me either."

"I've been in school all day."

"I didn't call you because you didn't call me."

"You're the one who walked out. That's stupid." It's so stupid, I giggle.

He sighs. "Neither of us are very good at this, are we?"

"No."

"And?"

"And ..." my voice cracks. "I left early. I'm having a really bad day, Ezra."

"Do you want me to come get you?"

"Will you? I'll meet you down by the park on the river, if that's okay."

His voice softens. "All right, give me ten minutes."

I run to Pecos Park, plunking down on a hill near the Pecos River when I get there. Moody as I am, my heart still jumps when I finally hear Ezra call my name. His voice lifts my spirits, and I fling myself at him as soon as he's within spitting distance.

"Whoa." He catches me in his arms, lifting me off the ground. "Are you trying to kill me?"

"I'm happy to see you."

Ezra sets me down and holds me at arm's length, staring into my eyes. Silently, he pulls me onto the grass and sprawls out, resting back on his elbows before speaking. "I'm really sorry about yesterday, Ruby. Can we agree that we're both head cases and be done with it?" he asks, dazzling me with a hopeful smile.

"If you tell me one thing."

"What's that?"

"Why you took off so abruptly."

Ezra's mouth twitches. "I'm good at pushing people away—force of habit." He looks at me sadly, but with an enormous amount of affection in his eyes. "I didn't want to leave, Ruby. I was afraid of what'd happen if I stayed. I don't want to mess this up."

"I don't mean to argue, but leaving made things better how?"

"It just did." He frowns again, then smiles.

"I wish you'd at least try to explain. I mean, I'm here, and I'm listening."

"You won't understand."

I drop my head on his shoulder. "Maybe, maybe not. I don't understand you half the time as it is. But I still love you."

Ezra turns and looks at me. On the surface, at least, he doesn't seem angry or happy, and his complete lack of emotion takes me by surprise.

"How can you?"

"Why do you always question everything I tell you?" I frown at him.

"Ruby, I think my heart just stopped."

I fill my lungs, holding my breath until they feel like bursting. "You were an ass yesterday. But I haven't been so great the last few days either. I'm not always good at admitting how I feel, especially lately. But I do love you, Ezra. Because you're you."

Ezra grasps my arm, pulling me closer. He kisses me gently, weaving his hands through my hair. After a few moments, he pulls back without letting me go, putting inches between our faces. "Say it again?"

Ezra's eyes are darker than usual, but they're also soft, and vulnerable, and completely intent on breaking my heart. "Later." I smirk. "After you earn it."

"You drive a hard bargain."

"Yeah—because I'm not a patsy."

Ezra laughs. "Amen to that."

I blush, hiding my face in his scratchy shirt. "Will you take me home now?"

He looks at the ground, letting a veil of hair fall into his eyes.

"I know what you're thinking, and I promise I won't jump you again."

Ezra runs a finger under my chin. "Ruby, I'd live inside you if I could. But sex isn't something you can take back."

"I'm not a child, Ezra. And it's important to me, too, you know."

"There's just ... things I need to get straight first."

"Things?"

"Things," he says resolutely.

"I hate it when you're cryptic." When he's cagey, and he wears cagey like a second skin, I second-guess everything. I analyze every word out of my own mouth and worry about what I should and shouldn't tell him.

"Maybe I'm just nervous." He smiles.

I raise my eyebrows suspiciously. "Ezra Lucero nervous? *Right.*"

"I know you girls think we're all about sex, Ruby, but you're not the only ones who choke when it comes to getting close." He looks flustered, which makes me giggle.

"So, you all, like, just want to be held?"

"You know, that's exactly why we don't share this stuff in the first place." Ezra pushes me flat on my back in the grass. He leans over my body. "You're gorgeous. You could wear rags and roll in the dirt, and you'd still be the hottest girl in New Mexico. It's not like it's easy for me to keep my distance."

"Thanks," I smile, pretending I'm not thrilled he thinks so.

He traces my lip with a rough thumb. "Why'd you leave school early?"

"Ashley spilled the beans about Mom's letter. The entire school, and I mean everyone, had me in their crosshairs."

"Give it a day. I promise, tomorrow they'll be on to someone else."

Ezra pulls me up off the grass and walks me to his truck. On the drive home, he clutches my hand like it's his lifeline, squeezing so hard it almost hurts, so hard our fingers feel indivisible.

"Will you come in?" I ask shyly when he stops the truck in front of my house.

Nervous tension bounces between us. I feel it physically, but I also know that whatever happens, until it happens, it'll have to be his call. Like the tide, I'll ebb and flow. Right now, I just really want to be near him.

Ezra agrees to come inside. He walks me upstairs and lies with me on my bed. His body has this tremendous pull, but I do my best to keep my hands off him. Instead, I vent about Ashley's "helpful" big mouth.

"Why is it so hard for you to let people in?" he finally asks.

"It's not. I just don't want to be known as the weird girl whose crazy mother committed suicide."

"Then don't be the weird girl whose crazy mother committed suicide."

"It's not that easy."

"It's exactly that easy. What other people think doesn't matter."

I mumble into his shirt. "Why are you so perfect?"

Ezra wraps his arms around me, pulling me snugly against his chest. "I'm obviously not."

I run my hand up his arm, letting it rest on his shoulder. His shirt is soft, like worn cotton, and I pull at it, rubbing the fabric between my fingers. "Ezra, yesterday when I tried to take your shirt off, why'd you stop me? Because of your scars?"

He shrugs against my pillow. "Insecure, I guess."

"What's the tattoo on your arm? Can I see it?"

After a pause, Ezra sighs and slowly unbuttons his shirt, sliding it down off his left shoulder. Colorful ink graces his skin. It's beautiful, and intricate, and a lot like Leo's. "It's a totem, right?" I reach out to touch it, but Ezra pushes my hand away. "Your Pecos clan?"

He twists his head to look at me, startled by the question. "How do you know that?"

"I looked it up at the library," I answer shyly, a little embarrassed to admit I've been so nosey. "I wanted to know more about you after that night at El Morro."

He lets his head drop back against the pillow. "Surprise, surprise."

"Are you mad?"

"No, should I be?"

"For snooping?"

He chuckles. "I'm used to that about you, Ruby."

"It looks a lot like another tattoo I've seen. Like Leo's. I asked you about him, remember? The guy I keep running into near the ruin."

"Yeah?" He pulls his shirt up over his shoulder and quickly buttons it. His expression is hard to read. But his voice is gruff and laced with just the tiniest amount of jealousy. He may be angry, and because I can't tell, I'm not sure whether or not to keep going.

"I don't like you going up to the ruin, Ruby."

"I got that the first dozen times you told me to be careful."

"I mean it." He cups a hand over my cheek, stroking my face. "I like it even less knowing about this Leo guy. Do me a favor. Don't go up there anymore."

"At all?"

"Yes."

I sit up all the way, staring down at him. "But I like sketching the ruin."

"You also like tripping and hitting your head, or fainting, or whatever. Just humor me."

I hate being told what to do. But enough of me is still sufficiently unnerved by what happened the last time, that for the time being at least, he doesn't have to twist my arm.

"What if I can get Racine or Angel to hike with me?" I ask cautiously.

"How am I supposed to answer that?" He cocks his head, looking exasperated. "Even if I liked Angel, my answer would still be no."

"Why don't you like him?"

Ezra clasps his hands behind his head, clunking back against a pillow. "Trust me when I say it's mutual."

"I got that. And I know why he doesn't like you. I just don't understand why you don't like him. Does it have to do with playing football together?"

"Actually, the *only* time we got along was on the field."

"Really?"

A lone ray of sunshine crosses my bed, catching his eyes, turning them golden violet. "He was good." Ezra shrugs.

"Wait, what?"

"He played fair. And he made sure the rest of the team did too."

I sit up, feigning shock. "Now you're going to tell me you have a wife and two children."

"I'm serious."

"Seriously?" I gape.

Ezra makes something like an oh-my-god-are-you-really-my-girlfriend? face. "You know, you're not making this easy." He flexes his fingers between mine, locking and unlocking each one rhythmically. "Angel trusts himself. I respect that."

"You say that like *you* don't trust yourself."

He pulls a hand across his face, leaving it over his mouth as if stopping himself from disagreeing. "I've never had faith in much beyond my reflection. I partly hate Angel for being what I'm not."

"You're so much more than your reflection, Ezra."

Ezra looks up at the woody knots in my ceiling, absently working his jaw. "Yeah, but Angel would never purposely hurt you."

"Neither would you."

"I'd rather die. But, at some point, I will."

Ezra hooks a finger under my chin. His expression is sad but resolute, and just thinking he may be right, turns my stomach. "Then love me until then and let *me* be the judge when it happens."

"I do love you, Ruby," he says quietly. "That's how I know it's going to happen."

CHAPTER SIXTEEN

THE STORM THAT BLEW MY HEART AWAY

I FIX EZRA'S AVOWAL TO MY HEART like a patch, ignoring the gloomier parts of his declaration. For a couple of days, those three words, "I love you," bridge the space in my chest that over the last year grew into a chasm. And because of it, on my birthday, I manage a whole morning of happy. But by late afternoon, as I wait for Ezra to come over for my Birthday-slash-Halloween dinner, I'm back to feeling sulky.

For one thing, the house is too tidy. Liddy spent the morning cleaning, and it's so immaculate now I want to throw up. For another, it smells too perfect, like cinnamon and roasting turkey. The worst thing, though, is that in two more hours Torrance, Angel, *and* Ezra will all be under one roof together.

Pacing the living room, I mess up a pile of magazines, and the boots lining the hallway wall, and the painting of Apache Canyon I painted that Liddy insisted we hang in the kitchen. I pull a log from the perfect stack beside the kiva fireplace, watching the rest roll into a flat pile. Shuffling and mumbling under my breath, I drive myself crazy until Liddy finally pokes her head into the living room and yells at me.

Disembodied by the wall, she shouts, "What the hell are you doing?"

"Rearranging."

"Ruby!" she yells. "Get out of my hair for a while."

"Fine," I sniff. "You've been like Martha Stewart on crack all day. I'm going for a hike."

"Just be back by five-thirty," she warns. "And I mean five-thirty, understand?"

Liddy doesn't have to persuade me. I grab my headphones and a jacket and head straight for the path behind the house, planning to head toward Apache Canyon.

As I hike, the stark contrast between my music and the quiet forest bothers me. Even with my headphones blaring, the eerie stillness is like a heavy wool blanket weighing me down. All around me, the earth gives off static that clings to my skin, as if the land itself suddenly discharged all its energy. It's unnerving, especially today.

On the plateau, my senses go haywire. The air smells sharp, like burning pine, and the earth pulls at my limbs like a magnet. Spooked, I sprint the last half mile, wondering as I run how I ended up near the clearing instead of Apache Canyon. By the time I reach the ruin, my heart is thumping like a drum line. Lightning flashes in the distance in time with the thunderclouds heading north toward La Luna. My head prickles. It feels as if every molecule in the clearing is supercharged, and as I step toward the center of the ruin, my body is suddenly, inexplicably weightless.

My eyelids flutter and the forest shatters in a white-hot

flash that erases everything on the mountain. For a few terrifying moments, I'm caught in-between under what feels like the heavy weight of inertia, completely blindsided. Then the surge fades and a radiant sheath of violet-blue night sky lights the forest. Soft blue hues brush the ruin, casting parallel shadows over the rocky ground. Cricket songs fill the air, and the trees rustle crisply, caught in a wind current.

Disoriented, I suck in pockets of air. The forest smells scorched, and when I look up, my eyes fall on a sapphire orb above the earth in an arc with four others, dipping beneath the horizon. I'm still on the mountain, but it isn't *my* mountain. It's more like my mountain the way Dali may have painted it after a night of heavy boozing.

When my eyes finally adjust, they land on my mother. She stands like a statue near a ruin wall, wearing the same yellow dress we buried her in.

Ruby. Her butterscotch voice echoes inside my head. *You shouldn't be here.*

Overhead, an enormous magenta comet shoots across the sky, expelling hundreds of green sparks into the atmosphere. They leave behind tiny fleeting rips in the night, like peepholes to other universes.

"Where am I?"

So many names ...

"Am I ... in Heaven?"

Her soundless laugh tickles my cheeks. *No, love.*

"Did I faint again?" I touch the back of my scalp, searching for a lump.

No.

"Am I dead?" I squawk.

You're alive, Ruby.

The air crackles as her body flickers, igniting a tiny shower of sparkles. I jump back and stare at her wide-eyed. "You're not real."

She points to her chest. *I'm still in your heart.*

Around me, the sky blazes a bright orange, swathing the pines in a sea of fire. For a moment, I can't see. Then she's there again, only this time as more of a light. Her body rises slightly off the ground, fading then pulsing to life. Everything around me, including me, suddenly levitates off the ground. My head spins, and I desperately reach out for her.

"Just tell me where I am," I plead. "This is a really shitty time to be obscure."

She shakes her head. *The Ancients sent me to guide you home.*

"The Ancients?" I croak.

You need to go back now, Ruby.

"I don't understand. Am I in the Otherworld?" My stomach defects, and I double over. My mother—my mother is standing in front of me. How is any of this possible?

You have a gift, and as long as you keep coming here, you're in danger. Grabbing my arm, she pulls me back to the middle of the ruin. *It's time, Ruby. And beware the Watcher.*

"Wait!" I plant my feet in the dirt, rustling up a dust shower that morphs into small silvery droplets of water. "You can't send me away yet. I have so many questions."

They know you now. There's no time.

"Make time!" I shout, covering my mouth when I realize I'm yelling. "You have to tell me."

Tell you what, love?

"Why you left."

Everyone leaves. It's the way of the universe, Ruby.

"You sound like Ezra," I whimper.

My mother's expression changes. She looks down at me through unreal lashes, narrowing her eyes. *Watchers aren't to mix with True of Heart.*

"What?" I croak.

It's forbidden.

I stare, completely dumbfounded. Mom's circuitous answers split me down the middle, fragmenting my ability to reason. All her words—The Ancients, Watcher, True of Heart—I've heard them before, but still they mean nothing.

The sky starts to fade as a deafening roar shakes the forest. She grabs my hand and pulls. *No more talking. You must go.*

"Don't ..." I sob.

Stay away, Ruby. Leave the gate to the Watcher.

I step back away from her, breathless, sick, and completely confused. "The Watcher, is it Leo?" I croak.

Another thunderous roar shakes the trees. Mom grabs my hand and pulls. *You must stay away!*

"You keep saying that! But I don't understand why!"

White clouds spread like snaking filament across the fading night, agitating the forest. Behind Mom, an enormous creature crashes into the clearing. Like a smudge against cream paper, its leathery grey contours fade against the incandescent sky. It opens its mouth, exposing wickedly curved teeth, roaring silently.

My mother stands very still. She grasps my hand so hard it hurts, then quickly shoots upward, cutting a path through the atmosphere. Light as a feather, I fly like a bird alongside her, grasping at the ribbons of her dress, soaring over the serpentine Pecos River. Thunderclouds explode over La Luna, and she closes her eyes, breaking away from me toward the mountains.

"Mom!" I scream. "Don't leave me."

Her body fades as she merges with the skyline, leaving me suspended. She flies east, fading to a speck against the grey sky. Dangling high above the pass, I open my hand, staring at the tattered yellow ribbon wound between my fingers. It smells like the ocean—briny, vast, and wild. Yellow like the midday sun, it flares in my palm, blinding me as I tumble to the ground.

"Ruby!" Liddy screeches. "Do you know where you are?"

"Morocco?" I squawk, bolting upright.

She chews furiously on a nail, staring between Torrance and Ezra, who look a lot like people who've gathered for a funeral.

"Wishful thinking?" I peer up at them, bleary-eyed.

"Jesus!" she yells.

Ezra sits down next to me on my bed, pale as a snowdrift. His eyes are near wild.

"What happened?" I look around my room, trying to remember if I walked home. My throat feels like sandpaper, and my body hurts the way bodies do after a killer hike.

"You never came home. Torrance, Ezra, and Angel went out looking for you."

"Angel?" I swallow.

"He's in the kitchen," Ezra says quietly, "trying to get through to the hospital."

"Storm knocked the phone lines out," Torrance adds. "It's the only place in the house picking up cell reception."

I try getting out of bed but decide against it when my brain explodes. "I went hiking."

"We found you up the mountain. Near the ruin. That was Ezra's call, and a good one. We carried you down," Torrance says.

Liddy wipes her eyes. "What were you doing up there, Ruby?"

Ezra shoots me a look but doesn't say anything.

"I saw Mom," I whisper.

Liddy holds a shaky hand over her mouth. I can tell she's been crying. "Sweetheart," she says tenderly, "you were unconscious."

"I saw her," I insist. "I was awake, Lid. I just ... went somewhere."

Ezra drops his head. He starts to speak, but Angel walks in. "I got through to St. Vincent's in Santa Fe," he says in a rush. "They're sending an ambulance, but it'll take a while. Until then, they said to make sure she doesn't have a concussion." He holds up a piece of paper. "I wrote it all down." Angel stops when he sees me, dropping down beside the bed. "Ruby, you're awake."

I try smiling, but it's difficult to do under Ezra's watchful, worried eyes. "Surprise," I rasp, wiping a tear off my cheek. "Best Halloween ever."

Angel clasps his hand around mine. "Thank God, you're all right."

Liddy plucks the paper off the bed and starts ticking through the hospital's list, making me recall my name, and the date I was born, and who the president is. When she's sure I'm not about to drop dead, she leans over me and rubs a hand across my forehead tenderly. "I think you'll probably live," she says, still apprehensive. "But at least one of us should stay with you until the paramedics arrive."

Torrance takes Liddy's hand. "Angel can stay and keep an eye on her."

Angel straightens up, smoothing his dirty, slightly damp dress pants with his palm. He looks worried but manages to smile. "Ezra should stay with her."

Liddy looks upset, like she doesn't want to go, and stands in the doorframe, wavering.

"I'm okay," I whisper, unsure if I believe myself.

"Way to turn eighteen," she says tearfully. "I'm sorry, Ruby. We'll make it up to you. Ezra, you come down if you need anything."

When the door closes behind them, Ezra shuts his eyes for a moment. "Ruby ..." he starts. He takes my hand and rocks his fingers between mine restlessly. "What were you doing up there? You promised."

"I wanted to be alone. But I didn't mean to go to the ruin. I just ended up there. Ezra, I ... I saw my mom again. It was like I was dreaming but not."

Ezra presses his hand against his head so forcefully he seems angry, but his soft eyes look thoughtful. He strokes my forehead. "Your mother's dead."

"I'm telling you, Ez. I went somewhere."

"*Ruby.*" He looks down at me sadly, oozing a kind of sympathy I hate.

"She was wearing the same yellow dress we buried her in." I open my fist, revealing the dirty yellow ribbon still in my palm.

Ezra stares down at it, but his expression is so impenetrable it's daunting. He looks away, breathing audibly, and when he turns back again his face is stony. "I know you want to believe you saw her. But it's just a rag. Something you picked up on your hike."

"You think I'm crazy?" I ask, waving the ribbon at him.

"No. I think you're exhausted." He shakes his head. "And that you're right that something is off. But I think it's *you*, Ruby. And I don't want you going to the ruin. Not with me, not alone."

"I didn't faint," I whisper.

Ezra lays out lengthwise next to me on the bed, pulling me to his body. "Call it what you want. I don't care. Just stay away from it."

"Mom told me to stay away. She said Watchers don't mix with True of Heart. I don't know what it means, but it reminded me of her letter."

An impossible tension mars Ezra's very dark eyes. "Ruby, it's your first birthday without her. And you're still angry. It's just the letter messing with you." He swallows before saying, "Let's just rest now. The ambulance will be here soon."

"You're acting weird, Ezra." I push up, trying to forge a pocket between us so I can see him better. "What's wrong?"

"Other than that, my girlfriend fainted—again?" he answers gently, rubbing a palm over his mouth. "You scared the shit out of me. My heart nearly stopped when I saw you lying on the ground."

"She must have brought me back ..." I trail off, feeling unbearably tired. "Where I went, it was like the forest was on fire, and there was this ... this thing, like a creature, and a planet . . . a bunch of planets. Like your Pecos Circle. They eclipsed the sky."

"Shhh." Ezra kisses the top of my head, stroking my hair.

"You don't believe me?"

"I already told you what I think."

"Ezra ..." I start to protest, but he shushes me again before I can finish.

"Quiet now. Stop talking. Just don't fall asleep, okay? Hospital's rule until we know for sure you don't have a concussion."

My head objects to every movement I make, every word I speak, even the light. Closing my eyes, I snuggle against his chest, feeling calmer with his strong arms wrapped around my sore body. "I'll try. But I still want to talk about it later."

Clutching the ribbon to my chest, I rub the satiny fragment with my thumb. It isn't just trash I picked up on the mountain. I know it in my gut the same way I know Mom *had* to be talking about Ezra's clan. *Watchers and Guardians of the Mountain.* Maybe she *was* warning me about Leo. Just because Ezra doesn't know Leo, doesn't mean they don't share the same background.

"Such a fitting Halloween." Dazed, I cling to him. "Happy Samhain, Ezra."

He pulls me closer, whispering into my hair, "Happy birthday, Ruby."

CHAPTER SEVENTEEN

AFTERMATH

EZRA AND LIDDY LINGER IN A CORNER of my room while EMTs take my vitals and shine lights in my eyes. After they give me a clean bill of health, Liddy lets Ezra stay the night. We don't talk much, but Ezra watches me carefully, as if trying to unpack my every movement and expression. It's unsettling but having him near also calms my mind, and I eventually drift off.

The next morning, though the paramedics assured Liddy everything looks normal, Liddy still takes me to an urgent care in Santa Fe. Like the paramedics, the urgent care gives me a clean bill of health—no bumps on my head indicating I fell, no hypoglycemic markers, no nothing, and I resist the urge to tell Liddy, *I told you so.*

Because I'm not about to die, I convince her that despite The Great Ruin Debacle, a title no one but me thinks is funny, it's okay to go hiking with Torrance out at Bandelier like they'd planned. And thank God. Her hovering is driving me for-real crazy.

Almost as soon as Liddy and Torrance are out the door, Ezra comes back over. But he's as morose as ever, and his disquiet is like a flashing neon sign.

"Will you please stop worrying?" I ask as I pat the bed.

Ezra crawls in beside me and snuggles against my side, warm and soft in all the right places. I'm tired, but also so aware of his body. He moves closer, and I search his face, visually tracing a scar from his chin to the neck of his T-shirt.

"I'm sorry," he says. "I just really love you."

"If I tell you *I* love you again, will you get naked with me?"

"Tell me and find out."

"It doesn't work that way," I joke. "I need incentive."

"Then don't tell me."

Ezra stares up at the ceiling, unsmiling. When he tries to sit up, I grab his arm and pull him back. "I love you," I tell him earnestly. I wind my arms around his neck, kissing his face, then his ear. "More every minute. I'll still love you even if you don't want to see me naked."

Ezra's stony face breaks. He props himself up on an elbow and leans over me, landing a kiss on my lips. I pull him down against my body, locking him in place with my legs, and he drops his weight, looking down at me all moony-eyed. "You're everything to me, Ruby. No matter what happens, I need you to know that."

Before Ezra can protest, I unlatch my legs and tug my T-shirt off, wriggling beneath him. Surprised, Ezra sits up. "What are you doing?"

"Following through."

"Ruby ..." he starts.

"Shhh ..." I put my finger to his lips.

I kick myself out of my jeans and push him on his back, then unbuckle his pants, moving his hands away when he tries to stop me. "It's not about sex, I swear," I promise. "I just want to be close to you. Will you let me?"

"Can we just ... do this?" he croaks, pulling me flush against him. "I'm not very disciplined."

"Look at me, at least," I swallow, laying out beside him. I take his hand and place it on my bare stomach. "Please."

Ezra turns on his side and runs a hand over my body. His eyes are wide and bright. "You're beautiful."

With a push, I roll him over and kiss his chest and stomach, bunching his shirt out of the way. I wind myself around his body, wrapping my bare legs around his blue jeans. Being so exposed yet connected is enough; I feel alive in his arms, and my love for him travels between us as if he's inside me.

"Are you good?" I ask a little breathlessly.

"Are you?"

"Better than good." I kiss his nose again, rubbing my lips against its waxy texture. "You're perfect." Ezra is the best medicine. Being close to him like this, it's like last night's catastrophe happened in another lifetime.

Ezra sits up a little, pulling me back against the bed with him. He picks up the tattered yellow ribbon off my bed stand where I left it and rubs it between his fingers. "Last night you mentioned Samhain. Do you know what that is?"

"Yeah. It has something to do with Halloween."

"It's the night the veil between the living and dead is thinnest."

"Right," I say, remembering my conversation with Leo. "I've heard that before."

He lets his breath out slowly, taking a minute. "I think that's why you fainted."

"You believe I saw her?" I sit up straighter, over him.

"I believe you saw *something*. Despite what I said last night, I do think the mountain is trying to tell you something. If you won't listen to me, then listen to her."

"You mean about the Watcher?" I stare at him, holding my breath while I wait for an answer.

"I mean about going up there." He sits up, inadvertently creating more space between us. "Do you trust me?"

"I'm sitting here practically naked." I snort. "What do you think?"

He frowns, inhaling deeply before letting out an audible sigh. "You asked me about the ruin. Why I don't want you up there. I know this won't make sense to you, but ..." He sighs again and closes his eyes. "I have to go away for a while."

"Why?"

"To tie up loose ends."

"What loose ends?"

"It has to do with my family. You'll have to trust me." He looks pained. "I swear I'll tell you everything when I come back."

"I do trust you. But I don't understand." I trace circles on a patch of smooth, tanned skin over his muscled stomach, closing my eyes for a moment while I try to refocus my mind. Ezra doesn't always mean exactly what he says when he says something.

He touches his chin, flicking a finger absently over the tiniest cleft still visible beneath the scarring. "You will, later."

"How long will you be gone for?" I whisper.

"A couple of days? A couple of weeks? I don't know." He moves his legs over the side of the bed, pulling his shirt down over his stomach. "A client offered me a job out in Las Cruces a couple months back. Restoring an old church. I've been thinking about taking it for a while."

"Wait, are you serious?" Every muscle in my body goes numb—just minutes ago we were on the verge of committing to something much deeper. Now he's talking about leaving? "That's your loose end? A client in Las Cruces? Bullshit. You're running away, aren't you?"

Ezra scrubs his forehead vigorously. "I'm not. I'm coming back. I just need time."

Angrier than I am confused, I bite my lip hard enough to taste blood. "When are you going?"

"Tomorrow, probably."

"Tomorrow!" I shriek. "You could have told me that *before* I took my clothes off and threw myself at you." I chuck a pillow at his face and jump up off the bed, pulling on my jeans and shirt. "Is it because of what happened last night?" I whimper, hating myself for being so whiny. "Because I went up there when you told me not to? Or because you're mad at me. Or afraid of losing me?"

Ezra stands and walks toward the window. "I am afraid of losing you. But it's going to happen anyway if I don't leave."

My heart beats so hard I feel dizzy. "Is there someone else, Ezra?"

"Ruby, no!" He turns toward me with real anguish in his eyes. "I'm in love with *you*. But my life ... the truth is ... shit, I don't know what it is anymore."

The truth. My feet wobble, decidedly uninterested in

supporting my weight any longer. I drop on the bed and stare wildly. Has he been lying to me about how he feels? Has he been planning his escape all along?

"Don't." Ezra sits down on the bed beside me. He rubs a thumb between my eyes, smoothing out a frown line. "Don't do that. If we're really in this together—and I want that more than anything—I need to set things straight. And I don't know how to do that yet. But I'm trying."

"How long have you been thinking about this?"

"Since the first time you told me you love me."

I stare at him incredulously. How do I answer? How do I stop him? "Fine, I *don't* love you. Will you stay now?"

"I'm coming back."

"What am I supposed to do until then? Sit around with my fingers crossed, hoping you'll figure out I'm not a waste of your time? Or that you're not a waste of mine? Ezra, whatever it is, we can work it out."

Ezra runs a palm over my head, softly over my hair. "I'm not running. When I come back, I promise you'll understand why I left."

I glare at him. "What if when you do, I don't care anymore?"

"Don't do that." He frowns. "Don't give me an ultimatum. I won't choose the way you want me to."

I try to stare Ezra down, but he won't look away. His eyes are hard and dark, and I know he means business. "Staying isn't an option," he warns me.

"How did we go from being naked and in love to breaking up?" I sniffle, holding in a sob.

Ezra throws his hands up at his sides. "We're not breaking up!"

"Yet."

"Not ever, if I can help it! Jesus, Ruby, don't be so dramatic."

"Me? Right, because you're just this even-keeled guy, *Ezra*."

Ezra stands up and turns away from me. He nods, then opens the bedroom door, stepping out into the hallway.

"What are you doing?" I yell at his back.

"Leaving."

"Ez, wait! Please." Sullenly, I follow him out of my room and trail him into the living room, then to the front door. Outside, my bare feet on the wood porch steps remind me it's freezing. "I really hate you right now."

Ezra places his hands on my cheeks. "I know you do. But I really love you. And I need you to believe we'll make it. I need you to want to."

"If I don't?"

He shakes his head. "Please, Ruby. You have to."

I close my eyes. Because how am I supposed to respond? My brain is still back in my bedroom, processing. All I know for sure is that I am completely, irrevocably heartbroken. "When you try, you're the kindest person," I plead. "Whatever mistakes you made we can get through them together. Don't go away. You belong *here* with me, Ezra, in La Luna."

His eyes flare, and I swear they turn a deeper shade of purple. "Stay away from the ruin while I'm gone."

"Ezra, I mean it."

Ezra scrubs his face and looks toward the mountains. "So do I."

"Did you even hear me?"

"Ruby," he says coolly, "you can't help me."

I smash my teeth together, trying so hard to stare him down

it makes me dizzy. "Why don't you just come out and say it then—this isn't working. You don't want to be with me."

"I won't say it because it isn't true! But that doesn't matter because no matter what I tell you, you refuse to listen." He pinches the bridge of his nose, breathing hard while he pulls himself together.

"Bullshit!" I bark. "You're so full of excuses."

Ezra drops his head. "Just stay away from the ruin."

"You can't tell me what to do, Ezra, especially now," I insist.

He steps down onto the walkway. "Promise me!" he nearly shouts.

"Fine!" I shout back at him.

Ezra wavers on the gravel, swaying forward like he wants to reach out to me. Finally, he takes my hand and pulls me into a bear-hug. I bury my face in his chest, trying to hold in my sob, then break out of his arms, making for the door so he won't see me blubber. Without hesitating, I run inside, slamming it shut before he has any kind of chance to change his mind.

CHAPTER EIGHTEEN

FOREST FOR THE TREES

MONDAY IS LIKE A BLACK CLOUD following me around school, raining constantly. Everyone has an opinion about Ezra's job in Las Cruces. Ashley acts like it's no big deal, but not Racine. She says as much when Marta mouths off about it during lunch.

"Did you just defend him?" Racine snaps, flicking breadcrumbs at Marta.

"All I said is that Ezra leaving isn't the end of the world. It's not like you guys are married." Marta shakes her head at me. "You can be really pushy, Ruby. I totally get why he needs his space."

Racine licks her lips. "So, it wouldn't bother you if your boyfriend ran off after you stripped naked and told him you loved him?"

"I told him I love him before I stripped," I mumble.

Marta snorts. "I'm just saying, he has commitment issues. He never was a lovey-dovey sort of guy. So yeah, you probably totally freaked him out. He asked you not to go up to that stupid ruin, and you did anyway, and then he had to carry your ass down a mountain. I'm sure he thinks you're mental. Anyway, if he *really* loves you," she looks right at me, "he'll get over it."

Marta is thousands of miles from being the kind of person I'd normally take advice from. And I really want to knock her out just to see her stupid head hit the floor. But I've been telling myself pretty much the same thing since Ezra left yesterday.

I chew on my lip, picking at my salad. "He's leaving for Las Cruces tonight. I called him and talked him into meeting me at Margarita's after school to say goodbye," I say, more to myself than anyone. "Maybe he'll change his mind."

Marta purses her lips together, smiling snidely. "If you're so sure he loves you, why stress? He'll leave and come back. End of story."

Because nothing's made sense since my mother died. "Because what I know and what Ezra thinks don't always coincide. Why are you all giving me such a hard time about it?"

"Because you're whining." Marta flips her hair, shrugging me off.

"Because we're worried about you," Racine corrects her.

I drop my head in my arms. Lunch is turning into my own personal grumble-fest and I feel despicable.

"Just let things ride." Ashley pats my head. "If Ezra's cool, he'll do what's right."

Marta and Ashley nod simultaneously. Racine chews on a nail, looking out the cafeteria window at the quad. But she keeps her mouth shut until after school, when she corners me near the flagpole.

"You're going to meet him now?" she asks, tapping her toe on the nearly frozen ground.

"That's the plan," I sigh.

"Ruby, I think it's fair to question this one. I agree. It doesn't feel right."

"Are you saying that you *don't* think he's a horrible guy? Or that you think he's up to something?"

"Both. I think he loves you. But that he doesn't know his mind. Whatever it is, you shouldn't have to settle for sitting on the sideline."

I can't help smiling. "I'm not crazy?"

"You're totally crazy." She wrinkles her nose. "But I also understand why." Her smile grows as she reaches out to hug me. "Call me later and tell me how it went?"

"I will," I promise.

Racine's support gives me the push I need to hop on a bus to Margarita's. At the diner, I go straight inside, early but anxious to meet Ezra. Just before four, Angel stops in. Except for my bomb of a birthday the other night, I haven't seen much of him since Marta's party. We haven't really talked, and I miss him. He's definitely a sight for sore eyes. But it isn't the greatest timing.

"Hey, you." He smiles down the aisle after Daisy hands him a Styrofoam cup of coffee. "Glad to see you're among the land of the living. What's up?"

"I'm meeting Ezra in a few minutes." I check my cell phone, double-checking the clock on the wall.

"I just stopped in for a caffeine fix. I'm still on duty," he scowls. "Chuck called in late. Bastard."

"Good ole Chuck." I smile. Chuck is the master of tardy. He almost always throws a kink in someone's, usually Angel's, night.

"So, how are you feeling? Torrance said docs gave you a clean bill of health."

"Okay. I mean, the damage isn't too bad. Two plus two is still six, right?"

Angel laughs. "I've really missed you, Ruby."

"We haven't talked much since Marta's party."

"No, we haven't. Want to grab a cup of coffee this week?" he asks, looking hopeful.

"That sounds great."

Angel holds up his coffee cup, saluting me before making his way back to the station. I check my phone again. Four-ten. Where is Ezra?

At four-thirty, I call him. Ezra's phone rings forever before rolling to voicemail. When it does, I have no idea what to say. My emotions are a jumble of anger, worry, relief, and despondence, and before I settle on one, I push the little red button on my phone cutting his voice off mid-sentence. At five-thirty, I lay my head on the table and don't look up again until someone slips into the booth beside me.

"Hey," Angel says. "I saw you through the window. Where's Ezra?"

"I think he stood me up," I tell the table.

"I'm off now if you want company."

My head is like a boulder, but I lift it anyway, for Angel's sake. "I'd like that."

"He probably got held up or something."

"He better have *literally* been held up."

Angel raises an eyebrow as he looks down at me. "What's going on, Ruby?"

The minute he asks, I start crying. "Hey." He winds an arm around my shoulder. "I'm sure he's fine."

"I wanted to say goodbye," I sniffle.

"Goodbye?"

"He's leaving to take some job in Las Cruces. Didn't you hear?"

"What? No?" He squeezes me tighter. "How long will he be gone?"

"I don't know, awhile? But he's going because of me. I'm sure of it. And I had this idea I'd talk him out of it tonight."

"Maybe that's why he didn't show."

"Because he can't resist me?" I snort.

"If you were mine, I'd have a hard time leaving. If I could even do it, I'd definitely have to slink off into the night."

I sniff at the image of Ezra slinking. "Nice try."

Angel throws an arm over the booth, pulling a knee up on the seat before pivoting toward me. "So, he's a jerk. But you already knew that. Better?"

"Much."

"I'm sure he'll call later, Ruby. Even we jerks get to feeling guilty after a while."

"We?"

He shrugs sheepishly. "Well?"

"You mean because of Marta's party?"

He nods.

"Angel, you helped carry me down the freaking mountain on Saturday." I try to smile. "I think we're even."

"Still friends then?" He shoots me a lopsided grin.

"Of course. Always." I rub my face, take a breath, and squeeze his hand.

"Don't worry about it." Angel nudges my shoulder. "It'll all work out. You'll see."

"How's your mom?" I ask, deliberately changing the subject.

"Swamped. I'm going into Santa Fe Saturday to help. You should come along."

"Maybe."

Angel cocks his head. Even after Daisy sets a cup of coffee in front of him, he keeps his head askew, staring at me.

"What?" I ask.

"I mean it. That I want you to come with me."

"Okay, I'll come."

Angel sits back in his seat, clearly satisfied. After ordering a burger, he tells me about all the criminal complaints that came into the station over the weekend, dramatizing the details. If I didn't know better, I'd think the town is a cesspool of flashers, thieves, and arsonists. Outside the window, the trees sway with the wind. I watch them while he talks. Then I spot Leo standing perfectly still on the sidewalk across the street, bathed in incandescent streetlight. I blink, and like that he's gone—if he ever was there to begin with.

Angel elbows me. "Ruby, are you listening?"

"Outside," I say to the window, pushing a finger against the pane almost desperately.

Angel leans over me across the seat. He cranes his neck from one side of Margarita's to the other and shrugs, looking at me with inquiring eyes. "I don't see anything."

"I thought I saw Leo."

"Who?"

"Forget it."

Leo. Why am I thinking about Leo?

Because it's six-fifteen. You're pissed at Ezra. He definitely stood your ass up.

"I'm in love with Ezra," I blurt out. "And I wish I wasn't."

Angel chokes on his water, coughing when it catches in his throat. "Which is worse?" he rasps, wiping his mouth with his sleeve.

I tap my nails on the table, then bite one, thinking. "You mean loving him? Or not wanting to love him?"

"Right."

"Not wanting to, definitely."

Angel cranes his head, looking at me thoughtfully. "My mom is fond of telling me I shouldn't wish for something I don't really want."

"How do you know I don't mean it?"

"Knowing you? If you didn't want to love him, I'm pretty sure you wouldn't."

"It'd be easier." I sigh.

"Easy isn't better."

"Are you taking his side?" I ask incredulously.

"No. If I had things my way, you'd be mine already."

Surprised by his honesty, I squeeze his arm. "I really miss you, Angel. You're a good friend. The best, seriously."

"Thanks," he says quietly. Grabbing my bill off the table, he averts his eyes. "Let's get you home. It's getting dark out."

"But what if he shows up and I'm not here?" I whimper.

Angel grimaces. We both know Ezra isn't coming. I'm dangerously close to being, That Girl in Denial.

Angel pays both our bills and pushes me out of Margarita's, wrapping an arm around my waist while he maneuvers me to his Bronco. He starts the engine, switches on the heater, and pulls off his gloves. "Things always look brighter in the morning. Even when you're minus your Prince Charming."

"More like Dr. Jekyll," I mutter.

"Play the game, Ruby. He'll come running back when he sees you've got the ball."

I throw my hands up, exasperated. "This isn't football. And if he's testing me, he can shove it." Except Ezra isn't testing me—I feel it. Something much bigger is going on. And despite Ezra's aptitude for being a jerk, I realize in bed later that it isn't at all like him to stand me up. One thing he isn't, is a coward.

The next day, worried Ezra is lying paralyzed in his workshop or pinned under a bookshelf in his living room, I skip school and trek over to his house. I haven't been there before and take my time walking up his long gravel driveway. Ezra's truck is gone, and a few newspapers litter his front porch. The doors are all locked, the shades are drawn, and he doesn't answer when I knock. Except for a basketball and a half-full can of flat Dr Pepper sitting on his driveway, the whole place looks abandoned.

After an excruciating week passes without a word, I finally break down and call him again. "Whether you meant to or not, you got me," his voice taunts when the call rolls over to voicemail. *Well, I did mean to*, I think bitterly. *But I don't "got" you.*

My head is a jumble of emotions. I mumble something about trust, and how it's okay that he left, and how I love him. But I feel like a total wuss afterward. The smart thing would have been to give him a piece of my mind—put his voicemail in its place like a gutsy girl would.

"Hey, love!" Liddy calls out from the kitchen after I hang up the phone. "Come sit. Your dinner is getting cold."

Shuffling to the table, I drop into a chair and stare darts at the chicken on my plate, still roiling inside.

"What's up? Still bummed about your birthday?" Liddy

reaches across the dinner table, grabbing a plate of asparagus while she motions at me peripherally.

Torrance catches my eye, looking between Liddy and me. He knows. I know he knows because of the way he's treated me all week—with kid gloves.

I push a baby potato around my plate, dragging it through a swirl of garlic and butter. "I miss Ezra," I tell Liddy blankly. "He's gone."

"Where'd he go?"

"Beats me," I shrug.

Liddy furrows her otherwise smooth brow.

"He took a job in Las Cruces," Torrance tells her.

"That so?" I ask him.

"That's what you told Angel, isn't it?" he says.

"I wish you wouldn't conspire behind my back," I snap. "You're not my father."

Torrance smiles apologetically at the same time Liddy chokes on her food. "Ruby!" she coughs out, "That was totally uncalled for!"

"But true," Torrance acknowledges. "You're right, Ruby. And I'm not trying to be. Although I have your back regardless."

Liddy looks both annoyed and concerned, which makes me feel guilty. "I'm sorry." I push my plate away and drop my arms and chin on the table. "I'm cranky. Torrance is right. He took a job in Las Cruces restoring an old church."

Liddy frowns. "Why didn't you tell me?"

I answer into the table, turning my face down so my forehead meets the wooden surface. "Between my birthday and Ezra leaving, I feel like a loser." I peek up at her. "We were supposed to meet before he left, but he never showed. He didn't even call to say goodbye."

"Oh." Liddy suddenly looks a bit moody herself. "That's lousy."

"Are you sure he left?" Torrance knits his brow.

"He isn't answering my calls. And he isn't home. I assume. Why?"

"I swear I saw him in Villanueva Thursday at the woodlot."

Ezra usually drives into Villanueva to buy wood when he starts a project. But that would mean he stood me up *and* lied about leaving. And, I guess, decided to avoid me as well.

Liddy bites her lip. They both look at me sympathetically, waiting to see if I'll fall to pieces at the table. I drop my head back into the little cavern I've created and mumble incoherently.

"Sweetheart." Liddy reaches over and strokes my hair. "I'm sure he has his reasons."

Right. Like he doesn't give a crap. Or he really is the deceitful jerk everyone warned me about. Or he's hiding something. Actually, that one's a no-brainer. Ezra is definitely hiding something.

After dinner, Torrance joins me on the couch in the living room while Liddy puts a pot of tea on, loudly scrounging for cookies in the kitchen.

"Liddy's right," he tells me. "Ezra's not stupid. I'm sure he had his reasons."

I pause, taking long, deeps breaths so I don't cry in front of him. "He claims he needs time to think, but I don't understand why he had to go away to do it."

"Ezra's cagey, Ruby. You knew that from the beginning."

"Angel thinks I should ride it out."

Torrance looks both amused and surprised. "Angel said that? Well, that's a new one on me."

"You don't think I should?"

"My nephew's a romantic. He wants you to be happy. But *you* have to decide whether you're willing to live with Ezra's silence."

"What if he just never calls me again?"

"Then I think you have your answer." Torrance sits back, smashing his lips into a frown.

"What?" I ask anxiously.

He moves closer to me on the couch, leaning forward to speak. "I went to school with Ezra's parents."

"And?" I ask, curious.

"Ezra's mom, Abigail Peña, was a looker, but she was reclusive. Folks used to say she was a little off her rocker, living up in the woods with her daddy, all alone."

"*And?*" I ask, this time expectantly.

"Ezra's dad moved to Pecos in tenth grade. George Lucero. Big jock. He found his niche pretty quickly. Then he met Abby. George was so gaga for her, folks started spreading rumors again about the Peñas being witches. Anyway, I'm just saying, my parents told me stories about the Peñas they went to school with. And their parents did too. The Peñas were, and always have been, a strange and secretive bunch."

"You think the stories are true?"

"What, that Abby cast a spell on George? No," he laughs. "I'm saying Ezra's family has history, that the boy may not be all right in the head."

"You're telling me not to trust him."

He looks me straight in the eyes. "I'm telling you to follow more than just your heart."

"What happened with George and Abby?"

"They got married after high school and had Ezra a year after. They stuck around La Luna but rarely came into town."

I scrub my face and search my knees, trying to make sense of Torrance's story. Nodding like I understand, I thank Torrance and walk to my room in a daze. La Luna has always shunned Ezra's family, and knowing it hurts almost as bad as his leaving. Why didn't he tell me more about his family's history himself?

Brushing my teeth, I ignore the mirror, even less thrilled by my reflection than ever. Lulled by the water hitting the porcelain sink, I let my mind wander. *Ezra, what is it you aren't telling me?*

Suddenly, all the hairs on my body stand at attention.

Give it time, Ruby. You'll understand soon enough.

I jump, dropping my toothbrush in the sink when I hear his voice as clear as a bell inside my head. His words ring in my ears as if he's standing right beside me.

Terrified I may actually be going crazy, I grab my robe and quickly make my way downstairs, bounding toward the kitchen. Near the bottom step, I overhear Liddy and Torrance whispering in hushed voices. Something about the conversation sounds urgent, so I stop, listening from the other side of the wall.

"I'm really worried about her," Liddy whispers.

"Ezra's her first love," Torrance answers softly. "She'll get through it."

"Ruby doesn't give up, Torrey. And after losing Sera, I'm worried she won't see the forest for the trees."

"Ruby's sharp. Eventually she'll figure out that Ezra's like every other schlep of a guy and move on." Torrance's firm tone drives his conviction home. "I think it's as simple as that."

"There's more to him than meets the eye," Liddy insists. "There's no way she'd be with him if there wasn't. *She* believes in him. *She* believes he can wrestle his demons. And I'm worried she'll fall apart if she's wrong."

Listening to them makes me sick. Hearing Liddy worry out loud and Torrance reassuring her that I'm a lovestruck child is bad enough. But knowing that neither of them have faith in Ezra sets me off. *I'm* allowed to be mad at him. He's *my* insufferable boyfriend. But *they* are not. They barely know enough about our relationship to speculate, much less prognosticate our future together.

"Do you trust him?" Liddy asks.

"About as much as I can throw him."

"I think he really loves her."

"Love doesn't always inoculate you from heartbreak." Torrance sighs.

The room is silent for a moment. Then Liddy purrs, "Why, Sheriff, are you worried I'm gonna break your heart?"

Torrance's voice drops an octave. "I don't know. Are you telling me you love me?"

I hear rustling, then giggling, and run upstairs before my head explodes. The last thing I want to know is that Liddy and Torrance are in love. Maybe I'll care later. But right now, if the earth cracked open beneath the living room and swallowed them both up, I'd sing hallelujah.

Seething, I lie in bed, wound like a clock. When the sky turns rosy and birds start chirping outside my window, I give up all hope of sleeping. Pulling my easel away from the wall, I prep a new canvas. For a few hours, I layer it with coats of acrylic, standing by the bedroom window, splattering black and grey over everything. I spend most of Sunday turning the creek, forest, and gentle slope up the mountain into something sinister and hostile. Then I prop it on my dresser and lie in bed, staring at it all night.

Monday, I ignore everyone. At lunchtime, I sneak off to the far corner of the cafeteria and sit alone, picking at my grilled cheese sandwich—until Racine spots me and marches over to my table, sitting down uninvited.

"What are you doing over here?" She picks up my tray and makes it halfway across the room with my lunch before I catch up, following her dejectedly.

"That bad?" Ashley asks when I plunk down on the lunch bench next to her.

"No, probably not."

Ashley scoots over and flings an arm around me. "He *still* hasn't called?"

I shake my head.

"He totally dissed you," Marta concludes. "Time won't change that he's a dog."

"Marta," Lisa growls. "Stuff it."

"Fact is," Marta continues. "Ruby's entitled to mope. Ezra's an asshole."

"I don't get it." Ashely squints. "I mean, really. Why wouldn't he call you?"

Marta smiles. "Because he's blowing her off."

Racine shakes her head at Marta. "Should I tell people you're still together? Or that you broke up?"

"I don't know," I sniffle. "Don't tell people anything, I guess."

"That boy should thank his lucky stars he's gone. Because if he were here, I'd maim him." Racine stabs at the air and makes squeaky noises, which makes me laugh.

I'm grateful to have Las Gallinas on my side. But this last week has sucked big time, and my head isn't in the game at all. As they continue to chatter, I can't stop thinking about Ezra, and what Mom said, and the ruin.

And Leo.

My gut says Leo has something to do with Mom's warning about the Watcher, and maybe even with what's going on with Ezra. And if that's true, I have to know. Ezra may have forbidden me from going up to the ruin, but Ezra isn't here. Besides, it's not like he's going to know — if he even still cares about me at all.

CHAPTER NINETEEN

CRASH COURSE IN FALLING APART

AS SOON AS THE BELL RINGS, I sneak off campus before Racine can catch me and slip on the bus. At home, I throw my boots on and hike straight up the mountain. I walk fast, feeling anxious. El Maldito and the ghosts of Glorieta are the least of my worries; after what Mom said, I'm most terrified of Leo and the ruin.

In the clearing, I pick juniper berries and draw sketches of the ruin while I wait for my ears to buzz, taking small, measured breaths when my nerves act up. It's eerily quiet for a long time, until Leo's voice cuts through the silence.

"Ruby!" He walks through the brush into the ruin's center.

I yelp, holding my hand against my heart.

"What are you up to?"

Looking around the ruin proprietorially, I say, "Thinking. Searching for answers. Maybe sacrificing myself later."

He doesn't laugh. "It'll be dark soon. You shouldn't have come."

I step back, further away from him. Leo's right. I shouldn't be here. Neither Liddy, Ezra, nor Mom would like it. Scowling, I close my eyes. What Ezra does or doesn't like shouldn't matter.

"What are you doing?" Leo asks.

I open my eyes and stare at him, furiously twirling a loose strand of hair around my already numb fingers. "Thinking. I do know how to do that."

Leo gazes into my eyes like he's latched on to my soul. Like he's just waiting to yank it out of my body and stomp on it. "What's wrong with you?"

"Me? What's wrong with *you?*"

He squints. "You're a mess, Ruby. What's going on?"

"Like you care."

"I do," he says, "try me."

I glare at him, partly to stop myself from crying. "I'm angry. And very confused about what to do with myself."

Leo almost grins, but he stops himself. "What are you *supposed* to do with yourself?"

"You think it's funny?"

"Not at all." He shakes his head. "I really do want to know."

Pulling my shoulders forward, I stand up straighter, trying to present a tougher front. "Ezra disappeared. I mean, he took off without saying goodbye. I don't even know if we're still together."

Leo steps up closer and grabs my hand. "*I'm* still here, Ruby."

Angry as I am, giving in to Leo seems like a perfect way to hurt Ezra. But Leo scares me. And if I did it, if I intentionally tried to hurt Ezra, I'd be exactly the kind of person I hate.

"I don't want you," I whisper.

Leo stands his ground. He closes the space between us, looking down into my eyes. "No?"

His lips are warm when they meet mine, and for a moment,

I pretend they're Ezra's. I kiss him, letting him pull me so close I can't breathe. Letting him push until something shatters inside. Abruptly pulling back, I drop my head, afraid to look at him. "I'm sorry."

"It was a good start," he says.

"No. It was terrible. I can't ... I can't do this."

"You're running away again?"

"Yes."

Leo looks sad for maybe the first time ever. I've never seen him look anything but handsome, and confident, and smug. "I wish you wouldn't."

"Do you?" I grimace, feeling spiteful. "You still want to get into my pants that bad?"

"It's not like that."

"I'm going now. You can go back to doing whatever it was you were doing."

"Wait." He grabs my arm. "Meet me here on Sunday? Around two?"

"Why should I?"

Leo's dark eyelashes flutter over his eyes, pulling purple threads through golden irises. He blinks, and I swear they change colors. "Because I asked you nicely."

Nervous, I step back, breaking loose from his grip. "So you can what, charm me, or try to talk me into leaving Ezra, or just generally take advantage of my broken heart?"

"I want to show you something."

"What?"

"You'll have to come back to find out," he insists.

"I don't think so, Leo."

"Please," he says earnestly. "You won't be sorry."

I shake my head no, slowly. Every time I see him, I'm sorry. Sunday won't be different.

"I'll be here, Ruby — if you change your mind."

Leo shoots me a perfect smile. Perfect like cardboard. Like he's cut it out and pasted it on and is so used to relying on it when the situation demands, it's automatic.

Before he has a chance to say more, I grab my things, turn, and head down the mountain, knowing he won't follow. Closer to the bottom, most of the trees stand bare or dormant, forming a canopy over the trail. Unsightly without leaves, they stir something visceral inside me. How does anything manage to look so majestic *and* imperfect?

Pulling my jacket tighter against the cool air, I follow the canopy of tree branches home, thinking about Ezra. Ezra is like the forest, scarred but still magnificent, rooted to his surroundings. I see him everywhere, in the pines, and shrubs, and rocks, reminding me that of all the feelings I've carried up and down the path for nearly three months, my feelings for him have been the strongest. Ezra embodies the pass, enigmatic and guarded. He'll never be my storybook prince. Things will never be uncomplicated.

At the end of the trail, I stop by the stream in our backyard. I drop my jacket and gloves on the ground and sit quietly on a rock, watching condensed plumes of my breath fill the air. I sit for what seems like forever, until I notice it. A mountain lion. Standing between the creek and my back door.

It rumbles low in its throat, twitching its tail as my mouth drops open.

Oh, god. Breathe, Ruby!

The lion growls, sending epic chills through my body. The sound, like thunder colliding with an atom bomb, stops my heart.

Shaky, I stand up and walk sideways, facing the lion while I inch toward the house, feeling for the Swiss Army knife in my pocket. I try to remember what I read on the internet, thinking, *If it attacks, go for its eyes, and nose, and haunches.*

Closer to the back porch, the lion leaps in front of me. It drops its head and looks up through menacing eyes. I yelp, frozen mid-step. Panicking, I wield my knife, holding it out as if it has some kind of superpower.

The lion sits back on its haunches, staring at my knife suspiciously. Curiously, it stops growling and lies down. Its eyes sweep the yard lazily. When I take another step, steadying my balance, it moves its head toward the door, almost as if assuring safe passage.

I bolt, grateful I forgot to lock the house up. Inside, I run to the kitchen window and search the yard. The lion sits near the brook, next to my jacket, looking less than interested in doing anything but enjoying the scenery. I watch while it scans the sky, occasionally swatting at something. When it finally lopes away, I drop into a ball on the ground, surprising myself by sobbing. Riding a wave of tears and adrenaline, I have the strongest urge to call Ezra. I know he won't answer, but it doesn't matter; I just want to hear his voice. I need to tell someone who isn't Liddy what just happened.

When Ezra's voice mail picks up, I clear my throat and speak. I tell him I miss him, then blubber about running into Leo and the mountain lion. Part of me hopes he'll be mad enough at me for going up to the ruin again to come back from Las Cruces. Most of me knows it'll take more than a run-in with wildlife to bring him running.

Over the next week, I tell myself I'm over him. I morph from mad, suspicious Ruby into Ruby the Impenetrable. It feels like Ezra has been gone forever, and I don't want to care. Mostly I refuse to let myself feel anything.

"How's it going?" Torrance asks me Saturday morning, dropping his newspaper when I sit down at the kitchen table.

"Why don't you guys ever stay over at your house?" Torrance is my second favorite adult, but he's always around. Sometimes it feels like I checked into a hostel.

"Liddy doesn't want to leave you alone overnight," he smiles. "Trust me, I've tried."

"She still asleep?"

"Yep. She's taking advantage of *my* day off. She wants to laze around the house in her pajamas." Imitating Liddy's voice, he smiles and says, "Because isn't that what Saturdays were made for?"

"Amen." I nod.

Torrance turns back to his paper. After what I'm sure he thinks is a proper amount of time, he closes it, smoothing the newsprint out against the wood table. Facing me, he holds his coffee mug in the air, gesturing while he speaks. "Any news?"

"You mean have I heard from Ez? No."

"Well, just in case, I put a call down to the station in Las Cruces. I'm sure he's fine. But it's one less thing for you to worry about."

"Really? Torrance, you're the best," I gush. "I mean, I know you don't like him."

"Thank Angel, it was his idea. Much as I'd like to take credit for it. And I don't dislike Ezra. I have reservations."

"Did they tell you anything?"

"Nope. But the station will keep an eye out for us. A friend of mine on the force down there said he'd be willing to go down to the church and check it out if I tell him which one."

I drop my muffin and pop up from the table, throwing myself at Torrance. Hugging him, I whisper, "You really are the greatest. Liddy's lucky."

He squeezes me and lets go, keeping his hands on my shoulders. "She is lucky, Ruby, because she has you. She may not tell you, but you're her guiding light. Though I guess I'm not chopped liver either."

"Rib eye maybe?" I tease.

Torrance grabs the paper and rolls it up, threatening to swat me. I take a potshot, swinging playfully for his shoulder, but miss completely. "Remind me to teach you how to throw a punch." He chuckles. "I'm going upstairs. Think I can trust you down here alone?"

When I nod, he smiles. "You're a good kid. Now go be a good kid on your own."

"Hey," I stop him. "Think it's okay if I take Liddy's car? I'm supposed to meet Angel for coffee."

"I don't see why not?" He shrugs.

He nods, fills another mug for Liddy, and heads for the stairs. After he's gone, I sit in the alcove trying to decide if sending someone to check on Ezra makes me a stalker.

A beam of sunlight shines through the window, slicing the alcove in half. Like the small sunny space, I feel divided. I'm not really sure what to do with myself and after spending too many minutes waffling, finally run upstairs, throw on clothes, grab my sketchbook, and drive to Margarita's.

By the time I get there, Saturday's lunch crowd is just starting to trickle in. My favorite booth in the back against the window is still open, so I grab an abandoned newspaper and sit down, waving at Daisy across the counter. Flipping slowly through the paper, I settle on the entertainment section just as Angel walks in.

"Ruby." He tips his cowboy hat at me down the aisle. "A fine Saturday to you."

"How's it going?"

"You swallow a lemon?" he jokes, sliding into the booth beside me.

"A crate of them." I frown my answer then drop my head on his shoulder. "Hey, thanks by the way. For suggesting that Torrance call down to Las Cruces."

"My pleasure." He sinks into the booth, throwing his cowboy boots up on the seat across the table. "I hate seeing you so worried."

Daisy shuffles over and takes Angel's order. She fills my coffee cup and asks, "Any word?" All of La Luna knows about Ezra's job in Las Cruces. No one ever cared about him while he was around, but they're all fascinated by his absence.

I give Daisy my perfunctory he's-probably-swamped-with-work answer, then listen while Angel tells me about his late shift the night before—how he jumped a truck stalled on Interstate 25 and called in another abandoned one in a field near Glorieta. That's it. For the better part of his shift, he and the other officers sat around and played Exploding Kittens.

"You want to rent a movie and come over? I've got frozen pizza," he asks when he's finished eating, pushing his clean plate aside.

"You just ate."

"For later. We'll have a marathon and nuke the pizza for dinner."

"Sure." I gather my stuff and throw it into my backpack. I could definitely use the distraction. "Just remind me to call Liddy in a little bit and tell her. She's been super protective since my birthday."

Angel leaves the table to pay, then stops and leans over the breakfast counter, looking down at something with Daisy and another customer.

"I can't believe you brought it!" Daisy shrieks at a guy sitting at the counter. "I can't find mine."

"Hey, Ruby. Come here," Angel calls to me.

I join them, leaning over to see what they're gawking at.

"Look at Gina!" Daisy giggles, pointing to a picture in the middle of what looks like a yearbook page. "I had such a crush on her. And Michael. And Angel!" She taps Angel's picture, smiling up at him. "You don't look a day older."

"It wasn't that long ago, Day," Angel laughs.

"Four years is long enough," Daisy argues.

"You look really good," I agree, leaning over to see his picture better. "What about you, Daisy?"

Daisy flips through the book. A small smile creeps across her face; I swear she even blushes a little. She leans over a page and points. "There."

Daisy tilts the book sideways. In the picture, she's wearing a sapphire dress. She looks pretty, but mostly she looks like Daisy. Four years has made no difference.

"Beautiful." Angel nods. Daisy blushes deeper, snapping him playfully with a rag.

"He's right," I agree.

I scan the page, looking at all the smiling faces. Near the bottom, a picture catches my eye, but it's partially covered by Daisy's elbow. Tilting my head, I nudge her arm out of the way.

"Oh my god!" I squeal, pulling the yearbook a little closer. "That's him!"

"Who?" Daisy and Angel ask in unison.

"Leo." I point to the picture in the bottom right corner. "It's Leo! Look!"

Daisy pulls the yearbook over, then looks up at me and scrunches her nose, bewildered. "Hon, that's Ezra. Before his accident. You've never seen a picture?"

"Give me that." I grab the book.

"I can't believe you've never seen a picture," Daisy marvels.

"I'm not surprised," Angel says. "I wouldn't show her either, if I were him."

I look down at Leo's beautiful face and try to make sense of the letters aligned beneath the square. *Ezra Lucero.*

As I read it over and over, the room spins. My face flushes and I swallow, trying desperately to rid myself of the lump lodged in my throat. Ezra Lucero. But the picture is most definitely Leo.

"Kind of shocking, huh?" Angel looks sympathetic. "I mean, if you didn't know."

I look up at him, horrified. "But ..."

Angel squeezes my shoulder. "Guess you can see why he's so touchy about it."

A tear slides down my cheek, and the air against my wet skin pulls me back into my body. "Does Ezra have a cousin, or a brother or something, who lives around here?"

Angel looks at me funny. "No. He's an only child. Not that it's not obvious. Why?"

"I ... Angel," I swallow, "I have to go." Frantic, I break free of his hold and pull my car keys out of my pocket, shaking as I grasp them.

Angel seems confused. "What about our movie?"

"Rain check, please," I mumble quickly.

I bolt out the door and rush to the car down the street, but I'm too shaky to drive. Instead, I make friends with the driver's seat, hyperventilating myself into a panic. When I can breathe without hiccupping, I pull away from the curb, heading home in a daze.

In what world could Leo and Ezra possibly be the same person?

Desperately, I try to remember everything about both of them. They're the same height and have the same coloring and similar hair, though Leo's is a little wavier and more kempt. But their voices are different. Ezra's is rougher, a little gritty; I've always just assumed the accident damaged his chords. And Leo has golden eyes.

It can't be possible. Ezra can't possibly, humanly, be Leo.

But if he is ...

The way people describe Ezra when he was younger, before his accident, is Leo to a T. Leo seems to know me in a way I never could put my finger on. And I'm painfully attracted to him, despite the fact he's so despicable. The same way I'm physically attracted to Ezra in a way I never could rationalize.

They have the same tattoo, Ruby.

A train wreck of irrational thoughts party-crash my mind. What if Mom isn't a hallucination and the Ancients are real?

What if Leo is a monster? Or what if Leo is just Leo but somehow stole Ezra's identity? What if Leo caused Ezra's accident? And, if by some crazy chance, Ezra and Leo are the same person, how in the world does that work? And just what—and this is a hard one—does it make *him*?

In my driveway, I park and sit, staring at the trees through the windshield. Remembering all the things I've said and done with Leo sends my heart crawling up my throat. If Ezra and Leo are the same person, it means Ezra knows how attracted I am to Leo's stupid face, and that I kissed him.

It means Ezra is still in La Luna.

CHAPTER TWENTY

YOU HAVE TO LEAVE TO COME BACK

LEO LOOKS ME UP AND DOWN when I step into the clearing, tearing his eyes away from a crumbling ruin wall. "I wasn't sure you'd come." He makes a show of looking down at his watch. "But here you are. Two o'clock on the nose."

I drop my backpack on the ground next to a tree, pointing to the wall he's examining.

"What are you doing?" I'm not sure what *I'm* doing or whether I should do anything at all. The whole idea that Ezra could be Leo is crazy.

Leo's perfect face and perfect golden eyes stare down at me. His perfect nostrils flare in amusement over his perfect mouth when I blush. Even if I'm right about him, he still affects me. "Just waiting for you, Ruby."

"I'm not even sure why I'm here. You do know I hate you, Leo?"

Leo's posture changes like Ezra's does when Ezra is uncomfortable, hunching sideways slightly. His eyes take on the same faraway look Ezra's do when he's trying to force himself to stop thinking about something. And he bites his lip. If I didn't know to look for Ezra's ticks, I'd miss them. But there they are, glaring at me. In a moment, I stop wondering. I'm certain. Leo is Ezra, just maybe not the same Ezra *I* know.

Leo steps closer, stopping at my side. "Want to talk about it?"

"No, I don't think so. I'm tired of talking." I sigh, then shudder. "We should make out instead."

Leo laughs until he sees I'm serious. "Really?"

"Truly."

"I don't think that's a good idea."

"For real?" I stand on my tiptoes and kiss him, using his jacket to pull his body against mine. Leo kisses me tentatively, then insistently, pushing me back against a tree. My hands run under his shirt down to his button fly. He groans when I unbutton it but makes no move to stop me.

"You're impossibly beautiful," I whisper. "I think about you all the time. Every day. Imagine what it's like being with Ezra when *you're* always on my mind."

Leo draws back, pulling out his plastic smile. "Aren't you still together?"

"Forget Ezra. I want you, Leo." I take his hand, pressing it against my chest, holding it there. "And since when do you care anyway?"

His eyes shimmer with what may be tears before he tilts his head forward, slowly pressing his lips against mine. He kisses me cautiously, but his heart beats as if he's just jogged ten miles.

"Why now?" he whispers in my ear, burying his face in my hair.

"You never had much of a conscience about it before," I answer breathlessly. "What's the big deal?"

"It's ... this isn't you, Ruby."

I pull my head back, meeting his eyes. "Look, you don't have to be my boyfriend. I just want to mess around. So can we get to it? Because you're starting to bore me."

"Did I do something?" His striking face crumbles, and for a moment, I feel terrible.

"Not yet," I say. "But we can change that."

Leo lets go of me, stepping backward. He buttons his jeans, but his eyes never leave my face. "Forget it."

"Since when did you turn all hearts and chocolate? It's perfect, Leo. Something meaningless with someone inconsequential."

"That's not fair."

I start laughing, nearing hysterical. The words sound so absurd coming from his mouth. *Fair.* What does fairness, or anything else involving reason, have to do with it?

"All's fair in love and war, right? You've spent the last couple of months toying with me. Now it's my turn." The fact that I've started crying makes me madder. "I hope it was worth it. Because messed up as things are, if you'd told me the truth, I think I could have loved you anyway."

"*Ruby.*" Leo looks stunned. He lowers his voice, pleading. "Let me explain."

"I don't want to know," I hiss.

"I wanted to tell you. I planned on telling you today. It's why I asked you up here."

"You're months too late! And you know what!" I shout, covering my ears like a child. "I don't care!"

Before he can answer, I turn and run down the mountain faster than I've ever run anywhere, leaving my backpack behind. I run past my house and keep on going down the road into La Luna, sprinting from the ruins into town without stopping. Trees and houses whoosh by, cluttering my already chaotic mind with fuzzy shapes and colors. I can't think or focus and don't even want to. Finally, I find myself on Luna Street, in front of the Sheriff's Department. Doubled over on the sidewalk, my lungs feel like I've inhaled acid as I work to slow my breathing.

Inside the station, it's warm and mostly empty. To the right of the lobby, I can see Torrance inside his office through an interior window, sitting at his desk reading. Of the five desks scattered around the front room, only one is occupied. Angel rocks side to side in his chair while he works at his computer. I rap on the reception window and he looks up, startled.

"Ruby! How long have you been standing there?"

"Aren't you supposed to have stealthy hearing, or like, know when someone's staring at you or something?" I ask through the window.

"I'm a deputy, not a spy." He laughs and stands up to unlock the door dividing the waiting area from the rest of the station. "Come on," he motions at me.

I follow him back to his desk, plunking down on an old wooden chair across from him. "What are you doing here?" He gives me the once-over. "You look wrecked, what happened?"

"I was up in the mountains ... and ... and ..." Like that, I'm overcome with sobs.

"Hey. It's all right. Breathe." He rolls his chair up next to mine. "What were you doing up there? Was it that stupid cat? Did you see it again?"

"No, Angel. No. I just ... I just." What do I say, that Ezra isn't Ezra but some ... something? "Yeah," I finally whisper. "I ran all the way here. Crazy, right?"

"You *ran* here? From your house?"

"From the ruin," I sob.

Angel looks at me like I've gone crazy, and odds are good he's right. He runs a hand over my arm and squeezes my hand. "Okay. Calm down." Gently, he unzips my jacket and slips it off my shoulders. "Come on, let's get you some water."

At the watercooler, he hands me a cup. Taking it, I mutter, "You think I'm a nut-job."

"Yeah, kinda," Angel answers affectionately. "The way you rushed out of Margarita's yesterday. And now, running here? Going up to the ruin again. What's going on?"

"I'm really sorry about yesterday. It was just ... seeing Ezra in the yearbook, I guess."

Angel holds his arms out. I let him hug me, grateful for his friendship.

"Hey, Ruby!" Torrance calls behind me.

I let go of Angel, turning around. Half of Torrance's body eclipses his office doorframe. "Hi," I answer softly.

"You okay? I didn't see much of you last night."

To Angel, I whisper, "Please don't say anything," under my breath, then tell Torrance, "Sure, I'm fine. Just stopped by to see Angel."

"I'm taking Liddy into Santa Fe in a couple of hours." He pauses. "Do you two want to join us? We can wait until Angel's off."

Angel looks at me, waiting.

"I don't think so," I say quietly. "But thanks for asking."

Torrance nods, waving out the door before he closes it.

Angel takes my hand and leads me back to his desk. "Sit," he says, and I sit down.

While Angel finishes his end-of-the-day paperwork, I fiddle with a game on his cell phone. Not an inch of me wants to think about Ezra-slash-Leo. Less than an inch of me knows where to start.

After Chuck finally shows up to relieve Angel, Angel leads me out of the station like a rag doll. He keeps an arm around my shoulder, maneuvering my limp body to his jeep, and drives me home.

"Do you want me to come in?" he asks after he pulls into my driveway.

"Yes, please."

He kills the engine. "Let's feed you then. Come on."

Angel makes us green chile grilled cheese sandwiches. We sit together in the window alcove with our plates on our laps, and the cramped space feels cozy.

"This is nice," I tell him. "Thank you."

"You going to tell me what happened today?"

"I did."

He gives me a look. "I mean what really happened."

"It's not a big deal."

"Ruby, you ran from the ruin to the station. You shouldn't have been up there. You know that. It must have been a huge deal."

I look down at my toes. "I spooked myself. That's all."

Angel sets his empty plate on the floor and scoots closer. "I'll get Torrance to put another call into the conservation office."

Out the window, only a sliver of moon lights the sky. The forest is blacker than the night. "Angel, I accidentally left my backpack up at the ruin today."

"I don't want you going back there alone."

"No," I shake my head, looking out at the dark forest. "I don't want to either."

"I'll go up with you after school tomorrow. I'm on duty until five. But I can pick you up at three-thirty. It shouldn't be a problem."

"Thanks." I nod gratefully. "I really appreciate it."

I gaze out at the trail leading up the hill. The ruin is a part of Ezra's history—I know it in my heart. But I'm terrified to go back up there and figure it out.

"You really miss him, don't you?" Angel asks softly.

"Yes."

"Think he's coming back?"

"I don't think he left," I say, holding back tears.

"What do you mean?"

"I mean, I think he's still here."

"I don't understand."

"You warned me to stay away from him. I didn't believe you. But you were right."

Puzzled, Angel shakes his head. "The way he is with you, I can't reconcile it with the Ezra I knew, but you're right that he's different, Ruby. Maybe you finally pulled him out of his shell."

"You have no idea," I stutter, "how right you are. Or how wrong." I suck in my breath, then blurt out, "What if I told you he's two people?"

"Isn't that what you've been saying all along?" He frowns. "That he's not really the Ezra *we* all knew? I'm agreeing with you. I'm saying you're right, maybe we never really knew him after all."

"I don't think there's a soul who *really* knows him," I whisper. "I'm not even sure he's human."

Angel leans forward. "Don't you think you're being a little harsh?"

"I'm dead serious."

He frowns, perplexed. "What is it you're not telling me?"

Angel's green eyes home in on mine. I try to resist his questioning face, but he won't look away, and I'm not stubborn enough to outstare him. "What?" I finally ask.

"You didn't run all the way into La Luna because you saw a lion, did you?"

"No," I admit. "I saw something else."

"What?"

"Ezra. Or Leo. I don't know, Angel. I'm so confused right now."

He sits up straighter. "Ruby, you have a lot on your plate."

"You think I'm crazy."

Angel's broad smile lights up his face. "Well," he teases, "maybe tonight."

"All right." I inhale sharply. "You want crazy, how's this?" My brain yells, *Don't do it, Ruby! Don't tell him*! But my mouth has a mind of its own, and it takes off running. "I told you about Leo. The guy I met hiking?" I clear my throat, unable to dislodge the lump that's grown from a pea to a golf ball. "Yesterday, when I saw your yearbook, when I saw Ezra ... the picture of Ezra, Angel, I'm telling you he's Leo."

Angel hasn't actually concluded I've lost it yet, that much is clear. But he really doesn't understand what I'm telling him either. "They look alike?"

"No," I whisper. "They're the same person."

His face cracks, breaking into a smile. "So, Ezra and this Leo guy ... you're saying they're one person?"

"Yes."

"Nice metaphor." He grins, crinkling his eyes and nose in delight.

"It's not a metaphor!" I shout. "They are literally the same person!"

Angel pulls back abruptly. "All right." He frowns. "That *is* crazy."

"I'd never seen a picture of Ezra before his accident. I freaked out Saturday when I realized it was him. And I went up to the ruin today because I knew Leo would be there. I can't explain how he does it, but when I watched him, really watched him, I knew. They *are* the same person."

Angel blinks a few times, then bobs his head. "Ruby." He puts his hands over mine. "You know that's not possible. I don't blame you for *wanting* to believe it but listen to yourself."

I've been listening the whole time. Until I said it out loud, I hadn't realized how insane it sounded. "Who is Leo, then?"

"There's an explanation, I'm sure. But not that one."

I pull my hands away and bury my face in them. "Not one person knows Leo. And I only see him in the forest. Mostly near the ruin. How can he look so much like Ezra but not be him?"

"I don't know." He shrugs. "But I promise, I'll help you get to the bottom of it."

"They have the same tattoo, of the same thing, in the exact same place on their arm."

Angel drops his head, fiddling with his class ring. "That is weird."

"But not weird enough?"

"Maybe Ezra has a twin?"

"That none of you knew about?"

His brows come together; I can tell he's seriously mulling it over. We sit together quietly, both unsure what to say. Now Angel knows everything I do.

"Can you stay?" I finally ask, disturbing the quiet hum in the still kitchen. "Liddy probably won't be back until late, and I'm too freaked out to be alone."

"Stay over?"

"Yeah—on the couch."

Angel agrees, and I head upstairs to change into pajamas before bringing him down one of Torrance's sweatshirts. We build a fire in the kiva fireplace in the living room, lying across from each other on separate couches, but we don't say much. Angel stares at the ceiling while I watch the flickering flames cast shadows on the wall. Neither of us mentions Ezra, or Leo, or mountain lions.

When Liddy and Torrance get home just past twelve, they walk in quietly, startling when I sit up. "Ruby!" Liddy gasps. "What are you doing on the couch?"

Torrance does a double take when he sees Angel. "You having a sleepover?"

"I asked him to stay," I answer. "I didn't want to be alone."

Angel clears his throat. "I can leave," he says softly. "I don't want to be a problem."

"It's fine," Liddy answers. She walks over, kisses my cheek, and whispers in my ear, "Are you okay?" When I nod, giving her a quick hug, she walks toward the hall and hooks her arm in Torrance's, nudging him toward the stairs before turning back to shoot Angel a look. "Just stay on *your* couch."

They go upstairs, and I pull the blankets over my head. My eyes are heavy, but my body feels weightless.

"That how you always sleep?" Angel whispers.

"No," I mumble under the covers. "I'm hibernating."

"Won't you get lonely after a while?"

"No," I grump.

"Don't you want to stick around and see if Ezra comes back?"

"If he even left."

I hear Angel shift on the couch. "Wouldn't it be weird if you were right?"

The near dark makes it easier to speculate about things that go bump in the night. Exhaustion is the worst kind of catalyst; it makes anything seem possible.

"Weird is an understatement," I answer softly.

"Completely insane then. How's that?"

My stomach sends tremors through my body. Because I don't know how to think about Ezra in any way that ends in some sensible argument, I don't want to think about him at all. Even though it would take an atomic bomb to completely erase him from my thoughts. So, I let my heart ache and keep my mouth shut.

"Ruby?"

"Can you maybe just come over here and lie down with me?" I ask. "I mean, platonically."

"Are you sure? I don't want to make Liddy angry."

I shake my head under the covers before I realize he can't see me and throw them off. Angel gets up and comes over, dragging his blanket with him, and I wriggle forward, patting the space behind me on the couch. Angel settles in, sandwiched between my body and the cushions. He winds an arm underneath my head and tucks the other around my waist, pulling me tightly against his chest.

"This work?" he asks.

"It does. Are you okay with it?"

When he answers, I can tell he's smiling. "I'm good—as long as you are."

Angel's arm is like a seatbelt protecting me from the unknown, securing me to something real and safe, if only for the night. Between us I feel an enormous amount of affection but no awkwardness. "I am. Stupid as it is, I feel protected."

"It means a lot that you trust me," he whispers into my hair.

I nod my head, snuggling as far into him as I can. Maybe the world is tearing at the seams; at least I can count on Angel to mend its fabric. My heart may be breaking, or broken, or completely wasted away already, but between Angel, Liddy, and Racine, I know I still have constants. For the next few hours at least, that'll have to be good enough.

CHAPTER TWENTY-ONE

PAPER HEART CUT FROM STONE

I MAKE MYSELF GO TO FIRST PERIOD. After Mom died, I learned the hard way that when things go south, I can't just drop out of life. But my concentration is at an all-time low, and by third period I'm obsessed; I have to know more about Ezra and his Pecos heritage.

By lunchtime, I've morphed into a basket case. The lunch bell rings, and I hide out in the girls' bathroom until Las Gallinas are safely holed up in the cafeteria. Then I sneak off campus and hop on a bus to the library.

Luckily, the same librarian who told me about the Pecos the first time I went looking for information is at the circulation desk. When she sees me, she waves me over. "Girlie," she says, "your book's been waiting here awhile." Her eyes twinkle as she holds up a finger and disappears below the circulation desk. She pops up again and hands me *The Enchanted Pecos.* "Only one copy left in Albuquerque. You lucked out."

"Thank you." I want to study the book in private, but she looks at me expectantly, so I take it from her and flip it open.

Near the book's middle, a collection of pictures catches my eye. I browse them casually, stopping on a small reprint of an old woodcut. Half-lion, half-man, the woodcut jumps off the page at me. Beneath it, a caption reads, "Shiankya—Mountain Lion. Watchers and Guardians of the Mountain."

As the words sink in, I struggle to swallow, and when the librarian shifts, I jump, sending the book to the carpet with a thud. A soft squeak escapes my lips, following a tremor that treks up my spine. Ezra wasn't joking when he told me Shiankya means mountain lion.

Shaky, I pick up the book. "Last time we talked, you told me some of your grandmother's stories," I say quickly. "You called the Otherworld a Bone Closet. What is it, exactly?"

"The way my grams told it, we go there to give back our terrestrial spirit and reunite with the spirit gods. But the way she described it, the place sounds like Heaven, Hell, and Purgatory all rolled into one."

"Did she ever say anything about Pecos Indians who could be two different people at the same time?" I ask breathlessly.

"Two people at the same time? I don't follow."

"I mean, like, maybe being able to switch back and forth between different bodies?"

"Shape-shifters?" She raises an eyebrow.

I shake my head and point to the picture of the half-man, half-mountain lion. "Yeah. I guess. Like this."

"No. Can't say she did. But shape-shifters aren't uncommon in native lore. The Hopi and Navajo have their skin-walkers, and plenty others speak of men in their tribes who turn into women, women who turn into mythical creatures, people who're half-man/half-beast. Given Grammy's Bone Closet," she chuckles. "I suppose I wouldn't be surprised."

Listening, my head swims with nonsense—nonsense that makes sense, especially when I put two and two together. But it's incredibly hard to let my mind go there. Ezra's clan dates back more than a thousand years. Watchers? Mountain lions?

I thank her profusely and run outside to call Angel, letting him know to pick me up at the library instead of school. While I wait, I ponder the possibility that my maybe-boyfriend-slash-shifter-slash-I don't really know what he is, may also be my mountain lion. If Ezra is a Watcher, much less the Watcher Mom called out, what exactly is he watching? Could the ruin truly be a gateway to somewhere ... different?

When Angel pulls up, calling me over when he sees me standing in front of the library shivering, I just about throw myself into his truck. He turns the radio down as I scurry into the front seat, trembling like it's thirty below outside.

"What's up?" he asks.

"I wanted to check out a book."

He cocks an eyebrow. "It couldn't wait?"

"No."

Angel drums his fingers against the steering wheel to some country song as we drive. Otherwise, he's completely silent until we pull into my driveway.

"What happened to school?" he asks almost paternally, letting the truck idle.

"Nothing. It's still there."

"*Ruby.*"

"Book," I say, holding the book up. "Library."

He snorts, nodding up the mountain. "You still want to go up there?"

"No," I say adamantly. "But I need my backpack. If you don't want to come with though, I understand."

"Uh-uh. You're not going up there alone."

"Come on, then." I pull the keys out of the ignition and toss them on his lap.

"Whoa." He grabs my arm. "What's up?"

"Nothing, I just want to get my stuff and be done with it."

"Is there something you want to tell me?"

"No," I say sharply.

Angel starts to say something, but I cut him off. "I'm sorry. I'm anxious. That's all. I just want to go get it. All right?"

He grabs his rifle, nodding curtly. "All right. Let's try to get back before dark."

"That why you bringing Tess?" I ask. "In case we don't?"

"Partly."

I can guess the rest. It isn't to shoot at ghosts.

Angel and I head up the mountain side by side. Holding his rifle against his chest, Angel walks deliberately, but at a quick enough pace to make my heart thump.

"It's quiet up here." He frowns. "Ever notice that?"

"Every time."

He squints down at me. "You edgy about running into Leo or the mountain lion?"

"Both."

Angel winds an arm around my shoulder protectively. I leave it there, letting it comfort me while we walk. After a while the trees thin, then change in variety, signaling we're nearing the plateau. Huge cotton candy clouds hang in the air overhead, their grey bottoms filled with rain, and the forest smells sharp like wet soil. The day is so beautiful, so *normal*, I find it hard to believe the ruin is anything more than a pile of crumbling blocks.

When we finally walk through the clearing, Angel sucks in his breath. "Wow. It looks completely different in the daylight."

"I think it's going to storm," I tell him. "We should hurry."

"Probably," he answers absently, staring at a crumbling wall.

"I left my backpack over there. Come on."

Angel lets me drag him to the tree across the clearing. It's like dragging a brick. He faces backward, staring at the circle like he's hypnotized.

"There it is." I point to my green sack, shaking him back to me.

Angel walks over to it and peeks inside, then picks it up and slips it over his shoulders. Mission accomplished, I nod toward the path, tugging him out of the clearing.

"You know, seeing the ruin in daylight, I almost believe what you said about Leo and Ezra. There's something about it that's ... odd. I didn't notice it last time," he says on the way down.

"Do you think it's possible? I mean, have you thought about it?"

"I have. All last night. All today. I just can't bring myself to believe Ezra's some—what? What would you even call him?"

"I don't know." I shrug, thinking about the book. "A shape-shifter?"

Angel clicks his tongue. "I stopped believing in things that go bump in the night a long time ago, Ruby."

"Yeah, but are you still afraid of them?"

"Depends on what you mean." He stops, looking up at the now-grey sky. "If we're talking about the kinds that hide in your closet and slither through drainpipes or suck the life out of goats, no. But up here, I'm somewhat more open to things like ghosts and witchcraft. Though I doubt it."

"The forest is the *only* place I've ever seen Leo."

It starts to drizzle, and Angel flips the rifle's barrel down. He shuffles his toe through a bed of wet pine needles, kicking them off his boot when they stick. "Ever think he might be a ghost?"

"Leo? Are you serious?"

"Partly," he laughs. "I guess."

"Yeah. I just ... why? I mean, what would be the point? And how does that explain Ezra?"

"Since when do ghosts make sense?"

Hearing him say it makes me laugh. *Since never*. And here I am asking him to entertain the idea that Ezra can shift from one person to another.

"I'm a dumbass. You're right."

When Angel grins, little drops of rain glint off his eyelashes. "Maybe it's the ghost of Ezra's grandfather or great-grandfather."

I shudder. "You're creeping me out. You're saying I made out with the ghost of his dead great-grandfather?"

"You made out with Leo?" he asks incredulously.

I frown-smile. "Mmmm, *maybe?*"

"Well." He shrugs, stifling a grimace. "Yeah."

We both crack up. Maybe because we're so strung out to begin with.

"You think Ezra will consider it cheating?" I joke.

"I don't know." Angel clears his throat and rubs rain out of his eyes. "In my mind, cheating's more about intent."

"I'm totally screwed then."

Angel pulls the rifle up and wipes the barrel with a shirt-sleeve. When I frown, he points up at the denser canopy of trees covering the trail. "It'll be fine. We're sheltered. But we should get ..."

Behind me the bushes crackle, distracting Angel. His almond eyes balloon as he slowly puts his hand out, nodding at me to stay put. Ignoring his warning, I twist around, searching for whatever it is that has him so distressed. Then I see it. Off to my left, an enormous mountain lion standing still as granite, watching us.

Angel's hand slides down to the rifle's trigger, but he keeps it lowered at his side. "Walk slowly, Ruby. Toward me," he says quietly. "I'm going shoot to its left."

The lion growls low in its throat. It turns its head toward me and hunkers down. As it crouches, my heart speeds into overdrive.

"What if you hit it?"

"Ruby!" Angel barks. "Move."

"Wait. Don't," I whimper.

"I almost have a clear shot."

"It won't hurt me."

The lion meets my eyes. Its whiskers twitch, and in an instant, I realize it has Angel, not me, in its sights. I jump in front of it just as it leaps at Angel. We collide midair, the lion crashing down on top of my body.

My chest contracts when I hit the ground, deflating as the lion's paw crushes my lungs. Pushing frantically, I tilt my head back and find myself looking upside down at Angel. He trains the rifle on the lion.

"Please," I plead breathlessly. "Please don't shoot it."

Tears fill my eyes and mix with the light rain, blurring the lion's face. I move to rub them away, and a low growl rumbles through the lion's body. It places a huge paw on my shoulder, nearly giving me a heart attack, and looks down into my eyes.

Angel cocks the rifle's barrel back. "Son of a bitch," he mutters.

"Angel don't provoke him," I beg, nearly sobbing.

Briefly, the lion's pupils contract, pulling threads of purple through its golden irises as it refocuses. It drops its head and growls fiercely near my face. The sound is deafening.

Terrified, I make myself meet its eyes, choking out, "Please, Ezra."

Behind me, Angel commands me to stay put. "Do ... not ... move ... Ruby," he enunciates, spacing out each word for emphasis.

"Please," I whisper. "Don't do this."

For the briefest moment, the lion's eyes turn completely violet. Then they fade back, blazing a brighter gold in the grey afternoon light. The lion wavers, then bolts toward Angel, knocking him to the ground just as Angel fires off a shot.

I scream, scrambling on my knees across the dirt. Angel is flat on his back, struggling to sit up, but the lion is gone.

"Ruby!" He pulls me to him. "Are you all right?"

Shaking my head, no, I start sobbing.

"What the hell did you jump in front of me for?" He yells. "I almost shot you!"

I'm crying so hard I can't speak. But it doesn't matter.

Angel doesn't believe Ezra is Leo. He'll never believe Ezra is also my lion.

"Did ... did you get it?" I stutter.

"I don't think so." He stands, pulling me up. "Come on. Let's get the hell out of here."

Angel drags me down the trail until I'm able to run the rest of the way. We reach my house quickly, but instead of going inside, we head straight for his Bronco. He opens the passenger door and almost shoves me inside.

"What are we doing?" I ask breathlessly.

"Unless I killed it, you're gonna have one pissed off cat on your hands. Either way, I discharged my rifle. I have to file a report, and I'm not leaving you here alone while I do it."

"I don't want to be alone," I whisper.

Mentally, I hurt so bad. Like someone pushed me out of an airplane, and I'm in that place just before hitting the ground, mourning my impending doom. Fury, fear, bewilderment, and a million other feelings tangle into a big ball, lodging in my center between my ribs. What if Angel hit his mark? What if he killed Ezra?

When I break down again, sobbing, Angel pulls my wet body across the parking brake, mingling his muddy jacket with my own. He looks down into my damp face and tilts my chin up to meet his eyes. "Hey," he says softly, pushing wet hair off my cheek. "It's all right."

Angel drives toward La Luna, keeping an arm around me the whole time. As we near downtown, the rain picks up, pounding the windshield. I'm grateful for the mind-numbing clatter.

Just like I know Ezra is Leo, I know for sure he's my lion.

Know it in my bones the way I know how to breathe and sleep. Still, there are so many things I don't understand. And I'm not even sure I want an explanation. I only know that Ezra terrifies me.

At the station, Angel ushers me into Torrance's empty office. Out front, the two deputies on duty are busy at their desks—everyone else has gone home for the evening. Angel closes Torrance's blinds, sits me down on a worn couch against the wall, and then fires up Torrance's computer. He takes off his damp jacket, sits down at Torrance's desk without saying a word and starts typing. Neither of us speak, but the tension in the room is palpable.

"You okay?" he finally asks, rubbing his face with both palms.

"No. But I'll survive."

Angel pushes back from the desk, swiveling sideways in his chair. He stands up and walks to the closet. "Let me get you something dry."

I shuffle over and stand very close to him, wanting more than anything to feel connected to something tangible.

"Do you want a sweater?" he asks, rummaging through Torrance's stockpile.

"Yes," I swallow, tugging at my wet shirt. "Help me put it on?"

When I move even closer, pressing myself against him, he dips his head, searching my eyes. "We've had a tough run today, Ruby."

"I ..." I stutter over a sob. "I don't want to be alone right now, Angel."

Angel's chin meets his chest, and I stand on my tiptoes,

pulling him closer. When our lips touch, I close my eyes, but all I can see is Ezra.

After a moment, Angel puts his hands on my shoulders, moving me back. He holds me at an arm's distance. "This isn't what you want, Ruby."

"Isn't it what you want?"

His nostrils flare. "You know what I want. But you're upset and confused. And you still love him."

"I want to forget him."

"It's not that easy. And I don't want to be your rebound guy."

He looks stricken. More than anything, I want to set what my heart feels aside. "You know you mean more to me than that."

Angel's phone rings in his jacket pocket, disrupting the tension between us. He turns sideways, dropping his hands. "I should get that."

Staring down at the brown carpet I mumble, "Saved by the bell, I guess."

Angel walks to his jacket and fishes his phone out. "Torrance," he mutters under his breath. He holds the phone to his ear and says, "Yeah. She's with me. Sure," then drops it onto the desk.

"Liddy?"

"Yeah," he answers wistfully, "she's looking for you. Torrance said to tell you she wants you home by twelve. And to leave a note next time you go out without telling her."

I cover my face. "What's wrong with this picture?"

"Too much," he answers. "I wouldn't know where to start."

Angel throws me the sweater, then changes out of his damp

button up. When he slides it off his toned shoulders, I turn away, hating that I notice how good he looks.

"Do you want me to drive you home now?" he asks, staring at me inquisitively.

"Don't you have to finish that report?"

"I'll do it later."

I go to him when he holds out his hand. He wraps me in his arms, and I let myself melt into his body. But he's right. Despite what I know, I still love Ezra.

"I'm sorry," I whisper into his chest.

Angel rubs my back. "Let's talk about it later."

Looking up into his thoughtful eyes, I hope to God I haven't lost him. I do love him, just not the way he wishes I could. "I didn't mean to ..."

"I'll call the state first thing tomorrow," he says, stopping me. "Think you can give me a statement later?"

"All right."

"We'll figure everything out," he assures me. "I promise."

I doubt we will but agree just the same. After Mom died, I gave up arguing certain things, like when people say everything will get better, and mastered the art of nodding.

"Hey." Angel grabs my hand and squeezes. "For real."

"Maybe I died, and this is Hell."

"You've had a crap time." He shakes his head. "I know things feel crazy now, but they won't always. Love makes you think and do funny things. Look at me," he chuckles softly. "I'm a prime example."

Maybe I should address what Angel just said. But I can't. And my guess is, he doesn't want me to. "I don't think it's that easy," I whisper.

Angel lets go of my hand and grabs his holster off the desk. "It's not that hard."

"Angel, I have to tell you something. You won't believe it. But I know I'm right."

"What?" He buckles his holster and waits for me to answer.

"I went to the library today, and I looked up Ezra's clan, and ..."

He cuts me off. "His clan?"

"His Pecos clan. His ancestors." I let my words loose in a rush, jumbling them together. "His clan, Shiankya, it means mountain lion. And Shiankya, they were known as Watchers, Guardians of the Mountain. And there are literally hundreds of folktales about shape-shifting in Native American lore."

"Whoa, slow down. What are you saying?"

"The lion, it's Ezra. I know it is," I rush out.

"Ruby, now you do sound crazy."

"Crazier than thinking Ezra's Leo?"

"Yes."

"It didn't attack me. What kind of lion just stands there over someone like that? Mountain lions are predators. They hunt for sport. Think about it. It's not the first time it let me go—*us* go. That's not normal. You said so yourself. And you don't see a lion the way we have, as often as we have, unless it's hunting you. And it wasn't hunting us. Tracking maybe, but not hunting."

Angel looks worried. He puts his hands on my shoulders, giving me one of those smiles people do when they think you're too bonkers to notice. "Sweetheart, you need sleep. This whole Ezra/Leo/lion thing ..."

"His name is Leo, for God's sake!" I shout. "*Leo*. I know

it's him, Angel! He's all three of them. You have to trust me."

"Let's get you home." He kisses my forehead and turns me toward the door, grabbing both our jackets on our way out of the station. I resist, but when he pushes me forward, I give in. Knowing he thinks I'm off my rocker makes me miserable. And I don't want to make it worse. I need Angel to hear me. I need to be someone who appears sane enough to be heard.

Outside, rain falls at an angle in sleety sheets. Angel spreads his jacket a couple of inches over our heads, opens the station door, and runs, linking his arm through mine. Beside him, I keep my head down, eyes focused on the sidewalk. I run until someone calls my name, and Angel and I freeze, paralyzed.

Under the incandescent streetlight, Ezra's eyes glow like oxidized umber. He stands near Angel's Bronco, soaked from head to toe. Wet hair clings to his face and set jaw. He looks distraught, but most of all he is astonishingly, heartbreakingly beautiful.

Angel steps back and grasps my arm, pulling me close. "What the—"

Ezra nods, holding his hand out toward me. "I need to talk to you, Ruby."

Thank God Angel is beside me. Trembling, I grip his arm, waiting for my legs to either give up and drop me or take off running. Angel squeezes my shoulder and steps forward, in front of me, keeping a hand over his holster. "You need to go," he tells Ezra.

Ezra looks up at the sky, letting rain hit his face before meeting my eyes. "I'm sorry."

Angel shakes his head incredulously. "You're sorry?"

"I didn't mean it—on the mountain."

Angel flinches.

"It *is* him! It *is* you!" I yell from underneath Angel's jacket. "They're all you. Leo. Ezra. The mountain lion!"

"I'll explain everything. Please, Ruby, just give me a chance."

"Am I right?" I shout.

Ezra looks stricken. He shudders and drops his broad shoulders, slumping forward. Meeting my eyes with a look that sets the remnants of my heart on fire, he nods. "I'm so sorry. I really, truly am."

He steps closer, and Angel un-holsters his gun.

"Put it away," I yelp, dropping Angel's jacket to grab his shoulder.

Angel raises his arm anyway, taking another step toward Ezra. Icy rain soaks my shirt, running in streams off the sidewalk into the gutter. It swirls around my shoes, carrying bits of thawing ice and decaying leaves back to the Pecos River.

"Put it away, Angel!" I shout, stepping beside him.

Ezra's long black eyelashes flutter, offsetting his narrowed golden eyes. Every scar, every last bit of damage is gone. But in his own way, he looks just as heartbreaking. I step in front of Angel and face Ezra, tears mixing with the rain on my face though I really want to be strong.

"You jumped Angel," I say accusingly. "You tried to hurt him. *You* ... whoever that is."

Ezra looks tortured, and angry, and most of all helpless. "I didn't. I wouldn't have."

"I don't believe you!"

"Jesus, Ruby. I was worried he might accidentally shoot you. I'm still me," he pleads. "I'm still in love with you. I told you, if you believe anything, believe that. Just give me one minute.

To explain. To make you understand."

Angel groans. "A minute? It'll take you a freakin' lifetime." He steps up next to me and grabs my arm. "Now back the hell off!"

Ezra looks at me, pleading with his eyes. "You have every reason to hate me. If I were you, I wouldn't understand. I probably wouldn't even try. But you're better than that. You know I love you. I'll go to the ends of the Earth for you, Ruby. Do whatever it takes. Please, just listen for a minute."

"I don't trust you, Ezra!" Nearly wailing, I cover my mouth, smashing my hand against my lips like a muzzle.

"This wasn't a choice. But I couldn't tell you either. Just let me explain."

For a moment, Ezra's eyes catch fire. In the dark night, they spark a brilliant orange, glowing violet at the edges, burning through me like a poker. I jump back and close my own eyes, pressing at them to block the flash inside my head. When I stumble, Angel grabs me. He takes my hand and pulls me close, telling Ezra something I don't understand.

"That's not true!" Ezra shouts.

"You landed on top of her!"

"I was angry. I lost control. But I would never hurt anyone."

I open my eyes, meeting his gaze straight on. "You did hurt me, Ezra. And I don't know how to forgive you. I don't even know how to begin to understand what's going on."

"Ruby ..." he trails off.

"This is unreal." Angel's voice sounds calm, but I feel him shaking. "You almost killed her."

"I wanted to kill *you*," Ezra answers coldly. "But I didn't."

"Because I had a rifle!" Angel links his arm in mine. "Come

on. I'm getting you the hell out of here." He turns to Ezra. "Move and I swear on my life, I'll shoot you."

Ezra holds his hand out, but he doesn't try to stop me. I walk backward, watching him watch me walk away. Lost as I am, he looks even worse. He looks heartbroken. I ache to reach out to him. But I also feel completely, irrevocably shattered inside.

CHAPTER TWENTY-TWO

FOLKLORE

"YOU READY?" Angel asks, shaking my knee.

His bloodshot eyes are a giveaway. He didn't sleep last night either.

"As I'll ever be," I sigh. I'm not sure how I'm going to get out of Angel's Bronco and walk around school all day like I don't know Ezra's some monster.

"Should I pick you up at three?"

"No. I'm okay. I'll walk home or take the bus."

"What if he comes looking for you?"

I shrug before jumping out of the Bronco, presenting a much stronger Ruby than I feel inside. I asked myself the same question all night, over and over. "Then he does. I mean, I can't hide, you know?" I squeeze his hand and open the door. "Thanks for staying with me again last night. For everything."

Inside the school's main building, students litter the hallways. Lockers slam, and papers rustle, and people mingle. Everything is so normal. Still dazed, I stand and stare down the hall until Racine rushes up behind me and grabs my shoulder, sending me to the ceiling.

"Gotcha," she laughs.

"Remember," I gasp. "If I suddenly drop, continuous pumping in counts of six."

"Ugh, you're not going to have a heart attack. You're so morbid, Ruby."

Racine starts to say something else, but Giovanni catches up with us, latching on to Racine's arm. "How's my girl?" He asks her, kissing her cheek before looking at me. "Hey, what's up, Ruby?"

"Ruby was just about to tell us about her date with Angel."

"What?" I stop short, jamming my hands against my hips. "It wasn't. Wait, how did you know?"

"He just dropped you off, didn't he?"

I'm about to protest again when Ashley catches up. "Ruby!" she yells. "Spill!"

Her eyes are moist and dreamy, and I instantly fear the rumor mill. "Okay ..." I start slowly. "Nothing happened. A mountain lion jumped us last night. Angel took me home, and I was so freaked out, I asked him to stay."

The three of them stop walking.

"Jesus. Are you all right?" Racine gasps.

"No. I don't know. It was really crazy."

"And?" Ashley demands.

"What do you mean 'and'? And Angel shot at it after it jumped on me, and then it jumped at him, and then we went down to the station," I say in a clipped rush.

Ashley slides her arm around my waist protectively, sticking by me all the way to class, even after Racine and Giovanni say their goodbyes. Before she leaves, she hugs me, whispering softly in my ear, "Katie told me that Chris told her that Jason called him last night and told him that you and Angel came into the station completely soaked. He said you guys holed up in Torrance's office in the dark for a couple hours. Jason told Chris you looked pretty messy on your way out. Like ... well, you know."

"And Katie told everyone, right?"

"I'm just warning you now because of Marta."

I rub my forehead, trying to stave off what feels like a massive incoming headache. "Should I hide in the bathroom during lunch?"

"Do you have a reason to?"

"No."

"Then you should tell Marta where to stick it."

"Maybe I'll just hide out in the bathroom," I sigh.

"Okay. I'll hide out with you. Me and Ray. I'll fix your hair or something. You can tell us what happened."

"Which bathroom?"

She picks at a nail, thinking. "North Quad. Not the bathroom. The storage room by the gym. We can eat while we talk."

"All right," I agree. "Lunch. North Quad."

Like the week before, and the week before that, and probably every week since I officially started dating Ezra, people stare at me and whisper through all four periods. By lunchtime, I want to make a big sign that reads, *Yes, I spent the night with Angel, and yes, my shape-shifter boyfriend 'disappeared,' and yes, my mother 'fell' off a pier last year*, and tape it to my back, along with *kick me* for good measure. To top it off, Ezra-slash-Leo's face is like a dirt stain that won't come out. It haunts me throughout every period.

I keep it together until I walk into the storage room. But the minute Racine sees me, she switches into Inquisition mode, bringing it all home. I drop my backpack on the floor, and she takes off running.

"Did *something* happen?" she asks worriedly.

"You mean between me and Angel?"

They nod.

"No."

"You should hear Marta. She's telling everyone that you and Angel are an item—like a you-did-it item."

I focus on the flecked linoleum floor, trying to shore up any tears. "He slept over because I was freaking out. Nothing happened. He slept on the couch again."

"Again?" Ashley squawks.

Racine looks puzzled. "Why were you together in the first place?"

"I left my backpack up at the ruin on Sunday. I didn't want to go back up alone." My head drops into my hands, hitting my palms with an audible *thwack*. I suck in a few musty breaths, trying to calm down.

"Hey." Ashley scoots next to me and gives me a hug.

Racine scoots to my other side, pulling a wad of tissue from her backpack. "So, you're upset about the rumor? Or the mountain lion? You look crazed, Ruby. It's starting to freak me out."

"Did you dump Ezra?" Ashley asks.

"No. I mean, yes. I mean ... I can't explain it."

"Ruby, just tell us!" Racine insists.

I stare at Racine, trying to focus. *Tell them. Tell them what?* "I can't," I sniffle, blowing my nose.

Racine gives me her best you're-a-pain-in-the-ass look, pursing her lips together.

"Fine." I throw my tissue at the ground. "But you'll never believe me."

She looks toward the heavens, letting her smooth bangs fall across her eyes. "You're soooo dramatic."

In one long breath, I explain everything, exhaling as it comes out. "The lion that attacked us last night, it was Ezra. And he's not ... he's normal now. I mean, he looks normal. Like Leo. Because he is Leo. Leo *and* Ezra. *And* the stupid mountain lion. It's unreal. But both Angel and I saw it."

Racine rolls her eyes. "Ohmigod. If you don't want to tell us that badly, just forget it!"

The warning bell rings, and Racine waits for Ashley to leave. Then she blocks the doorway, cornering me. "What's really going on?" she demands.

"I told you."

"Ruby, I know you miss him. But you're being really freaking crazy."

Looking her dead in the eyes, I steady my voice. "Racine, Ezra's something ... different. He knows how to do things. Weird things, like, turn into things, weird things."

Racine shakes her head at me sympathetically. "I'm really worried about you."

"Ray, I'm serious. He has Pecos heritage. And there are stories about the Pecos being magic. And old rumors about his family."

"Sweetie, it's called folklore. I mean, do you believe in vampires? Or the Chupacabra? Or aliens in Roswell?"

"How is this any different from ghosts and haunted forests? You believe that."

"Ruby ..."

"I saw it—him. So did Angel."

"Angel saw it?" she asks skeptically.

I nod my head.

"I want to talk to him then." She throws her arm around me, leading me out to the hall. Before we get to our classroom, she stops and pulls me away from the door by my shirtsleeve. "Look, I believe you saw something weird. Okay? But I'm sure there's a logical explanation."

Maybe she's right, but the answer doesn't suddenly materialize during fifth or sixth period. While the teachers lecture, I stare out the window, thinking about Dr. Jekyll and Mr. Hyde. My own Dr. Jekyll and Mr. Hyde, wondering who, is who. When sixth period ends, I almost clap. My torturous day is over. Finally, I can go home and finish my nervous breakdown in private.

I try to exit the classroom quickly, keeping my head down. Unfortunately, I'm not quick enough. Racine catches up outside the room and asks if I want to go to Margarita's for a shake, before mock chastising me for trying to sneak out of class without her. When Giovanni and Marta catch up, Racine nudges my side. "Well?"

"You could bring Angel." Marta grins. "Since Ezra's obviously out of sight out of mind."

Nervously hopping from one foot to the other on the front quad, I flip Marta off.

She smiles slyly. "That the best you can do?"

"Come off it, Marta," Racine snaps. "Don't be such a bitch."

Marta tosses back her long hair, opening her mouth to say

something snotty, I'm sure. But she stops mid-syllable, staring at something behind me.

"Holy shit!" she sputters.

I turn, expecting to see a couple in full-blown make-out mode or some tricked-out hotrod in the parking lot. Instead, across the street, the new-old Ezra leans casually against his black truck, thumbing the round silver belt buckle, he's wearing. He stares at me from under his straw cowboy hat as if one of us might spontaneously combust.

"Ruby!" Racine grabs my forearm, holding it in a death grip.

"No f'ing way," Marta gasps.

I stare back, mesmerized by his face, while Racine shakes me.

"What the hell is going on?" she asks.

"I ... I told you," I stutter.

It's hard enough to swallow, much less talk. I manage to croak out, "I'm sorry," before taking off. I run away from the school, away from my friends, and away from Ezra. I run until I find myself feeling weak and breathless on the old Frontage road.

A big oak finally slows me down. Its branches, like thick knots of twine, hover over the side of the tarmac. It reminds me of Ezra. The old Ezra. My Ezra. I stop under it to rest, catching my breath before making myself walk the rest of the way home.

Up my driveway, Ezra's black truck idles near my front door. Terrified, I stop in my tracks and turn in circles. Tucked into the foothills so far from our neighbors, I suddenly panic. I'm not afraid of him, exactly. But I am scared to face him. Especially alone.

"Ruby," Ezra says quietly, stepping down from his truck as I walk up the driveway, "I just want to talk."

A violent shudder rips through my body and I wrap my arms around my shoulders, trying to hold all my feelings inside.

"Don't be afraid," he pleads, looking stricken.

"I *am* afraid."

"Please, Ruby. I love you." He takes my hand, squeezing it between both his own. "I can't lose you."

"You love me?" I yank my hand away. "You lied to me. I don't know who you are—*what* you are."

"I'm me," he whispers. "Just different."

Ezra has the most stirring golden eyes. He looks sincere, like he'd rather throw himself off a cliff than lie to me again.

"Go away."

"That's not what you want," he insists.

"I hate you," I sniffle.

"You don't."

"For now, I do."

"For now?"

"It's possible I'll hate you less next week." His face softens, and I see the Ezra I love inside the boy I was so taken with. Making the switch is hard—trying to reconcile the two. On the outside at least, they're so different. "You're the Watcher my mother was talking about, aren't you?"

He pauses, searching my face before answering. "Yes."

"Shiankya. Mountain lion. Watcher and Guardian of the Mountain," I recite.

"Yes."

"I read about you."

He shakes his head slowly, narrowing his fine eyes. "You

have every reason to think I betrayed you. But I swear I haven't. I'll do whatever it takes to make this work. But you have to let me explain before you decide."

"I don't have to let you do anything."

"Please," he pleads. "Give me five minutes."

"Who are you?"

"My name is Ezra Leonardo Lucero. I *am* the guy you fell in love with—*and* the guy you met at the ruin."

"And the mountain lion?"

He nods.

"A shifter?" I whisper.

"Something like that."

The fact that both Ezra *and* Leo are standing in front of me makes me reel. "Leo is everything I hate in a person. You were just the way you described yourself in high school."

He runs a perfect hand through his perfect hair and sighs. "I had trouble reconciling my two halves, Ruby. And you got the worst of both. I'm flawed, obviously."

"I don't understand ... how could you be ... how long were you ..." I have no idea where to start.

Ezra's eyes bore holes into the gravel. When he looks up again, his face seems troubled. "It's such a long story. But I'll tell you. Let's go inside."

I want to. I really do. But anger runs through me like ice water when I think of everything that happened between Leo and me, and I'm not scared anymore, just pissed. "You made a fool of me. You let me make a fool of myself! You had me completely, Ezra. You *knew* you did. Why didn't you just tell me? Why run away and then meet me at the ruin like," I point at his face, "like that?"

Ezra closes his eyes, breathing deeply before opening them again. "I never thought it would get this far."

"But it did. And you had to know how I'd feel when I found out." I keep my voice low, clenching my fists to keep from yelling.

"I wanted to know you better from the moment I saw you in the market that first time. In the beginning, I just wanted to be around you. I thought you'd like Leo better. Later, I needed to know you liked me. The real me, flaws and all."

"Leo wasn't better."

"I didn't think you'd pay attention to me looking like I did. Then you dragged me to Pecos. After that, I couldn't stay away."

"I don't understand. Once you knew I liked you anyway, why keep pretending to be Leo? Why couldn't you just be Ezra?"

"Ruby, it was me you were with. I am Leo—and Ezra."

"He ..." I sigh and look away. "You weren't the same."

Ezra looks stricken. "They're both a part of me."

I sniffle, wiping a tear out of my eye. "You toyed with me."

His face collapses, crumpling in a way that crushes the remains of my shattered heart. "I suppose I did." He sighs, and a tremble moves through his body. "But I couldn't control the change. On my own land, on Pecos land, they let me keep my face. Outside the forest I couldn't have been this for you if I'd tried. Not until you told me you love me."

"Th ... they?" I stutter.

"The Ancients."

My hands lock my temples in a vice grip, pushing back waves of nausea. "Ezra," I say. "You're not making sense."

"I was angry and self-centered. And I wasn't a good Watcher.

I didn't care anymore, not until you came along. You were my test, Ruby."

I look down at my toes. "I don't understand."

He grabs my limp hand again and presses it to his chest. "You trusted me. You believed in me. You wanted me despite my face, not because of it. You made me want to be more than a shell. It had to be of your own free will. But I had to give you enough of a reason. Loving me, it's no small feat. I know that. But you do anyway."

I rip my hand away, hating myself for feeling so vulnerable. "Did."

"You still do," he says confidently. "It's the one thing I know for sure."

I stare openmouthed, wanting to argue, to make him spell everything out. But I don't even know what I'm arguing about. Nothing he's saying makes sense.

"Are you even human?" I scoff, stepping back.

His eyes flare like I've slapped him. "Mostly."

"Mostly?"

"Plant. Human. Animal. They're just words, Ruby."

"No, they're a classification. Plants are not human. Animals are not human. Cells and bacteria and viruses are not human. Normally, living things fall into one of three categories," I answer curtly.

"And I'm saying it's not cut and dry."

I want to cover my ears and close my eyes. The world has to be consistent with what I know. It has to be, or everything I've ever believed will come unraveled.

"The things you've been taught, they're not fixed like you thought. The universe is full of wonder."

"You can read my mind too?" I ask sarcastically.

"Sometimes."

"I ... you ..." I stop, completely dumbfounded. "For real?"

"Yes."

"But how?"

"I think it has something to do with the ruin."

I cross my arms over my chest, gripping my sides, tethering myself to the planet. "Ezra," I say, breathing out to stop my voice from shaking, "what do you *watch?*"

He stands up straighter, his already taut body stiffening. "That's an even longer story."

"My mother ..." I trail off.

He nods, maybe reading my mind. "Said Watchers don't mix with True of Heart."

You are true. One day you'll be True of Heart. That's what Mom wrote in her letter.

"I don't know what that means, Ezra."

"I don't either. But I'm in love with you. And you're in love with me. And I can't believe the Ancients would let that happen if it wasn't meant to be. Ruby, you gave me my life back. Maybe I'm wrong, but if I am, I don't accept it."

The ground shifts beneath my feet, pitching me forward and back. "You have to go," I whimper. "I can't ... I can't do this."

"I'm not giving up. You don't just walk away from destiny."

"Destiny?" I shout. "Are you serious? How am I supposed to wake up tomorrow, and love you, and live my life now like everything is normal? It's not going to happen!"

Ezra digs his hands into his pockets. He stands in my way, blocking the pathway to my house. My eyes ache, and my lungs burn. I can't breathe. I'm not even sure I want to. All I know is, if I don't get away now, I'm going to fall apart.

"Move," I whisper.

Ezra doesn't budge. He stands in front of me, stubbornly forcing my hand. After a moment, he reaches out and I push past him toward the house. I run without looking back, trucking up my front steps.

CHAPTER TWENTY-THREE

BOLD NEW WORLD

AS LAS GALLINAS GOSSIP ABOUT EZRA, I do my best to ignore him standing across the parking lot. Just like yesterday morning, he's outside near the quad, propped up against his truck, hands tucked into his pockets as he stares at me.

"You still haven't talked to him?" Racine asks when she notices me frowning.

"No."

"What is he doing?" Ashley squeals.

"Trying to wear me down?"

She glares. "He's insane. The Devil."

Marta snorts. "He's insane alright. Insanely good-looking."

"He's not the Devil, Ashley," I assure her.

"No?" Racine says guardedly. "How do *you* explain it, Ruby?"

"I can't, yet. I just know he's not evil. He's ... Ezra."

"Whatever," Marta scoffs. "I forgot how flipping hot he is."

"Funny how you hated him so much when he wasn't handsome," I snipe at her.

Racine eyes me suspiciously. "You aren't going to let him

off the hook, are you? I mean, he doesn't look even remotely apologetic."

"He's Ezra." I grimace. "Was he ever?"

"Yes, well. That?" She points to him as we walk across the quad toward the main building. "Has stalker written all over it."

"Ray, you all grew up with him. He's still the same boy, whatever that means."

She stops, yanking me to the side, away from Las Gallinas. "What if what people say is right?"

"He didn't cast a spell on me! Torrance told me about the Peñas. They sound tragic, but I seriously doubt they're actual witches."

She looks past me, at the steady tangle of students trudging to class. "Your boyfriend disappeared and came back *different*, and then you tell me you think he's a shape-shifter, and then he starts stalking you. Everyone and their mothers are talking smack about the Peñas and how Ezra cast a spell on all of us, especially you. Get the picture, Ruby?"

"I know you think I'm crazy. But I don't think he's evil. I think he's ... different."

"Ruby, none of us think you're crazy. We're just worried."

"Is it so terrible I want to believe he's good?"

She shakes her head dismally and taps the tiled floor with a red Converse. "And if you're wrong?"

"Then I am." But I hope to God I'm not. My mind doesn't know how to think about alternatives. A bad-seed Ezra just isn't an option. "I know you're worried, Ray. I'm worried too. But I need to know who he is before I decide. I need to know what's really going on. I *am* going to talk to him eventually."

"Don't you mean *what* he is?" She purses her lips together.

Bumping Racine with my hip, I push my face underneath hers awkwardly, trying to make cross-eyes at her. "It'll be okay. Trust me."

"Cut it out," she laughs.

"I love you, you know."

Racine throws her arms out and hugs me. "You're not scared to find out?"

"I'm terrified."

She locks her arm in mine, walking us down the hall. "I don't like it. But since you're going to talk to him, anyway, will you at least tell me before you do it?"

"Yeah," I lie.

I put on a good game face. But I know I'll probably fold when it comes time to follow through. My heart believes Ezra is good, but my head is pissed *and* terrified, and since Mom died, it's gotten really freaking excellent at shutting my emotions down. I'm not sure I want anyone to know what I'm doing beforehand, especially if it doesn't go well.

After sixth period, following a too-long day spent trying to pretend I don't notice people staring and a lot of nervous fingernail biting while Las Gallinas pretend to forget Ezra's a freak over lunch, Racine and Ashley walk me out to the front quad. Marta and Giovanni are already at the flagpole waiting, and when Angel spots us huddled together, he honks his horn and waves from his cruiser, motioning me over.

"You've got 'em all wrapped around your little finger," Marta says sourly. "You sure *you're* not a witch, Ruby?"

"Want to test me?" I glare at her.

"Where are you going?" Ashley asks.

Racine looks out at the mountains. "Didn't you say you and Angel and Torrance were going into Santa Fe after school?" she lies.

"Right. To meet Liddy," I improvise.

"Liddy and Torrance seem really tight," Ashley says.

"Yeah, I think he may move in."

"That's great." Racine smiles, winking at me conspiratorially. The last thing I need is Marta spreading some rumor about how I've run into Angel's waiting arms, and Racine knows it.

"Then we'll all be one big, happy family," Marta snips sarcastically.

Not at all in the mood for Marta's crap, I pull myself up straight and step in front of her. "You know, it's hard enough without your stupid attitude dogging me everywhere. I'm really freaking tired of it. Can you just shut up for once? *Please*."

Marta smacks her lips together. "I didn't realize you think I'm such an overbearing bitch."

"You didn't?" I ask, feigning sincerity.

Racine pulls me back and pushes me toward Angel's Bronco. "Go. Call me later!"

Nodding, I run off toward Angel without another word. Marta isn't worth it. Compared to Ezra, my issues with Marta are rosy.

"You okay?" Angel asks as we pull away from the high school.

"Noooooo ..." I draw out. "But I'll be better if you buy me pie."

A smart girl would probably stay away from Angel right about now. The last thing I want to do is feed the already rampant rumor mill. But Angel believes me and trusts what I say without bombarding me with questions, and at the moment, what I know doesn't really care about what I want.

Angel grins his assent and drives us straight to Margarita's. After stopping to talk to Daisy, we find a booth in the back, far enough away to catch up about Ezra in private. Angel sits down next to me and slips an arm around my shoulders. He orders pie and coffee for both of us, then tells me about the crimes and misdemeanors he faced earlier, how he helped Mr. Jensen pull a lame horse out of an arroyo, and how he filed a bunch of fish and game papers.

"Exciting, right?" He smiles at me.

I start to nod yes, but Daisy yelps, "Holy shit!" from behind the counter.

She drops a pot of coffee onto the countertop, shattering it, startling the heck out of everyone. As Ezra saunters down the aisle toward our table, his gaze fixated on me, a hush settles over the diner.

Angel scowls, speaking through his teeth when Ezra stops at our booth. "Go away."

"This is between me and Ruby," Ezra answers, looming stiffly over the table.

"You're standing in the middle of Margarita's with a brand-new freaking face. You ask me, you just made it *everyone's* business," Angel growls.

Daisy walks out from behind the counter. A few people stand up in their booths, trying to get a better view.

Ezra's irises shift almost imperceptibly, turning just the slightest bit violet near his pupils. "Ruby," he says, ignoring Angel, "we really need to talk."

"No way." Angel jerks his head, vehemently against it.

Ezra glares down at him. "I didn't ask you."

Angel starts to stand, but I grab his shirtsleeve, pulling him back to the seat. "Angel's right. I told you, I don't want to talk."

Ezra's eyes flare as if someone lit a fire behind them. "You can't just undo your feelings, Ruby."

"Watch me," I lie.

"She's not going back to you," Angel says, straining to keep his cool.

"She never left."

"You're right," I snap, staring up at him. "Because you can't leave someone you never had. I don't know you. You're a stranger."

"You do know me. You understand me better than I do. Except for this," Ezra points to his face, "I've always been honest with you. One way or another, I've always been myself."

I believe him. And I can tell he knows I'm thinking it. But the hurt is still overwhelming, leaving little room for forgiveness.

Ezra draws his body up like an arrow. "If it takes you forever to trust me, Ruby, I'll wait. But I'm not giving up. Because this—me and you—it's right."

My heart jumps, and I try to make myself speak, to say something like, "I forgive you." But all that comes out is, "Go away. Please. I meant it when I said I don't want to see you anymore."

Ezra's beautiful face twists into a grimace. He reaches out to touch my cheek, closing the distance before quickly walking away, sending a wave of regret through my body.

When Margarita's front door closes behind him, a collective

sigh ripples through the room. Daisy turns and stares at our booth like we descended from the Heavens in little silver spaceships. Everyone starts talking. Loudly, insistently, asking a million unanswerable questions. I cross my arms over my chest and try and sink beneath the booth as people stare. It's like I'm stuck in Hell—if you pulled Hell inside out, dipped it into liquid nitrogen, and then smashed it into a billion tiny pieces.

As if Ezra's unmasking in Margarita's isn't bad enough, gossip about his new-old face makes it back to Liddy. At dinnertime, she walks into the house with a big bag of takeout food and Torrance.

Torrance plunks down onto the living room sofa, interrupting the already intense conversation I'm having with Angel. Pitching forward on the couch, he grabs a magazine off the coffee table, flips through its pages for a few seconds, then abruptly tells Angel to go grab silverware.

"Well?" he asks me after Angel walks off.

I do my best to look dumb. "Well, what?"

"All the talk, Ruby. I'd call it crazy, except we saw Ezra when we picked dinner up."

Liddy sits on the edge of the couch. "We just want to know what's going on."

"We? Since when did you two become *we*?" I snip.

Liddy gives Torrance a look. "Well," she says softly. "That's not the point now."

I drop my chin, shaking my head at the coffee table.

Torrance sits back, popping open a takeout carton after Angel dumps a pile of forks and spoons in front of him. "I'm not your father. But I do care. You're a good kid, Ruby."

I look at him questioningly.

"I don't know how to figure Ezra's new face. Maybe you can help me out?"

"Leave Ruby alone." Angel stabs at his food, forking the bottom of the takeout carton. "She's been through a lot this week."

Torrance groans. "And of course, my nephew's involved."

Playing stupid isn't going to get me far. But there isn't any way to explain Ezra's baffling, incomprehensible change. Upset, I stare out the window, scrubbing fresh tears off my cheeks. "I don't know how it happened. He wants to explain, but I won't let him."

"People think he's a goddamned witch," Liddy snorts. "It's ridiculous. You'd think we'd regressed to the Dark Ages."

Torrance looks uncomfortable. He opens and closes his mouth, wavering before finally asking, "He *is* Ezra, right? Not some relative, or long-lost twin, or look-alike?"

"Yes, he's really Ezra."

He picks at the edge of a magazine, flicking it absently. "Then I'll be damned if *I* can explain it."

"He knows how to change ... to shift," I stutter.

Both Torrance and Liddy gape at me with the funniest expressions. Angel shoots me a cautioning look. He doesn't want me to say it, I can tell. But I can't lie to them anymore, even if they do think I'm crazy.

"Liddy," I swallow, "I mean it. The boy I met up at the ruins, Leo, he's Ezra. Only I didn't know then. I'd never seen a picture. But it's not just his face ... he can also ... turn into an animal. He's the mountain lion Angel I and kept running into."

"We think," Angel interjects.

Torrance and Liddy give each other a seriously solemn look. Her brow furrows so deeply, I think she may sneeze.

"You're joking," she half asks.

"I'm not. It's crazy, I know. But you have to believe me. Us." I nod at Angel.

"That's just not possible."

Torrance leans forward, his face immobile. "Assuming you're right, and I have to tell you it sounds more than crazy, how does he do it? And why?"

"It has something to do with the ruin. I'm sure. Think about it, Liddy. Almost every time I went up there, I ran into Leo. And when I fainted on Halloween, Ezra knew where to find me. That's what you all said, that he knew exactly where to go."

"Impossible," Liddy murmurs.

"I hear it sometimes. I mean, now I realize that's what it is. I *hear* the ruin. And I read this book about the Pecos. Ezra's clan protected the forest—they watched the mountain. And his Pecos clan name, Shiankya, it means mountain lion. They're called Watchers, and when I saw Mom, she said something about a Watcher. There's no way it's all just coincidence."

Torrance scrubs his chin. "Shape-shifting? Magic ruins? I have to tell you, it's hard to swallow." He leans closer, staring at me. "You've been working hard in school. Liddy told me. You sure you're not leaving something out?" He squints. "Sleep deprivation? Or drugs maybe?"

"What?" I squawk. "No!"

"You saw him, Torrey." Angel paces the room, speaking quickly. "How else do you explain it?"

Liddy's eyes are the size of pomegranates. If she wasn't such a skeptic, I know she'd be terrified. "Sera is dead," she says sharply. "And magic ruins, *really?*" She balls her hands into her lap, squeezing them together nervously. "Ruby, you know that's impossible."

"Except it's true!" I almost shout at her.

She tips her head to the side disbelievingly. "Then how do you know he's not dangerous?"

"He's the same Ezra. Sort of. Maybe."

All three of them look at me peculiarly. Angel scratches his head. "He's gone out of his way to get Ruby's attention. But if he wanted to hurt her, by now I think he would have."

"He says he still loves me ..."

"Forget it!" Liddy snaps. "I want you to stay away from him until we make sense of all this craziness. You hear me?"

I've been afraid to let myself think about being with Ezra again. But the second she tells me to stay away, I know I can't. "If I let him, he'll tell me everything."

"No!" Liddy's answer is categorical.

"Liddy, I love you. You know that. But you can't really stop me."

"Ruby's right." Angel shoots me another look, silently telling me to chill. "It's the only way we'll understand—and we need to understand. That or come up with a darn convincing story. The way people talk, they'll be gathering a lynch mob soon."

Torrance sniffs, hunching his shoulders. "What makes you think they shouldn't?"

"Torrance!" I yelp. "How can you say that? His family has lived in the pass longer than any of you. You said it yourself; weird as they were, they've always been harmless."

Torrance pulls his chair closer, leaning forward. "There aren't many people left 'round town that put much credence in the Peñas' family history, but the ones who do will be quick to judge." He pivots toward me. "Listen to me and listen good; think long and hard about this. The Peñas are broken people. Even if there isn't an ounce of truth to those rumors, you're fighting an uphill battle."

I stand up, moving to the fireplace. "It's not like it was easier before, Torrance."

"Ruby, no matter the truth, certain folks are bound to think he cast some kind of spell on you. That he *used* you to do whatever it is he did."

"Let them," I tell him. Ezra never made it easy to love him. Even if it is over, I have to know the truth. "I'll talk to him. He's just waiting for me to give him a chance."

Liddy grimaces, shooting me her fiercest don't-you-dare look.

"Mom would tell me to do it. She'd say, 'Don't jump the shark, Ruby, grab it by the fins.' You know she would."

"I don't like it, Ruby." Liddy's eyes soften. They water a little before she sniffs.

"You can trust me."

"It's not you I don't trust, love."

Underneath, I'm as unsure as she is worried. But I have to know. I won't be able to concentrate on anything else until I do. "I'll go see him tomorrow after school."

Torrance coughs. "At his place?"

"It's really not the kind of conversation you have in public."

Liddy interjects again. "Forget it!"

"You're going to have to handcuff me to my bed then, Liddy."

Her mouth drops open as her eyes narrow to fine daggers. "Don't tempt me."

Torrance places a hand on her knee, squeezing gently. "It may be for the best." When she shoots him an even harsher look, he adds, "I'll drive her there and stay while she talks to him."

Liddy looks at me, contemplating. "That's the deal. You go, he goes." She nods sideways at Torrance, then back at me.

"Fine," I sigh. "Tomorrow. You can drive me there after school."

Torrance holds out his hand. When I take it, he pulls me into a bear-hug. "Thank you, Ruby."

My consent buys me the consensus I need, but the next afternoon, when the sixth-period school bell rings, even I'm not convinced. After Torrance picks me up out front on the quad, he fixes his gaze on the street, going out of his way to avoid my questioning stare. Tense as he is, it doesn't take a rocket scientist to figure out he's still unhappy with my decision. And I'm not sure I blame him.

"Hey," I say, trying to lighten the mood as we merge onto the highway. "I've been meaning to tell you I really appreciate how much you do for Liddy. She's the greatest, Torrance. I'm glad you found each other."

"I'm crazy about her."

Torrance glances sideways, shooting me a smile so small it could be a tick. Worry uproots his expression, and I love him for caring. "I know you are. I am too."

We drive in silence for a few moments, and I turn in my seat, examining Torrance's profile. He has a strong jaw and kind eyes, and seeing the concern creasing their corners, it's clear he's a kindhearted person, not to mention exactly what Liddy needs. Someone who respects her and knows she's an equal.

"You know how I said you weren't my dad?" I ask.

"Listen ..."

"Wait a minute." I shush him with a hand. "What I want to say is that I can't imagine having a better one. I wish you were my dad. You're exactly the kind of dad I'd want. I know you're here for me. I haven't said it, but that means a lot."

Torrance's bright eyes beam. He smiles shyly at me for a second. "Thanks, kid."

At the entrance to Ezra's long gravel driveway, he slows the cruiser, letting it idle. "Should I drive up?"

"No, I want a moment to think while I walk."

Torrance grips the steering wheel, keeping his eyes forward for a moment. After a few seconds of what looks like serious contemplation, he turns back to me. "All right. I'll be here the whole time. Call or text if something goes down."

I force a smile, trying to convince us both I'm not terrified. "Is that, like, cop-speak for let me know if something bad happens?"

"Yes, Ruby." Torrance winks at me. "It is."

Shaky, I smooth my palms over my hair, sneaking a quick peek in the visor mirror. *So, you want to know Ezra. Do you even know yourself?*

Stepping out of the cruiser, I take a deep breath and close the door.

No, a voice in my head replies, *but I suspect you're about to find out.*

CHAPTER TWENTY-FOUR

ROAD LESS TRAVELED

TALL PONDEROSAS LINE EZRA'S driveway. I follow them, moving slowly toward the rustic front porch, checking out the massive lavender bushes growing along the pebbled walk that leads to his front door.

Ezra sits on a porch step. He twirls his hat on the wooden planks and runs another hand through his hair maniacally, combing it over and over. He looks agitated, but when he sees me walking up the driveway, he stands up, waiting on a step still as a board.

We meet face-to-face and he pulls me into his arms. There isn't time to protest; one minute I'm stepping up to the porch, the next I'm pressed against his chest in a suffocating hug. Flustered, I push back, breaking his iron grip.

"Not so fast."

"I'm sorry. I'm really happy to see you." Despite his brash smile, he still manages to look sheepish.

"How do you know I'm not here to tell you it's over?" I frown at him.

"You're not."

I look him over, struck by how cocky he is, even when he's trying to be charming. "You're so sure?"

"Yeah." He grins.

"You know." I shake my head and climb past him, up the stairs to the top step so we see eye to eye. "I'm beginning to think I would've hated you a couple of years ago."

Ezra stares at me earnestly. "You would have. Good thing for me it's not a couple years ago."

"What are you doing out here anyway?" I ask, flustered.

"Waiting for you."

"How did you know I was coming?"

"I didn't. I heard Torrance's cruiser pull up."

On my tiptoes, I try to look down the driveway, but I only see trees where the slope drops off. "You heard it?"

"And I smelled you."

My eyes pop along with my heart. "You what?"

"On the wind." He points up. "It's in the air."

"But we were all the way down the driveway, in his car."

Ezra shrugs.

"What do I smell like?" I ask.

He leans in close, sticking his nose in my hair. "Like lilacs and sun."

I push him back, carving out breathing room. "I don't understand. How can you smell me from so far away?"

"You came here for a reason, Ruby. Why don't we go inside and talk?" He walks past me to the front door.

Holding back, I stare at him apprehensively, suddenly worried about being alone in his house. My heart feels sure and it muffles the alarm inside my brain, but I still hear it going off.

"Or, if you're not comfortable, we can stay outside," he backtracks.

"Do you have, like superpowers on top of everything else?" I ask.

Ezra laughs quietly. "No. Just really heightened senses."

"Oh." I gulp, hovering near the door. "So, yeah, Torrance is going to wait down at the end of the driveway. In case ..." I feel stupid for saying it. "You know."

He arches a dark eyebrow. "In case I do something?"

I look down at the steps, ashamed to admit it. "Yes."

"Would it be better if we just sat on the porch then?"

"No," I mumble. "Let's just go inside."

Ezra holds out his hand, dropping it when I walk past him into the foyer. Inside the house, an exquisite hand-carved archway crisscrosses the ceiling. Tiny flowers, and trees, and corn maidens leap from its surface, turning the entry into a wonderland.

I point at the beam and spiral around. "Did you do that?"

"No. My dad did."

Ezra almost looks proud. He leads me into a living room filled with pieces of furniture from every era—full of mismatched chairs, and arm tables, and cabinets someone painstakingly restored. In one corner, near a window, an ornately detailed cabinet fills the wall. I go to it, running my fingers over polished mahogany.

"That one's mine." He smiles. "It was on its last legs when I found it."

"It's beautiful."

He pats an old restored sofa, then sits down in an antique chair beside it. "There's really no easy way to begin," he says.

"To put it mildly."

"I love you. That's the most important part—though I know you need more."

I nod, waiting for him to go on.

He leans back in his seat, stiffly crossing one leg over the other. "Outside of my family, I've never talked about it."

"The Peñas, your family, are they witches?" I ask softly. I've been so busy being angry that Ezra lied to me, I haven't given much thought to why he lied. It never occurred to me that he may have been the guy everyone hated in high school *because* he was different. That maybe it wasn't easy keeping his secrets secret.

"No," he sniffs.

"Shifters?"

Ezra grimaces and twists in his chair. His face contorts, and as he stares at me, his eyes change colors; dark purple seeps from his pupils, spreading through his irises, turning his golden eyes lilac.

"Your eyes," I murmur, startled.

"The Peñas have lived in the pass forever."

No one really takes the stories seriously anymore. At least they didn't until I came back." He shakes his head. "I should have listened to my mother. She told me my family embraced its fate a long time ago, that I should learn to keep to myself and accept it isn't reasonable to expect anyone outside the forest to understand."

"But maybe they would have."

He shakes his head sadly. "They wouldn't. Look how people are acting now."

"People don't know what to think, Ezra. Can you blame them?"

"A real conundrum, huh?" He looks at me, fluttering his long lashes. "It's my town too, Ruby. I can't leave it, and I wanted to see you, and I'm real damned tired of hiding." He stares at me longingly, pinning me to the cushions with his now buttercup eyes. When I don't answer, he continues. "I've always known I'm supposed to stay here and guard the ruin like my mother, and every generation before her, has. I knew but I never accepted it. I really believed I'd beat the curse. I wanted to get out."

"Curse?" I whisper.

"That's what my dad called it. Shiankya: the curse." He scowls. "I just wanted to be normal. I wanted a normal life."

"Your mother, she, um, changed then too?"

Ezra seems amused by my choice of words. "Mom *and* Dad both did. It's passed down on my mom's side since the beginning of time. My dad though, that was sort of dumb luck. Shiankya's *only* form is mountain lion. But my dad, he could mimic anything. He just didn't know he could until he met my mother."

"I ..." My mouth drops open, frozen mid-word.

"I know it's a lot to take in."

"How? I mean," I swallow, uncertain what to ask, "Your dad didn't know he could shift? Was he Pecos too, or," I pause again, feeling a little numb.

"Shifting isn't unique to the Pecos. But even people born to it, if they don't have a guide, it often just lies dormant inside them. My dad was probably the first in his line for hundreds of years to discover he could do it."

"How'd he figure it out?" I exhale.

"My mom sensed it in him when they met."

I stare at him. How impossible.

"To hear him tell it, my mom let him loose on the world. But he wasn't bound to the ruin like she was. He wasn't a Watcher. And once he understood what he'd have to give up to stay with her, when he understood she *had* to stay, he felt burdened."

The implication, that generations of Peñas have been slaves to the ruin, settles in my stomach like a boulder. "Because you were in the picture?" I ask softly.

"She couldn't leave the pass, Ruby. *I* can't leave, not until my children are old enough to watch the ruin. He wanted his freedom. I understand that. It was much easier for my mom to accept her fate growing up, knowing her place in the world. But Dad was essentially ambushed. To him, his ability really was a gift. It took him a while to understand that as far as Mom was concerned, shifting is utilitarian. She never embraced it, and she never quite accepted that he did."

When Ezra pauses, wiping a tear from his cheek, I move from my seat to sit beside him. Gently, I squeeze his hand, encouraging him to go on.

"Things could have been different all around, but they both refused to meet in the middle." Ezra tentatively rubs a thumb across my palm, slowly closing his hand around mine as if asking permission. "Neither of my parents were particularly easy people to be around."

"That must have been really hard for you." I gently pull my hand away. My heart aches for him, but it doesn't change that he lied to me for months.

He shakes his head. "He resented her. I think he planned to leave her after high school, but Mom got pregnant. I knew he wasn't going to stick around after the first time I shifted. He'd hoped with all his heart it wouldn't pass on. He's the reason I hoped with all my heart it wouldn't." Ezra blows out, pitching his head back onto the couch. "He should have just left way before he decided to check out."

"That's why you hate him," I whisper. *That's why you hate yourself.*

"My dad filled my head with garbage. I wanted a life outside the ruin. And for the longest time, he let me believe it was possible. When I realized it wasn't, I hated him for that more than anything. It split me down the middle. You have no idea how much I envied 'normal' kids like Daisy and Angel."

My emotions are all over the place. Unsettled, I stand up and walk to the window, turning my back to hide that I'm crying. "Why'd you come back then, Ezra?"

"To spite myself, I guess."

I press my forehead against the cool glass windowpane, letting it soothe me. Every question Ezra speaks to unearths twenty more. There are so many, I'm not sure I'm ready for all the answers.

"Watching the ruin, it's your *duty*?"

"It's my birthright."

"Don't you believe in free will?" I ask softly.

He sighs so heavily, I feel it move through me. I turn again to meet his eyes, as unguarded as I've ever seen them. "When Mom found out I planned to go to college in Boston, she accused me of being like my father. And she was right. I believe I'm accountable for my actions and their consequences, Ruby. And turning my back on the ruin comes with consequences—ones I'm not willing to live with, especially now that you're around. There has to be a Watcher. And my mom has already done it for years." Ezra walks over to me. He takes my hands and places them on his chest as though shielding his heart. "What happened after Caroline left set everything in motion."

I wipe tears out of my eyes. "You mean your accident?"

"It wasn't an accident."

Ezra's eyes change again. It isn't much, just a slight shift toward yellow, but I know he's wondering how much he should share. Instead of continuing, he reaches out and hugs me so hard, I'm aware of how every inch of him fits against my body.

"After the breakup, I came back here to punish myself." He sniffs. "I drank too much one night and ended up at the ruin. I turned my pockets inside out on that stupid altar. I basically threw myself over the boulder and begged the Ancients to make things different."

I break away and hold my breath, hearing Angel's voice. *Be careful what you wish for, Ruby.*

"And?" I whisper.

"Nothing happened. So, I went home. But when I woke up in the morning," he shakes his head, bewildered, "I looked like a monster."

"You woke up ... like how you were when we met?"

"Yes." He lets his breath out in a long, steady stream. "The Ancients must have known my heart. I guess they wanted me to know I was ugly on the inside. That my true face isn't the one I was lucky enough to sport around all my life. I'd been acting like a selfish, ungrateful ass—they made that clear. I do believe in free will, Ruby. But it took me a while to figure out free will isn't an excuse to do whatever I like."

"They punished you." I exhale.

"They taught me a lesson." He takes my hand and presses my fingers to his lips. "But you were willing to look past my surface. When you found something worth loving," he taps on his chest, "I started to see things in a different light. You believed in me. And I gradually wanted to be a better person for reasons that never dawned on me before." Ezra and I lock eyes, and his intense gaze is almost frightening. "I never meant to toy with you, Ruby. But my face was all I had for years. And I saw the way you looked at it—even when you hated Leo. I didn't know how to trust that you liked me entirely for myself. Not until you told me you loved me."

I pull back. Remembering how I kissed him in the canyon makes me queasy. He'd been Leo then. Calculated, and cool, and full of bravado. "Once you knew though ..."

"I was scared shitless you'd stop if you knew the truth!" It comes out in a rush, almost like he's angry. "And by the time I figured out what was going on, I was in love with you. I didn't care about anything else after that except staying together. I wanted to be me again desperately, but in the end, I would have stayed like that forever if it meant keeping you."

"This was all about getting your face back?" I choke.

"No! Listen to me. The Ancients didn't give me guidelines. I'd resigned myself to being like that forever. I'm just saying that once I realized it was a test, it didn't matter. I'd give this face up forever to save what we have. I just worried it wasn't enough."

"I *was* attracted to Leo." I step away from him, feeling sick. "But I was attracted to the you inside from the very first day you went with me to Pecos. I loved you despite your face. I've always been clear about that."

"I know that now." He drops his head. "Honestly, Ruby, I wasn't all myself with you either way. It's like they sheared me in two, and I couldn't reconcile either half. It was awkward, and I felt awkward, and that awkwardness made me even more insecure. The only thing I knew for certain was that being with you was changing me. If I hadn't fallen in love with you," he says softly, "If you hadn't fallen for me, I'm not sure who I'd be right now. I think I had to find a reason to be a better person. And I think you had to love *that* Ezra first."

"Maybe the face you ended up with had to do with the path you chose. You say they were both you—maybe one of them just won out."

His eyes darken, turning a deep violet. "Which me do you think that is?"

I sigh, hating the truth even as I hear myself say it. "I don't know yet."

CHAPTER TWENTY-FIVE

EVERYTHING UNKNOWN

"YOU'RE ANGRY."

I stare at Ezra, wide-eyed. "Is that a question?"

"Do you think you can forgive me?" Ezra's voice is steady, but his irises are like an ocean, churning out shades of deep, inky violet.

"I want to, Ezra. But Leo was awful. And you were gone for so long. And you still haven't explained the ruin or why you left."

"You're right," he says, closing the gap between us. "But I will if you give me a chance."

My mind is fraught with old wives' tales and wonder. I want him to keep talking, but my brain feels like it's caught in a meat grinder, and my stomach is grumbling.

"I'm hungry," I tell him.

Ezra's face contorts, twisting into a question mark. "That's not the response I expected."

"If you feed me, I'm a lot more likely to forgive you."

Ezra snorts and takes my hand, leading me to the kitchen.

He sits me down on a stool near the counter and opens a window before pulling bacon and lettuce out of the fridge. While he quietly putters around the stove, I take deep, measured breaths, inhaling sizzling fat, and forest, and piñon. The silence between us feels heavy, but it gives me a moment to think through some of what he's said.

"I don't understand how *either* of us are tied to the ruin. All those unknowns, they scare me, Ezra."

Ezra stops cooking and looks up, focusing his now nearly lilac eyes on me.

"Your eyes," I whisper. "They keep changing colors."

He smiles apprehensively. "My cellular framework is erratic; it's how I shift so quickly." His eyes flash, and he blinks rapidly. "They usually change with my feelings. I *can* control it, Ruby. I'm just a little out of practice."

I raise my brow, astonished. "Like a mood ring?"

"Sort of." He nods, and his eyes turn an even brighter gold around the violet.

"Is it just lion?" I breathe out, mesmerized by his irises. "I mean, can you do anything else?"

"Shiankya is the most natural. The easiest." He averts his eyes again, concentrating on our bacon sandwiches. "But I *can* change into other things. I inherited that from my father. It's just much harder."

I stare at him as he comes around the kitchen island, struck by his sudden vulnerability. On the surface, I don't recognize this Ezra. But I trust my gut. And my gut says to stay and hear him out.

Ezra places two plates on the counter. "There's something I want to do before we eat," he whispers in my ear.

"What's that?"

"This." He wraps a palm around the back of my neck, pulling me forward.

I let him, and when he kisses me my lips sting, sparking a fire in my lungs that burns all the way to my fingertips. Breathless, I rest a palm on his face and another on his chest, whispering against his soft mouth, "This doesn't mean everything's fixed."

Beneath his tight tee and too-perfect chest, his heart beats like it's shifted into overdrive. "I know," he murmurs. "You just drive me crazy."

Agitated, I break away and take a bite of my sandwich.

"I missed you, Ruby."

"I missed you too," I say grimly, thinking about all the times he met me as Leo. "But I'm guessing you already know that."

"Well, there were the phone messages." He grins.

"And the things I told Leo. And the mountain lion." I frown at him.

"Ruby ..."

"I feel betrayed, you know. And stupid."

"That was never my intention."

"How come you followed me around the forest?" I drop my sandwich on my plate, half expecting his answer. "The stories you told me, were you protecting me from the ruin?"

"From yourself." I stare at him, biting my lip furiously, and he adds, "You visited Ottomundo. Even Watchers can't do that."

My heart thumps out an uneven beat, and I inhale to slow it down. "It's really a gateway?"

"Yes." He smiles warily.

I suck in my breath, almost inhaling a piece of bacon.

Ezra sets his mostly finished sandwich on the plate in front of him. "I know you need more. But let's take a break. My head's spinning. Yours must be on Jupiter." When I nod, full of a thousand questions, he takes my hand. "Let me show you my workshop."

Ezra leads me outside to the outbuilding beside his house. Pieces of unfinished furniture and stripped wood hang on the walls, smelling like Ezra sometimes does, of wood shavings, and turpentine, and beeswax. He shows me his tools, giving me brief lessons on how to use band saws, and rasps, and drill presses. For a little bit, I let him pretend things are normal.

Afterward, Ezra walks me through his house, stopping upstairs. Opposite his bedroom door, a four-post bed takes up space under a large window facing the mountains. On the other side of the room, a small, ceramic-tiled hearth protrudes from the sienna-hued wall.

Ezra sits down on his bed and pats the space next to him. "Should we build a fire and curl up?"

I blush but meet his stare. "I should call Torrance."

"Of course," Ezra smiles.

I nod when he stands up and dig my cell phone out of my jeans pocket, holding my breath while I dial.

"What's up?" Torrance asks warily.

"We're just talking."

Torrance coughs. "Ruby, you've been in there awhile."

"I'm good, Torrance. Really. But you should probably leave. I'm going to be here for at least another couple hours."

Torrance is silent for a moment, and I notice Ezra fidgeting with something on the dresser in the corner of his room, acting like he isn't listening.

"You call me again if you need anything, understand?" Torrance finally says. "I'm just going to hang out here a little longer."

"I will," I promise. "But tell Liddy I'm staying the night?"

Ezra looks up at me, stifling what may be a smirk.

"We still have so much to talk about," I add.

I hang up before Torrance can reply, feeling like a million tons of dynamite just went off inside my heart. It flutters erratically, fearful of all the things Ezra still hasn't told me.

"You want to stay?" He asks hopefully.

"I want to trust you, Ezra. I haven't let myself trust anyone since Mom died. Not even myself."

Visibly more relaxed, Ezra hums out loud, building a fire as I dig around his dresser for something to sleep in. When he walks into the adjacent bathroom to look for a spare toothbrush, I look his room over. Photos litter his dresser. In one, a miniature Ezra teeters on a huge boulder in the middle of the desert between two people: an attractive woman, probably his mother, and a handsome man. In another picture, the same man holds a tiny baby. The man resembles Ezra, and I'm struck by his joyful expression.

Ezra steps out of the bathroom and hands me a toothbrush. He catches me staring at the picture and moves behind me, whispering over my shoulder, "That was the day I was born."

"I was just thinking he looks really happy."

Ezra nuzzles my neck. "Right now, I'm happy."

"Both of them ..." I drop my head back against his chest. "Your dad killed himself because he *was* special, and my mom killed herself because she thought she wasn't."

"Dad believed in Ottomundo. He wasn't afraid of dying."

"You think that's where I went when I fainted?" I shiver.

"The way you described it, yes."

"But maybe it really was just altitude sickness."

He looks down at me, calling my bluff with his eyes. "You don't believe that."

"I'm not sure what to believe. I mean, you saw me. I didn't go anywhere."

"It's a spirit portal," he says quietly. "My guess is your spirit left your body." He cocks an eyebrow and pulls me closer. "When the gate's about to open, I feel it in my bones like a song or vibration. That humming you keep talking about? That's the gate gearing up. It resonates every time you're up there."

I turn and bury my head in his shoulder, clinging to him like a straitjacket. "If you can't *see* spirits, Ezra, what are you watching for?"

"I didn't say I couldn't see spirits." Ezra strokes my hair. "I said I couldn't see yours. I *can* see spirits that don't belong here."

"That don't belong here?" A shudder runs the length of my body, freezing my insides.

"Call Liddy. I don't want her breaking down the door in the middle of the night." He holds up the shirt I pilfered from his dresser. "Then go change. I'll be right here waiting, and when you're done, I'll tell you everything."

Inside Ezra's bathroom, I nervously change into Ezra's old Pecos High gym shirt, then call Liddy *and* Racine, telling them between protests that I'm staying the night. When I step out of the bathroom, Erza, who changed into a pair of flannel pajama pants and nothing else, motions for me to join him on the bed. I sit down beside him, and he wraps an arm around me, pulling the comforter around us as we settle in together.

Wriggling closer to his side, I say, "All right, tell me."

Ezra tucks a stray lock of hair behind my ear. After a quiet moment, he says, "All spiritual beings start in Ottomundo, and all beings go back. But not everything in Ottomundo was human before it died. The Otherworld is made up of *all* the universe's life forces. There are worlds out there we can't begin to understand. Everything from the souls of gods to creatures we can't fathom live there, waiting for the Ancients to send them somewhere else. But not all of them want to go where they're sent. Sometimes they look for ways out."

"That's why you kept an eye on me?" My throat suddenly feels like I just walked through the Sahara, and the words come out all crumbly. "Because you think the ruin is dangerous?"

From my periphery, Ezra looks serene, but when he turns on his side, his eyes shift colors like a prism. "That and the fact that you seem to be able to open the gate. That makes *you* dangerous—to you, me, and everyone else."

His eyes churn in a flurry of motion. They fade to gold, then flash violet, then turn a very deep purple. He looks tired, and I'm not sure I even want to hear the rest. "Ezra, who *are* the Ancients?"

"Gods? Angels? Beings from another universe? All I know is that the Pecos worshiped them and that they're immortal. They rule over all the matter in all universes and together form Ottomundo's spine." His voice wavers for a moment. "Ottomundo is made of different realms, each controlled by

364

separate Ancients. They make up a council that decides where, if at all, to seed spirits. The council changes every couple thousand years or so. But they're always made up of Ancients and their descendants."

Ezra's explanation is so insane, I feel giggles coming on. "You're saying you protect an interdimensional nexus to other universes?" I ask through my fingers. "And it's right there," I point toward the window, "Like Heaven but just up our mountain?"

"Yes."

"*Ezra.*"

"Except it's not Heaven. How you've lived one life doesn't affect where you go next, or even in what form. And for some of us, it's also a terminus."

I'm so perplexed it's a chore to hold back hysteria. Whoever said ignorance is bliss was a genius. "Reincarnation?"

"Yes, Ruby. If you want to call it that. Though beings move between trillions of universes and just as many spirit forms." He sniffs, then covers his face with an arm. "Okay, it does sound kind of crazy, doesn't it?"

"The librarian at school called it the Bone Yard. But you're making it sound more like, I don't know, New York or something," I say lamely.

Ezra laughs, shaking the bed. He looks at me with bright, hesitant eyes. I stare at the ceiling, trying to equilibrate. Having faith in anything unseen is hard enough. He's asking me to believe in something so unfathomable, it's mind warping.

"I can hear you," he chuckles. "And I'm not trying."

"My thoughts?"

"I'm sorry."

"Oh." I blush. "Maybe now would be a good time to tell me how your powers work."

"Powers." He laughs. "You're funny."

"Whatever you call them. I just need to know." I squeeze his thigh. I want to climb under his skin and be his bones, to consume every inch of him. But his differences also scare me.

"I'm not Superman. It's pretty basic. I see well, especially at night. I smell things from a fair distance. And I can hear for miles when I focus. I run fast. And I'm stronger than most people, more impervious to injury. Basically, I'm equipped with the skills you'd expect I'd need to guard the ruin, but that's it. Sorry to disappoint."

"Disappoint?" I make a face at him. "Right, because being able to shift into another life-form isn't enough."

When Ezra grins, I'm struck by how different his face is—as near to perfect as a face can come. Yet looking at him is still an adjustment. I miss my old Ezra, whose craggy countenance I grew to love.

"Can you really read my mind?" I ask.

"Yes, there really are times I hear your thoughts."

"Great." I hold my breath, not at all liking the idea. "Explain that."

"I can't." He shrugs. "But I'm sure it has to do with the ruin. I don't mean to listen in, Ruby. But I think you project. And it helps that I can read you well. You wear your heart on your sleeve, you know."

"I don't know how to feel about that. I don't think I want you inside my head."

"If it's any consolation, I try really hard to tune you out when it happens."

"How can you be so human, and yet, so different?" In some ways, he's still every bit my Ezra. In others, it's like meeting a stranger from another planet.

Ezra scratches his head thoughtfully. "Humans are a bit clueless when it comes to understanding themselves. Maybe I'm perfectly normal. Maybe it's the people who aren't so tuned in that are different."

"Like my mother."

"Or my father."

Ezra wraps his arms around me and throws the quilt over our heads, blocking the light. The dim space is a welcome relief. Up close, I see his face and his face alone, and realize I love it in any form, moody or happy, confused or confident, marred or beautiful, lion or man.

Part of me is still mad at him for all the crappy things he's done. But looking at him, my heart knows Ezra is what it wants, who it wants, no matter how much trouble comes with the package. Thick or thin, bad or good—it's just going to take my head a bit to catch up.

"Ezra, if I am True of Heart," I gulp, closing my eyes, "what Mom said ..."

"That you should stay away from me?"

I nod.

"Like I said, I don't accept that. And I don't believe we'd be together right now if being together was wrong."

CHAPTER TWENTY-SIX

WHAT MATTERS

SUN FILLS ALL FOUR CORNERS of the room with crimson light. I feel buoyant and lazy, and I'm comfortable being lazy, so I keep my eyes closed, barely aware of the heavy weight across my shoulder. Yawning, I roll over, disturbing what turns out to be Ezra's muscular arm locked around my body.

"Hi," he whispers when we're face-to-face.

"Hi," I answer sleepily.

"Have I told you how much I love you?"

"Not since last night."

Ezra's eyes twinkle playfully. "I love you, Ruby." He traces my lips with a finger, then grins. "Want to see me turn into a fox?"

"No!" I squeal. "Right now?"

"I'm kidding. I've never been a fox."

Still bleary-eyed, I look at him incredulously. "It's impossible to wrap my mind around."

"What if I show you after school? You can see for yourself."

"Really?" I swallow. "It's not all secretive or something?"

"I don't have any secrets left. Not with you."

I close my eyes and move closer, pressing up against him, savoring how intimate it feels. How could I have hated him just three days ago?

"You don't mind?" I mumble contentedly.

"I've never changed in front of anyone who wasn't related to me. It may be a little weird, but that doesn't mean I don't want to."

Ezra's eyes dance, pulling threads of purple across his golden irises.

"What?" I ask, suddenly feeling self-conscious.

"How do you feel about being late to school?"

When I blush, he throws the sheet over our heads and growls playfully, nuzzling my neck. I hadn't paid much attention to the fact that he went to bed shirtless, sleeping in nothing but flannel pajama bottoms. We stayed up so late, and he filled my head with so many stories, I wasn't even aware of my own body by the time I finally closed my eyes. But under the covers now, so close, I'm painfully conscious of him.

Ezra is incredibly strong. His beautiful arms and smooth, tanned skin just about glow. Next to him, I feel a mixture of lucky, and inhibited, and completely anxious.

"What?" he asks shyly.

"What *what*?"

"You're staring."

I swallow and bury my face in my hands. "I'm so embarrassed."

When I look again, he's smiling. "You make me nervous, too, if it makes you feel better."

"Um, no. Doesn't help," I giggle, flushing furiously.

"Why don't you just come here and hug me then?"

Bashfully, I snuggle up against his chest, fitting against him flawlessly. The old Ezra was perfect in his own way. But this Ezra has it all, and it's hard to know exactly how to feel about such perfection.

"Ezra," I say shyly, "before you didn't want to ... you didn't want ... you know."

He cocks an eyebrow. "Is that a question?"

"Yeah. I think so."

"I wasn't all together. Being with you that way wouldn't have been right. I wanted to, Ruby. God, I wanted to, trust me. I still want to. But I also wanted you to know the truth before things got that serious. I promised myself I wouldn't let it happen until I told you."

"And now?"

"Now you know who I am. I'm not hiding anything."

"What if after everything, I want to wait?"

"Then we wait." Ezra touches my brow, running a hand down over my cheek. "When it happens, it'll be right for both of us."

Ezra said "when," not "if." He wants me, and the idea fills my heart. "I think I need a little time. I do forgive you, but I don't want it to happen while I'm even remotely angry."

"And you still are." He says it like he knows it's not a question.

"A little bit."

"I understand."

"I have another question." I pause, letting it all sink in. "You didn't really go to Las Cruces, did you?"

Absently, his hand travels to his head under the sheet, messing an unruly cascade of staticky dark hair. "No. I went up to the ruin and begged. Every day. I promised to stay and do my job. I asked them to look into my heart."

"And they did."

"They must have." He sighs, then grimaces. "Ruby, the day I asked you to meet me back at the ruin ... I *was* going to tell you. That *was* my lofty plan. But then you got there, and it was clear you already knew, and you ran to Angel, and I kind of lost it. In that way, I guess I'm as human as it gets."

"Ezra Leonardo Lucero," I tell him, "your world is very strange, and I feel like I'm sort of drowning in it. But I'd really like it if you'd just go back to being my boyfriend. I'm still mad at you. And I'll be mad for a while. But I don't think I could love you more than I do this minute if I tried. *Because* you are who you are. *Because* you aren't perfect."

"Ruby Brooks," he tells me. "You have no idea how relieved I am to hear that."

Out his bedroom window, the sun shines above the mountain. I can tell by the shadows it casts on his wall that I've already missed first period. But for once, I'm not really worried. Compared to Ezra's secret, AP English and Physics suddenly seem insignificant.

"We should get you to school," he finally says, pulling away a little.

"I don't want to leave. What if I wake up? What if this is all a dream?"

"I promise it's not." He kisses me, sitting up ruefully before standing up and pulling on a T-shirt. After I dress and scarf down a bowl of Fruit Loops, he drives me to school. If I miss third period and the school calls Liddy, she'll worry. If I miss fourth and Racine notices, *she'll* go ballistic.

As Ezra drives through the pass toward Pecos high school, he takes my gloved hand, squeezing my fingers. "Can I ask you something?"

"You're going to anyway, aren't you?"

He chuckles softly. "Yes. I'm just being polite."

"You're not always the best at it, you know. Being polite."

"And?"

"And I'm just saying." I smile.

"Of course you are."

"So, are you going to ask?"

He looks at me, pensively pulling his head to the side. "Are you going to Stanford next fall?"

"Is that a trick question?"

"Don't be difficult. Just answer it."

"I applied to the University of New Mexico. I haven't told anyone yet."

"But you're not going, right?"

"Well," I pause, "I got in."

Ezra's face looks a mixture of surprised, unsure, and unhappy.

"I'd think I'd like to stay here, with you and Liddy. The U's a good school, Ezra, especially if I major in anthropology. And you can help me 'study.'" I grin.

He looks away, at the craggy mountain peaks surrounding us. As if looking at me will influence what he says next. "I don't want you to stay."

"You don't want me?" His words stab at my heart.

Ezra inhales. His golden irises change, and his jaw softens at the edges. "Are you crazy? I said I don't want you to 'stay.' I don't want you to throw your life away."

"I'm not throwing my life away. I don't feel like I'm stuck here, Ezra."

"You may regret it one day. You deserve the best, Ruby."

I stare at him, wishing he saw what I did. "The University of New Mexico is a good school. Plus, it's cheaper. It's the best of both worlds. I can stay here with you *and* Liddy. I'll save money. And I can live in La Luna. It's only an hour into Albuquerque."

"I want you here with me. More than anything. But the ruin is dangerous to be around, and *if* something happens," he turns again to glance at me with sad, beautiful eyes, "I don't know for certain I can protect you."

"'If' is a tenuous word, don't you think? Sort of a long shot."

"Where you're concerned, 'if' is good enough."

Reaching out, I twist a lock of his midnight hair around my finger, tugging playfully. "It's my life. Shouldn't I be able to choose?"

"Free will." He sighs, then chuckles. "Not if you don't choose right. I can't force you to move away. But if you stay, you have to promise you won't go up to the ruin."

I pause for a moment, staring up at the snow sparkling in the sun on the side of the road. I don't want to promise. But I also know he's right. Hastily, I rush out, "I think we should find out why I'm able to cross over."

"No," he answers, almost as quickly as it's out of my mouth.

Ezra's expression twists my heart. But I'm still determined. "If we go back together once, *just* once, for like a couple minutes, maybe I'll see my mom again."

"No," he says more sternly.

"I believe everything you've told me. And I'm trying really hard to wrap my mind around the Otherworld and Ancient thing. But I need to know what being True of Heart means and why I'm able to cross over. Aren't you even a little bit curious?"

"I've told you before, curiosity killed ..."

"The cat." I cut him off. "Yeah, I know. But I'm not a cat, you are. So maybe you need *me* to protect *you* up there."

He mashes his perfect lips together and frowns a frown that despite its downward trajectory could still light up the pass.

Only slightly deterred by his tenacity, I shift gears into sweet-talk mode, batting my eyes for good measure. "Please, Ez. Not knowing—it'll drive me crazy. You're so strong, so fast. I know you can guard me. You can watch to make sure nothing happens. And if something does, I completely trust you to stop it."

He sighs, long and hard. "I said no, Ruby. Twice now."

I meet his sideways stare. "We can go after school today. You can shift there."

Ezra's eyes change, narrowing as they turn deep violet. "Which of the words I just used do you not understand?"

"All of them," I say as deadpan as I can.

"You have that much faith in me?"

"Yes. Except it's not faith exactly. Faith is like stabbing at something in the dark. It isn't the same as knowing. And I *know* I can count on you."

Ezra leans sideways and touches my chin, tilting my face upward as he pulls in front of the high school. "Fine, Ruby." He shakes his head as he leans in to kiss me. Under his breath, he grumbles, "Talk about a double whammy."

"We *need* to know." I kiss his cheek reassuringly before hopping out. "It's a good thing."

Though I'm nearly three full periods late, it's hard to say goodbye. Still, I let him go and beeline into the school, running down the hall to my classroom. When I walk into French class and Racine sees me, she does a double take before giving me the stink eye. I sit down, and she leans sideways over her desk.

"Later, Ray," I whisper into the aisle. "I'll tell you at lunch."

Racine nods curtly and turns back toward the teacher. But by the time lunch rolls around, she's a crazed beast. Seconds after I walk into the lunchroom, she grabs my arm and pulls me out into the hall.

"Well?" she shouts loudly enough for everyone inside the cafeteria to hear. "Tell me!"

"Everything's fine," I assure her.

"Fine. Yeah, you already said that. Twice. Last night and this morning, both times on the phone from Ezra's bedroom."

"Okay, everything's great. Calm down."

"First, I can't believe you spent the night. Second, you called this morning and said you'd be here by second period. And then you weren't. I was freaking out."

I feign stupidity, shrugging. "Why?"

"What do you mean 'why'? A week ago, Ezra was MIA, and you were all heartbroken and hating him. Then he—poof—shows up looking completely hot, and you say you think he might be some kind of super-freak or something." She rolls her eyes at me. "It should be a no-brainer, Ruby. Things are not *fine*."

"Are you sure you're not my mom reincarnated?" One day, Racine is going to make a seriously formidable mother.

"Did he explain everything?"

"Sort of. I mean, it's kind of mind-boggling. I can't say it all makes sense."

"Jesus." She crosses herself. "And his face?"

"Surgery," I answer without really thinking.

As soon as it tumbles out, I know it's for the best. Gossip around town is both crazy and rampant. People need a story to hang their hats on, and surgery makes more sense than shape-shifting or an enchanted ruin.

"What?" she screeches.

"He had some kind of fancy plastic surgery, really cutting edge. That's why he left. He didn't tell me because he wasn't sure it'd work out. It was supposed to be a surprise."

"Bullshit!" She grabs my arm, stopping me cold.

I shrug, trying my best to look clueless. "It's true."

"I don't believe it."

I shoot her a stern look, shaking my head. "It's true enough, Ray."

Racine looks completely cynical, plus a little peeved.

"Look. It's crazy. *Really* crazy. I admit it. But it's complicated. And I promise I'll do my best to explain. Just not now, all right?"

"But you will tell me about his 'surgery' later," she insists.

"Later—in private. If you promise it stays between us."

"Fine," she nods, pulling me into the lunch line. "I'll run with surgery if that's what you want. But you better work on your delivery. You're like cellophane. Only more transparent."

I squeeze her arm. "Thank you."

"So then are you still *together* together? Because people are going to ask."

"Yes."

She bounces in place impatiently, shifting two different kinds of Jell-O around on her tray. "He knows how much he hurt you, doesn't he?"

"He knows. But he couldn't exactly help it. And we all make mistakes, right? He's only human."

She raises her eyebrows high on her forehead. "Is he?"

"Yes," I answer adamantly, glancing toward Las Gallinas at our table across the cafeteria. "Way more than Marta, for instance."

Racine giggles. "Touché."

Lunch tray in hand, I twine my arm in Racine's, pulling her toward our table, determined to act as if the last couple of weeks have been nothing more than a small bump in the road. Lunch ends, and the last two periods of the day crawl by. I can't concentrate, probably because all I can think about is visiting the ruin and seeing Ezra shift. I'm not sure which is scarier, but just thinking about both injures my brain.

After school, I huddle on the front quad with Las Gallinas, pretending like the rest of them to be interested in the conversation we started over lunch about winter break. We're all really just waiting for Ezra to arrive, but I play along, feigning cluelessness, determined to downplay his sudden metamorphosis back to perfect.

"Surgery, huh?" Marta *tsks* when Ezra pulls into the parking lot.

"I can't believe how good it came out." Ashley gapes, letting her mouth fall open as he parks and walks toward us. "I mean, he looks almost exactly the same. It must have cost a freaking fortune."

"Modern technology." Racine shoots me a look, smiling slyly. "Imagine what they'll be able to do in twenty years."

Marta ogles Ezra shamelessly. "Whatever he did, damn, he's hot. Good luck keeping him."

Ezra stops on the sidewalk about twenty feet from our huddle and winks, amplifying his already crackling wattage. He stands there with his hands in his pockets, tilting his head to the side while he waits, preening.

"He's still a cocky SOB, isn't he?" Ashley asks.

"A little." I smile.

Rushing out my goodbyes, I run over to him and throw my arms around his neck. Ezra lifts me off my feet, holding me close before planting a kiss on my lips. "You ready?" he asks, reluctantly unlatching my arms.

"Yes. But I'm nervous," I admit. Though 'nervous' is a gross understatement.

Ezra drives us up to my house. After going inside to exchange my school backpack for my hiking gear and listening to Ezra tick off all the reasons hiking to the ruin is a bad idea, we start walking up the mountain.

"Read my mind," I tell him as we trudge over dirt and dried twigs.

"I thought you told me not to."

"Just do it."

He closes his eyes and smiles, shaking his head curiously. "Do you really believe in forever?"

"With you?" I nod. "It seems possible."

Ezra stops and kisses me. My head spins, and when he finally pulls away, whispering, "Could you do it? Live here in the forest until we're both old and infirm and you have to wheel me everywhere?" it feels like his lips and my lips are still connected. I laugh to mask the small earthquake inside me. "I don't know. Ask me again after everything."

Ezra nudges me gently. He winds an arm around my shoulders and pulls me to his side, locking us together at the hip.

"Should I do it here?" he asks.

"You don't want to wait until the ruin?"

"I don't even want to go to the ruin."

"Then, yes." I exhale. "If you're ready."

His eyes change, turning a brilliant buttercup as he stares into mine, searching. They flicker to periwinkle, then settle on lilac. "Okay," he says smoothly. "Step back."

I break out of his arms. "Good kitty," I tease.

In my head, I've already played out a bazillion different mind-blowing scenarios. But none of them are like how it happens. For a second, he looks like a blur—like a vibrating blur. Then I blink. And quicker than I can gasp, a huge mountain lion stands at my side, looking me almost in the eye.

I screech and jump, tripping on a root that sends me flailing backward. My backpack hits the ground, and my breath escapes my body. Filling my chest to capacity, I sputter, looking up to find him standing over me. Ezra growls, sending a rumble forward from the hollow of his neck. When he opens his mouth, dipping his head toward mine, a set of very large, very sharp teeth make my acquaintance. I reach out and touch an incisor, gently pushing a finger against its tip.

"Don't bite me," I warble.

Ezra's eyes contract; he blinks and the long golden whiskers above his eyes flutter, tickling my forehead. When I giggle, he rubs a furry jowl against my cheek.

"You know I almost peed in my pants when you cornered me near my house. You're lucky I didn't shank you."

Ezra steps back and sits down on his haunches, looking as immensely pleased as I imagine a mountain lion can. He flares his coral nose, sending his whiskers upward.

Sitting up, I lean into his golden fur, running a hand over his soft, bristly head and ears. I throw my arms around his thick neck and hug his sturdy, warm body. At first, I can't wrap my arms all the way around him. Then my arms suddenly encircle him completely.

"Jesus! You are fast," I yelp.

"Which me do you like better?"

"The one who won't eat me." His eyes are like shiny objects, mesmerizing. I stare, watching him watch me. "I'm completely speechless."

Ezra kisses me hard, pressing me back against the ground. "The trouble with changing around you is how much lion you bring out."

I bite my lip, holding back a smile. Energy bounces between our bodies. His skin is charged, giving off small shocks when I touch him. "You're like a spark. You know? Like when you touch something electric and it runs through your body."

"That's exactly it," he whispers gruffly.

"Seriously? You're shocking me?"

"It'll die down in a couple of minutes."

"That's wicked. Have you ever ..."

"Ever?"

"You know."

Ezra grins at me, then unzips my jacket. He runs a hand

underneath my shirt, over my bare skin, making me crazy. "Not right afterward."

The air outside feels cool against my body. In contrast, Ezra is warm and galvanized; electricity bounces between his fingers and my stomach. For a moment, I feel him, and only him, as though we've merged molecularly.

"Why do you do that?" I shiver.

He brushes hair off my face with his free hand. "Everything inside me speeds up when I shift, all my cells, every process. I slough off electricity until everything slows down. I often have to stay outside for a few minutes afterward or I short everything."

"Really?" I giggle. "Does it hurt?"

"Like being mildly electrocuted or burned." He kisses my nose.

I move my head against the scrubby ground, searching the sky while my mind turns. "How do you get used to something like that?"

"How do you get used to anything?"

I stare at him, feeling like a child, trying not to sniffle. My emotions are all over the place.

Ezra chuckles, stroking my cheek with electric hands. "Did you know there used to be animals that could shift into humans? They ran around naked until they found pants or an outfit to steal, at least that's what my grandfather told me. He called them Foes with No Clothes. Back in the day, people hung cloth outside their dwellings or wore cloth bands around their wrists to keep the Foes mollified."

I sock him in the shoulder playfully. "You're messing with me."

"Am I?" Ezra grins secretively. "Supposedly, before the portal was restricted millenniums ago, all sorts of creatures came here from Ottomundo. Then, I guess, they all had their purpose."

Ezra makes my head hurt. Every time he opens his mouth, the world suddenly seems so much more complicated. "What about vampires and werewolves?"

He laughs out loud. "Werewolves, maybe. And Skin-walkers. But vampires? I doubt it. The Ancients gave humans gifts because we *weren't* monsters. They honored goodness and rewarded it with certain freedoms, like having an animal spirit. Believe me, if the Ancients wanted us to know real evil, we would."

Ezra kisses me again, letting his fingers linger on my stomach until the electric sensation peters out. He doesn't say another word, but his eyes never leave mine. We lie together under thick, defined clouds, watching each other as the sun skirts across the horizon. My skull is so numb I barely notice the little pebbles and pinecones that have found shelter beneath my head. But I'm more comfortable on the ground beside him than I've been anywhere else for a very long time. And because of it, more hesitant than I was earlier to visit the ruin.

"Want to shift again and go up to the plateau now?" I ask, trying to re-talk myself into going up there.

He sits up. "No."

"You sure, Ez? You could lead the way. I'll just follow."

He gives me a look. "You're not a follower, Ruby."

After a few awkward moments, Ezra helps me up off the ground and wraps one of my arms around his waist, securing it with a broad hand. He holds onto me tightly, as if I may break away. Between the trees, under an open parcel of sky, his beautiful face glows, rivaling his emotive eyes.

"Ruby," he says earnestly. "Before we get there, I want to ask you something. I think you should go to Stanford. But if you do stick around after graduation, will you consider moving in with me?"

I open my mouth to answer and end up stammering.

"Cat got your tongue?" he whispers.

I take a deep breath and start again.

"You don't want to?" He cuts me off. "No, I mean, I understand. I shouldn't have asked."

"Please be quiet," I tell him, pausing when my throat catches. "I was going to say that you don't have to ask me to live with you because I want to stay. I don't expect ..." I let my voice trail off, holding my breath. "I want to, Ez. Someday. But suddenly everything's different from what I thought it was. I need to know who I am. And I want to know *this* you better. Plus, I don't like thinking you're asking because you feel like you're stuck with me."

Ezra's laugh startles me. It goes deep and shakes his body. "Are you kidding?"

"No." I swallow. "Don't make fun of me. Just tell me you'll wait until I'm ready."

Ezra drops down on one knee like he might propose, looking up into my face. "Ruby Brooks," he starts, "I want you to move in with me. And I will most definitely wait until you're ready."

I pull him up and lock my arms around his neck, holding on for dear life. When he lifts me off my feet, I whisper, "But you get to tell Liddy."

He laughs near my ear. "Always negotiating."

"If *I* tell her, she'll kill me. Then this conversation will be pointless."

"All right." Ezra's voice hums with both apprehension and affection. "If the ruin doesn't change your mind, it's a deal."

CHAPTER TWENTY-SEVEN

THE HERO NEVER DIES

WE HIKE THE REST OF THE WAY to the ruin, winding through bare brush and swatches of trees to the plateau. At the edge of the clearing, Ezra stops and shakes his head at me. "I can't believe I let you talk me into this."

Dumping my backpack, I sit down on a patch of dry pine needles. "I'm starting to wonder why you let me talk you into this."

He drops down beside me. "Should we go back?"

I grab his forearm, digging my nails into it to steady both of us. "No."

Beneath the setting sun, the ruin blazes, sparkling like wet gold. My heart slows while I watch a wall shift from yellow to orange, highlighting a circle of micaceous stars like Ezra's Pecos Circle. "Look." I point at it. "It's sparkling."

Ezra's smile looks strained. "Did you know that's why Coronado thought he'd found Cibola in New Mexico?"

"You mean one of the Seven Cities of Gold?"

"Yes," he nods. "It's the micaceous clay. It makes everything glitter."

Ezra stands up and walks to the ruin. He runs his fingers over an eroded patch of adobe, scratching at its pebbly surface. Overhead, the sun turns the long clouds languishing in the low sky to scarlet ribbons. I sigh, looking upward. "Have you ever seen anything so beautiful?"

He turns sideways, examining my face. "Yes," he answers softly.

I blush, whispering, "Read my mind."

"Now it's a novelty?"

"Just do it."

"You could?" He sounds puzzled. "Oh ..."

"You asked me a question before you shifted. I don't need to visit my mom first. I know the answer. It's yes, I could stay with you until we're old and infirm and I have to wheel you everywhere."

Violet seeps through his golden eyes. He walks over to me and taps the side of my head with a finger. "I heard you."

"I still can't get over it."

Ezra wraps his arm around my shoulders, pulling me back against his chest. "Ruby, we had to carry you home on your birthday. And that first time you fainted, you just hit the ground. I've been thinking about that all day. I know I promised I'd come here with you, but I think crossing over is a really bad idea."

I smile, pretending to be a lot less anxious than I feel. "If I'm out too long or whatever, just wake me up."

Ezra catches me at the wrist as I move away from him. "I *really* think it's a bad idea," he stresses, pulling me back a little. "What if something happens? What if I can't protect you?"

"It won't. And I know you can. I believe that even more now that I've seen you shift."

He frowns and lets go, standing as motionless as the still air around us, bristling with anticipation. As I close my eyes and concentrate on Ottomundo and my mother, I feel Ezra's physical pull. His strength fills me with courage, encasing me like a sheath of new skin, as though it came from my own soul.

"Wait," he says abruptly, breaking my trance. "I have to tell you something."

I open my eyes. Ezra's face is ashen; he looks sick. "What?"

"Watchers and Trues exist on different sides of the gate now for a reason," he rushes out, "at least they're supposed to. It's dangerous for a True and a Watcher to associate until a Watcher passes on. Their allegiances should be to the Ancients, not each other."

I stare at him, bug-eyed. "Ezra, why are you telling me this now?"

"Because your mother probably will. And if you are True ..." he stops and stares at the ground, rubbing the back of his head.

"What?"

"Watchers and Trues used to share sort of a symbiotic relationship until a Watcher killed a True and let half the Otherworld out." He grimaces. "It's common knowledge. We're selfish bastards who'd rather escape to Ottomundo than do our jobs here on Earth. And we'd do anything, including charming the pants off a True to get there."

"Ezra!" I gasp.

"I mean, it's not like it's documented history. And it was thousands of years ago. And it may have been an accident." He stares at me, obviously mortified. "I could never hurt you, Ruby."

"I don't even know what being True means," I say, dumbfounded.

"It means you'd be part of something bigger once you leave this world. Until then," he shakes his head, "everything I've ever learned says Trues are born in, and die in, Ottomundo. All I know for sure is that you're not an appointed True. Not yet. Maybe you're a True-in-waiting or ... something like that. Whatever the answer, you are an opportunity. There are things in Ottomundo that won't think twice about using you, hurting you if they think you can get them out. Part of my job now should be protecting you from that. It's just one of a thousand reasons I don't think you should do this."

My jaw clenches, reminding the rest of me to stay strong. "I don't care what my mother says about you or us. Because *I* finally trust *myself*. But we need to find out, Ezra. I need to find out who I am ... *what* I am."

"Let's go back, Ruby." His solid voice is soft and pleading. "We'll figure it out some other way."

Ezra is genuinely worried about my safety. But beneath that I see a different kind of fear. He's scared to lose what we've managed to salvage between us. "Ezra," I reach out to him. "Everything we know is folklore and stories passed on through your family. You're not even sure how much of it is real. But no matter what I learn, I'll still love you."

Ezra pulls me in for a hug, and I bury my head against his chest, breathing in wood shavings, and pine, and lavender along with his laundered shirt. As he stands there looking forlorn, I push away from him and close my eyes again. I'm anxious and sad he may be right and try forcing it all out of my head.

Around me, not one thing stirs—not a leaf, or the wind, or even my heartbeat. The forest and every atom of its fabric is inert. In an instant, the sky sheds its color, draining fast like a tub. For one brief moment, the day is so bright I only see Ezra's outline. Then the sky burns out and trees glow beneath the same bluish, luminescent chain of orbs I saw over the mountains last time.

"What the hell!" I yelp.

I told you not to come back.

At the sound of my mother's voice, I whip around, gawking at the same yellow dress she wore the night we went flying. Her voice is a singsong gust, but it comes out sternly, brushing my ears and cheeks like a cold breeze.

"Well, *you're* supposed to be dead." I swallow, suddenly panicking. "And *you're* here."

My mother's grave face breaks into a smile. It grows deeper when I put my hands on my hips, trying to convey my frustration.

I am dead. She puts her hands on her hips, mimicking me.

I take a deep breath and hold it in, counting silently until it feels like I might explode. *Yeah, you are.* "I need to ask you something."

You need to go.

I shake my head. "Am I True of Heart?"

True of Heart, she repeats in a singsong voice. *Yes.*

"And that means?"

It means you must go back to Earth until your time's up.

"That's not very helpful." Her convoluted answers are about as informative as a dagger through the eye. Perplexed, I take a deep breath, trying to make sense of her words. "Is that why I can open the gate?"

One day, you'll have a place here. That's all I can tell you.

Until then, stay far away from the ruin—away from the Other-world. Leave it for the Watcher. You can't come here again until you crossed over naturally.

"Am I ... in Ottomundo?"

You're in Tamoanchan: The Otherworld's skeleton, the Under-world, the Land of the Dead. Where souls come first before moving on. Her diaphanous body explodes in a crackle, pulsing to life in a rainbow shower of color. *The Ancients have a plan for you. But you must stay away from the ruin until it's your time.*

"What plan? What if I don't want to be True of Heart?"

The choice isn't yours. But you have a long life ahead of you. What you do with it now is for you to decide. On Earth at least, you have free will. Unless the Descended find you, the Ancients are the only ones who can affect your ultimate destiny.

"Find me?" I choke out, feeling faint. "The Descended?"

Her mouth opens in an extended yawn. *Cipactli, Tiamat, Mictlan, Omacatl. Until you cross over, you're not impermeable to irreversible spirit death. If the Descended find you, they'll use you to open the gate. And if they see fit, snuff your soul. Without you in the picture, the chain will break. Earth will be closed to the Otherworld, and the gate will remain sealed until the Ancients find their next True of Heart.*

I bite the inside of my cheek hard, balling my fists at my sides. It feels like every atom of oxygen has been sucked from the mountainside. My lungs shrink and I fear I may start hyperventilating. "Trues open and close the gate from your side?" I garble out.

They're the only ones who can.

"And Watchers protect the gate from Earth?"

That's enough, Ruby. It's time to go back.

I shake my head adamantly. "Not until you tell me why you did it."

Did what?

"Jumped. Off the pier. It's pretty clear from your letter it wasn't an accident."

Letter?

"The one you gave to Liddy last year. The one Liddy gave me before my eighteenth birthday."

Her face softens around her sad eyes, but she just floats in front of me, silent.

"Mom?"

Mom lowers her eyes, and my skin prickles. I feel a sudden shuffling in my head, like something, or someone, is picking through it. When she looks up at me, she smiles, but her face is more like a mask of my mother's.

I choke on the air, tasting bile. "You're not my mom, are you?"

She shakes her head.

"Oh, god." I cover my mouth with my gloved hands, breathing heavily.

Think of me as your guide. It's easier this way, Ruby.

"But why?" I near sob. "And why Mom?"

You trust her. She's in your heart.

"Is she there with you?"

She shimmers against the blue night, rippling in waves. *She loved you. It wasn't her intention to hurt you. She traded her life for yours. To keep you safe. So you'd have the opportunity to live out a full life.*

My body feels weightless, like it might float away. I step back toward a tree and grab a branch, breathing erratically. "I don't understand."

You will one day.

"But ... but how ... how did she even know about the Otherworld?" I stutter breathlessly.

She shimmers, blotting in the middle as her sides spill out in diaphanous tendrils, but she doesn't answer.

"Please," I beg.

She turns quickly, blending into a smudge that suddenly shoots above the trees, spreading like a gossamer curtain over the plateau. She hovers for a second, then in a flash pulls back, dropping down in front of me.

You must go!

My heart beats so fast my eyes blur. "And Ezra?"

You can't trust him.

"But last time you said he can protect me."

He can, if he's not entangled. Your will is your own, Ruby. But that doesn't mean it's what the Ancients want.

"That doesn't make sense. They gave him his face back."

Mom 2.0 shoots forward. She locks a cold but concrete hand around my wrist, tugging me toward the ruin. *Their lesson distracted him from his most important job; he'll protect you better if he's not whining about his losses. That you feel for each other is unfortunate happenstance. Though not entirely surprising. Watchers and True share the same universal cloth, and on this side, at least, have always walked a dangerous road together. That's why it's law here now. Watchers aren't to mix with True of Heart. He'll protect you, Ruby, but if you let him get too close, he'll also tear your heart out. It's in his nature.*

She pushes me toward the center of the ruin, and I shiver so hard my teeth rattle. "He won't!"

You think that now. But you can't be certain.

"I am certain. He'd never do anything to hurt me. I'd bet my life."

If you stay with him, you are betting your life. I don't know the Ancients' intentions. But I do know that Watchers live in the shadows. They hide their true heart. They're the opposite of everything you are, Ruby. Whatever you think now, you'll never know him entirely.

From the bushes behind us, something screeches, sending a flock of huge birdlike creatures from the trees. I cough, choking on my spit as if it contains thorns. Whimpering, I wrap my arms around my waist as my heart speeds up, then down, then up again, beating hard enough so that I hear it outside my body.

Behind Mom 2.0, tall pines bend at an angle one by one, groaning under unseen weight. A brilliant magenta flash lights up the sky as their tips pop forward like springs, rustling discordantly in the distance, igniting a vortex of swirling color above the mountain.

Go, now! It won't take them long.

"Please, tell me what to do," I sob. "Now that I know, how am I supposed to live my life?"

Look inward to find the answer. Even here, there are no guarantees, love.

The sky bubbles above the trees, popping holes in the night that look like celluloid melting in the atmosphere. For a moment, I can't see her, and then she's there in front of me again, only this time more light, than matter. She rushes me, pushing me back, then grasps my shoulders and shoves me toward the ruin's stone altar.

I hold my hand out to her, desperate to hold on. "Until I die, what's the point of being True of Heart?"

393

Her diaphanous body explodes in a crackle. But she doesn't answer. All I hear is, *They're watching you both closely, Ruby.*

I squawk, throwing my arms out to find purchase. Around me, the sky's purplish cast fades to eggshell. The sky is so bright I cover my eyes, screaming over the growing roar that surrounds us. As everything fades, a creature the size of a car pushes through the trees, mowing them down beneath its flowing gunmetal body. It cuts through the forest just as my fingers start to burn like someone stuck them with hot pins, and the searing rips through my arms.

The creature's low-timbered gurgle shakes the ground, throwing me off-balance. As it leaps high into the air, sailing at me in long ribbons like a jet stream, I fall backward. It soars over me, baring rows of teeth the size of lawn stakes, and then suddenly it's gone. Everything disappears. I hang suspended in a void, weightless, unable to feel my own body.

"Ruby!" Ezra shouts.

As I hit the ground, a huge rhino-like creature bounds out of the empty sky. It cuts through the air, crashing to the earth so hard my teeth rattle. I scream for Ezra and scramble behind a ruin wall, gasping for breath.

In a flash, Ezra shifts. He jumps at a creature so enormous Ezra looks like a kitten beside it. Off to my side, he backs the creature against a tree, pushing into it with his skull. I scream again, and in my head hear Ezra yell at me to run.

My legs are like tree trunks rooted to the ground. But it doesn't matter; the creature can tear me to shreds for all I care. There's no freaking way I'm leaving Ezra.

The creature moves stealthily, breaking free of Ezra's hold, its grotesque silver eyes glowing in its head. It mews a low guttural mew that rattles the trees around us, knocking Ezra back, laying him flat so fast the creature has time to pounce. Pinning Ezra to the ground with a tire-sized paw, it rips at his shoulder with its teeth. As Ezra's golden fur turns red, I scream, and the creature lifts its streamlined head, opening its mouth to reveal sets of long serrated teeth set in a massive, pointed jaw.

The creature pauses for a second, long enough for Ezra to get it together. As it stares at me, Ezra twists himself around its muscular haunches, burying his teeth into the hollow near its ankle. The creature snarls and steps back, and Ezra springs at it so quickly he's a blur. He jumps and lands on the creature's back, scratching thin lines of blood into its oily sides with his paws.

The creature flings Ezra about wildly, whipping him around like a chew toy. My stomach revolts, and I double over, certain I'm going to vomit. I'm so afraid if I look away for even a second, he'll be gone.

Ezra holds on until the creature rolls over, pinning him under its body, screeching so violently my ears pop. I cover them and close my eyes, feeling like my eyeballs might explode. In my head, I call out, shouting, *No, no, no!* above all the noise. I feel Ezra inside me. I hear his thoughts and feel what he feels as he fights. He isn't scared for himself, only of what the creature may do to me if he loses.

As I listen, Ezra's voice peters out.

Ruby, he says, *run!*

Piles of rocks cover the ground near my feet. Without thinking, I grab the largest and rush the creature, yelling in a pitch that matches its strange mewing. The rock collides with its rubbery leg, bouncing back, sending my arm flying so far behind my head I feel my bones protest. I scream again, or at least I think I scream, and then the clearing goes black. For what seems like the thousandth time, I hit the ground. My head smacks a rock, and I lie in the dirt, inert, deaf, and sightless.

"Ruby!" Ezra shakes my shoulders, rattling my teeth and skull.

"Cut it out," I swat at him.

All around, everything falls into order: the ruins, and pines, and setting sun.

"Ruby!" Ezra yelps. "Jesus, you stopped breathing."

I shoot up frantically. "Ezra! Are you all right?"

He lets out a long breath, looking into my eyes. "Yes. I think so. If you are."

I try sitting up straighter, but my head pounds inside my skull. "I'm fine," I lie.

"You're as white as a ghost."

"What happened? Where'd it go?"

He swallows, obviously shaken. "You dropped, and it just ..." he shrugs, making a question mark with his body. "Disappeared. Ruby, I heard you shouting something inside your head. I think you willed it back to wherever it came from."

"Oh, Ez, I went there. To ... to Ottomudo ... to the Otherworld."

Ezra looks dumbstruck and tremendously worried. "You just ... you hit the ground. I mean, you closed your eyes and fainted. When you came to, that thing flew out of nowhere."

"I met my mother, and I saw ... god ..." I rub my eyes.

"You saw God?" he squawks.

"No ... I mean, like *god*, I can't describe what I saw because it's completely indescribable. *God*, I don't even know if what I saw was real." I realize I'm doing a mixture of babbling and hyperventilating and slow down, gasping for air. "It was crazy. But not as crazy as that ... thing."

Ezra's eyebrows come together in the center of his forehead. He wraps an arm around my shoulder and pulls me closer, wincing as he moves to support my frame.

"Hey." I push him back, searching his chest. There's a huge red stain on his jacket near his right shoulder. "Ezra!"

"Flesh wound," he grimaces.

Ezra pulls me closer, surrounding me with shaking arms. He holds me like we're about to face Armageddon.

"It's okay," I whisper, unsure if anything will ever be okay again.

"It's obviously not."

"If I stay away from the ruin, it will be. My mother said." *My mother. Not my mother.* But he doesn't have to know that.

"Are you True of Heart?"

When I don't answer, he stiffens. He holds me rigidly, breathing rapidly in my face while his eyes shift colors.

I try smiling, as if a giant, Otherworldly hellhound attacking us is the most natural thing in the world. But like everything else about my body right now, it hurts. I run a hand down his arm and tilt my head back, brushing my lips against the tip of his jaw. "It just means I can open the gate, that's all."

"That's all?" He pinches the bridge of his nose, inhaling deeply. "A thing the size of a bus followed you out, and you say, 'That's all'? It's obviously enough."

"She told me to leave the moment I got there, but I didn't. I refused until she answered my questions. It's my fault."

Ezra shakes his head like he's shaking off a thousand pounds of doubt. He presses his lips together, and digs his fingers into my shoulder, tightening his grip. "Liddy could have moved you anywhere, but she brought you here. Now that we know, it can't be a coincidence."

I remember Mom's letter. How in retrospect, she must have known before checking out that my fate would travel this path—a path apparently only she understood. "All I know is if I stay, Mom said you can protect me."

"You asked her about me?"

I want to tell Ezra everything. But I know better. If I say she thinks he's a danger to me, he'll do something crazy. Besides, I don't accept what she said. I may be True one day, but here on Earth, I'm not. There's no real reason to believe Ezra and I shouldn't be together. "Yes," I tell him. "She said the Ancients have their eyes on us. Guess we better be good for a while."

Ezra holds me for a moment, latching on as if I might float away. His strong heartbeat, muffled by his jacket, thumps out of sync like fireworks going off. He's still charged, and I feel every little pulse that moves through his body.

"Hey, are you okay?" I burrow into his good shoulder, speaking into his neck.

"I'm fine." He grabs my hand. "Can you stand?"

I nod, and he pulls me up, groaning as he shifts his weight. I rest a hand on his stomach and look down at his leg, staring at a red stain seeping through the denim.

"I'm fine. It'll heal."

"It ... it doesn't look fine," I stutter, swallowing to keep from crying.

"I'll be fine. But, Ruby, *you* can't come up here again—ever. I don't want you anywhere on this mountain. Do you understand?"

I wind my hand into his, twining our fingers together tightly. "Yes."

Ezra pulls me to him. He stares down into my eyes, and a strange tingling migrates across my forehead.

"Don't do that!" I pull away from him. "You promised."

"Because I didn't think you'd lie to me."

"Ezra, I told you everything."

"I'm sorry," he says softly, examining my face. "But I don't believe you."

"You're going to have to. Because you can't go sneaking around my brain whenever you think I'm hiding something."

He drops his head. "I need to know whether it's safe for you to stay with me, Ruby."

"Mom said to follow my heart. And my heart says you're mine, Ezra. End of story."

Ezra pulls me back to him, silently letting the tension between us settle. He holds me tightly against his chest, flexing his arms around my shoulders. Finally, his heartbeat slows, thumping in sync with my own as we both calm down.

"I didn't mean to snap," I say gently. "I just need you to trust me."

His golden eyes gaze down at mine, worriedly searching.

Can you hear me? I ask in my head.

Yes.

They trust you to watch the ruin now. I trust you. Trust yourself, Ezra.

Ezra wraps an arm around my waist and directs me toward the trail, hobbling a little. We hold each other up on the way down the mountain. He wipes an eye here and there, and I shiver, but neither of us admit how scared we are.

Near the bottom, his arm stiffens around my shoulder. Softly, he says, "I'm a Watcher, and you're True of Heart."

"Yes." I lean my head against his jacket, slowing down a bit. "But we have free will. We decide whether or not to love each other. Here at least, we get to decide whether it's right."

"And if it turns out they don't want us to be together?"

"I don't know. And I don't care. This is my life, right now. If they want me in Ottomundo someday, they'll have to deal because I won't do it *here* without you."

He looks me over, holding me hostage with his violet-golden eyes. "You're willing to live with the consequences?"

"Aren't you?" I ask.

"I've never been so sure." His bright smile lights his already animated face, tugging at my heart. "I'm okay with consequences, as long as you're safe and in my life."

"How about you take care of me now, and I'll watch your back in the Otherworld?"

Ezra looks at me with wide, hopeful eyes. "You're a believer now."

"I believe in *us*, Ezra."

Ezra laughs, and the sound warms my freezing body. He looks up at the sky and chews on his bottom lip before looking down at me again. "I think you should leave La Luna when you graduate. But if you decide to stay, I swear on everything I am to do everything in my power to keep you safe." He speaks softly. "Just remember, a leopard doesn't just change his spots."

"But you're not a leopard, you're a lion."

"I am a lion. And I know what I want, but I'm not always

levelheaded when I'm emotional. I'm rusty when it comes to relationships. You'll have to bear with me for probably more than a while."

I stop him and kiss his cheek, then his nose, then his mouth. "I know, and I will. Besides, it's mutual."

"I scare the pants off you too?"

I laugh and squeeze his arm.

"Well, *that* I like."

When we get to my house, Ezra stops short, standing stiffly by the creek in the backyard like a Greek statue. He pulls my hand, tugging me back, lining me up with his substantial body. "Before we go in, promise that from now on, you'll tell me if something feels off. Even if *you* think it's nothing."

"Define 'off.'"

"Just promise, Ruby."

"Okay. I promise."

"And you won't ever go up there again."

"Never."

He kisses my nose. "You will always be my first priority."

"What about the ruin?"

"You, Ruby. Always." He leans in and whispers in my ear. "Given the choice, I'll knock it down before I'll ever risk your safety."

I look up at his sun-kissed face and sleek, rounded cheekbones. Ezra may as well have been chiseled by Michelangelo. In a million years, I'll never get tired of looking at him.

"You're beautiful," he tells me.

"I was just thinking that about you."

He points to his head. "I got that."

Knowing there's something bigger out there makes it easier

to decide. Maybe in the next world, Ezra won't be mine. Maybe in this world my friends and family will decide I'm crazy. Maybe being together and living so close to the ruin *is* dangerous. Maybe a scary creature will eat me before I have a chance to find out. Or maybe I'll cross the street tomorrow and be hit by a car. But he could also be my happily ever after. I know now—life doesn't come with guarantees. Betting on Ezra is just the start.

COMING SOON

Ruby and Ezra's story continues in *Wild Open Faces*, book two of the *Wild and Ruin* series. Stay tuned ...

ACKNOWLEDGMENTS

A special thank you to my husband, Greg. From reading all of my many manuscript iterations to holding my hand when I broke down, convinced I'd never write again, you've stood by my writing. My love for you is immense and the words 'thank you' alone don't cut it, so pretend I have the power to grant you the Awesomest Husband in the Universe award and that it comes with a trillion dollars, an unlimited supply of calorie-less, still to-die-for pizza and Doritos; and never-ending effortless hikes through the American Southwest—for starters. Likewise, to my boys, Elijah and Gabriel, and my parents, Tamar and Abram. You've been wonderfully supportive in so many unique and immeasurable ways, I don't know how to thank you with the full force of how I feel. I love you all enormously. Without your ongoing support and encouragement, I might have given up writing altogether, which means you would not be holding this book in your hands!

Much gratitude to my beta readers and friends Carolyn, Susan, Lisa, and Margaret who loved this book fiercely and with a passion from the start (and me, thankfully), and who gave me brilliant advice over the many years I took to finish Ruby and Ezra's story. Lisa, thank you especially for your thoughtful feedback, as well as for encouraging me to keep on going each of the thousand times I threatened to throw in the towel while I went through the prepublishing rigmarole. Many thanks also to my Santa Fe writing group, especially Melissa, Sue, George, and Rachel for your continued advice and support throughout the publishing process. Also, to Amber, who has steadfastly championed my endeavor to publish overall and given me more spot-on advice than I could hope for. I could not have done it without all of you and appreciate all your advice and goodwill, not to mention the many mornings and evenings you listened to me fret or complain about my writing. You mean everything to me, and I hope you'll find as much joy in this story as I have in being a part of your lives.

This book would not be what it is without my amazing editor, Alexandra O'Connell. And it would not be where it is without my wonderful manager, Kirsten Jensen. Thank you both so much for helping bring this story to fruition and for being such supportive, smart listeners. Because you never doubted me, I never lost faith in the story or the journey, no matter how arduous the process. Thanks also to Heather Giffin-Vine, graphic designer extraordinaire, for this amazing cover. You rock, girl! And a special shout-out to Shoshana Bettencourt, who patiently took a bazillion photos over the course of a day to capture what has got to be some of the more flattering author pictures I've encountered (and is also just a really awesome friend and person).

To all my friends and extended family that I don't have room to mention by name (and there are a lot of you), I thank the Powers That Be every day for you and want you to know you're the absolute best. Seriously. I'm a writer, and writers know these things; we operate from the heart.

Though untraditional, I'd also like to thank all the naysayers I've known throughout the years who either implied or outright said I'd never be a successful writer. I hate the word 'no' with a passion and telling me I can't do something is the most surefire way to ensure I succeed. You are the best motivation!

A million thanks to all my readers, whom I value, respect, appreciate, and adore! Don't EVER give up. ALWAYS ignore people who come to you armed with a list of reasons why they think you can't or shouldn't do what you love. Don't let anyone convince you, you're not good enough. And when in doubt, fake it. Pretend you know you are, wear that knowledge like your second skin, and soon enough you will be.

Thanks also to all my online writing groups and social media peeps and peers. Your support has meant a lot, and your demonstrable interest and involvement in my writing from afar has encouraged me forward. Your support goes to show that the kindness of strangers is not a myth or lost art. There are plenty of selfless, incredible people in this world, and if you put yourself out there, it isn't as hard as it sometimes seems at first glance to find them.

To my Bobe and Zade. You believed in me from the start and always encouraged me to keep writing. I don't have enough room here to thank you for all the ways you've touched my life. But you know and I know, and wherever you are now, I'm betting you can read my mind.

Finally, but never the least, thank you to my sis, Libby, for your affection, love, friendship, advice, and never-ending adherence to the sometimes difficult but always worthy sister-code. I love you with all the force and energy of a bazillion supernovas and will worship and adore you until the end-times.

To paraphrase a quote from Carl Sagan, "In the vastness of space and immensity of time, it is my joy to spend a planet and an epoch with you all."

Jennifer G. Edelson is a writer, trained artist, former attorney, pizza lover, and hard-core Bollywood fan. Originally a California native, she currently resides in Santa Fe, New Mexico with her husband, kids, and dog, Hubble after surviving twenty-plus years in the Minnesota tundra (but still considers Los Angeles, the Twin Cities, and Santa Fe all home). Other than writing, Jennifer loves hiking, traveling, Albert Camus, Dr. Seuss, dark chocolate, drinking copious amounts of coffee, exploring mysterious places, and meeting new people—if you're human (or otherwise), odds are she'll probably love you.

For more information, please visit Jennifer's
Author Page at:
    www.JenniferGEdelsonauthor.com.

You can also find Jennifer on:
    Twitter: @JGEAuthor
    Facebook: www.facebook.com/JenniferGEdelsonAuthor/
    Instagram: @JGEAuthor

All comments, mail, and inquires, including book-club requests, speaking engagements, and signing inquires, may be addressed to Jennifer at: BadAppleBookinfo@gmail.com.